HEART OF FIRE

In a daze Marquis walked toward Valentina. Her back was to him and he reached for her hand, turning her to face him. "I could so easily love you," he whispered, surprising not only Valentina but himself as well.

Valentina stared at him, unable to look away. There had been something strong and electric between them from the start. His words danced through her mind and she knew she could easily love him also.

"You should not say these things to me. It isn't proper."

The dark eyes that caressed her face and finally rested on her lips were compelling, pulling at Valentina. "I do not know what is proper where you are concerned, Valentina Barrett. Do you know I dreamed about you last night?"

She shook her head. "I don't think you should—"

He placed a finger over her lips. "Shh, do not say it. You and I both know there is something powerful between us, something over which neither of us has any control."

Valentina was unprepared for Marquis's next action. When he pulled her tightly against him, she felt as if a bolt of lightning had jarred her body. Dozens of scalding remarks formed in her mind, but she could not utter them, not while his hard, lean body stirred and stoked the fire within her . . .

MARIA LUISA YEE

GOLDEN PARADISE

CONSTANCE O'BANYON

ZEBRA BOOKS
KENSINGTON PUBLISHING CORP.

MARIA LUISA YEE

This is for you, Sharon. You came to me as a daughter—not from pain of birth, but through marriage to my son, Rick. I love you for your sweet nature, for your kindness and consideration to others. Most of all I love you for the happiness that twinkles in my son's eyes.

Against A Golden Sky

In the land of the golden sun, life bursts forth anew.
Where blue sky touches golden hills, destiny waits for
  you.
Cry not for what you leave behind in the icy, barren land.
Sorrow will soon disappear like a trickle through the
  hourglass sands.
Dance, Valentina, whirl, Valentina, with beauty to
  inspire the poet's eye.
Your tears will all be washed away, against a golden sky.

—Constance O'Banyon

Prologue

San Francisco . . . 1848

The golden sun beat down on the beautiful green countryside, warming the air with its soft glow. A small sea otter awkwardly made its way down the beach toward the shimmering, blue Pacific Ocean. Diving into the water with a clean splash, the creature soon became lost from sight in the swirling tide. A sea bird circled in the sky as though carried on the wind. Suddenly the bird spotted his prey and swooped down to catch an unsuspecting fish that had leapt out of the water.

A lone observer sat astride his prancing black steed, taking in the beauty around him. His dark eyes moved almost caressingly over the land, with the soft gaze of a lover. This golden California was his land—the land of his ancestors, and, if God were willing, the land of his sons. Gazing out to sea, he watched the whitecaps washing gently past the inlet to splash white, frothy foam upon the shore. His eyes lifted to a mission that stood on a distant hill, a sad reminder—as well as a glowing triumph—of a time when the mighty Spanish Empire had established her hold on this young land.

Marquis Domingo Vincente was of noble blood. He was

pure Castilian Spanish. At thirty-five years of age, he cast a tall shadow. His body was lean and hard, his complexion dark, his face handsome. He was dressed in Spanish trousers that flared at the bottom. Silver weaving ran down the outside seams of his trouser legs and across the front of his matching bolero jacket.

Marquis's great-grandfather had first come to California in 1769 with the explorer, Gaspar de Portala. The Vincente family had been granted land from the Spanish king and had passed it down through the generations. The Vincente Ranch, Paraíso del Norte, now belonged to Marquis's grandfather. One day it would pass to Marquis as a sacred trust for generations to come.

The Vincentes were a proud family, steeped in Spanish tradition. Marquis had seen many changes in this land he loved. He had watched California pass from Spanish to Mexican rule, and he remembered the day the Mexican flag had been lowered over the customs house and the American flag had been hoisted in its place.

A frown narrowed Marquis Vincente's dark eyes as he glanced down the steep slopes, past the clump of scrub oaks, to his right, where he could see the small village of Yerba Buena—or, as the American intruders had renamed it, San Francisco.

His lips curled in contempt at the changes that had taken place in his beloved California. Hordes of people crowded the streets and byways of San Francisco, changing her from a small, sleepy little village, to a bustling, foul pesthole.

He could feel the growing unrest, the disappearance of a gentle way of life—a life in which Spanish grandees ruled their land like kings; a life in which families dwelt amid bountiful Nature's hand of plenty. Tradition and honor were being trampled in the mud, beneath the boots of greed.

The sun went behind a cloud as Marquis watched the

restless waves lap against the shore. He did not know that soon his honor would be tested and that he would be challenged to give up his way of life, to turn his back on family customs.

There was a strange restlessness that stirred within Marquis's breast. He turned his mount toward Paraíso del Norte and nudged the animal into a steady lope. Marquis soon pushed aside the unsettling feeling that something was about to happen to him that would change his life forever.

Cornwall, England

Valentina Barrett stood atop a jagged rock formation and gazed down at the churning sea that washed up on the rock-strewn shoreline. It was damp and cold, and she pulled her wool cape tightly about her and shivered. The day was bleak and gloomy. The gale-force wind picked up the sleet from the ground and hurled it into her face as a frenzy of white seemed to drop out of the sky. The winter-white world held no appeal for Valentina. She thrived in the warmth of the sun and had always detested the cold.

Valentina was unaware that she was a beauty. She did not know that her silver-blue eyes would soon reflect a deep fascination for three very different men in a far distant land. How could she know that her sweetly curved body would soon inspire men to worship her like a goddess? She was miserable and unhappy, feeling loneliness in the very depths of her soul.

Chilled to the bone, Valentina made her way toward the family home, dreading the solitude she knew she would find there. Stopping to glance back in the direction from which she had come, she noticed the snow was beginning to pile into high drifts along the roadway. No one would come calling in this storm, she thought miserably. Not that anyone ever came anyway.

11

This land was almost cut off from the rest of the world. The sea was too treacherous for visitors to reach her home from that direction, and the roads were rocky and craggy—even in summer they were often washed out and in bad repair.

Valentina sighed heavily, feeling a chill that was only partially induced by the cold. Walking up the front steps, she entered the dark, gloomy house, knowing her ever-faithful maid, Salamar, would be waiting for her. She longed for the time her father and mother would return to England. They were traveling the world and she never knew where they were until an occasional letter arrived from some distant country.

Valentina had been living with her grandmother, who had died the night of Valentina's nineteenth birthday. Now Salamar was Valentina's only companion. She had never felt so alone in her life and she hoped fervently that her parents would soon come home or arrange for her to join them.

Forces were already at work that would bring together this daughter of the cold North land and this son of the golden country. The time would come when Valentina would stir Marquis's Spanish blood to the boiling point and their lives would be played out amid the splendor of a golden paradise.

Chapter One

Cornwall, England . . . 1849

The hauntingly exotic music sounded strangely out of place filtering through the windows of the English cottage. A dark-skinned woman, sitting cross-legged on the faded rug and plucking the strings of the *oud,* watched as her pupil whirled around the floor in a flurry of red silk.

The knowledge that Valentina had far surpassed her teachings made Salamar's dark eyes sparkle with wonder. The young English maiden had a wonderful talent that one rarely found in a dancer. Each movement she made was like poetry. Valentina's waist-length, golden hair swirled around her in a soft curtain of sunlight. Her eyes were such a light color blue that they seemed almost transparent silver. At the moment, those eyes were gleaming with wild abandon and excitement. As Valentina turned and whirled, her well-shaped legs were faintly visible through the filmy material of the costume Salamar had made for her.

Salamar realized for the first time that her charge had grown into a lovely young woman. As she observed Valentina moving her hips so that the beads at her waist made a jingling sound, Salamar wondered why she had not noticed before how beautiful the girl had become.

As Valentina dipped down in a final, graceful curtsy and the last chord of music faded away, Salamar laid her instrument aside and smiled proudly.

"You are magnificent. I have never seen anyone dance as well as you—not even your mother. If you were in a harem, the sultan would make you his favorite, perhaps even his wife."

Valentina's cheeks were flushed with excitement, and she took a deep breath to slow her exhilarated heartbeat. "Do you mean it, Salamar? Am I really that good?"

"Yours is a true gift."

Valentina dropped down on the floor, unfastened the tinkling bangles from her wrist, then handed them to Salamar. "I love dancing, but I will never be as good as Mother was when she danced. She was the best."

Valentina's mother, Evonne, had been born and raised in a small village in southern France. Evonne's father had been a dance master who had taught his daughter to dance the ballet. Her talent had been boundless. When Evonne was but nineteen, she became the rage of Paris. Since it was considered *risqué* to dance on stage, Evonne had changed her name to Jordanna. As the dancer Jordanna, she had obtained fame and had been heralded as the greatest dancer who had ever lived. She had been courted by dukes and princes alike; she had been showered with jewels and expensive gifts. She had danced for kings and queens all over Europe. Once she had danced in Saint Petersburg and Czar Nicholas had come to every performance.

One day, with no warning, Jordanna simply dropped out of sight, taking her maid, Salamar, with her. Her audiences were never to see or hear of her again. A search was made to find her, but no trace was ever discovered— she had just disappeared. What the people did not know was that Evonne had met and fallen in love with a handsome, dashing, Englishman, Ward Barrett, who had swept Evonne across the English Channel, where they had married. Theirs had been a magical romance. Valentina was the result of their union.

"You are a much more dedicated dancer than your mother ever was," Salamar stated. "She danced only because her father expected it of her. You dance because you love it. You are not restricted to just the ballet as your mother was. You have mastered all the dances I taught you."

Valentina glanced at her maid, her only friend and companion. Salamar's story was a sad one. She had been born in a sultan's palace in Turkey. Her mother had been one of the sultan's favorites, and Salamar was their daughter. After the old sultan died, his jealous young son had rounded up all his father's women, selling them into slavery.

Valentina had often been told how Salamar had first come to her family. Twenty-one years had passed since Valentina's grandfather had been traveling in Arabia. When he chanced upon a slave auction that was being held in a public street, he had been horrified that people could be bought and sold like cattle. He was never to know why he bought the young fourteen-year-old who was being degraded and poked by many leering men. Perhaps it was because the young girl had been the same age as his daughter. Valentina's grandfather had purchased Salamar with the intention of giving her her freedom. But at the time he could not make Salamar understand that she was free to go where she wanted.

Alone and frightened, in a foreign land, Salamar had followed him, not understanding what was happening to her. Finally, Evonne's father decided he would send the girl home to France as a maid for his daughter. Salamar had been educated with Evonne and had proved to be

15

eager and intelligent, mastering several different languages. When Evonne had run away to marry Ward Barrett, she had taken Salamar to England with her. Since the day Valentina had first drawn air into her lungs, Salamar had loved and cared for her.

Valentina's father, Ward Barrett, was a wanderer. The only son of a wealthy English family, he was too restless to settle down in one place. Evonne adored her husband and gladly went everywhere with him. Even Valentina's arrival did not stop the young couple from traveling; they simply bundled up their daughter and took her and Salamar with them. By the time Valentina was ten years old, she had seen half the world.

When Valentina was twelve, she, Salamar, and her parents came home to Cornwall for a visit with her English grandmother. As they were preparing to leave, Valentina's grandmother had insisted that her granddaughter remain with her so the child could receive a proper education. Valentina had been devastated when her parents had reluctantly agreed.

The long years passed with Valentina seeing her parents only at the Christmas season. Letters would reach her from faraway places and she received gifts from all over the world. Valentina's growing-up years would have been very lonely if it had not been for Salamar. The maid created fun for her charge. They talked about distant places they had visited, and both longed for the day when they would join Valentina's parents again.

While Salamar had lived in the harem, which had consisted of women of many nationalities, she had learned the dances of many countries. She had passed on her knowledge of those dances to Valentina. Valentina could perform the Dance of the Seven Veils, Gypsy dances, Spanish dances, and endless others. And Valentina's mother had instructed her daughter in ballet.

Because it was so isolated in Cornwall, Valentina had

16

been allowed to wear the gauzy veils and costumes that Salamar had made for her. Slipping on the finger cymbals, she would swing her hips in an enticing manner while dancing her loneliness away. Valentina's grandmother had not approved of her dancing, but she had loved the child and had been very indulgent. She had seen that her granddaughter was wasting away with loneliness, so she had finally allowed her to practice the dance. She had insisted, however, that Valentina finish her other lessons each day before commencing the instruction in dance. Now Valentina was nineteen and Salamar insisted that she could outdance her mother.

Last spring Valentina's grandmother had taken ill and within three weeks had died, and still Valentina grieved. The loneliness was almost like a physical pain. She had the feeling she and Salamar were living on an island, alone and deserted.

Now Valentina rose and moved across the room. "I'm going to change my gown so I can meet the mail coach. Perhaps there will be a letter from my parents today."

Sadly, Salamar watched Valentina leave the room. Shaking her head, she felt heartache for this girl who had been all but abandoned. Salamar knew Valentina's parents loved her, but they were like children chasing rainbows, forgetting that they had responsibilities in England.

When Valentina returned from meeting the mail coach, there was no need for Salamar to ask if she had received a letter. The dejected look on her face told the grim story.

Following Valentina into the kitchen, Salamar watched her remove her cape and hang it on a hook. "I have some nice hot stew for you, Valentina. After you have eaten, you will feel much better about everything."

Valentina shook her head. "I'm not hungry. I don't want anything to eat."

Glancing out the window, the young girl thought how dreary the landscape was. The dark storm clouds grimly predicted it would snow again before morning. The sun had not come out in over a month. Even the cheery fire blazing in the kitchen hearth did little to dispel the gloom that hung over the house.

Salamar took Valentina's arm, gently pushing her down in a chair. "You must keep up your strength. When your mother and father send for you, you will not want to be suffering from ill health."

Valentina nodded in agreement but ignored the stew and hot bread dripping with butter and wild honey in favor of a cup of steaming, cream-laced tea. Rising from the table, she carried her cup over to the window and stared down the road, wishing someone—anyone— would come to see her. She had not seen anyone besides Salamar and the mail carrier in over three months.

"You must come away from that window or you might become chilled," Salamar scolded mildly.

"What does it matter? Who would know or care?" Valentina answered in a rare burst of self-pity. Usually her disposition was sunny and she smiled readily, but today she was overcome by misery.

"It is not good to dwell on unhappy thoughts, Valentina. Think instead of pleasing things. In my father's harem, I knew a woman who could project herself into any place she wanted to be. If she wanted to be atop a mountain, she would just close her eyes and describe it to us in detail. She could describe a sunset and actually make us see it. She taught me how to do this, and I will teach it to you."

"No. I do not want to live in a world of dreams and shadows. I want to feel life through every pore of my skin. I want to feel the sun on my face. I want to be in a land green and alive with life."

"Perhaps it is better that I do not teach you to project your thoughts," Salamar agreed. "I believe that you will soon be happy without weaving magic dreams."

Valentina's face brightened. "Tell my fortune, Salamar. Please tell me what will happen to me in the future," she begged, knowing Salamar sometimes had the uncanny ability to predict coming events.

"No, I will not. I told you many times before that I will not look ahead for you. If it is bad, I do not want to know about it."

"Why?" Valentina demanded. "Perhaps you will see something good."

"You know that I never tell the fortunes of the people I love," Salamar declared stubbornly.

Valentina frowned, aware that once Salamar made up her mind about something it was useless to try to change it. "Could anything be worse than the life I'm living now?"

Seeing Valentina's disappointment, Salamar reluctantly motioned for the girl to join her at the table. "Very well, but I will not tell you if I do not like what I see." When they were both seated at the kitchen table, Valentina watched Salamar's face closely, expectantly.

The maid picked up Valentina's slender hand and gripped it tightly. Valentina had expected Salamar to study her open palm, but instead her grip tightened and she stared into Valentina's face.

"I see in the near future a long journey by sea," Salamar began. "The way is not clear, but you will enter a golden country . . . this is not clear either."

Valentina stared at Salamar's arresting face, trying to see past her heavy-lidded eyes. "Where in this world is there such a place as a golden country, Salamar?"

"It is a far journey to a new world. You will search for that which is lost to you." Salamar's voice was trancelike and sounded far away.

"I don't understand; what new world?"

"I see sadness. . . ." Salamar's voice trailed off. "This isn't clear. . . ." Salamar tightened her grip on Valentina's hand. "I see fame, adoration. You will be worshiped by many men, but you will love only one. This man will love you as two people, then he will reject you as both."

Salamar's face whitened, as if she had been drained. Releasing Valentina's hand, she leaned back in her chair, trying to regain her strength.

"What does it all mean, Salamar? What golden country, and who will worship me? Will I end up with the man I love? What do you mean, he will love me as two people?"

"I will say no more than this." Salamar lowered her dark eyes, and watched Valentina closely. "Tomorrow will bring a letter, and soon you will begin your journey."

Valentina's heart was beating with excitement. "Will you come with me, Salamar? I will not leave without you."

"Yes, I will come with you."

"Can you not tell me what the prediction means?" It made no sense to Valentina. What was the vague promise of love? Where was the golden land?

"No, I will tell you no more. It was a mistake to have gazed into your future. It does no good to see these things." Suddenly Salamar smiled and it seemed to ease the troubled wrinkles about her mouth. Reaching out, she drew Valentina into her arms. "You are the child I could never have. I will stand by you in all your troubles. I will help you all I can."

No matter how Valentina begged, Salamar would say no more on the subject. That night in bed, Valentina stared into the darkness, wondering what the future held for her. Perhaps Salamar was only playing a game with her. Yes, that was it, she reasoned. She had just been trying to entertain her so she would forget about her loneliness. Valentina would know tomorrow if Salamar had indeed seen into the future. If the mail coach brought her a letter, she would believe.

Valentina tried to imagine what it would be like to leave this cold, barren country. It had been her world for so long. The Barretts' roots were deep in this land. Morgan's Folly had been in the Barrett family for generations, for the house and several hundred acres had been deeded to Valentina's family over five hundred years ago.

The present Duke of Warrick lived in the large, formidable castle five miles distant. At one time Morgan's Folly had belonged to the wealthy, powerful Warrick family. A distant ancestor of Valentina's had fought bravely at Lord Morgan Warrick's side during the Crusades. When her ancestor saved Lord Morgan's life, his reward had been the land Valentina's father now held in trust. Many generations of Warricks had tried to redeem the land that had once belonged to their estate, but Valentina's family had always stubbornly held on to it.

Valentina remembered her father telling her how Morgan's Folly had gotten its name. Some two hundred years ago a London newspaper had published an article about the land Morgan Warrick had deeded to the Barrett family. In the article the land had been called Morgan's Folly, and today the house and grounds were still referred to by that name.

While the lonesome-sounding wind howled and groaned, hurling icy particles of sleet against the windowpane, Valentina released all thoughts of generations past, snuggled beneath the warmth of her covers, and fell asleep.

21

Chapter Two

Valentina had washed her hair and was sitting beside the fire drying the long tresses when she heard the front door open and saw Salamar enter. Valentina looked at her expectantly, hardly daring to hope she had received a letter from her mother and father as Salamar had predicted.

"Did it come?" she asked in a soft voice. "Did I get a letter?"

Salamar reached into her apron pocket and withdrew a letter, handing it to Valentina. "Did I not tell you it would come today?"

With trembling hands Valentina took the letter. She immediately recognized her mother's delicate handwriting. As she carefully opened the envelope, her eyes sought Salamar's. "I wasn't certain that you were serious yesterday. I thought you might have been trying to cheer me up."

"I never play games with the sight," Salamar replied. "I will only tell what I see."

Valentina excitedly tore open her mother's letter and began to read aloud:

Dearest Valentina,
    Your letter caught up with your father and me in

23

San Francisco, California. Both of us were sorely grieved when we learned of your grandmother's death. I know how alone and abandoned you must be feeling. Your father has written a letter to our solicitor in Plymouth, instructing him to advance you the money for a boat trip. I am told by your father that you should employ Merland, the gamekeeper, to board up the house and sell the stock. You are to instruct the village seamstress, Mrs. Grover, to make a wardrobe for you. Spare no expense and use the best materials. You will need clothes for all occasions. Salamar is also to be outfitted as befits her station. You and Salamar will book passage on the *Berengaria* on the first of March. Your father knows the captain very well. He does not usually take passengers but has assured us that you and Salamar will have every comfort. Your father and I will be waiting for you. It has been so long since I have seen you, my darling. You will be all grown up now. What fun we shall have when you arrive. This is an exciting country, unlike any other you have seen. You will determine this for yourself when you first catch sight of this golden land.

Valentina glanced quickly at Salamar. "How could you have known about the golden land? How could you—"

"Is there more to the letter?" Salamar asked, smiling ever so slightly.

Valentina was dazed by the accuracy of Salamar's prediction. It took her a moment to clear her mind and continue with her mother's letter.

Valentina, your father and I own a half interest in a gold mine where we hope to make a big strike. Gold is so plentiful in this land that many people have been known to scoop it right out of the water.

Our partner, Samuel Udell, believes that we will make a strike any day now. Take care, my love. Before too long I will hold you in my arms.

Love,
Mother

Valentina's eyes sparkled with happiness. She jumped to her feet and whirled around in a wide circle; then, grabbing Salamar, she danced her around the room. "We are going to be together as a family again, Salamar. Who knows what new adventure awaits us in this California."

Salamar smiled at Valentina and her eyes took on a mysterious glow, reminding Valentina that she might know exactly what awaited them in San Francisco.

The six weeks before Valentina could board the *Berengaria* passed in a busy haze of happiness. The house had to be put in order; the animals had to be sold. Hours were spent with the seamstress, fitting new gowns. At last the day came when the furniture was covered with dust sheets and the trunks were packed with new gowns, bonnets, and shoes.

Valentina felt no regret the moment she finally stepped into the buggy that would take her and Salamar to Plymouth, where they would board the *Berengaria*. There was no sadness in her heart as they pulled away from the house in which she had spent the last seven years of her life. She did not even turn back for a last look before they topped a hill and passed out of sight. Valentina's spirits were soaring and joy filled her heart; she could hardly wait to be reunited with her mother and father.

Valentina stood on the deck of the ship, watching the

billowing canvas struggling to catch the wind. The *Berengaria* was a sharp, clean vessel supporting three masts. So far the journey had been uneventful. They had been blessed with a fair wind all the way from Plymouth. Now the *Berengaria* was in sight of the dreaded Cape Horn. Valentina remembered reading in books that no sailor—be he a seasoned traveler or a young cabin boy— ever breathed easily until he was safely around the Horn.

Valentina stared in awe at the beauty of the magnificent sunset. The sun seemed a big red ball of fire being swallowed up by the sea. Her eyes followed the fleecy clouds that were scattered across the horizon, and she mused that they looked much like the frothy foam that danced on the waves. Raising her face to the heavens, she was unaware that she was being observed.

Captain Nathan Masterson was spellbound as he watched Valentina Barrett with her golden hair flying in the wind. She was bewitching—a lovely creature, small boned, with delicate beauty. Captain Masterson had come to know the beautiful Evonne Barrett, and the daughter had classic beauty, not unlike her mother's.

Valentina's eyes were a crystal blue, with seemingly infinite depths. Since she had come aboard, Nathan Masterson had found himself making excuses just to engage her in conversation. Indeed, it seemed he had thought of little else but her on this run. Since Valentina and her maid were the only females on board, they kept to themselves, spending most of their time below in their cabin.

The crew always went out of their way to be polite to both women. Even though they never dared approach Valentina or speak to her, they worshipped her with their eyes. She seemed unaware that she was stirring the sailors' hearts with admiration and devotion.

On his last voyage to San Francisco, Captain Masterson had met Valentina's mother and father. He had become fast friends with the Barretts after he discovered that Ward Barrett had come from the same part of England as he. The captain had consented to bring Valentina and her maid to them in California. Now, after seeing her, he was glad he had.

Wanting very much to talk to Valentina, Nathan Masterson decided to use the approaching danger of Cape Horn to engage her in conversation.

Valentina turned at the sound of heavy footsteps. Looking up into the rugged face of the captain, she smiled slightly. Captain Masterson was not handsome in the traditional sense; his skin was tanned from long hours in the sun and his blond hair was bleached almost white. There were laugh wrinkles about his sparkling blue eyes and the smile on his lips was genuine. He was of medium height, but, nonetheless, he was a commanding figure in his blue jacket and white trousers. He looked every inch the captain he was.

"I see you are taking advantage of the calmness of the sea, Miss Barrett. I feel it my duty to inform you we are in for heavy weather as we approach the Horn."

A smile curved her lips. "I feel it my duty to inform you, Captain, that I am a seasoned traveler. By the time I had reached by sixth birthday, I had stood beneath the pyramids of Egypt and walked through the ruins at the Colosseum in Rome. While I have never been around the Horn, I have been on board a ship in a typhoon, while on route to the Orient."

"I know all about your travels. Your father told me a great deal about you."

"How long have you been acquainted with my parents, Captain?"

"Ours has not been a lengthy friendship, but a solid one. We found we had much in common. As a matter of fact, your father and my uncle went to school together."

Captain Masterson watched as the dying sunlight played across the beautiful face. He was awed that anyone could look so perfect. Valentina Barrett was every man's dream of what a woman should be. She was gracious, and her manner of speech was cultured with deep, rich tone. She moved with the gracefulness of a swan floating across water.

"It's my guess that your father would have made an excellent explorer had he been born in another time, Miss Barrett. I was astounded at all his tales of adventure—and it isn't easy to astound a sea captain."

Valentina's laughter was musical. "I know what you mean, Captain. My father is, for want of a better word, a wanderer. He and my mother have covered the globe several times over. When I was younger, I traveled with them. Once I reached my twelfth birthday, my Grandmother Barrett insisted that my parents leave me with her so I could be brought up as a well-educated English miss. My father argued that the world would be my classroom, but my grandmother won in the end."

Captured by the sound of Valentina's voice, Captain Masterson leaned against the ship's rail as her story unraveled. "And were you happy to give up the wandering life, Miss Barrett?"

"Never. I detested needlework and was a total disappointment to my grandmother. She liked to say it took years for her to hone me into a proper young lady; even then she wasn't sure she had altogether succeeded."

His eyes twinkled. "Don't you think you are a proper young lady?"

She returned his smile. "I'll leave you to judge, Captain."

His heartbeat quickened as he watched the teasing

28

light in her eyes turn to one of inquiry. "Oh, yes, Miss Barrett, I would say you are very definitely a proper young lady."

The captain shifted his eyes out to sea, fearing he would say too much. Valentina was weaving her way into his heart and he had to keep a clear head. He searched his mind for a safe subject. "Tell me, Miss Barrett, are you not just the merest fraction frightened to have embarked upon such a perilous journey alone?"

"I'm not alone, Captain. Salamar is with me."

"Ah, yes, the maid. I would venture to guess that she came to your family from one of the foreign ports you visited. Perhaps from India."

"You are almost correct, Captain. Salamar was born in Turkey, but when my grandfather found her, she was in Arabia. She is not only my maid, but my closest friend and confidante as well."

"Are you excited about being reunited with your parents in California?"

"Yes." Valentina lowered her eyes. "My grandmother has just recently passed away, making it necessary for me to join them."

"I see. California is a wild place since they discovered gold. There are so few women, I wager you will be the center of attention when you go ashore."

"Tell me what you know about California, Captain. I know very little about that part of the world."

The captain turned his eyes out to sea. "California is a golden dream for some, a nightmare for others. Since gold was discovered in 1848, at Sutter's Mill, people have flocked to her shores from all over the world. To my way of thinking, they are trampling beneath their feet the greatest treasure, if they could but see it. I believe California is the land of milk and honey. All a man would have to do is poke a seed in the ground and it would take root."

"You sound like you love the land. I wonder why you took to sea, Captain."

He laughed down at her. "I took to the sea because my family owned three ships and had three sons. As you see, I had very little choice. I will tell you this, though; if I were a young man starting out, I'd go to California and buy land—not to dig for gold, but to cultivate and watch things grow. The Spanish dons have the right idea."

"There is a great Spanish influence in California, isn't there?"

"Indeed, yes. The land once belonged to Spain, and later Mexico. Many of the Spanish still live there as if they were kings. Some are of high birth. They are of pure blood and speak Castilian Spanish. If this land boasts of having nobility, it is the Spanish grandees."

At that moment a huge wave slammed against the side of the ship, giving warning of things to come. Valentina gazed at the monstrous, blue-black outline in the distance and knew they were in sight of the Horn. Pulling her cape tightly about her, she shivered from the cold and a dread of the unknown.

"You should go below now, Miss Barrett. The closer to the Horn we get, the rougher the sea will become." Captain Masterson was sorry that the conversation had to end. He had been thoroughly enchanted by Miss Valentina Barrett. But duty called. The Horn waited for no man.

Valentina glanced at the rolling, churning sea and felt a flicker of fear. Raising her head to the heavens, she saw that ominous clouds were blackening the sky, completely hiding the sunset. "How long will it take to make the voyage around the Horn, Captain?"

"If luck is with us, we will be around it in little more than a week. It could take longer—one never predicts time when facing the unpredictable Horn. It's bad luck. 'Tis said by sailors of old that if the Horn hears you, your

30

ship will not make it around at all."

Valentina caught the humor in his eyes. She smiled and nodded her head. "If you will excuse me, I will go below." She could sense that Captain Masterson had already turned his attention to the *Berengaria* and the task at hand. Moving away, she made her way back to her cabin, knowing the captain was needed at the helm.

The gale intensified before morning and the moanful howling sounded almost like a woman's scream. Sleet and hail unleashed their fury, pelting the ship, driving against it with all the forces of hell, aided by the churning waves that splashed across the deck.

Valentina lay on her bunk wide-eyed, wondering if they would make it through this terrible night. Salamar, seemingly undisturbed by the storm, slept as peacefully as a baby, while Valentina lay shivering and afraid.

Throughout the next day the violent storm continued. All the power of the unpredictable sea released its fury on the *Berengaria,* her passengers and crew. The sea was running high and, by nightfall, the ship's decks had to be cleared of snow and ice.

By midnight the sea fell to a flat calm. Valentina was overcome with relief. She was drained emotionally, feeling small and insignificant. She had lived through a storm that had controlled her life by playing on her fears. Never again would she underestimate the power of a stormy sea.

In the week and a half it took to round the Horn, the weather vacillated between calm and storm. Once the Horn was behind them, Valentina and Salamar ventured forth from their cabin. They watched the crew replacing splintered wood, mending torn sails, and repairing the damage that had been wrought by the storm.

Valentina stood on deck shivering beneath a sun that gave off no warmth; even so, she was enjoying the calmness of the sea. In the distance she watched as a flock of albatross soared on the wind. She was delighted when they landed on the sea to be playfully washed about by the motion of the waves.

When the *Berengaria* entered the bright blue waters of the Pacific, the warming sun was most welcome and a balmy trade wind gently helped the ship on its way. Valentina's happiness soared like the playful albatross, for she knew each day brought her closer to her mother and father.

California

Marquis Vincente's black boots were soundless as he descended the stairs, moving across the indoor courtyard and entering the archway leading to the main part of his family home. The day he had been dreading for so long had finally arrived. He was to meet the woman to whom he had been betrothed since his twelfth birthday. Even though the Estrada ranch adjoined Paraíso del Norte, Marquis had never met his betrothed, Isabel Estrada. Her father, Don Jose, he knew quite well; her mother, Doña Maria, he knew not at all. Doña Maria had hated California, refusing to live in what she termed "that wild, heathen country." She had reared her two daughters in Spain. Now she had come to California to escort her daughter Isabel so that she and Marquis could be married.

Marquis did not look forward to a life with a wife who had been chosen for him. What if she were ugly? Worse still, what if she were boring? The Spanish traditions ran deeply in Marquis's blood. He might not like the woman who had been chosen for him, but he would marry her. His grandfather had taught him that Vincentes always did what society expected of them—what propriety demanded of them.

At the door of his grandfather's study, Marquis could hear his grandfather apologizing to his guests because his daughter-in-law and his granddaughter had traveled to a distant mission and would not be home until late in the day. "Had they known you were arriving today, they would surely have stayed home," he assured them.

Marquis wished he had gone with his mother and sister. He turned the knob and stood in the doorway. His eyes went first to his grandfather, who was beaming with happiness. Don Alonso was a tall man, unstooped by his seventy years of living. Illness had robbed him of his strength and had left him pale, but his eyes were always bright and keen. He was from the era of the proud grandees—the last of a dying breed. Marquis realized with a heavy heart that his grandfather's health was deteriorating. Yet, still head of the Vincente family, the old grandee held onto life with a vengeance.

There were four other people in the room and Marquis assessed them all, one by one. There was his betrothed's mother and father. Don Jose, a man of medium height, had nothing outstanding to recommend him other than the fact that his ranch raised some fine blooded horses. The man was lazy, always depending on others to look after his interests.

The mother, Doña Maria, seemed a shy, nervous creature who appeared ready to take flight. She had a thick waistline and a nervous twitch in her right eye. Marquis found himself hoping that the daughter did not resemble her at all. He spoke politely to Señor and Señora Estrada, wishing himself hundreds of miles away.

Hearing a rustle of silk, Marquis moved his eyes past the mother to collide with seeking eyes that were also

33

assessing him. The tall, sumptuous woman had skin the color of a magnolia blossom. Her shimmering, black hair was pulled back from her face and fastened with bright yellow combs. Her mouth was red and curved up in the slightest smile. He noted only briefly that her gown was white trimmed with yellow velvet. There was no doubt that this woman was beautiful. Marquis felt some of his worries dissipate and he flashed her a smile.

Advancing across the room, Marquis approached his grandfather. His eyes went to the other girl in the room, and he saw that she was too young to be Isabel Estrada. Judging from her looks, he placed her in her early teens. She was as uncomely as her sister was beautiful. Her hair hung lankily about her shoulders, her skin was sallow, and she was uncommonly small, coming only to her sister's shoulder. The one thing that struck Marquis about the girl was the softness in her eyes. Sadness was reflected in their shining depths, a sadness that touched his heart. Marquis wondered what cruel twist of fate had cast this young girl opposite the beautiful Isabel. He found no humor in the fact that the girls wore identical gowns, calling unnecessary attention to the differences between them.

Don Alonso stood up, leaning heavily on his cane. "Come in, Marquis. There is someone here you have been waiting a long time to meet. Come and greet Señorita Isabel Estrada, your betrothed."

Marquis moved forward, taking Isabel's hand and bowing graciously. He felt her grip tighten on his, and her bold eyes stared straight into his. She might look like a lovely, demure young lady, but the eyes that stared at him were certainly not those of an innocent—they gleamed with raw passion that seemed ready to ignite.

"I am glad we meet at last, señorita Isabel," he said politely. "I feel I have known you for a very long time."

Isabel could hardly believe her good fortune. She had

not been looking forward to today, for she had not known that her betrothed would be so handsome. It had been drilled into her head that Marquis Vincente was from one of the wealthiest and most influential families in California. She had been told by her father how fortunate she was to be marrying a Vincente.

How fortunate indeed! She had not expected him to have velvet-soft eyes, a smile that would melt any maiden's heart, shoulders so broad and hips so narrow. He was arrogant, noble, sensuously male. She felt her skin tingle as his dark eyes swept across her face.

"Yes, at long last," she breathed, lowering her eyes with maidenly shyness, knowing it was expected of her. "My father often wrote me about you. You see, even in Spain we know about Marquis Vincente."

Marquis nodded his head, suddenly feeling trapped. He could imagine the net closing around him. When he thought of spending the rest of his life with Isabel Estrada, he experienced a sudden sense of . . . repugnance! Yes, he mused, that was the word. But why? There was no denying she was beautiful—many a man would be proud to offer her his name. Why was he feeling forced into a situation over which he had no control? Why did the thought of touching her make his skin crawl?

Don Alonso cleared his throat and smiled at the younger Estrada daughter. "Marquis, I would now like to present you to Isabel's sister, Señorita Eleanor Estrada."

Marquis bowed to the young girl politely, giving her a warm smile. "I am delighted to make your acquaintance, señorita," he said gallantly. Again he noticed the sadness in her dark eyes and was touched by it.

Marquis was aware that everyone around him had been talking at once and that his mind had been wandering. The look his grandfather gave him clearly said that he was being rude. "Isabel asked if you cared to show her the garden, Marquis." The reprimand was clear in Don

Alonso's voice.

"It would be my pleasure to conduct you on a tour, Señorita Isabel," Marquis answered politely.

Isabel folded her fan with a snap and used it to tap her sister's head. "Eleanor will have to accompany us since I have no *dueña*," she said, lowering her lashes coyly.

Marquis tilted his head. "But of course." Opening the door that led to the hallway, he motioned for the ladies to precede him.

There was a heavy silence as the three made their way down the corridor and out into the inner courtyard. They were greeted by the sweet aroma of the many tropical flowers as it wafted through the air tantalizingly.

"How delightful!" Isabel exclaimed, turning around in a circle, viewing the garden. "This is magnificent."

Again Marquis's heart was touched with pity for the ugly sister as she seated herself on the marble bench and folded her hands in her lap. The poor creature was so short that her legs dangled in the air and she was unable to touch ground.

Eleanor was watching Isabel try to work her magic on this tall, handsome Californian. She had seen her sister weave spells about men many times in the past. While growing up in Spain, Isabel had always been surrounded by admirers.

Through veiled lashes, Eleanor saw the pity reflected in the eyes of Marquis Vincente when he looked at her. At that moment, he did a strange thing that would endear him to the young girl for life. Marquis picked a delicate purple bloom and handed it to her.

"The beauty of the flower will soon fade, but the beauty of one's heart will long endure," Marquis said. Eleanor blinked in astonishment. He had just recited her favorite poem. None of her sister's gentlemen friends had ever paid the slightest attention to her. This man was different from all the others. She was loath to see him

36

caught in Isabel's web.

Isabel snapped her fan open and shut in irritation. "One would think you wanted to marry my sister instead of me, Señor Vincente," she hissed. "Do you find my sister more desirable than I?" she asked spitefully.

Marquis did not try to hide the look of disbelief that spread over his face. He could not understand Isabel's uncharitable attitude toward her own sister. Did she not care that the young girl was living under her shadow, torturing herself because she was not beautiful?

He thought of his young sister, Rosalia, who had been raised with love and understanding. His smile was warm as he lifted Eleanor's hand to his lips, softly placing a kiss on the palm. "I believe there is more to your sister than meets the eye, Señorita Isabel. I would like to be her friend."

Isabel raged on the inside as her sister giggled in delight. Knowing she must cover up her anger, Isabel tried to smile, hiding her fanatical rage. "Is this where we will live when we are married, señor?" she asked, lowering her lashes, again pretending maidenly shyness.

"Yes, of course. The west side of the house has always belonged to the oldest son of the family. The next time you come for a visit, I will show you around the house. You may want to do some rearranging or redecorating."

"Why are we not to occupy the main part of the house?" Isabel asked.

"Because my grandfather is the grandee, that is still his domain."

Marquis Vincente was polite and said all the correct things, but Isabel could sense that he was not drawn to her as so many other men had been. "I'm sure the west wing will be lovely, señor," she said, meeting his glance with boldness. "Will this garden be accessible from our rooms?"

"Yes. If you will look over to the right just above the

fountain, you will see the balcony off the master suite. There are stairs from the balcony leading into the garden." He paused. "It has always been the custom for the Vincente men to bring their wives to the west wing."

"Is it not wrongly called a wing? Your home is built in a square around a courtyard," Isabel observed.

"I know it appears so, but the way it is set up on the inside makes it a wing." Marquis knew they were saying unimportant things, feeling each other out.

"Could we not see the rooms today?" Isabel urged. She wanted to spend time with this man who was to be her husband. She wanted to make him fall in love with her. She had the strangest feeling he didn't like her. She had had many lovers in Spain but had always been discreet, and she hoped Marquis hadn't heard about her past.

Suddenly Marquis felt an urge to get away from Isabel. He knew he would face his grandfather's displeasure later for being rude, but he would chance it. "I hope you will accept my apology, Señorita Isabel, but I have to leave right away. I told my mother I would meet her at the mission and escort her home."

"Must you go?" she asked with a pout on her lips.

"Unfortunately, yes. I would not want my mother and sister traveling on the road alone. As it is, it will be dark before we can get home."

"Is it dangerous?" Isabel asked, wanting to keep him with her as long as possible.

"Indeed it can be. One of my *vaqueros* saw bear tracks beside the road this morning." Marquis knew he was making excuses. True, he had promised his mother he would ride out to meet her, but it would not be necessary for him to leave for at least two more hours.

Isabel's mouth dropped and her eyes were like glittering ice. "There are so many things I want to ask you. We should be getting acquainted. Would you rather be with your mother than spend time with me?"

His smile was quick and his teeth flashed. Shrugging his shoulders, he explained, "Alas, I fear I must. It grieves me to leave two such charming ladies. May I escort you back to your mother and father?"

Now Isabel made no attempt to hide her ill humor. Her face grew rigid with displeasure. "No. I will just stay in the garden. You can take my sister back inside since you seem to prefer her company to mine."

Marquis laughed and winked at the young sister. "I understand you will be here for dinner. I will see you both then." With a nod of his handsome head, Marquis turned and walked away.

Isabel watched him until he was out of sight. Her anger had been ignited and needed to be vented on someone. There was an enigmatic gleam in her eyes as she turned on her sister. Grabbing the flower blossom Marquis had given Eleanor, she threw it on the ground, stomping it beneath her shoes. Her face was distorted with fury as she raged at her sister.

"How do you like the flower now, Eleanor? Does my betrothed make your heart swell with lust? Do you covet him for yourself?"

"No, Isabel. I would never do that." The tears that fell down her sister's face had no effect on Isabel, nor did they stay her hand from striking Eleanor hard across the face, leaving a red handprint.

"I will teach you to flirt with my betrothed. You cannot think he found you pretty, can you?" Isabel taunted. "Could you not see the horror in his eyes when he looked at your ugly face? He felt pity for you, nothing more."

Eleanor wiped her face with a lace handkerchief and shoved it into her pocket. "He is the only man who has known how to talk to me. He was not awkward and uneasy because I am not beautiful like you. I do not know why you are so cruel. I think Marquis liked me. I am no threat to you, Isabel. Why do you find pleasure in tormenting me?"

"No woman, not even you, will come between me and Marquis Vincente. I have dreaded meeting him for years. I feared he would be ugly and fat, but after seeing him today, I have decided I will like being his wife. He is wealthy beyond belief. I was told this house was grand, but it exceeds my expectations. After Marquis's grandfather dies, all you see here will belong to me. With the Vincente land and ours connected, we will have more land than any family in California."

"What will Marquis do on your wedding night when he finds out his wife is less than pure and has been with many lovers?" Eleanor foolishly asked.

Isabel whirled around, grabbed a handful of her sister's hair, and twisted it tightly around her hand until it brought tears to Eleanor's eyes. "You are not going to tell him anything, my sister. Besides, do you think me a fool? I have ways of preventing Marquis from finding out about my lovers." Isabel's face was twisted with wrath. "Be warned, little sister. I will kill you if you ever attempt to come between me and Marquis."

Eleanor was whimpering in pain as her sister yanked her backward, and she fell off the bench, hitting her head on the stone patio. "Swear you will never utter a word about my other lovers to Marquis!" Isabel pressed her foot against Eleanor's throat. "Swear!" she screamed out in rage.

"I swear," Eleanor whispered, her voice hardly audible since the pressure from her sister's foot was cutting off her breathing.

Isabel removed her foot and walked toward the arched doorways that led to the house. Halfway there, she turned to her sister. "The day anyone comes between me and Marquis is the day that person dies!"

Chapter Three

It was early morning when Valentina stood on the deck of the *Berengaria* watching Captain Masterson and his crew scurrying about, making preparations to drop anchor. As the ship sailed through the bay past a small island, Valentina chose not to look at the tangle of ships that cluttered the inlet; instead she trained her eyes on the distant shore.

She drew in her breath, so struck was she by the virgin beauty that assailed her senses. It was as if she were looking upon a land time had forgotten—a new land for new people. The sun spread its light over the land, turning the grassy slopes a spectacular yellow. This really was the golden country, she thought. With great anticipation, Valentina looked past the wooded area toward what she knew would be the town of San Francisco.

The *Berengaria* made her way slowly forward to avoid scraping one of the many ships that rode at anchor. Valentina had never seen such an awesome sight; there were so many ships in the bay that their masts cluttered the sky, blocking out the full view.

As the ship moved closer to shore, Valentina strained her eyes, searching for some sign of her mother and father. Excitement stirred within her breast. Soon . . . soon they would be a family again!

No sooner had the anchor clanked into place at the bottom of the ocean floor than Valentina's trunks and boxes were loaded onto the longboat. Valentina was learning that little time was wasted on board a ship. She and Salamar were helped down the rope ladder into the boat. Then Captain Masterson climbed in beside them and directed the oarsmen to make for shore.

Nathan Masterson's warm smile rested on Valentina. "I trust you will find all you desire here in California, Miss Barrett."

"Thank you, Captain. And let me also thank you for an exciting voyage. I will tell my father about the courtesy that was extended to me and Salamar on board the *Berengaria.*"

Captain Masterson looked pleased at her words, and Valentina could have sworn that he blushed. "I will be anchored here for a fortnight, Miss Barrett. Should you have any reason to need help, I stand ready to assist you."

She blessed him with a smile that made her eyes dance. "I expect to be in the safe hands of my mother and father as soon as we reach shore. But I thank you for your kindness." Again her eyes were sweeping the distant shore, searching for the beloved faces of her parents.

When the longboat bumped against the wooden pier, Valentina still had not spotted them. As Captain Masterson helped her ashore, she scanned the faces of the crowd, unaware of the many looks of admiration directed at her by the men on the dock.

"I don't see your parents," the captain observed, glancing about the crowd of people who had gathered to meet the *Berengaria.*

Valentina's legs felt wobbly but she knew from experience that the sensation would pass as soon as she

42

became accustomed to being on land again. She met the captain's eyes. "No," she replied with a sinking heart, "I don't see them either. Perhaps they didn't know I would be arriving today." Her disappointment showed on her face. She glanced at Salamar as if she wanted her to decide what they should do.

Captain Masterson, seeing Valentina's distress, offered her reassurance. "I suspect your mother and father are waiting for the crowd to clear out, Miss Barrett. I would suggest that you move farther down the pier while I see to your baggage. If by that time your parents haven't come, I will send one of my men to make inquiries for you."

"Thank you. That would seem the best thing to do," Valentina admitted, glad to have him take charge for her.

Slowly Valentina realized she was the center of attention. She blushed at some of the bold stares the men cast her way. She felt as if she were on display. Never had she been on the receiving end of such close scrutiny.

Seeing Valentina's discomfort, Captain Masterson took her arm to assist her across the wooden planks that served as a dock. "Let's get you and your maid out of this heat," he said, clearing a path through the mob.

Valentina did not see the tall, gangly figure of a man making his way toward them until he spoke. "Pardon me, would you be Captain Masterson of the *Berengaria?*" The stranger's eyes swept Valentina with interest before resting for a brief moment on Salamar.

"I am indeed Nathan Masterson, sir. How may I be of service to you?"

"I am Reverend Percival Lawton," the man introduced himself, speaking in a stiff New England accent. "I was asked by Mrs. Barrett to meet her daughter, Miss Valentina Barrett. I have been watching every ship that came in for the last two weeks. Very tedious business, I must say."

Valentina wondered why her mother and father had not come to meet her themselves. Why had they sent this stranger? When she looked into the reverend's serious grey eyes, she extended her gloved hand. "I'm Miss Barrett, sir. Why aren't my parents here to meet me? Has something happened?"

"I thought you must be her," he said, ignoring her question as he took her hand for the briefest moment; then he dropped it as if it burned him. Reaching into his coat pocket, he removed his handkerchief and nervously dabbed at his face. "Nothing to worry about. I hired a buggy, so if you will put me onto your baggage, I'll see it's loaded."

Valentina pointed to the collection of trunks and boxes that was being stacked nearby. "You will find everything there, Mr. Lawton," she answered before she turned her attention to Captain Masterson. She was anxious to be away so she could see her parents. "I want to thank you again for everything, Captain. I'm sure my parents will want you to take a meal with us before you sail."

He took her proffered hand. "I will be honored, Miss Barrett. You have only to send word on the appointed date, and I will be there."

Nathan Masterson was reluctant to turn Valentina over to the nervous stranger who called himself a preacher. When the man returned, the captain saw that he was directing several dock workers to load the trunks in his carriage. Percival Lawton seemed anxious to be on his way and was irritated when Masterson pulled him aside to question him.

"I don't understand all the secrecy. I want to know exactly where you are taking Miss Barrett. I know her mother and father quite well. It doesn't sound like them to send a stranger to meet their daughter."

The man nodded his head toward the west. "I have a small place just across town where I live with my sister.

At the back of my place we have a small cabin that the Barretts have rented from us. Ask anyone where I live and they can direct you. If you will excuse me, I'll lash Miss Barrett's baggage down."

Valentina watched Percival Lawton dart after her trunks, while Captain Masterson pulled one of the dock workers aside and questioned him about the reverend. After he was satisfied that Mr. Lawton was who he claimed to be, he returned to Valentina.

She held out her hand to him, feeling somewhat nostalgic about their parting. "I will miss the adventure, Captain. Perhaps I will sail again on the *Berengaria*. I certainly hope so."

Captain Masterson bowed slightly and touched the tips of her fingers. "I would deem it an honor to have you sail with me at any time, Miss Barrett."

He watched her turn away, knowing he would always remember her. After she was lost in the crowd, he made his way back to his men who were unloading cargo onto the pier. He was not really saying good-bye; he would see her again, he decided.

When Valentina and Salamar reached the buggy, Mr. Lawton made no attempt to help them inside. Puzzled, they looked at each other before climbing aboard, taking precautions not to show too much ruffled petticoat.

Reverend Lawton spoke not a word as he guided the mules into a steady stream of traffic. A heavy, uncomfortable silence hung in the air and Valentina was worried about her parents. Where were they? Why had they entrusted her to a man she didn't know? Suddenly she felt the comfort and warmth of Salamar's hand on her shoulder. The reassuring touch seemed to be telling her, Don't worry, everything will be all right.

With a sigh of relief, she turned to her maid and smiled at her. Then she turned her attention to her surroundings. She became fascinated by the sights and sounds

45

around her. San Francisco was a ramshackle town, teeming with people from all walks of life. There were wooden buildings, many half finished. Canvas tents dotted the landscape, some of which had been turned into businesses. Large quantities of goods and wares were piled in front of buildings because there was no room to store them. The muddy streets were filled with masses of humanity hurrying about their daily lives. There were Chinese, Mexicans, Frenchmen, Spaniards, Russians and many other nationalities that Valentina did not recognize.

There was a strange excitement about them, as if the very air they breathed was filled with gold dust. Valentina turned to Mr. Lawton, determined to find out about her mother and father. "I was wondering why my mother sent you instead of coming herself?" Valentina watched the man's face as she worked her fingers out of her gloves, then clutched them in her hand.

"Your father and mother rented a cabin from me several months ago. Mrs. Barrett's been real sick. Mr. Barrett took off to the gold fields and left her alone. Me and my sister thought it only Christian for us to look after her until you arrived." His mouth thinned, and he turned watery eyes on Valentina. "Folks that come to this place seeking gold deserve what they get. It's the devil's work."

Valentina's head was reeling. No, he couldn't be telling the truth. "My father would never desert my mother when she was ill, as you suggest." Valentina glared at the man, knowing she was on the verge of losing her temper.

"I didn't mean to imply that your father deserted your mother. I believe she was supposed to join him when he had a suitable shelter built for her at his diggings."

Valentina stared at the man, hardly breathing. She was almost afraid to ask the question that went round and round in her mind. "How ill is my mother?"

"Could be worse; probably will be. She's got what they call the Panama fever. Must have got it coming overland through the jungle."

Valentina gripped her hands together tightly. "What are you saying?"

"Misery is born of misery. Your folks committed a great sin by coming to this land and trying to desecrate it. That's the folly of greed."

Valentina felt her anger rise to its zenith. "How dare you say such a thing about my mother and father! My mother is a good woman, and my father is an honorable man. You have no right to criticize them. Take me to my mother at once."

Percival Lawton's watery eyes moved over Valentina's face. "I have the right. I'm God's messenger, and he speaks through me. Your father paid the price for his sins; now it's your mother's turn to pay."

Valentina's breathing seemed to have stopped for the moment. "Are you saying that my father is . . . ?" She clutched her gloves, twisting them tightly. "No, it isn't possible."

Percival Lawton looked away from her. He was concentrating on guiding the mules past a wagon that was bogged down in the mud, blocking the road. "I'll not be the one to bring you ill tidings. When you see her, you must ask your mother to tell you about your father."

Valentina clamped her teeth together and brought her anger under control, but she could not control the fear that nagged at her heart—fear that something dreadful had happened to her father. "I insist that you tell me where my father is," she demanded in a shaky voice.

Mr. Lawton looked sideways at her. "Well, if you say so, but your mother wanted to be the one to tell you. She took ill right after your father left for the diggings. Your father had paid my sister and me to look after your mother. Then he left with his partner—a man some believe to be of dubious reputation. Your mother got a letter saying they struck gold; shortly thereafter it was learned that your father was killed in a cave-in."

"No!" Valentina cried, reaching out for Salamar's hand. "No, it cannot be!" Tears blinded Valentina and rolled down her cheeks. Trying to control her emotions, she gripped Salamar's hands tightly. "Was . . . did anyone find my . . . father's . . . body? Is there proof he is dead?"

"The proof is whether or not you believe Samuel Udell's word. Your mother refuses to admit he's dead. She says she'd know it if he wasn't coming back."

"Since we only have Samuel Udell's word that my father is . . . dead, and you implied that he might not be trustworthy," Valentina concluded, clutching at straws. She could not accept that her father might be dead. He had been so alive. She loved him so much.

"Well . . . if you want to look at it that way; not many men trusted Mr. Udell. I tried to tell your father he was unscrupulous, but he didn't heed my warning. Be that as it may, your father is most assuredly dead. Why else would he stay away so long? Your mother needs to face the truth or she won't ever get well. She's too weak to get out of bed, just lays there moaning. It was like she gave up when she heard about your father. She's been counting the days until you arrive." He gave Valentina a tight little smile. "I believe I have won your mother's soul to the Lord and she sees the error of her wicked ways."

Valentina was weighed down by emotions she could not ignore. Her heart ached for her father; she was worried about her mother. She wanted to strike out at this hateful pious man. "My mother's soul doesn't need saving, Reverend Lawton. Don't you ever dare say that she had wicked ways."

He gave her a condescending glance. "We can all do

with a little soul-searching, miss. You might do well to remember that."

Valentina glared at the man. She had no intention of being in his company any longer than was necessary. She felt an urgency to be with her mother, but the buggy wheels seemed to turn so slowly.

By now she realized Salamar had not spoken a word. Looking into her companion's face, she saw her concerned frown. "We will have a doctor look at your mother, Valentina," Salamar said with assurance. "As for your father, I, like your mother, will not believe any harm has come to him until there is proof."

"Yes!" Valentina cried. "We won't believe the worst unless we have to. Mother would know if anything dreadful had happened to Father."

The mules were straining at the bit as they maneuvered the steep hill. "Will the animals not go faster?" Valentina urged frantically. "How much farther is it to your house?" She was beginning to think they would never arrive at their destination.

Percival Lawton glanced at Valentina, hoping her temper had cooled. She sure was stubbornly defensive of her parents, he thought. That spoke well of her in his eyes—even if the parents didn't deserve her blind trust. "It's just a short ways now. Right over that next hill. Patience is another of God's virtues, Miss Barrett," he reminded her.

Valentina was using all her strength at the moment to hold onto what shred of patience she had left. Realizing it would do no good to try to reason with this man, she tried to concentrate on the scenery. Vaguely she noticed the bars and saloons they were passing. Loud music filled the air and she could hear the shouts and laughter of merrymaking. The whole atmosphere had a feeling of unreality.

When Percival Lawton drew the mules to a halt,

Valentina glanced at the small house. It was neat and shining with a fresh coat of paint. She was surprised that his house was so near the business part of town. There was a general store across the street and what appeared to be a saloon next door. She thought it a strange place for a man of the cloth to live.

As if reading her mind, Mr. Lawton spoke. "We search for lost souls wherever we find them, Miss Barrett. It is better to live among the wolves as a sheep than be torn apart by their fangs."

It crossed Valentina's mind that this man who claimed to be a messenger of God could learn a valuable lesson from the kindly vicar in her church back home. It was on the tip of Valentina's tongue to ask him about the scripture that mentioned casting one's pearls before the swine, but she refrained.

Climbing out of the buggy, she ran up the rock strewn walkway toward the house. Not bothering to knock, she pushed open the door and looked about her in desperation. The room was small and neat, though sparsely furnished.

The woman who occupied the sofa cast her knitting aside. Coming to her feet, she stared at Valentina with astonishment and disapproval written on her face. Valentina guessed this would be Reverend Lawton's sister, the one of whom he had spoken. One glance told Valentina that this was the female counterpart to Mr. Lawton—watery eyes and all. The gown the woman wore was of black broadcloth with a stark, white lace collar. Her dark hair was pulled back in a severe bun and her stingy little mouth was drawn into a tight frown.

"Where is my mother?" Valentina blurted out.

"And who, pray tell, would you be? Am I to assume you are Miss Barrett?" Prudence Lawton asked, looking down her nose at Valentina most disapprovingly.

"Yes. Please forgive my rudeness. In my concern for

my mother, I forgot my manners. I am sure you will understand I am most anxious to see her."

Suddenly the woman's attention was drawn away from Valentina. She stared, with gaping mouth, at Salamar, who stood in the doorway. "I will not have an Indian under my roof," she screeched. "Get her out! Get her out! We will all be massacred!"

Salamar seemed undaunted by the woman's outburst. She walked slowly and deliberately to stand beside Valentina. "Salamar is my friend and companion, ma'am," Valentina explained. "You are in no danger from her."

Reverend Lawton chose that moment to enter the room. Having heard the conversation, he intervened. "Now, Prudence, you mustn't make snap judgments. Even the unworthy deserve our consideration. Perhaps this heathen woman was placed in our hands for a reason."

In spite of the look of amusement on Salamar's face, Valentina ground her teeth together. Had the whole world gone crazy? What in heaven's name would make this man and woman believe they were the salvation of the world? Anger burned like fire in Valentina's chest. "I can assure you, sir, and madam, that Salamar has not been placed in your hands for any reason." She felt rage at the pious assumption that Salamar was a heathen. "For your information, Salamar's soul is already in good hands. And I can tell you one more thing about her; she doesn't judge people before she knows them, and then only sparingly." Valentina's breasts were rising and falling with each breath she took. She did not notice the covetous way Percival Lawton was staring at her, but Salamar noticed. When Valentina looked at her maid, she saw humor dancing in her eyes.

"Now, now, let us all begin again and see if we can't make amends," Reverend Lawton said, dabbing at his face with his handkerchief. "Prudence, I would like you to be acquainted with Miss Barrett. Miss Barrett, my sister, Prudence. As I told you before, my sister has been looking after your mother."

Valentina acknowledged the woman with the merest nod of her head. She was becoming angrier by the moment. All she wanted to do was find her mother. Drawing herself to her full height, she spoke authoritatively. "I will see my mother now if you don't mind."

Prudence Lawton was still glaring at Valentina and said nothing, but her brother smiled and nodded his head. "You will find your mother in the log cabin out back. Just go down the hallway and out the back door. You go ahead while I see to your baggage."

"No, leave everything in the buggy," Valentina said. "We won't be staying in your cabin. I intend to take my mother away from here as soon as possible."

Prudence snorted. "It's not likely you will find a decent place that will take you in, even if you could afford it. There isn't a room to be had in this whole town."

Valentina hurried past the woman and made her way down the hallway with Salamar in close pursuit. She passed a kitchen, then two closed doors that she assumed to be bedrooms. Pushing open the back door, she moved quickly in the direction of the small log cabin. Rushing up the wooden steps, Valentina slowly lifted the crude latch and the door swung open on creaking hinges. Though the sun came through the cracks between the logs, the room was in darkness. She could only see vague outlines.

"Mother," she called softly. There was no answer.

As she stepped inside, her eyes slowly adjusted to the darkness. There appeared to be crates and boxes stacked against one wall, leaving very little space for anything else. Valentina's gaze fell on the small cot be-

52

neath the window.

"Mother," she called again, this time louder. There was an answering moan, and Valentina flew across the room, dropping down on her knees beside the cot.

With trembling hands she touched the dear face that was no more than a dark outline. "Mother!" she cried, feeling the heat of her mother's skin. She was burning up; her temperature was much too high!

"Valentina, is that you?" Evonne Barrett's French-accented words were no more than a weak whisper.

"It's me, Mother. I'm here and everything is going to be all right now."

"Oh, my dearest child, I thought you would never get here. I waited so long . . . so long. Please let in some light so I can see your face." Evonne Barrett was becoming excited, lapsing into her native French.

Salamar moved across the room and jerked down the heavy paper that had been blocking out the sunlight. The room was instantly flooded with a warm glow, and Valentina could see the tears on her mother's cheeks. She was horrified at the change in her mother. Her once shining, golden hair was streaked with grey; her skin had a yellow cast to it; her eyes were dull and lifeless. Valentina's heart ached so severely that she wanted to cry out, but she knew she must put on a brave front for her mother.

"Don't worry, Mother. I'm here now and I'll take care of you. Salamar and I will have you well in no time. You'll see."

Suddenly Evonne Barrett gripped her daughter's hand with a strength that surprised Valentina. "Did Reverend Lawton tell you about your father?"

Valentina nodded. "Yes. Can it be true that father is . . . ?" She couldn't bring herself to say the word.

"No, I don't believe it for a moment. I would know it inside if my husband were dead. You must promise me

53

that you will do everything you can to find him. Promise me, Valentina! Promise!"

Evonne seemed so upset that Valentina feared for her health. She knew she had to calm her down or she would become hysterical. "I promise, Mother. I will not rest until I find Father."

For the first time since entering the cabin, Salamar spoke up. "This place is dirty. It isn't healthy for a well person, let alone someone who is ill."

Valentina glanced about her, gritting her teeth at the condition of the cabin. It was dusty and looked as if it had never been cleaned. The bed covers were soiled and Valentina felt her blood boil. Was this what the Lawton's called taking care of a sick person?

"The first thing I want to do is get a doctor out here to examine you, Mother," she said, trying to organize her thoughts. "I'm going to get you out of this place. We will go to a hotel until we can find a proper place to live."

Evonne closed her eyes as if keeping them open was too great an effort. "We can't move from here, Valentina. It costs a hundred dollars a month to rent this cabin. Wade paid for it a year in advance. The rent runs out in three weeks. I don't know what we will do then. I want to stay here so when your father returns he will know where to find us."

"A hundred dollars a month! That's outrageous!" Valentina declared. "I will find somewhere far better than this. You can't get well here."

Evonne took her daughter's hand. "You don't know, dear. There are people sleeping on the streets for want of a roof over their heads. We are very fortunate to have this place. The money is all gone. . . ." her voice trailed off.

Valentina noticed Salamar had already begun to stack the dirty dishes that littered the crude table. The woman cast her a resigned glance before picking up a pail and walking outside to find the well. Valentina noticed that the cabin consisted of two rooms. The only furniture was the cot her mother lay upon and a rickety table with two chairs. There was an open hearth, but no fire burned in it to ward off the dampness of the cabin.

"We will stay here for awhile, Mother, but only until we can find something better. I am going to talk to Mr. Lawton about a doctor."

Glancing down, Valentina noticed her mother had already drifted off into a restless sleep. Now that her mother could not see, Valentina's tears flowed freely. In the days to come, she would have to call on all her strength because she was the head of the family now. Everything rested on her shoulders. To add to her troubles, it did not appear that her mother had much money, and Valentina had very little. It didn't matter, she thought. She would find some way to take care of her mother.

Standing up, she glared in the direction of the Lawton house. She did not intend to allow Mr. Lawton and his sister near her mother again. They had shamefully neglected her mother's care. How dare they treat her gentle, sweet mother in such a shabby manner.

Valentina had promised her mother she would find her father. That was one promise she intended to keep. Whatever it took, she would do; wherever she had to go, she would go. Wiping the tears from her eyes, she squared her jaw and rolled up her sleeves. The first order of the day was to clean this filthy cabin.

Watching her mother's eyes slowly flutter open and then close again, Valentina knew she had drifted off to sleep. She placed a soft kiss on Evonne's fevered cheek, then moved to the door to see Salamar returning with the wooden bucket full of water.

"What are we to do, Salamar?" she asked, looking into her sympathetic dark eyes.

"You will do what you must," came the assured answer. "You always have."

Valentina's shoulders drooped; she felt a sob building deep inside. "My father, he can't be . . . dead."

Salamar's eyes moved over the dank and dingy room with a look of disgust. "I do not know about that, but for now we must look after your mother's needs. This place isn't fit for a pigsty."

Valentina raised her head, knowing she must push her grief aside for the moment. She would not cry for her father, because that would be admitting he was dead. Salamar was right; she would take care of her mother first, then she would try to find her father.

Chapter Four

Salamar was a wonder at accomplishing the impossible. In no time at all she had removed the crates that had cluttered the cabin and had stacked them outside the door with orders for Mr. Lawton to store them elsewhere. The cabin was clean, delicious aromas were coming from the caldron that bubbled over the open hearth, and Valentina's mother had been moved into the other room, away from the cooking noises, so she could rest undisturbed. Evonne Barrett now wore a fresh, clean nightgown and was reclining against snow white bed linens.

Valentina placed another log on the fire. Lifting the lid on the iron pot, she sliced onions into the stew and smiled as the wonderful aroma drifted through the house. She had not been idle either. She had scrubbed the floors until they shone, cleaned the windows until the reflection of the sun sparkled on each pane.

Now that Valentina was sure everything had been done to make her mother rest more comfortably, she would seek out a doctor and persuade him to come to the cabin and examine her mother.

* * *

Valentina watched Doctor Cline lean forward to listen to her mother's heartbeat. He cast Valentina a grim look as he straightened. "How long have you had this fever, Mrs. Barrett?" he questioned in his stiff professional manner.

Evonne Barrett, looking pale and listless, tried to lean forward but fell back weakly against the pillow. "I felt wonderful on the ocean voyage to Panama," she said, gasping for breath. "I was well during the hazardous boat trip on the jungle river that took us to the small village of Gorogona. It was on the trek through the jungles to the city of Panama that I first fell ill. At the time, my husband feared I had eaten something that had disagreed with me. After a few days of fever and chills, I seemed to recover. Later the fever recurred. Each attack seems worse than the last, leaving me weaker, sapping my strength."

Doctor Cline nodded. "It's just as I thought. You have the Panama fever. Many get the disease while in the tropics. There is no cure—it recurs every so often. I could have done more for you if you had contacted me sooner, Mrs. Barrett. Why didn't you?" There was reprimand in his voice, accusation in his gray eyes. "Why did you suffer when I could have given you relief?"

Evonne drew a shallow breath. "I was waiting for my husband to return and my daughter to come from England."

"With the right medicine you will be feeling better in no time. While I can't cure the Panama fever, I can treat the symptoms and get you back on your feet."

Valentina clasped her mother's hand, knowing the torment she must have lived through. She had been alone and helpless, with no family or friends. Her heart ached for what her mother had suffered. "The doctor will have you feeling well in no time, Mother. I'm here now and you aren't to worry about anything. I will take care of you." A tear ran down Evonne's cheek and she sighed contentedly. Her worries had been placed in the capable hands of her daughter. Her eyes drifted shut; she could rest now.

Doctor Cline snapped his black bag closed and cleared his throat. "Walk me outside, Miss Barrett, and I will explain the treatment to you."

Valentina noticed that her mother had fallen asleep. The doctor followed her as she tiptoed to the door. Stepping outside, she waited for him to speak. For the briefest moment he looked uncomfortable and cleared his throat once more. "I think I should inform you, Miss Barrett, that the medicine your mother will need is very expensive."

Valentina felt a sinking feeling deep inside. "How expensive?"

"A bottle will last about six weeks. The cost is one hundred dollars a bottle."

Valentina gasped in disbelief. "Surely you jest. That is totally unreasonable."

His eyes looked tired; his shoulders sagged. "I agree with you that it's unreasonable, but there is nothing I can do about it. The plant from which the medicine is extracted comes from the South American jungle. The price has been blown out of proportion by unscrupulous dealers. I am loath to pass the cost on to my patients, but I have little choice in the matter."

Valentina knew he was telling the truth, and she could see he felt embarrassed about the cost. She was frantic, wondering where she would get the money for the medicine. Pushing her fear aside, she realized this was her problem, not Doctor Cline's. "What do I owe you for your visit, Doctor?" she asked.

He shook his head and his kindly eyes took on a deeper sadness. "I am not looking to rob you, if that's what you think, Miss Barrett. I know some of my colleagues are charging exorbitant fees, but my fee is still four dollars a visit, like it always was."

"I believe you," she told him, knowing he was a compassionate man.

Doctor Cline smiled readily. "Your mother must also have red meat. This is almost as important as the medicine." He was hesitant, as if he hated to lay another burden at her door. "Meat is very expensive, Miss Barrett. I hope it will be no hardship on you."

Valentina's eyes met his with a spark of determination. "I have the money to pay for the medicine and the meat. Before my mother needs a refill, I will have the money for that also."

He gave her a warm smile. "San Francisco is a hard place for three women alone. Prices are outrageous. The men outnumber you a hundred to one. Is there no way you can take your mother back to England?"

"No, not until we find my father."

"Out here men have been known to disappear and never be heard from again. I wish you luck in finding your father, Miss Barrett."

"I will find him. If he is alive, I will bring him to my mother. If he is dead, then I will find his body or his grave. My mother needs to know if he is dead or alive. If he is dead, she needs to grieve. They are very close, Doctor Cline. I don't know if she can survive without him."

The doctor's eyes held a hint of admiration. "You will not find the life here easy, Miss Barrett. I would warn you to exercise extreme caution. These men are a rough lot. They aren't accustomed to seeing a beautiful young woman in their midst. If that alone weren't enough, allow me to inform you about the cost of living hereabout. Flour is forty to a hundred dollars for a hundred-pound bag; beef is a dollar a pound. Bacon and ham are a dollar

60

to a dollar and a half a pound. A man's shirt is going for anywhere from fifty to a hundred dollars. Those prices are the rates at the mines; they are only slightly less here in San Francisco."

Valentina felt as if all her courage were draining out of her bit by bit. She did not know how they were going to survive, but she would fight to give her mother whatever she needed to get well. She would not give up until she had learned what had happened to her father. Withdrawing money from her green silk reticule and carefully counting out the coins, she handed them to the doctor. He, in turn, handed her a bottle of the precious amber liquid.

"You will want to give your mother half an ounce first thing in the morning and last thing at night. If you have any problems, send for me. I will drop by as often as I can to check on your mother's progress." He gave her a tired smile, turned, and walked away. His boots made a crunching sound as he disappeared down the rock-strewn pathway.

Valentina felt tears of hopelessness and frustration building behind her eyes, but she refused to cry. If she did not do something soon, they would be destitute. She stepped back into the house. As always when she was troubled, she sought Salamar.

Salamar was spreading a pallet near the fireplace for Valentina. Without looking up, she spoke. "I have made my bed in the bedroom so I can be near your mother in case she needs me during the night. You will sleep here undisturbed."

Looking up, Salamar saw Valentina's troubled expression. Standing, she held out her arms and Valentina went into them seeking comfort. "Everything will work out for the best, Valentina. Things always look the darkest when one is weary. You must rest, my sweet child. You will be the strong one now. Your mother does not have your father to lean on; she will now lean on you."

Valentina had been in California for a week. Her mother seemed to be growing stronger and the fever attacks had become less frequent. In spite of the shabbiness of the cabin, it now had taken on a homey glow. Among Salamar's many talents, she was a wonder with a needle. Out of one of Valentina's old yellow-and-white-checked gowns, she had made curtains, which hung at the windows in the front room as well as in the bedroom. Valentina had painted the kitchen furniture white, and a bright yellow cloth covered the imperfections of the rickety old table. To make her mother's bedroom more cheerful, Valentina daily placed wildflowers near her bed.

It was still dark when Valentina buttoned her white blouse and pulled on her green velvet jacket. By the light from the outer room, she could see that her mother was still sleeping. She was relieved. Valentina knew her mother would worry when she discovered that she had gone to her father's mine, but she must. She wanted to stand face-to-face with Samuel Udell and have him tell her what had happened to her father.

Pushing her foot into a pair of black riding boots, Valentina stood up and adjusted her green velvet bonnet. When the rap came on the door, she rushed to the front room, hoping her mother had not been awakened by the noise. She pulled aside the curtains to glance at the short Mexican man who waited on the steps.

"Salamar, that will be the guide that Doctor Cline sent to take me to Father's mine. It will be up to you to convince Mother that I will be perfectly safe. I should be home within four days."

Salamar took Valentina's hand and held it for a long, silent moment. It was as if she were in a daze, and her strange eyes appeared to see things that no one else could. Smiling slightly, she dropped Valentina's hand. "I will convince your mother that you will be safe. You are starting out on the road to your destiny."

Valentina was accustomed to Salamar's talking in riddles, so she shrugged off her words. She glanced back at her mother for a moment, then went out the door.

The little man removed his *sombrero* and bowed to her. "I am Santiago, señorita. Doctor Cline has sent me to guide you." The dark-skinned man grinned from ear to ear, and his eyes danced merrily.

"Did Doctor Cline tell you where we are going, Santiago?" Valentina asked, warming to his open friendliness.

"*Sí.* I know the country where your father's mine is located like I know my mother's face, señorita. You will be safe with me looking after you." His assurance was comforting, his manner gallant.

When Valentina and Santiago walked down the path to the front road, they passed the Lawton house. As they rounded the corner, Valentina almost collided with Prudence Lawton. The woman was peering over the rim of her glasses, striving for a better look at Santiago. Prudence gave Valentina her most disapproving glance.

"I know what you are up to, miss. I questioned this man when he knocked at my door asking for you. Am I to understand that you are going off into the wilds with only this man for company?" Prudence asked in a horrified tone.

"Yes, that is my intention," Valentina said, trying to step around Prudence only to have the woman grasp her arm in a vicelike grip.

"You are a foolish young woman to go off without a chaperon. I don't know how it is where you come from, but in this country a decent young girl would never go off alone with a stranger. If my brother was at home, he

63

would heartily disapprove of your actions."

Valentina gritted her teeth, trying to retain her temper. "I am not subject to your brother's likes and dislikes, Miss Lawton. My mother and I rent a cabin from you. That doesn't give you the right to dictate to us."

"Well, I never!" Prudence declared with an air of indignation. "I will certainly bring pressure to bear on my brother to have you put out of our cabin. I have already spoken to him about the disrespectful way that foreign-looking housekeeper you have speaks to me. She won't even allow me to pay my respects to your mother."

"The doctor has advised us to see that my mother has plenty of rest. He has asked that we keep her visitors to a minimum. Salamar was acting on my orders when she turned you away."

Valentina jerked free, sweeping past the astonished Prudence Lawton. She did not look back as she made her way to the waiting buggy. Santiago had to run to catch up with her. When he reached the buggy, Valentina had already climbed in and arranged her green skirt. Santiago smiled brightly, picked up the reins, and guided the matching buckskin horses onto the roadway.

Valentina was determined to find her father, and no one was going to stop her. She realized it was unconventional for a young woman to go off with a man with whom she was not acquainted, but she was desperate and had no choice. Besides, she reasoned, Doctor Cline must trust Santiago or he would not have recommended him to her. Valentina was aware that Prudence Lawton stared after them until they were out of sight.

"How long will it take to reach the mine, Santiago?" she asked, pushing all other thoughts from her mind.

"If the warm weather holds out and it does not rain, señorita, we will be at the mine late tomorrow afternoon. The last ten miles of the journey will be through rugged country. We will have to leave the buggy at a friend's *hacienda* and go on horseback." He looked at her questioningly. "Can you ride, señorita?"

"Yes, I can ride very well," she admitted, gazing at the clear golden sky. A flock of blue birds soared into the heavens, and a soft wind kissed her cheek. Now that they were leaving San Francisco behind, the land was an unspoiled paradise. Valentina felt a kinship with this land. Everything would be wonderful if only her mother would regain her health and she could locate her father alive.

Marquis Vincente and his grandfather reined in their horses at the corral to watch several vaqueros breaking wild horses. It was the first day in weeks that Don Alonso had felt well enough to ride horseback.

Out of the corner of his eye, the older man glanced at his grandson, wondering what went on in his mind. He had been silent and brooding lately. This was not the way he had expected Marquis to behave after learning his future wife was beautiful. Of course, he reasoned, Marquis was a handsome young man and had been spoiled by beautiful women all his life. Perhaps he was not looking forward to being tied down to just one woman. It was common knowledge that Marquis had a mistress in town and saw other women besides. The thing that worried his grandfather was the lack of interest Marquis had displayed toward his betrothed, Isabel Estrada.

"You are very different from me when I was your age, Marquis. I was so much in love with your grandmother that I gave up my mistress, insisting that the wedding take place two months sooner than was arranged."

Marquis smiled at his grandfather. "Yes, but my grandmother was an exceptional woman. All the men in the country were in love with her. Did you never

65

question that she was the right woman for you, Grandfather?"

Don Alonso frowned. "No. But even if I had, I would have married her anyway. Once a Vincente has given his word, he never breaks it." The old man's eyes glittered with feeling. "Do you hear me? A Vincente never breaks his word, Marquis!"

Marquis stared into the distance. Was this what his life was going to be like? He could not picture himself rushing home to Isabel every night. She was beautiful—as an icicle was beautiful—and with about as much substance and warmth. Where was the woman who would touch his heart? Was he cold inside? Was his heart surrounded by ice also? Would he never feel really alive?

He drew in a resigned breath, smiling at the old grandee. "You do not need to worry, Grandfather. I will never break my word."

"Good, good. I want many great-grandsons to keep me company in my old age. You are the last of a proud line. I do not want to see the Vincente name die out."

Marquis tried to think of a baby coming from his and Isabel's union. He could not picture her as a mother—not the mother of his sons. "I do not love Isabel, Grandfather. I do not even like her."

"What has love or liking to do with anything? I admit that if love comes with marriage it is a good thing, but it isn't necessary."

Marquis gazed at the distant Sierra Mountains and felt a chill in his heart. Deep inside there was a part of him that wanted to know love—if the emotion really existed. So far he had found love to be a fabrication that singers sang about and poets wrote about. It had never touched his heart. He doubted that it ever would.

Chapter Five

The coast had been left behind; Valentina and Santiago now traveled in heavily wooded country. Valentina would have enjoyed the beautiful scenery if she had not been so troubled. She stared blankly at the profusion of wildflowers that grew on the grassy hillsides. She was unmindful of the tall pine trees that scented the air with a bracing aroma. As the horses clopped along the dusty road, her thoughts were on her father. She wondered what she would say to her mother if she discovered her father were indeed dead?

It was shortly before sunset when Santiago pulled off the road, stopped beside a gurgling stream, and unhitched the horses. Valentina walked along the grassy slopes as he set up a canvas tent for her to sleep in. She was touched by the little man's thoughtfulness. He seemed to anticipate everything that would add to her comfort.

Valentina patted each of the bay horses that were tethered nearby. Walking downstream, she allowed her eyes to wander past the woods, drinking in the beauty of this land. She stooped down to pick up a pinecone that was the length of her arm, marveling at its size.

As the sun splashed its last dying colors against the

western sky, she returned to camp. Santiago smiled widely, motioning her to sit on the camp stool so he could serve her dinner. Valentina was not hungry, but to keep from hurting Santiago's feelings, she ate the beans and *tortillas* that he had prepared for her.

Later she entered the tent and lay down on the downy soft bed Santiago had made for her. She fell asleep almost immediately and did not awaken, even when the distant sound of a wolf pack echoed through the dense valley. Valentina felt safe with the little man, Santiago, who had gone out of his way to please her.

As the next day progressed, the road took on a steady upward grade, becoming no more than a rutted trail. The team made slow progress climbing the foothills of the Sierra Mountains. The fog was so dense it was impossible to see the horses, let alone the road. Santiago slowed the animals to a walk and strained his eyes, trying to watch the road. The chilled wind that blew down the mountainside was biting cold. Valentina pulled her cape tightly about her and pushed her hands into its pockets, trying to keep warm.

"When we started out this morning, the sun was shining. What happened, Santiago?" she asked, straining her eyes in the swirling fog.

Santiago adjusted his poncho about his throat before he answered. "We are at a higher elevation. The weather is often unpredictable in these mountains. I have often seen it snow up here in the month of August, señorita."

They passed beneath tall pine trees, their ghostly images colorless against the foggy sky. The day seemed endless. It was impossible for Valentina to judge time or space since she could not see the sun. A sudden gust of wind blew the swirling mist and it thinned just enough for Valentina to catch a glimpse of a deep crevasse that ran the length of the roadway. Clasping her hands nervously, she tried not to think what would happen if the buggy veered off to the side. She was amazed that Santiago could keep to the road at all since she could not see where they were going. The one thing that kept her from calling a halt until the weather changed was the burning desire to reach her father's mine.

Suddenly there was a rumbling noise in the distance that made the earth tremble. The sound was somewhat muted by the mist and it was hard to tell where it came from. Valentina felt the hair on the back of her neck stand on end when Santiago called out, "Hold on, señorita! It is a landslide!"

Before Valentina had time to think, the horses reared into the air. Rocks and debris crashed down the mountainside right in front of them. Valentina heard the animals cry out in pain as the buggy lurched before being flung into the air by the impact of the rock slide.

Amid pain and fear, Valentina felt herself being tossed about as if she were no more than a rag doll. She rolled and slid down the mountainside, until finally she came to a halt at the bottom of a deep, craggy ravine. Valentina found to her agony and dismay that she was being pressed between the buggy and a wall of solid granite.

At first, Valentina's senses were dulled with amazement that such a freak accident could happen. Gradually, she became aware of the pain that shot through her leg every time she tried to move. In the distance, she could hear the horses thrashing about and knew they had been injured and were in pain also. Between big gulps of air to keep from fainting, she tried to call out to Santiago to see if he had been injured. No sound would come from her throat; the inside of her mouth felt like cotton.

"Señorita," she heard his voice coming from somewhere out of the fog. Wetting her lips, she tried to answer but could only moan. "Answer me if you are able,

Señorita Barrett," Santiago yelled.

Strangely enough, the fog seemed to disappear in one great swirling tide, as if it had been sucked up into giant lungs. Valentina's eyes slowly adjusted to the dimness. She reached out her hand when she saw Santiago making his way down the slope toward her. Her eyes moved up the ravine and she could see the wheel marks where the buggy had left the road to slide down into the gully.

By the time Santiago reached her, she could see the concern mirrored in his eyes. "Can you move, señorita? Are you badly hurt?"

"I seem to be pinned against the rock, Santiago," she managed to say in a painful whisper. "I do not know if I am badly hurt."

The buggy had turned over and its wheels were still spinning in the air. The back part was pressed against Valentina so tightly she could scarcely breathe. Santiago leaned into the buggy, pushing against it with all his strength, but it did not budge a fraction of an inch. His expression was troubled as it became clear he could not free her. Removing his poncho, he placed it between her head and the hard stone, hoping to make her more comfortable.

"I cannot move the buggy, señorita. I am going to have to go for help."

Valentina's heart pounded with fear and her mouth felt dry. "Must you leave me all alone?"

"It is the only way. I cannot free you by myself. The ranch of Don Alonso Vincente is no more than five miles' distance. I will go quickly there and enlist his help to free you."

For the first time Valentina noticed that Santiago's right pant leg was blood soaked. "Santiago, you have been hurt yourself. You shouldn't walk on that leg until you have had medical attention."

"It is nothing, señorita. The wound looks worse than it

70

actually is. I hardly feel any pain." In spite of his brave denial, Valentina noticed the grimace of pain that moved across his face when he spoke. "I will leave the canteen of water with you, señorita. Before you have had time to miss me, I shall return."

"How many bullets do you have in the gun, Santiago?" Valentina asked. She could still hear the horses' agonized cries of pain. His eyes followed hers up the slope. "I will put the horses out of their pain," he agreed to her silent plea. "Take comfort that I will soon be back with help."

Feeling as if she had been abandoned, Valentina watched helplessly as Santiago made his way slowly up the slope. She wished she dared call him back. She had no way of knowing how badly Santiago was injured, and she prayed he could make it the five miles to get help.

After Santiago had disappeared, Valentina held her breath. She cried out when she heard the two shots, realizing he had mercifully put the horses out of their misery. Afterward, an eerie quiet settled over the land. Valentina was sure there had never been such a silence. Even the wind had died down; not a needle stirred on the pine trees.

Searching for a more comfortable position, Valentina tried to shift her weight, only to find she could not move. After catching her breath, she decided the greatest injury seemed to be to her left leg. Laying her head back against Santiago's poncho, she wondered if she would ever be able to dance again. Hysterical laughter bubbled from between her lips, and she shook her head to clear it.

"Foolish Valentina," she whispered. "You don't even know if you will ever walk again and you are worried about dancing. You may die here, deserted and alone, Valentina Barrett." The sound of her own voice did nothing to alleviate the aloneness that weighed heavily on her.

Time meant nothing. It seemed that Santiago had been gone for hours. The sun had come out and burned off the last remaining patches of fog. The heat was now so oppressive that it beat down on her like the inside of an oven. Valentina could feel her face burning, but there did not seem to be anything she could do to protect her tender skin. Santiago had placed the canteen within her reach so she picked it up, splashing water on her face, but that did not ease the burning sensation for very long. Her throat became parched, and she took a deep swallow from the canteen.

Valentina tried to shade her eyes against the sun's harsh glare. Glancing about her, she began to panic. Suppose Santiago was so badly injured he couldn't find help? What would happen if no one came to her aid? Would she die here pinned beneath the buggy?

Valentina realized she could not lose control or she would be lost. She had to keep a clear head and push back the panic that was sweeping into her thoughts. Think of something pleasant, she told herself. Closing her eyes, Valentina forced herself to imagine that she was dancing. She went through the motions in her mind, first taking herself through a Gypsy dance and finally to the dance steps of a graceful ballet. Before she knew what was happening, she felt herself nodding off. Soon she was lost in a world of dreams where she danced across a hot bed of flaming coals.

Santiago fell facedown into the dusty road, his leg throbbing in pain, his energy spent. Struggling to his knees, he tried to rise, knowing he was the only hope Señorita Barrett had. If he lost consciousness, she might die before anyone could find her. His head was swimming, and he felt himself falling forward just as he

72

heard the thundering horses' hooves coming from over the hill in front of him. His ears were ringing, and he fought to remain conscious.

Marquis Domingo Vincente was the first to see Santiago's body stretched across the road. Holding up his hand, he called for his vaqueros to halt. He jumped from his horse amid the jingling of silver spurs and the creaking of saddle leather. Going down on his knees, he lifted the wounded man's head and stared into his face.

"Santiago Garza, what has happened to you?" Marquis asked as the little man slowly opened his eyes. Marquis took the canteen that one of his vaqueros offered and held it to Santiago's lips, allowing him to satisfy his thirst before answering.

"Do not be concerned about me," Santiago said, licking his chapped lips. "There was a rock slide and my passenger was swept off the road and down into the gully. Please go to her at once. She is pinned beneath the buggy, several miles back down the road."

Marquis was a man of action and quick decision. Standing up, he ordered two of his men to take the wounded Santiago to the ranch house, while he and the others mounted their horses and rode off in a cloud of dust.

Valentina groaned as she reached for the canteen. With trembling hands, she raised it to her lips and discovered it was empty. Tears of frustration welled up in her eyes. What would happen to her mother and Salamar if she died? she wondered. Hearing the whinny of horses and the sound of men talking, she turned her head toward the roadway. A shower of pebbles sprayed into her face as a man made his way down to her.

Wiping a grimy hand across her face, she felt her fears

73

fade. The man bent over her and she gazed into compassionate dark eyes. Orders were given in Spanish, which she understood because she spoke it fluently. Ropes were tied onto the buggy, and it was soon dragged away, freeing her from her prison.

Valentina would have fallen forward but for the strong hands that held her. Those same hands were gentle as they ran the length of her body, feeling for broken bones. Valentina was in too much pain to feel embarrassed by the man's exploring fingers.

"She is a *gringa*," Marquis observed in a flat voice. His dark eyes roamed at will over the soft curves. It was hard to tell much about her features, but he was amazed at the silver-blue eyes and the golden curls that were plastered to her cheeks with perspiration. Her face was blistered from the sun, and her mouth was cracked and bleeding. Pouring water onto his snowy white handkerchief, he dabbed at her swollen lips.

"I have never seen a young *gringa* before," one of the vaqueros stated, looking Valentina over carefully. "She is not very beautiful. Her skin is very red, and her eyes are a funny color."

Marquis twisted his head, giving the man an irritated glance that immediately silenced him. He scooped Valentina tenderly in his arms. "Be silent, fool; she may understand you. Find anything that belongs to her and bring it along," he ordered in a clipped tone. "I will take her to Paraíso del Norte where my mother and sister can look after her."

Valentina found herself on horseback, held in the arms of the man who seemed to be the leader. As her head fell back against his chest, she could hear the comforting sound of his heartbeat. A feeling of well-being washed over her, and her eyes shut as she drifted off to sleep.

As if from a great distance, she heard his deep voice as he spoke in halting English. "You are safe, Silver Eyes," he whispered against her ear. "You no longer have anything to fear."

Valentina stirred and her eyes fluttered open. For a moment she was dazed, wondering where she was. As her eyes moved across the sun-drenched room, she blinked in astonishment. The walls were white and the floor was dark, shiny wood covered with a mint green rug. She lay in a huge bed amid soft pillows. The covers were snow white and a lace canopy hung overhead. The room was large and airy with high, beamed ceilings.

Slowly Valentina began to remember the accident. She sat up slowly, experiencing vague memories of a man cleaning and dressing her leg wounds and applying ointment to her sunburned face. She had tried to protest when the man had given her bitter-tasting medicine, which she now assumed had made her sleep. She must have slept the night through because the bright sunlight pouring into the room proclaimed it to be early morning.

Valentina threw the covers aside and gingerly placed her feet on the floor. She was surprised to find someone had dressed her in a soft cotton nightgown. Her clothes were nowhere to be seen. When she tried to put her weight on her leg, pain shot through her foot and she gasped.

There was a soft tap at the door, and Valentina swung her feet back onto the bed and pulled the covers up to her neck. The door was opened by a smiling, dark-skinned woman carrying a breakfast tray. Even though Valentina had never seen one, she assumed this woman was an Indian. She had high cheekbones with eyes and hair as black as a midnight sky.

"Where are my clothes?" Valentina asked as the woman placed the tray on her lap. "I want to get dressed."

"Perdone, señorita, no hablo inglés."

Valentina knew she must switch to Spanish. She was silently thanking her father, who had insisted she learn other languages. "I would like to have my clothing please," she explained, the Spanish flowing easily from her tongue.

The woman beamed happily at Valentina. "Your gown was badly torn and is being mended. I have been instructed to say the doctor wants you to stay in bed, off your foot, for a few days."

Valentina shook her head. "I thank you for your hospitality, but I cannot remain here. I have important business to attend to. My mother will be worried about me."

"I do not know about such things. I am only the maid. My mistress will be in to see you soon."

"Can you tell me about my guide, Santiago? Is he all right?"

"I know nothing of such things."

Valentina realized she might as well save her breath. This woman would tell her nothing. She would just have to wait until the mistress of the house arrived. Picking up an orange slice, she took a bite and found it delicious. She was hungry and in no time at all had eaten the whole orange. She then started on the spicy omelette that melted in her mouth. As the maid busied herself straightening up the already immaculate room, Valentina bit into the fluffy biscuit that was dripping with butter. Already she was beginning to feel much stronger and wondered about her host and hostess.

Suddenly Valentina had a vague memory of dark eyes that had enveloped her with their warmth, hands that had gently soothed her, a voice that had assured her that everything would be all right. Who was the man who had rescued her? she wondered. Was this the man's home? If so, was he married? He must be. The maid had spoken of a mistress.

Valentina did not have long to reflect on her dilemma. There was a tap on the door and two women entered. There could be no mistaking the noble blood that flowed in the veins of the white-haired woman. She was dressed all in black from the top of her *mantilla* to the toes of her soft leather shoes. The woman's smile was friendly but guarded, somehow suspicious.

Valentina glanced at the younger girl and saw a soft twinkle in her dark eyes. Her lovely face was enhanced by the white gown she wore. Valentina judged her to be no more than fifteen or sixteen years of age. Neither woman seemed to be the right age to be the wife of the man who had rescued her.

When the maid picked up the tray and moved out of the room, the young girl approached Valentina almost timidly. "I am to extend a greeting to you and say that you are welcome in the home of my grandfather, Don Alonso Vincente. My brother, Don Marquis Domingo Vincente, also extends his welcome as do I and my mother." The girl spoke in halting English, as if she were weighing every word before speaking.

"I am in your debt," Valentina answered, smiling at the young woman and then extending the warmth to the older woman as well.

"I am Rosalia Vincente and this is my mother, Doña Anna Vincente."

"I am pleased to meet you both," she said, inclining her head. "My name is Valentina Barrett. I apologize for taking advantage of your hospitality. It seems I had little choice in the matter."

Rosalia smiled and her whole face lit up. "I am so glad you have come to our home. Please know you are a most welcome guest."

Valentina smiled at Rosalia and then turned to her mother, speaking to her in Spanish. "You are most

77

gracious, Señora Vincente." The older woman seemed taken aback for a moment when she heard Valentina speak in Spanish. "Can you tell me about my guide, Santiago?" Valentina pressed. "I am very concerned about him."

Doña Anna moved closer to Valentina's bed. "Santiago is well. He had a cut on his leg, but it was not deep. He said to tell you he was going back to town and would inform your family that you will be staying with us until you are strong enough to return home."

"Can you tell me the extent of my injuries, Señora Vincente? I only feel pain in my ankle."

"The doctor says that you have a strained ankle, minor cuts and bruises, and sunburn on your face and neck. My son says it is most fortunate it was not much worse."

"Was it your son who rescued me?"

"Yes, it was Marquis."

"I don't know how I shall ever repay your family for their kindness. It was most generous of you to take a stranger into your home, Señora Vincente."

"Are you an American?" Doña Anna asked, brushing aside Valentina's thanks.

"No, I am English."

Suddenly the coldness left Doña Anna's eyes and she smiled for the first time. "Ah, I have a fondness for the English. When I was a young girl, I spent one summer in your country. I have an aunt who married an Englishman."

"I admire your country," Valentina said. "I have only been here a short time, but already I have fallen under California's spell."

Doña Anna stared at Valentina for a moment. "I am not sure this is our country any longer. My son seems to think it belongs to the Americans."

"Do you not like the Americans, señora?" Valentina realized too late that she was asking a personal question, but it had just slipped out.

"I am holding off judgment until I know more about them. My father-in-law believes the time will come when the Spanish and American races will blend into one. He thinks they will raise fine sons and this land will flourish as when the white grape grows beside the red grape. Each in its own way will make fine wine." Doña Anna frowned. "I do not believe this. He even insists that we all speak English, but I will not. I think the Americans will spoil this land."

"Let us hope not, señora. It would be a tragedy to spoil this wonderful land."

The Spanish lady looked at Valentina suspiciously. She did not trust any of the *gringo* race. To Valentina, it seemed as if a coldness passed through Doña Anna's eyes. "I have many duties to attend to. If you need anything you have only to ask the maid."

"May I inquire as to when I will be able to continue my journey?" Valentina asked. "It is most important that I leave as soon as possible."

"It is best to wait until your ankle is completely healed," Doña Anna stated authoritatively. "You would not want to be sorry years from now that you did not take proper care of your injury."

Valentina would have thanked Doña Anna again, but the woman moved quickly across the room and out the door.

Rosalia had been watching Valentina closely. When her mother left, she pulled up a chair beside her bed and sat down. "I have never seen anyone with silver eyes and golden hair before. I believe if your face were not so burned you would be very lovely."

Valentina smiled at the young girl. "My grandmother always told me that 'pretty is as pretty does.'"

Rosalia giggled. "My grandmother was said to be very kindly, but she thought a woman was frivolous if she ever glanced into a mirror. In her time, there were no mirrors in this house. I never could understand that because she was very lovely."

"How very odd," Valentina observed. "Perhaps only the very beautiful do not need to look in mirrors."

"Will you tell me something about your life in England?" Rosalia asked. "I would love to see the world, but I have never traveled out of California."

Valentina was charmed by the lovely young Spanish girl. She not only told her about England but described many of the places she had traveled. Rosalia told Valentina what California had been like before the Americans had arrived and gold had been discovered. Valentina learned that the Vincente family had come to California over a hundred years ago. They had helped build the missions and had stayed to cultivate the land and raise blooded horses and cattle.

"My grandfather is very ill. My brother has taken on the running of Paraíso del Norte," Rosalia said sadly. "Marquis will one day be the grandee. He has been pledged to marry Isabel Estrada since childhood. They will marry in the late summer."

After Rosalia left, Valentina tried to remember the face of the man who had rescued her, but all she could remember was dark, flashing eyes and the tinkling sound of silver spurs. She hoped the time would come when she could thank Marquis Vincente for saving her life and bringing her to his house.

Staring at her foot that was bound with bandages, she felt impatient to mend. She had to renew the search for her father. It was her last thought before once more falling asleep.

The rain pelted the red tile roof and ran down the thick windowpanes. Valentina tossed and turned on the bed, moaning in her sleep. She dreamed she was falling over a cliff and a hand reached out to her from the darkness. She took the hand, feeling safe and secure. Dark eyes looked deeply into hers and she heard a deep, clipped voice with a heavy Spanish accent murmur in her ear, "You are safe, Silver Eyes. You no longer have anything to fear."

Chapter Six

Valentina would have been bored to tears if it had not been for Rosalia. She found herself looking forward each day to the young girl's visits. Doctor Agustin Anza had seemed a kindly man. He had examined Valentina twice and so far had refused to allow her to get out of bed until he was satisfied she was sufficiently healed. It was not until the fifth day after her accident that the doctor gave permission for Valentina to venture out of the bedroom.

Today Rosalia had brought one of her gowns for Valentina to wear. While Valentina sat before the mirror winding up her hair in a coil and fastening it at the back of her neck, she noted that Rosalia looked troubled about something. Her eyes kept seeking Valentina's in the mirror.

"Is something wrong?" Valentina asked, turning to face Rosalia.

"It is just that I am worried because one of our vaqueros was mauled by a bear yesterday. My grandfather says the bear is a rogue and is wandering too close to our ranch. My brother and some of the vaqueros will have to hunt the animal down and slay it."

"Was the man seriously hurt?"

"Marquis hopes the man will not lose his arm. He does

not believe that he will lose his life unless an infection develops." Suddenly Rosalia smiled. "It's much too nice a day to speculate on such gloomy subjects, Valentina. I wish you could stay with us forever. I have become so fond of you while you have been with us. I have never had a friend I loved better than you."

Valentina was moved by Rosalia's words. The Spanish had such a passion for life, and Rosalia had infected Valentina with some of her enthusiasm. "I have become very fond of you also, Rosalia. I will miss you when I go away."

Rosalia shook her head. "I cannot think about your going away." Standing up, she moved over to Valentina and picked up a mother-of-pearl comb, which she arranged at the crown of Valentina's head. "My brother inquires about your health each morning. Since it is not proper for him to come to your bedroom, he has asked to talk to you as soon as you are able. He is expecting to see you today. Doctor Anza told him you could get up."

Every night Valentina had dreamed of velvet-soft brown eyes and a deep voice that caused her heart to beat rapidly. What was it about Marquis Vincente that aroused her womanly interest? She had been fascinated as Rosalia had talked about her brother. Perhaps she had been affected by the young Spanish girl's hero worship of her brother. Perhaps when she saw him again, she would find he was nothing like the man she had dreamed of so often. She was almost shy about meeting Marquis Vincente. What if he could read her mind and discovered her infatuation with him?

Glancing in the mirror, Valentina studied her image critically, turning from side to side. Other than its being too short, she thought, running her fingers over the light blue gown with its dropped waist and ruffled skirt, it fit very well. She was thankful that the redness of the sunburn had disappeared, but she did not like the soft golden tone it had left on her face. Sighing heavily, she hoped Salamar would know how to bring the whiteness back to her skin. She prayed she would look presentable when she met Marquis Domingo Vincente.

"Come," said Rosalia, taking Valentina's hand. "I will now take you to my brother."

As she walked through the house and descended the wide stairs, Valentina was awed by the beauty of the Vincente home. She saw that most of the ground flooring was polished brick. At one time it must have been red brick, but over the years it had mellowed to a soft pink. The walls were of thick white adobe. Heavy Spanish furniture completed the picture of cool openness and grace. The house was like nothing she had ever seen before. Not even when her parents had taken her to Spain had she seen a house to rival this one. The rooms they moved through were filled with vases of fresh flowers that saturated the air with a sweet, lingering fragrance.

Rosalia led Valentina through a wide, arched doorway and, to her surprise, into a huge inside garden courtyard. The golden sun danced on the water of a huge fountain from which a fine mist filtered through the air. Valentina caught her breath at the beauty of the tropical flowers and trees that grew in the garden.

Glancing about with awe and delight, Valentina saw that the house had been built in a square and each room on the inside had a door leading to a courtyard. Her room had been on the outside of the house so she had not known about this marvelous indoor garden. Drawing in the sweet aroma that reached her nostrils, she allowed her eyes to drink in the beauty. There were strange and brightly colored tropical plants, fruit trees, and climbing vines.

Valentina heard a loud chattering and squawking sound, and her eyes moved to the huge cage in the middle of the courtyard. It reached some seven feet in the air and was at least fifteen feet wide. Made of iron, the cage contained a number of colorful exotic birds.

Her heart was filled with the loveliness that surrounded her and she was assailed by the strangest sense of *déjà vu*. It was as if she belonged here and had come home after a long absence. Before she had time to shake her strange feeling Rosalia led her to her brother.

Marquis was sitting at a table with a glass of wine in his hand, staring up at the blue sky that was like a bright canopy overhead. When he heard approaching footsteps, he glanced up, his dark eyes resting on the golden-haired English woman. He had almost forgotten about her. Seeing her in the flesh was like a physical shock. He had pictured a homely girl with beautiful hair and incredible silver-blue eyes. The woman who stood before him now, nervously waiting for him to acknowledge her presence, was the most stunning creature he had ever seen!

Speechlessly he rose to his feet, staring all the while into those strange eyes. He had the feeling that they were bottomless pits of splendor and, if he weren't careful, he would be forever lost in their depths.

Valentina could now put a face to the melting dark eyes that had haunted her dreams. His hair was the color of a raven's wing. His face was strong and finely chiseled, and his deep olive complexion made his handsome features even more prominent. He was somehow foreign looking—different from the men of her own race. He stared at her with the boldness of an unsheathed blade. Dressed all in black from his jacket to the heels of his shiny boots, he was a commanding figure. Tall and lean, he moved forward with a casual grace.

"Señorita Barrett, I am happy that you have recovered from your accident." He spoke English with a clipped accent; the sound of it vibrated through her body, and Valentina knew she would hear his voice in her dreams forever.

How should she react when she had just met a man who filled her heart with new, frightening, unexplored feelings? she wondered frantically. Lowering her eyes to avoid his probing brown eyes, Valentina hoped she was behaving normally and not like the fool she felt.

Struggling to regain her composure, she spoke carefully, weighing each word. "As I have already told your mother and sister, I owe you a debt that can never be paid, Señor Vincente. You saved my life."

Marquis took her delicate hand in his, feeling a warmth surround his heart. When she raised her eyes to him, a series of shocks raced through his veins that fired his Latin blood. No, he thought, he wasn't an icicle. He most definitely could react to a woman—this woman anyway. She was every man's dream of the perfect woman. Delicately small boned, hauntingly beautiful, it was almost as if she were not of this earth. She was an angel, pure and sweet.

"You owe me nothing, señorita." Marquis had always been so sure of himself where women were concerned. Now he was hesitant, as if groping for the right words and trying not to express his bewilderment. How could he stand here making polite conversation when his heart had just taken wing. Pulling his thoughts together, he spoke gruffly to cover up his feelings. "It is you who have graced my humble home, Señorita Barrett."

Valentina could not seem to tear her eyes from Marquis's. He applied no pressure to her hand, and yet she felt as if he were drawing her to him. "I have always heard that the Spanish of California are famous for their hospitality. I now know that to be true," she said, wondering if she were babbling like an idiot.

He inclined his dark head, releasing her hand. "Will you sit with me for a moment? I would like to ask you some questions. Santiago told me you search for your father. I would like to know more about it."

Valentina dropped down in a chair while her mind whirled with confusion at what she saw in his dark eyes. Marquis suddenly looked away from her. Snapping his fingers, he summoned the servant who stood in attendance and ordered her to bring Valentina a cup of hot chocolate.

Saying that her mother needed her, Rosalia politely excused herself, leaving her brother and Valentina alone.

Valentina nervously watched her go, wishing she did not have to be alone with this disturbing man. Licking her lips, she spoke. "I suppose Santiago told you the details about my father's disappearance, señor."

"Yes, he did. I confess I pressed him for information about you. I know the precise location of your father's claim. It is not far from here." Marquis's dark eyes moved over the face that he knew would be imprinted in his mind forever. "Why do you have the feeling your father is not dead, as his partner informed your mother?"

Valentina was very aware that something was happening between her and this man, but she did not understand what it was. "I . . . my mother and father were very close. She feels she would know if he were . . . dead. Does that sound like a flimsy reason to you?"

His dark eyes flashed. "Oh, no, señorita. I did not always believe in the power of love, but I do now." At her sharp intake of breath, his eyes flickered. "I will help you find out about your father."

"I have imposed on your kindness long enough. I . . . this isn't your affair. Why should you want to help?"

He crossed his legs and toyed absentmindedly with his spurs, spinning the cylinder so it made a soft, jingling sound—that familiar sound Valentina was beginning to associate with Marquis Vincente. "You have become my business, Señorita Barrett. Anyone who is in trouble and seeks the protection of the Vincente roof will find a friend at Paraíso del Norte. It has always been so, since the first Vincente came to this land."

"Paraíso del Norte. That means Paradise of the North, does it not?"

"Your understanding of Spanish is very good, señorita. I am told, by my mother and sister, that you speak my language well."

"I understand it better than I speak it." Glancing at the fountain rather than into his disturbing eyes, she took a steadying breath. "I thank you for your offer of help, but I will find my father by myself. This is something I have to do for my mother."

"You haven't succeeded thus far," he reminded her. "It is dangerous for a woman to go about this country without proper protection."

"The accident was most unfortunate, but it could have happened to anyone. I will not let a minor accident stop me from searching for my father."

Marquis's eyes rested on the slim curve of her neck and moved up to her rose-petal lips. "You have a strong mind, but you are only a woman."

Valentina's eyes turned to shimmering ice as she swung her face up to him. "You say that I am a woman as if it were some dreaded disease for which I should apologize. The fact that I am a woman is an accident of birth. Because I was born a mere daughter instead of a son, should I care less about my father?"

Marquis's lips parted in an amused smile. "I feel it would have been an unforgivable waste had you been born your father's son. I hope your pride will not stop you from accepting my offered help. I may be able to open certain doors that would be closed to you."

Suddenly she felt deflated. Why was she fighting him? "I am not too proud to take your help, Señor Vincente. I just feel that you and your family have already gone out of your way to help me. After all, I am but a stranger to you."

His eyes caught and held hers for the briefest moment. Lowering her lashes, she stared at his hand that ran caressingly over the wine glass. "Are we strangers, Señorita Valentina Barrett? Do you not feel we have known each other all our lives?"

Was he admitting to the same feelings she was experiencing? she wondered frantically, glancing at him. Hoping her voice would sound natural, she answered cautiously, "I don't know what you mean." She shifted her gaze from his and turned to the fountain. She was sure Marquis had not missed the blush that had rushed to her cheeks.

He was quiet for so long that she turned back to find him studying her closely. "No," he said at last, "perhaps you do not know what I mean."

Valentina was relieved when the Indian maid approached and placed hot chocolate on the table in front of her. Lifting the cup so she would have something to do with her hands, she took a sip and her eyes lit up. "What is the flavor in this chocolate that makes it taste so different?" she asked, glad for any excuse to speak of other things.

"Do you like it?"

"Yes, very much."

An amused smile touched his lips, as if he knew she was purposefully turning the conversation. "You are referring to the *canela,* or cinnamon, as I believe it would be called in your country."

"I never would have thought to put cinnamon in chocolate. I can't wait to fix this for my mother. She has always been fond of spices."

"Tell me about your life," he said, leaning back in his chair and watching her closely. "What did you do before you came to California?"

Valentina placed her cup on the table and allowed her eyes to move over Marquis. His black leather bolero jacket and tight-fitting black leather trousers outlined his masculine body. Soft, knee-length black boots fit snugly about the calves of his legs. His shirt was white, calling attention to his dark skin.

"There isn't much to tell," she began. "When I was younger, I traveled the world with my parents. As I grew older, my grandmother insisted I stay with her in England and be educated while my parents continued to travel. My grandmother recently died, so I came to California to join my mother and father. On my arrival, I discovered my father . . . missing and my mother in ill health."

Marquis's eyes traveled across her face, down her neck, to watch the rise and fall of her breasts. He felt a strange stirring in his blood—a fire that had begun to burn and that would soon be out of control if he did not take care. His heart recognized that this woman would be perfect for him. No woman had ever fired his blood as she was doing. He found himself wondering what it would be like to hold her in his arms, to kiss her soft lips, to allow his fingers to tangle in her golden hair.

Valentina was the antithesis of all other women in his life. Her pale skin was a stark contrast to that of the dark-skinned women of his race. Her golden hair was beautiful to behold, and so very unlike the dark tresses of the other women he had known. He felt he could spend the rest of his life gazing into her silver-blue eyes. She was like poetry—like the beautiful heroine of a romantic ballad. Valentina Barrett was wrapping him in a world of enchantment. He knew that if he never saw her again after this day, he would always keep an image of her in his heart.

Marquis reminded himself that he was betrothed to Isabel and had no right to want this woman. A woman of her obvious good breeding and grace would never be any man's mistress, and that was all he could ever offer her. It was better to put her out of his mind—she wasn't for him. He must steel his heart against her.

"Do you like California, señorita?" he asked, thinking how foolish it was to be making polite conversation when all he could think about was how beautiful she was—how he would like to taste those rosebud lips . . .

"Indeed, I find California wondrous fair. It is a golden paradise. Even the air I breathe seems washed in gold dust."

Marquis was pleased by her assessment of his land. "You have been here such a short while. Do you think with the passing of time you might be disillusioned with California? Do you not miss your home in England?"

How could she tell this man that since landing on the shores of his California she felt as if she were home for the first time in her life? "No, I do not miss England. Wherever my family resides will be home to me." Valentina did not realize how raw her feelings were until the words came spilling out of her mouth. "I just want to find my father so my mother can be happy again—so we can be a family again."

Marquis was quietly studying her. He read the many different emotions that moved across her lovely face: sadness, loneliness, desperation to find her father. Slowly he stood up as if ready to dismiss her. "Let us hope that with the passing of time you will see your mother reunited with your father."

Valentina glanced up at him. "I fear I must impose on your hospitality even farther. As I told you, my mother is ill and I must return to San Francisco as soon as possible. I wonder if you could provide me with transportation?"

"Do you feel that you are well enough to travel such a distance?"

"Yes, I have to be. My mother will be worried about me

as it is."

"I shall see that you are safely on your homeward journey in two days' time. By then your ankle will be sufficiently healed."

Valentina could feel Marquis's coolness to her now. It was as if he were deliberately trying to be rid of her. She knew so little about men, and even less about this one. Perhaps he was bored with their conversation and was dismissing her.

She stood and extended her hand to him. "If I don't see you again, let me say how grateful I am to you and your family for taking me in. I shall always remember your hospitality."

He lightly clasped her hand and she felt almost giddy from the contact with his skin. "You will see me tonight. We are having a *fandango* in honor of my betrothed. You are, of course, to be invited."

Valentina withdrew her hand from his warm grasp. "What is a fandango?" she asked with interest.

"I suppose you would liken it to one of your balls, but a little less formal, with more gaiety. There will be food and dancing."

Feeling she had already taken up too much of his time, she nodded. "I will leave you now. Thank you again, sir."

He flashed her a smile. "If you do not stop saying thank you, I will believe that you have a very limited vocabulary."

Valentina felt the sting of his words. "I . . . yes, of course, you are right. I must seem very boring to you."

"No, not you, señorita. You are eternal springtime— you are all that is good and beautiful in this world—but never boring."

She dropped her eyes, unable to look into the passionate brown depths framed with long, sooty lashes. "If you will excuse me, señor, I have taken up enough of your time. I will return to my room."

She would have turned away, but he reached for her hand and held it tightly. "Are you very sure your ankle is no longer bothering you?"

"The pain is all but gone."

Feeling as if he were losing something very precious and rare, he released her hand and watched her move away. His thoughts turned to his betrothed, Isabel Estrada. She was from a noble Spanish family and with their marriage one of his grandfather's fondest dreams would come true. It was best that Valentina Barrett would soon be leaving. She made him want to forget his obligations to his family. Perhaps tonight he would ask Isabel if they could move up the wedding date to June. He did not trust the way his mind was beginning to work.

Valentina hurried through the archway, down the hallway, and up the stairs. The house was so large—there were so many twists and turns—and she was glad she found her bedroom without getting lost.

Sinking down on the soft bed, she touched her flushed face. Her thoughts were bewildered. In God's name, what was happening to her? Marquis Domingo Vincente had turned her whole world upside down; he had made her aware of the fact that she was a woman, and very aware that he was a man.

Chapter Seven

Valentina could hear the magical sound of violins and Spanish guitars that filled the night air. As she brushed her hair away from her face, her toe tapped, keeping time with the music. Again she was dressed in one of Rosalia's gowns. It was a lovely lavender sprigged muslin with off-the-shoulder ruffles and yards and yards of ruffles on the skirt. Her tiny waist was enhanced by the bell-shaped hoop she wore.

Rosalia had insisted that Valentina wear her hair down. The golden tresses spilled across her shoulders and down her back in a profusion of curls. As they walked into the courtyard where the *fandango* was being held, they laughed and chatted of nonsensical things young girls talk about when they are together.

The aroma of exotic flowers mixed with the delicious smell of roasting meat. There was a lighthearted festivity in the air. Valentina felt excitement churning through every part of her body. She had the ear of a dancer, and the music was calling to her.

Marquis had been talking to his grandfather when he glanced up and saw Valentina walking down the flowered path. The last dying rays of the sunshine fell on her like a golden halo of light, and Marquis was struck dumb as he watched her. Valentina's whole body appeared to scintillate. Like a diamond in the sun, she absorbed the soft, golden glow. She was so alive, so radiant. He stood transfixed through an endless moment, held by a spell that was broken only when his grandfather spoke.

"Angel de oro."

"Yes, Grandfather," Marquis whispered passionately. "A golden angel."

Isabel was standing by the bird cage talking to Doña Anna and turned to watch the golden-haired woman approach. "Who is that?" she demanded to know.

"She is Valentina Barrett, the one whom Marquis rescued from the overturned buggy. She is nice enough for a foreigner," Marquis's mother observed.

Isabel glanced quickly at Marquis, noticing the way he stared at the woman. Her fingers balled into fists and her nails cut into the palms of her hands.

"Bring this golden girl to me. I want to speak to her," the old grandee told his grandson. "I will see what there is about her that turns the ice in your veins to fire."

Marquis paid no heed to his grandfather's stab at humor. Slowly, like a man in a trance, he walked toward Valentina. His heart was pounding against his ribs and his eyes flashed like wildfire.

As one caught in a dream, Valentina watched Marquis approach. He was dressed in black velvet and moved with the lethal grace of a panther stalking his prey. His soft eyes bore into hers, as if drawing all the secrets from her mind and body. She took a deep breath but was still unable to get enough air into her lungs.

When they stood at arm's length, Marquis bowed without taking his eyes off her. "Until this day, beauty such as yours was only imagined. You have brought it to life this night, Señorita Valentina Barrett."

Rosalia glanced quickly at her brother, wondering if he had lost his senses. Why was he acting the fool? She had never known him to make pretty speeches to a woman. Did he not know that his betrothed was glaring at him from across the garden? The anger in Isabel's eyes was apparent even from a distance.

Valentina felt flushed and feverish. She had no way of knowing it, but her young body was coming to life under the tutelage of dark Spanish eyes. "I do not . . . like such compliments," she said in a breathless voice. "They make me shy and embarrassed."

"I would never want to embarrass you, Silver Eyes." He smiled and extended his arm to her. "Come. My grandfather wants to meet you."

Valentina placed her hand on Marquis's arm, and he escorted her across the courtyard. She dared not look into his eyes but glanced instead at the beautiful Spanish woman who was glaring at her. Valentina did not need to be told that the woman was Marquis's intended bride. It was easy to read the jealousy on her face. Her eyes spat fire and her red mouth drew up in a pinched frown to reveal sharp white teeth. Valentina saw hatred come to life with such force that it distorted the woman's lovely face.

Valentina's eyes moved to the younger woman who stood beside Isabel. The poor creature was as ugly as Isabel was beautiful. Her hair was limp and thin and her lip was drawn up in such a way that her protruding teeth were always showing. To Valentina's astonishment, the small woman wore a gown identical to Isabel's, making the stark contrast between the two of them more apparent.

Valentina realized she had been staring and tore her eyes away from the two women. Her glance moved to the white-haired man with dark, shining eyes. No one had to tell her she was standing before the mighty grandee himself. His years of living were carved in his bronzed face. Laugh lines fanned out from his mouth and eyes.

The gleam in his eyes told Valentina he had an appreciation for the ladies. Yet the blue veined hand that rested on the handle of his cane trembled with weakness.

"Grandfather, may I present Señorita Valentina Barrett," Marquis introduced them. "Señorita Barrett, my grandfather, Don Alonso Vincente."

"I am pleased to meet you, señor," Valentina stated warmly, feeling the need to dip into a curtsy. She had the impression that she was standing before royalty.

"So," the old man said, speaking in stilted English, "you are the one my granddaughter chatters about incessantly. I was told you have the most extraordinary eyes; I can see my grandson was not exaggerating."

Before Valentina could reply, Isabel and her sister appeared. Don Alonso introduced the sisters to Valentina, but neither Isabel nor Eleanor greeted her in return. Isabel linked her arm through Marquis's possessively while Eleanor stared past Valentina.

Don Alonso was aware of the slight to Valentina and he reached out and took her by the arm. "I am told you speak Spanish, Señorita Barrett."

"That is true, señor," she said, lapsing into Spanish. "However, as I told your grandson, I understand it better than I speak it."

"I think you are much too modest, my dear," Don Alonso declared. "You speak our language very well. You must have had a remarkable teacher."

She blessed the old man with a smile, knowing he was trying to put her at ease. As she began to lose her nervousness, she found Marquis's grandfather to be charming. "My father was my remarkable teacher, señor. He also taught me French, Italian, and some Cantonese."

Don Alonso patted the chair beside him. "Sit with me, Señorita Barrett; I will hear more about you. I expect to be charmed, since I have never before seen so many accomplishments in one small girl."

Valentina's eyebrow arched and her pupils dilated. "I warn you, Don Alonso, I will not be talked down to just because I am a woman. My father brought me up to believe a person should be respected for his mind rather than his sex."

Don Alonso threw back his head and roared with laughter. "Did you hear that, Isabel? This charming English woman thinks females should be respected for their minds. How about you, Marquis? Could you admire a mind behind a face as lovely as this one?"

Marquis's eyes locked with Valentina's. "Perhaps," he whispered. "One can always find much to admire about the English, Grandfather."

Isabel gave Valentina a look of pure poison. "I believe a strong mind would be very boring in a marriage bed," she observed boldly, a sullen pout on her lips.

If Don Alonso was shocked by his future grand-daughter's words, he did not show it, but Rosalia's gasp of dismay could be heard. "I have never found stimulating conversation boring," Don Alonso remarked, "but I have yet to meet the woman who could name the planets . . . or play a decent game of chess."

Isabel saw her chance to prove Valentina an imposter. "If Señorita Barrett has such a fine mind, perhaps she can play chess, Don Alonso."

The old grandee's eyes danced merrily. "Do you play chess, Señorita Barrett?"

"I know the basics, but I would be no competition for you, Don Alonso," Valentina replied modestly. In truth she was an excellent chess player and had on occasion beaten her father, who was considered a master of the game.

"Remarkable," Don Alonso stated, feeling elated that Valentina was able to hold her own against Isabel. "Is it possible that you might also know the names of the planets, my dear? I would be impressed if you could name only one of the planets."

"You expect too much, Grandfather," Rosalia spoke up. "Very few men, let alone women, have your passion for the stars. And no one but Marquis is your equal at chess."

The old grandee's eyes locked with Valentina's. "Do you know about Sir Isaac Newton?"

Valentina nodded. "Of course. Was he not an Englishman?"

Don Alonso looked doubtful. "What theory did he prove?" he asked, testing her.

Several people had gathered around, listening to the conversation. Isabel cast Valentina a glance that clearly told her she had dug a hole and was in over her head. She was waiting for Valentina to be taken down to size by Don Alonso's knowledge of the planets.

"My father was a student of the planets. I confess he infected me with his enthusiasm at a very early age," Valentina admitted.

Still unconvinced but hoping Valentina could redeem herself, Don Alonso pressed her farther. "What theory did Newton subscribe to?"

Valentina smiled. "My father may have taught me about the planets, Don Alonso, but it was my mother who warned me against showing off to men. She taught me that gentlemen do not like a woman with a brain. I was warned by my father that it is unconventional for a woman to let others see she has a mind and can think for herself."

Isabel tossed her raven hair. "You are just stalling because you do not have an answer. You know no more about the stars and planets than I do."

Somehow Isabel's words hit a sore spot. She had issued a challenge that Valentina could not ignore. Even though Valentina knew her mother would not approve of her being ostentatious, she decided to display some of her knowledge without flaunting her accomplishments. "Sir Isaac Newton discovered the law of universal gravitation. He proved the sun's pull on the planets."

Don Alonso clapped his hands delightedly. "*Brava,* that is correct! You are an exceptional young woman indeed. I wouldn't be surprised, Señorita Barrett, if you knew the names of the planets as well."

Valentina met Isabel's glance and felt the need to go a step beyond what her mother would consider good taste. She could feel Marquis's eyes on her, but she dared not look at him. "I will name them in order: Mercury, Venus, Earth, Mars, Jupiter—"

As the color drained from Isabel's face, it seemed to suffuse Don Alonso's. "*Brava, brava.* You are a woman after my heart," he interrupted, needing to hear no more. "If I were fifty years younger, I would woo and win you, Señorita Barrett."

Valentina smiled at the old grandee, unaware that she was being provocative for the first time in her life. "I have always preferred older men, Don Alonso."

"Ah ha, I believe you are flirting with me. Would you be after my money or my mind?" His laughter was deep; he was delighted with his young house guest.

Isabel burned, knowing this English woman was receiving the attention that should have been showered on her. Spitefulness and hatred burned in her black heart.

Valentina's laughter joined the grandee's. She was unaware that she was stirring turmoil, creating a tempest that would soon rage out of control. "Money . . . I do not think so, señor. But perhaps I could be after you for your mind . . . or perhaps I only need a good chess partner."

Don Alonso shook with laughter. "With that kind of talk, you will surely wring a marriage proposal out of me, lovely señorita."

Isabel noticed the way Marquis was staring at Valentina and she did not like it at all. The Spanish guitars were playing softly and she decided to draw his attention to herself. If there was one thing she could do well, it was dance. The puny English woman might have captured Marquis's attention for the moment, but no woman in the past had been able to hold a man when she started dancing. Her hips swayed and her heels tapped. She would fire Marquis's blood tonight. Perhaps she would even allow him to make love to her.

Eleanor knew her sister so well she could read her thoughts. She was jealous of the English woman, and Eleanor was aware that Isabel would grudgingly guard anything that she considered hers; she would stop at nothing to keep her hold on Marquis. Could any man resist her beautiful sister when she started dancing? Eleanor watched Marquis force his eyes away from the beautiful guest to watch Isabel's dance. Eleanor could feel Marquis's torment. He was drawn to the English beauty, but duty marked his destiny. Perhaps she alone was aware of the undercurrents that were sweeping Marquis and Valentina along.

Valentina spent the evening talking with Don Alonso. He kept her beside him, introducing her to his friends and neighbors. She found the Spanish people gracious and polite. She admired their passion for living, their love of the land, and their feeling of loyalty. Once in a while Valentina's eyes would stray to Marquis Vincente. He was always with Isabel. She watched them dance together with a strange ache in her heart. She was glad she was leaving tomorrow. There was nothing but sorrow for her in this house. If she were to stay too long, she would be hopelessly in love with Marquis Vincente. That would never do because he belonged to Isabel Estrada.

Valentina sat beside Don Alonso at dinner. She enjoyed his sharp wit and winsome ways. He was charming and attentive. She could only imagine the number of women who had fallen victim to his charm in his younger days. He must have been every bit as devastating to the female heart as his grandson was now.

As the evening progressed, the guests began taking their leave. Suddenly the guitars slowed, and one of the men began singing a beautiful love song. Valentina was startled when Marquis appeared at her side and held out his hand.

"Will you do me the honor of dancing with me, señorita?"

Valentina hesitated only a moment before taking his hand. She was in a daze as he led her across the flagstone walkway to the fountain. Slipping his arm about her waist, he moved her into a slow Spanish dance step. The music was hauntingly beautiful, the night sky reflected a thousand twinkling stars, and Marquis's eyes were as soft as black velvet.

Valentina gave into the gentle enchantment that drew her under Marquis's spell. She could feel herself falling in love with him. Could love come so quickly? Would she ever be able to forget this dark man who had taken her heart without even being aware of it? Hurt and heartbreak would come later when reality settled in, but for now she was caught within a magic moment of time.

Over his shoulder Valentina could see Isabel's face distorted with anger. Glancing up at Marquis, she smiled slightly, breaking the enchantment. "I fear your lady love is not happy that we are dancing together. It is not my intention to cause trouble for you."

His eyes moved to her creamy lips, and she felt a shiver of delight run the length of her spine. "I believe you will cause me much trouble if I am not on guard."

"I don't know what you—"

"Do you not?" he interrupted, tension clouding his expression. "You cannot tell me a woman with your intelligence does not suspect when a man is fascinated with her."

"I believe I have been a nuisance to you," she said, choosing to misunderstanding his meaning.

He smiled down at her and shook his head. "A nuisance? Not hardly." A shiver of astonishing delight ran through her body at his deep, caressing tone. "If I kissed those lips, would I lose my heart for all eternity, Valentina Barrett?"

Her face flamed, and she looked into the depths of his eyes to see if he were jesting. There was no laughter or mockery in the velvety depths, only a soft glow of sincerity that made Valentina's knees turn to water. "I don't believe you should be saying these things to me." The words were spoken breathlessly, without reprimand.

"Must one hide the truth behind the false face of deception? Must I pretend that you have not disturbed me beyond reason?" he asked in a sharp tone. "Do not pretend you do not know you have been tying me in knots all day."

Valentina was young and inexperienced. She had never before had a man make love to her with words. She had no doubt that Marquis was accustomed to making pretty speeches to all the women of his acquaintance. He would not know that he was breaking her heart by pretending to feel something for her that he did not feel.

"Please, don't," she pleaded, staring into his eyes. "Don't do this to me."

Her words did not deter Marquis. She felt his hand tighten on hers. "If only I could hold you like this for all time. If we were alone I would kiss you." The soft sound of his voice vibrated through her body, wreaking havoc in her tortured mind.

"Beautiful English rose," he whispered, fanning her face with his warm breath. "Silver-eyed goddess, why do you torment me?" Valentina trembled all the way to her toes. She felt his hand move across her back to still the motion. "You have nothing to fear from me, Silver Eyes. I will never do anything to harm you."

His words were not very reassuring to Valentina. She feared what he was doing to her safe little world. He was turning her from an innocent to a woman fully awakened by frightening longings.

While he spoke, he was assessing her every feature. Her facial structure was delicate, each shape existing in perfect harmony with the whole. She would be beautiful carved in stone. She was a thing from which dreams were spun. But a second look told him a sculpture could never capture the true Valentina. She was brimming with life, vitality, and hidden passion.

She was so beautiful to look upon that it took his breath away. His eyes roamed across her bare shoulders where the skin was as soft and white as alabaster. As the soft moonlight touched her hair, making it sparkle, Marquis could feel himself falling more in love with her. Her eyes, reflecting silver, were soft and innocent. She was fascinating and he could not keep his body from trembling at the thought of making love to her. He saw uncertainty in her gaze, as if she did not know what his intentions were regarding her. It pained him to know she was frightened of him. He smiled, wanting to reassure her, but she pulled back in fear.

"I would sooner cut off my arm than cause you distress, Señorita Barrett. If I have frightened you, forgive me."

"I do not admire insincerity," she said, finding that her voice came out in a breathless whisper. "I do not want to be told the things you probably tell all other women. You would do well to save your praise for the woman you are to marry, Señor Vincente."

His smile was soft as he cocked his head. Valentina had not noticed that he had danced her to the far side of the fountain, which was out of sight of the others.

Before she suspected his intentions, he pulled her up on tiptoes, and softly touched her lips with his. Valentina melted against him, feeling as if her whole world was whirling and spinning out of control. Her heart was thundering against her ribs and she had the strangest feeling of unreality.

Raising his head, Marquis frowned at her with eyes like swirling storms. "Does that not prove that I was not being insincere?" Reaching for her hand, he placed it against his chest. "Feel the beating of my heart, Valentina. Feel what you have done to me."

She heard the ring of longing in his voice. Tears sparkled in her eyes as she felt his heart beneath her fingertips beating as wildly as her own. Pulling her hand away, she shook her head, unable to speak.

In that moment he saw the hopelessness of their situation. They could never be together. They were not meant to fall in love. She could never belong to him. "Perhaps it would be best if I take you back now."

Valentina did not wait for him to accompany her. Lifting her skirt, she hurried away, fearing her heart would burst with the frightening new feelings Marquis had awakened in her.

When she saw Rosalia standing beside her mother, she hurried in that direction. She was so confused that she hardly noticed when Marquis excused himself. In the periphery of her mind, she heard Doña Anna excuse her son's departure, explaining how one of the vaqueros had been attacked by a bear the day before and that Marquis needed to see to his comfort.

No one seemed to notice that Valentina was unusually silent the rest of the evening—no one but Isabel and Eleanor.

Isabel elbowed her way past her mother and father to stand beside Valentina. "Tell me, Señorita Barrett," she

106

asked, artfully opening her fan and running delicate fingers over the ivory carving while her dark eyes pinned Valentina with their heat, "is it usual for a woman from your country to go about in the company of a man, without a proper chaperone?"

Valentina's glance was drawn to Eleanor. She saw the smile of encouragement, as though the younger Estrada were offering her sympathy. Apparently she did not approve of her sister's rude tactics.

"It would be most unusual in England, Señorita Isabel," Valentina answered, "but, you see, I had no choice in the matter. I had no one to accompany me but Santiago, whom I consider a very able guide."

Isabel smiled spitefully. "A woman in Spain would never be allowed to travel alone with a man, even if he were an old man," she said, snapping her fan shut.

Rosalia, who was seated near Valentina, leaned forward and whispered in her ear, "Do not let anything Isabel says trouble you. She is only jealous that my brother finds you beautiful."

"I hardly listen to her, Rosalia." It was true. Valentina had been so deep in thought about Marquis that she paid little heed to the barbed remarks Isabel had made.

Don Alonso and Doña Anna watched the woman who was to marry Marquis. They both realized that Isabel did not have a sweet disposition. She was deliberately being rude to Valentina Barrett. Don Alonso shrugged his shoulders and lowered his voice so only his daughter-in-law could hear. "Marriage has changed many a young woman into a suitable matron. I am sure the same will happen when Marquis takes Isabel as his wife."

Doña Anna nodded her head in agreement. It did not matter overmuch if Isabel had an ungracious temperament. Once she became mistress of Paraíso del Norte, she would change. Opening her black lace fan, Doña Anna whispered behind it so only her father-in-law could hear, "I cannot really blame Isabel for being in an ill humor tonight. Marquis did pay marked attention to our house guest. It was shameful and unforgivable."

The grandée blinked his wise old eyes. "Let it be, Doña Anna. Marquis could have behaved no differently." There was more to it than rudeness on Marquis's part. It was as if the young English maiden had brought his grandson to life. Marquis had been stunned and overwhelmed by her beauty. Don Alonso could feel in his bones that trouble lay ahead.

"Valentina, would you like to go riding with me tomorrow?" Rosalia asked. "I am sure the doctor would allow it." Feeling she should include Isabel and Eleanor, Rosalia quickly added, "The two of you would be welcome to come along too if you like."

Isabel's eyes narrowed thoughtfully. "Will Marquis be going with you?" She had no wish to ride with Rosalia and Valentina. However, she had no intention of allowing Marquis to go with them unless she also went along. Marquis belonged to her. This woman with delicate beauty and strange silver eyes would never take him away from her.

"No, he will be hunting the rogue bear that is stirring up trouble for the nearby ranches," Rosalia answered.

Isabel shrugged her shoulders. "My sister doesn't ride, and I don't care for horses. I prefer to do my riding in the inside of a coach."

Valentina had seen Eleanor's eyes light up only to become empty moments later at her sister's refusal on her behalf. Eleanor had wanted to go, but evidently her sister controlled her so completely that she dictated what she could and could not do. Valentina felt pity for Eleanor but knew it was not her place to interfere.

"I would be delighted to ride with you tomorrow, Rosalia," Valentina declared, wishing herself a hundred miles away from here. There was trouble brewing in this house just below the surface. Valentina knew it would take very little to bring it all to a head.

Marquis had awakened feelings in her that would have been better left untapped. She had been subjected to Isabel's poisonous barbs all evening and was relieved when she could politely excuse herself and retreat to her bedroom. Soon she would be on her way back to San Francisco, and perhaps she would be able to forget about today.

In the early morning hours, too troubled to sleep, Valentina stood by the window watching the stars disappear one by one. She looked at the fading silvery moon that cast shadows over the landscape. She could see the road that led away from the house. Soon she would take that road and disappear from Marquis Vincente's life forever. He would marry Isabel, they would have children, and she would be no more than a memory to him—if even that. Running her hand down the window casement, she wondered if she would ever be able to forget the things Marquis had said to her tonight. She would have to have been a fool not to know he had been attracted to her.

She wished Salamar were with her so she could ask her if there was a difference between attraction and love. Turning away from the window, she moved to the bed. Valentina knew she was treading a dangerous path. Soon she would be with Salamar, who would help her regain her perspective so she could put her priorities in order.

Chapter Eight

Beneath a bright canopy of blue sky, with fleecy clouds floating lazily by, Valentina and Rosalia rode away from the *hacienda*. It appeared to have rained during the night because the grass and trees sparkled with dampness and gave off a freshness that filled Valentina's nostrils. The dun-colored mare she rode pranced and tossed its silken mane, showing its superior bloodlines.

Laughter and lightheartedness overcame all else as the spirited horse Valentina rode covered the distance with wide strides. She felt invigorated, alive. She had not enjoyed the freedom of riding across grassy meadows since she had left England. An expert horsewoman, Valentina gloried in the feel of the wind in her hair, and her cheeks were awash with excitement as they moved out of sight of the house. Galloping up hills and across valleys, she felt she could ride forever and never come to the end of this wild, unpredictable land.

When they topped the next hill, Rosalia pulled up her horse and pointed down the valley. "Look, a herd of antelope," she cried excitedly. Valentina leaned against her saddle and watched the graceful animals as they grazed on the sweet, grassy slopes. Her heart was pounding from beholding such beauty. Nature had splashed blue across the heavens, thrown in green for the trees and grasses, adding a multicolored kaleidoscope of wildflowers. Truly this land was blessed. The perfume of lavender, mint, and heliotrope filtered through the air, alluring, tantalizing the senses. It took very little imagination for Valentina to envision mounted *conquistadors,* their ranks marching behind with clanking armor.

"This is Vincente land as far as you can see," Rosalia announced with pride. "God be willing, it will be in our family until the end of time."

Valentina nodded. "I, too, have land that has been in my family for many generations. I am sorry to say my family does not cherish our land as you Vincentes cherish Paraíso del Norte."

Rosalia looked astonished. "My grandfather says land, like God, is eternal, it being the one thing a man can bequeath to the children of the future."

"Your grandfather is right. I envy your family your sense of belonging."

Rosalia nudged her horse in the flanks and laughed back at Valentina in order to overcome the awkwardness of the moment. "I will race you to the river," she challenged.

Valentina dug her heels into her mount and the two girls raced down the hill, scattering the herd of antelope. As they neared the river, Valentina could feel her horse tense. The animal whinnied and shied to the right, almost unseating her. Before Valentina had time to wonder what had spooked the horse, a loud growl came from a clump of scrub oaks just ahead. She held her breath when a huge brown grizzly bear came lumbering toward her.

Rosalia's horse reared on its hind legs and began racing back toward the *hacienda.* Rosalia tried to pull up the frightened animal to no avail. Twisting around in her saddle, she screamed back at Valentina, "Follow me. That is the rogue bear!"

Valentina tried to spin her dancing horse around and follow Rosalia, but the dun mare had a mind of her own. With rolling eyes and laid-back ears, the horse reared up on its haunches. Valentina lost her grip on the saddle and felt herself slipping. At that instant the mare took a frightened leap into the air and sent Valentina flying. She landed with a heavy thud on the rocky ground, which knocked the breath from her body. She did not take the time to find out if she was hurt. The grizzly had paused, as if sniffing the air, and Valentina scrambled to her feet, then made a dive for the horse's trailing reins. With a frightened snort, the horse twisted and whirled, pulled the reins from Valentina's hands, and galloped away in a cloud of dust.

Fear sharpened Valentina's wits. She was alone with the bear and there was no one to come to her aid. The grizzly was standing up on its hind legs and still sniffing the air. At the moment, it seemed he had lost interest in her, leading her to believe he had caught another scent. She took a cautious step backward. A thin sheen of perspiration covered her body and she recognized the bitter, acid taste of fear in her mouth.

There was a tree about fifty yards to her left and she could see what appeared to be the river just beyond that. Valentina did not know anything about a bear's habits. If she made her way to the tree and climbed into the branches would the animal follow? she wondered. Would it be better to run for the river and plunge into the water? She weighed her options carefully, all the while taking cautious steps backward.

Now the bear returned his attention to her. Bellowing and snarling, he dropped down on all fours and clumsily plodded in her direction. Valentina's legs suddenly felt rooted to the spot. What should she do? God help me! she silently cried, unable to move.

With flared nostrils and reddened eyes, the brute

quickly closed the distance between him and Valentina. Somehow finding strength she did not know she possessed, she forced herself to turn around and run in the direction of the nearest tree.

Seemingly from out of nowhere, a rider appeared. Simultaneously a shot rang out, and the rider caught Valentina about the waist, lifting her onto his horse and placing her across his lap. Marquis held Valentina against his body while he murmured huskily into her ear, "Easy, do not panic. You are safe now, Silver Eyes."

Her strength drained, her courage wilted, she melted in his arms, pressing her head against the lapel of his coat. Tremor after tremor shook her body as he ran a soothing hand across her back. "Must I spend my life rescuing you from trouble?" he asked with amusement in his tone.

"It does appear to be the case, doesn't it?" she replied in a little-girl voice that endeared her to him, wrenching his heart. Marquis had the overwhelming desire to take care of her, to always protect her from harm. "I do seem to get into a lot of difficulty, don't I?"

He smiled down at Valentina, warming her with his soft glance. As his eyes looked deeply into hers, she saw his pupils dilate darkly. "You can stop trembling, Silver Eyes. You were never in any danger. We have been tracking the bear all morning. I saw you fall from your horse and had the bear in my rifle sights the whole time."

"Rosalia—was she hurt?" Valentina inquired, looking in the direction Rosalia's horse had taken.

"No, she was not hurt. I saw her bring her horse under control. I told one of my vaqueros to see her safely back to the house."

Hearing the bear's loud bellows of rage, Valentina turned to find that several of Marquis's vaqueros had thrown a heavy net over the beast. With pointed sticks they were urging the grizzly up the ramp and into a heavy cage that rested in the back of a wagon. "Was the bear wounded?" she asked.

Marquis swung around in his saddle to see his men herd the animal into the cage and lock the door behind him. "I did no more than graze his head, dazing him so my vaqueros could easily get him into the cage."

Already a man had climbed onto the wagon and was driving the horses forward. "What will be done with the bear?" Valentina wanted to know.

"He will be used in the bear and bull fight later in the year. The bear will be allowed to recover from his slight wound before he is matched against one of our bulls."

Valentina's mouth flew open in horror. "You cannot mean . . . you wouldn't have a bear and bull fight against each other?" Her eyes sought his questioningly. "You wouldn't do such a thing, would you?"

His mouth quirked upward briefly. "Indeed yes. It is one of the sports enjoyed by my people. I can assure you it is a more even match than you may suppose. A bull can hold his own with a bear."

Valentina shuddered, thinking about the cruelty of such a match. She tried to remember she was a guest in this country and had no right to challenge the native customs. "I . . . thank you for coming to my rescue," she said, glad to change the subject. "Again I am in your debt."

"Are you hurt?" he inquired, looking her over carefully.

Her smile was like a breath of springtime. "No. Only my pride in my horsemanship was wounded when I fell off the horse."

Marquis helped her to the ground and dismounted beside her. "Under the circumstances you did well. As I said, you were never in any danger. I am going to give you a few moments to compose yourself before I take you back to the *hacienda*."

Valentina realized for the first time that she and Marquis were alone. So she would not be tempted to look into his wonderful, probing eyes, she gazed at the river. It was so peaceful here. The glittering torrent swept the rushing water past the riverbank where Marquis's horse grazed on the fresh green grass, swishing its tail to ward off the insects.

Marquis was leaning against a wide-based oak tree. When Valentina turned sharply to look at him, she found he was staring at her. He shifted his stance and frowned. "You are an enigma to me, Señorita Barrett. I have never met anyone like you before."

The sun had already dropped behind the mountains and there was no warmth in the blood-red sky, yet there was fire and warmth in the dark eyes that assessed Valentina. She felt vulnerable under his intense scrutiny. If she were an enigma to him, he was a complete mystery to her. His dark handsomeness was in startling contrast to all other men she had known. He was like this land that had bred him—wild, beautiful, and totally unpredictable.

His eyelids flickered and the dark orbs stared at her. "What is it that makes you stand apart from other women I have known?" he asked softly, almost to himself.

"My maid, Salamar, would say it's my capacity to rush headlong into trouble without the means of getting myself out."

His laughter held amusement, delight. "Do you often find yourself on the wrong side of a carriage or left behind by a fleeing horse?"

"No, this was my first time for both those experiences. But you have already been warned that I am always in one kind of trouble or another. Salamar says I can't seem to keep my feet on the right path."

Marquis was completely enchanted by Valentina. Even

the sound of her voice was uncommonly sweet to his ears. He found himself wanting to see her smile—really smile so that her silver-blue eyes would light up with laughter. He wanted to know everything about this charming creature—her past, her present . . . her future. She had aroused his desire, but he knew his passion would have to go unsatisfied. She was an angel, untouchable and pure. There was fire in her veins, but he would not be the one who would bring it to the surface.

In a daze, Marquis walked toward Valentina. Her back was to him and he reached for her hand, turning her to face him. "I could so easily love you," he whispered, surprising not only Valentina but himself as well.

Valentina stared at him, unable to look away. There had been something strong and electric between them from the start. His words danced through her mind and she knew she could easily love him also, if indeed she was not already in love with him. It never occurred to her to question his sincerity. She had the strangest urge to reach out and touch the dark lock of hair that fell carelessly across Marquis's forehead. Fearing she would do just that, she clutched her hands tightly behind her back.

"You should not say these things to me. It isn't proper." Her voice sounded unconvinced, her words meaningless, even to her own ears.

The dark eyes that caressed her face and finally rested on her lips were compelling, pulling at Valentina. "I do not know what is proper where you are concerned, Valentina Barrett. Do you know I dreamed about you last night?"

She shook her head. "I don't think you should—"

He placed a finger over her lips. "Shh, do not say it. You and I both know there is something powerful between us, something over which neither of us has any control. Do not bother to deny it." The yearning that lingered in his eyes caused the denial to die on her lips.

Color crept up her neck and suffused her face. She did not answer because she did not know what to say. She was unprepared for Marquis's next action. When he pulled her tightly against him, she felt as if a bolt of lightning had jarred her body. Dozens of scalding remarks formed in her mind, but she could not utter them, not while his hard, lean body stirred and stoked the fire within her.

Time and space fell away when he bent his dark head and ever so gently brushed her lips. Valentina was trapped by soft feelings of being wrapped in lamb's wool—she was safe, warm, secure.

Yet all too soon he raised his head and rested his face against hers. "Forgive me, Valentina. I had no right to do that. But like last night in the garden, I was compelled to kiss you," he whispered huskily. "Now if we never see each other again, I will remember the touch of your lips for the rest of my life."

Before Valentina could say anything, Marquis moved away, reached for his horse's trailing reins, and climbed into the saddle. Reaching out his hand, he lifted Valentina up beside him.

As they rode toward the *hacienda,* both realized they might be seeing each other for the last time. Aware that their bodies were touching, Valentina tried to hold herself rigid, though all she really wanted to do was melt against him.

As if it could not stop itself, Marquis's hand drifted up to touch her hair, and he pulled her back against him. They were both silent as the sun splashed its final dying rainbow of color across the horizon.

When they reached a hill that provided a magnificent view of the *hacienda,* Marquis reined in his horse. "I have decided that I will see you again, little Silver Eyes," he said. His hand moved to her face and he cupped her chin, raising it up so their eyes could meet.

Valentina shook her head. "I don't think that would be wise. We are from different worlds, and each of us has his own destiny to follow. This will have to be good-bye for us, Marquis."

His eyes took on a sadness. "Perhaps what you say is wise, but I will see you again, never fear." Nudging his horse forward, Marquis propelled him homeward. Valentina knew that the world was about to come crashing in on her. She wished she could stay forever in Marquis's arms.

When they reached the house, they were given no time to say more. Rosalia and Doña Anna ran to them, inquiring if Valentina was all right. Marquis helped Valentina down and she was hurried into the house by his mother and sister. Valentina had the strongest urge to turn around for one more look at Marquis, but she did not give in to her desire, though she could feel his eyes burning into her back. When she reached the top step, she heard the jingle of spurs, the creaking saddle leather, and knew he was riding away.

That night at dinner, Marquis and his grandfather were both absent from the table. Valentina was told Don Alonso was too ill to come downstairs, but no one explained to her why Marquis was not there and she did not ask. Even though Valentina knew she had no right to feel so, she was hurt because Marquis did not make an appearance on her last night at Paraíso del Norte. After dinner Valentina accompanied Doña Anna and Rosalia into the parlor, where she attempted to prolong the evening, hoping Marquis would come. When it was time to say good night, Marquis still had not appeared. Finally, with a sinking heart, Valentina excused herself and went to her bedroom.

119

When she entered the darkened room, she dropped down on the bed and covered her face with her hands. She wished the next morning would hurry and arrive so she could leave this place forever. She did not belong here. Valentina thought of her mother and hoped the medicine had helped her overcome the fever. Valentina had made her mother a promise that she would find her father and somehow she intended to keep that promise.

Her hand brushed against something soft that was propped against the pillow and she glanced up. There in the middle of the bed was a single crimson rose with a note attached to it. Her heart skipped a beat. Even before she read the note, she knew it was from Marquis. Her eyes devoured the words:

Silver Eyes, I will not see you tomorrow, having chosen this form of communication to say my good-bye. I have a feeling I was by far too bold with you last night and then again today. I beg that you forgive any offense you feel I have committed toward you. I assure you I have the greatest respect for you. As I promised, I will see what I can find out about your father. Never take it upon yourself to try such a dangerous venture on your own again. You will hear from me before too long.

Don Marquis Domingo Vincente

Valentina held the rose to her nose, breathing in the delicate fragrance. Tears of heartbreak and hopelessness fell on the crimson petals. In that moment, if anyone had asked her why she was crying, she could not have told them.

Valentina thought of Salamar and the strange predictions she had made about California. She tried to recall all that Salamar had told her, but her mind was in a muddle. She could only remember Salamar's speaking of a man whom she would love. There was very little doubt in her mind that Marquis Vincente was that man.

To Valentina's surprise, Santiago was waiting downstairs for her the next morning to accompany her back to San Francisco. She was glad to hear that they would be traveling on horseback rather than by buggy.

On her walk through the house, she mentally said good-bye. She would often think of the beautiful garden and remember the Vincente family's graciousness toward her.

Saying farewell to the Vincente family proved harder than she had thought it would be. Rosalia cried and Valentina felt her eyes sting with unshed tears. Doña Anna, as always the matriarch of the Vincente family, stood stiff and unyielding, and Valentina sensed she was glad to see her go. Valentina was greatly touched when Don Alonso got out of his sickbed to see her off. He made her promise that she would come to visit them again so he could take her on in a game of chess.

Marquis did not appear, but then she had not expected him to do so, since he had made his good-byes in his note. The rose he had given her was tucked inside Valentina's gown. She knew she would treasure it long after the color had faded and the fragrance had disappeared.

As Valentina and Santiago rode away from Paraíso del Norte, she could not resist halting her mount and gazing back for one last look. The rolling hills were bathed in golden light. The red-tiled roof gleamed brightly against the background of blue sky. In the distance, the mighty Sierra Mountains shadowed the land as a reminder that man was but a speck against the giants of nature. Her heart ached at the thought that she might never see the Vincente family again.

Turning her horse, she rode away with a deep feeling of

121

loss. She had no way of knowing that Marquis, astride his prancing black steed, watched her departure from a distant hillside. After Valentina disappeared from sight, he turned his mount and rode back to the house.

The trip back to San Francisco passed uneventfully. Valentina and Santiago rode hard each day, stopping only to rest the horses. The first night they dined on food prepared by the cook at Paraíso del Norte and slept beneath the stars. After that, they dined on their usual fare of beans and *tortillas*.

Valentina spoke little, trying to clear her mind of the past few days. She had visited a land and a people as different from her as day was from night. Yet a dull ache reminded her that she had left a part of herself behind.

Chapter Nine

It was dusk when Valentina and Santiago reached San Francisco. The town was coming to life as Valentina dismounted and bid the little man good-bye. Watching him ride out of sight leading the horse she had ridden, she raised her hand and waved to him. Out of the corner of her eye, Valentina saw the curtain move in one of the windows of the Lawton house and knew she was being watched. Easily dismissing her landlord and her sister from her mind, she quickly made her way toward the cabin, eager to see her mother and Salamar.

Salamar watched Valentina come up the path and met her at the door. Raising her finger to her lips, she cautioned her to be quiet. "Your mother is sleeping," she whispered, her face beaming a welcome. "How is your ankle?" Salamar inquired, glancing down at her riding boots, satisfied that since Valentina walked without a limp, she must be fully recovered.

"I have no pain at all. The Vincentes's doctor was a very cautious man, but he made too much fuss." Valentina smiled and hugged Salamar. "Was mother very worried about me?"

"Not after Santiago came by and told her what had happened. Doctor Cline convinced her that the Vincente family was very respectable and that you could not be in better hands."

The night was chilly and Salamar steered Valentina to the hearth and seated her in a chair. Valentina leaned back and closed her eyes while Salamar brought her a bowl of meat and vegetables. They talked in low voices so they would not disturb Valentina's mother in the next room.

"How is Mother feeling, Salamar? I have been so concerned about her."

"Some days I think she is growing stronger, then the next day she can become weak and listless again." Salamar shrugged her shoulders and shook her head sadly. "It is not your mother's physical health I am worried about. She has very little will to rise from her sickbed. I take it, from what Santiago told us, that you never reached your father's mine."

"No, but I shall try again. I promised Mother I would learn the truth about Father, and I will."

Valentina had not been eating, so Salamar took the spoon from her and raised it to her lips, daring her to refuse the bit she offered her. "All in good time, Valentina. We have a more pressing problem at the moment."

"Money," Valentina said, understanding Salamar's concern. "We are running out of money."

"Yes, for medicine."

"I don't suppose it helped Mother any when she heard I was in an accident."

"She was upset at first, but Santiago was very convincing when he told her you were all right. As I told you, Doctor Cline helped assure her that you were in good hands. He said the Vincentes were considered California nobility. He told your mother that when the history of California is recorded, the Vincente name will head the list for important families."

"I found them to be the kindest, most gracious people I have ever known. They made me feel so welcome. They treated me as if I were doing them a favor by staying with them."

"The Californians are known for their hospitality. It is said that when the first Europeans came to these shores, the Spanish welcomed them with open arms. The Spaniards had been dissatisfied with the corrupt Mexican rule for some time. This is their country, but many of them are willing to give the Americans a chance. They hope for something better for California than what the Mexican government offered."

Valentina took the last bite of her meat and smiled at Salamar. "I can see you have done your homework. You have only been in this country a short time and already you know the history. I am constantly amazed by your ability to glean knowledge."

The maid smiled slightly. "I got my thirst for knowledge from you, Valentina. You have made me aware that there are not enough years in one's lifetime to learn all the facts a hungry mind craves." Salamar took the empty bowl from Valentina and stood. "The doctor often brings the newspaper to your mother. Since you have been away, I have been reading it aloud to her; that is how I learned about California."

Feeling drained, Valentina leaned her head back against the wooden chair. "I don't know what we are going to do, Salamar. As you pointed out, we are running out of money. If it weren't for mother's ill health, we would move to the mine and I would work Father's claim."

Picking up the kettle of hot water from the hearth, Salamar watched the flickering firelight play across Valentina's face. "I didn't want to tell you this until you had rested, but I fear things are much worse than before. Two days ago your mother bumped against the table, knocking her medicine off and spilling the contents on the floor. I had to buy another bottle from Doctor Cline and it took almost all the money we had left. There is very little money for food, Valentina; when we have eaten what is in the house, there will be no money to buy more. I was reminded today by Mr. Lawton that the rent on this cabin comes due in less than a week."

Valentina felt as if the walls were closing in on her. "Does Mother suspect that we are running out of money?"

"No. I have kept it from her." She moved across the floor until she stood in front of the table.

Valentina held out her hands to the warmth of the fire, feeling the weight of the world pressing upon her. "I will just have to find employment of some kind."

"That would be the solution, but what are you qualified for?" Salamar asked bluntly.

"I could teach school." Valentina heard the splash of water as Salamar filled the basin; then she heard the clatter of dishes.

"There are no children here. This is a gold field town. The miners have not yet sent for their families. Whom would you teach?"

"I suppose I could become a seamstress."

"The kind of women who live in San Francisco either work in the saloon or are like Prudence Lawton."

Valentina shook her head in defeat. "The only thing I am qualified to do is dance. That is the one thing I do well. I fear there is no demand here in San Francisco for a dancer with my qualifications."

Salamar plunged a bowl into the soapy dishwater. "I already thought of that. I, myself, went to the Crystal Palace Saloon next door and told the owner, Tyree Garth, that I was a dancer. He was not unkind, but he readily pointed out the fact that I am past my prime."

Valentina stared at the leaping flame, despairing that

126

there was no solution to their plight. "I would rather not, but tomorrow I will talk to Reverend Lawton and see if he will allow us to stay on here until I find employment."

"He claims to be a man of God, but there is something about him I do not like. Be careful around him."

Valentina felt the same way. Percival Lawton seemed much more eager to condemn his fellow men than to teach them about the love of God. She dreaded the thought of facing him and asking for charity. She did not want to be under any obligation to the man or his sister. Valentina would have to find employment as soon as possible.

"How much money do you have, Salamar?"

"Four dollars."

"I have five. It will take all we have to buy meat for Mother. The doctor stressed how important it was that she have red meat. I believe for the first time in my life I am frightened, Salamar."

Salamar sat down near the hearth and poked at the fire with the heavy tongs. As the sparks scattered into the air, a glazed look came into her eyes, the kind of look she always got when she was looking into the future. "Do not fear, Valentina. You will soon know your way . . . tomorrow you will learn what you must do."

"If you know what will happen, then tell me, Salamar," Valentina pleaded. "Believe me, I could use the assurance of knowing the future at this moment."

Salamar shook her head. "You will know when the time comes. Tell me this, Valentina. Did you meet the man with dark eyes?"

"Yes, you foresaw this, didn't you?"

"Yes."

"Will he play a part in my life . . . or will I never see him again?"

"I believe at this moment he searches for something on your behalf. Is this not so?"

"That's true. He said he would try to find my father."
Valentina's voice rose excitedly. "Please tell me if—"

"Ask me no questions, Valentina. It is not good to
know too much about the future. Allow things to develop
as the Lord intends."

"Sometimes I feel like I have my back against a wall,
Salamar. Would you tell me if you knew my father's
fate?"

"Of course I would tell you that if I knew, but I do not.
I do not see everything in the future. The sight is a little,
like a door barely cracked to let in light. Your mother
seems to believe he is alive, and I trust in her feelings for
him."

Valentina stood up and began to undress for bed. Her
thoughts were of her meeting with Reverend Lawton the
next day. Something about him made her feel very
uncomfortable. When he touched her, it made her skin
crawl. She was so weary that she pushed all unpleasant
thoughts out of her mind and fell asleep almost the
moment her head rested on the soft pillow.

Valentina had washed her mother's hair, braided it in
one long braid, and tied it with a green ribbon. After
giving her mother a dose of medicine, she sat beside her,
holding her frail hand.

"I was glad to find you home when I awoke this
morning, Valentina. I feel it is my fault that you put
yourself in danger."

"Nonsense. I was never in any danger." Valentina
looked into her mother's soft eyes, seeing a beauty that
time could not erase. "You are very lovely, Mother. I can
well see why Father fell in love with you."

Evonne Barrett raised her daughter's hand to her
cheek. "I will always want to look beautiful for your
father. I must get well so when he returns I won't look

so pale."

"You could never be anything but beautiful," Valentina said, glancing at her mother's lovely face, which was unmarred by her illness. "You have what one would call a timeless beauty, Mother. When you are eighty, you will still be very lovely."

Evonne smiled at her daughter. "You are the lovely one, my dearest daughter. You don't know how lovely you are, do you?"

"I believe I am passingly pretty."

Evonne laughed for the first time in days. "Stay modest and sweet, my love. It is very becoming in a beautiful woman."

"What does it feel like to be in love, Mother?" Valentina wanted to know. "You and Father were in love from the first moment you met, were you not?"

Evonne raised her hand and touched her daughter's cheek. "Yes, the very moment our eyes met. To know love is to feel pain; it is also to know great happiness. It is loving one person so much that his happiness comes before your own."

"How can one know if she is in love?"

Evonne's eyes clouded and she took an unsteady breath. "You will know when the real thing comes into your heart. You will be willing to make any sacrifice for that love. There was a time when, as Jordanna the dancer, I was the rage of all Paris. Men stood in line just to have me say hello to them. When I met your father, I turned my back on fame with no regrets. I never missed the excitement of dancing; all I wanted was to be Ward's wife. I believe that is what will happen with you, Valentina. You will be like me and know the man you love the moment you see him."

Valentina thought of the velvet-eyed Spaniard and knew he had most certainly touched her heart. But was it love? she wondered. If so, it was a love that was doomed

129

to failure because he was soon to marry. Not wanting to think about Marquis, Valentina leaned forward and touched her lips to her mother's flushed cheek. "I am no beauty like you, Mother. I may never know the kind of love that you and Father have shared."

Evonne took her daughter's chin in her hand and raised her face to the light. "Oh, my dearest daughter, you are fairer than I ever was. You are so beautiful that you will make all the men fall in love with you. If you were dancing in Paris, you would be a sensation, for your talent far exceeds mine. Many gentlemen would offer you the world. But you must be wise and wait for just the right man."

Valentina laughed delightedly. "So speaks my mother. You look at me through eyes of love. You don't see my imperfections."

Evonne tugged at Valentina's hair. "Think what you will. All too soon, men will shower you with attention."

Valentina was thoughtful for a moment. "Are you sure you never miss being Jordanna, the *prima* ballerina of Paris, Mother?"

"Not one day of my life. Loving and being loved by your father was all I ever cared about. I know there were times when you felt cut out of our life, Valentina, but I had to go with your father. I will never regret that I spent all my time with him. You will understand this one day."

"Strangely enough, I never felt cut out of your life. I have always known that you and Father loved me. Of course there were times when I could have died of loneliness, but I believe I took some kind of satisfaction in your love for each other. However, I do not think when I marry that I shall leave my children with anyone."

Evonne's eyes drifted shut and she murmured, "No, I do not think you ever would. You will make a far better mother than I, for not only are you lovely, but you also have a kind and loving heart. Your nature is such that you don't even realize that you are lovely beyond compare."

Seeing her mother was tiring, Valentina moved quietly out of the room. Salamar was preparing lunch, and the cooking meat sent out a delicious aroma. Valentina tried not to think about the emptiness in her stomach. She and Salamar would eat only the broth, hiding the fact from her mother that she alone would have meat to eat.

"I am going to see Mr. Lawton now," Valentina told Salamar. "Pray that he has a kind and understanding heart." Salamar glanced up at Valentina and snorted. They both knew the good reverend had very little heart.

Reverend Lawton answered the door to Valentina's knock. His shadow fell across her face as he stepped onto the front porch. "I was saying to my sister just this morning that I was expecting a visit from you," he said, dabbing at his face with his handkerchief, a habit of his that was beginning to irritate Valentina.

"I have come to talk to you about the rent, Mr. Lawton." She could not help compare the way he was watching her to the way a cat watches a mouse.

Valentina instinctively drew back when he picked up her hand, turned it over, and studied it intently. "You haven't done much hard work in your life, have you, Miss Barrett? I would say you have been spoiled."

"I haven't worked as a field hand, but I have done my share of housework. I was not brought up much differently from most English girls."

"You haven't labored very hard; you have a maid to do that for you. I'm sure that isn't the case with most of your English misses. It certainly isn't the case in this country."

"I suppose there is some truth in that," she answered,

131

not knowing what point he was trying to make. She could not afford to offend the man if she were going to ask him to allow her more time to pay the rent.

"Idle hands are the devil's playthings, you know, Miss Barrett."

"I have heard that saying. My grandmother was always fond of saying 'busy hands are happy hands.' I believe I prefer her expression." Valentina knew she was saying anything that popped into her head, trying to avoid the subject that was foremost in her mind.

"So you have been taught about the sins of idleness." Percival Lawton smiled wholeheartedly. "Come into the house, Miss Barrett. There is something I have been wanting to speak to you about."

Valentina reluctantly walked into the small parlor with its dark, gloomy furnishings. There was no cheerful color in the room. Decorated in drab browns, it was stiff, formal, and uncomfortable. She had a feeling that nothing would grow in this darkened room. She felt the oppression, the lack of air.

"Won't you have a seat, Miss Barrett. My sister is away or she would offer you tea."

Valentina stood near the door. "I shouldn't come in if your sister isn't at home," she said nervously.

"Nonsense. I am a man of God. It is perfectly acceptable for you to be alone with me. It is much more proper than your wandering around the country with that native, Santiago."

Valentina knew it would not be wise to argue the point. Her grandmother had once remarked to her that those who ask favors are not in a bargaining position. Valentina now understood what her grandmother had meant. Deciding the best way to proceed was to get right to the point, Valentina took a deep breath and dropped down on the stiff horsehair sofa.

"I know the rent on the cabin is due at the end of the

week. I was wondering if you would mind waiting a few days until I can find employment."

Reverend Lawton seated himself beside Valentina, sliding so close that his leg pressed against hers. "You should have thought about looking for work instead of traipsing off to look for your father. With your mother's illness, you have a big responsibility."

"I realize that. I intend to find a job as soon as possible."

Glancing at her through watery eyes, Percival Lawton spoke. "The road to glory is paved with good intentions. What would I do in my business if I asked poor sinners to wait a bit." Valentina noticed that the reverend was staring at the neck of her gown and she shivered with disgust. His mouth was saying one thing, but his eyes were speaking another language. They were leering eyes—lecherous eyes.

"Will you give me a week to get the money?" she asked, resisting the urge to move away from him.

He was quiet for a moment, as if he were pondering the idea. "I tell you what I will do," he said at last, reaching out his hand and capturing Valentina's. "I have been looking for a wife. I believe, with my sister's training, you could be a proper helpmate for a man of God."

Valentina almost choked on her surprise. She had expected anything but this. "I hardly know you, sir. Besides, I cannot marry anyone at this time, Mr. Lawton. My mother is my responsibility. She needs me." She fought down the nausea that assailed her at the thought of being this man's wife.

"If . . . you become my wife, your mother will become my responsibility," he said meaningfully. "I wouldn't object if she were to live in the cabin out back, rent free, if we were married. I wouldn't even object to that foreign-looking maid of yours staying with her."

Valentina stood up on shaky legs. "I do not believe you

and I are suited to one another, sir. You would need a wife who would be subservient to your will. I am told that I am too strong minded for my own good. I am opinionated and not at all meek. You would tire of me quickly."

Percival stood up and, to Valentina's disgust, ran his hand down the front of her gown before cupping her firm young breasts. She jumped back and gave him a look of horror, but he forestalled what she was about to say. "I am a man with strong needs. Just because I carry God's cross doesn't mean that I'm not a man with feelings like everyone else."

"You go too far, sir," she declared. "No man has ever laid a hand on my person before." Valentina had rarely been so angry. How dare Mr. Lawton act so forward with her. "I will never forgive you for taking such liberties."

He seemed to take no exception to her angry words. His amused laughter surprised her. "You have told me what I wanted to know. I had to find out if a man's hands had touched you before, and that was the only way I could be sure." His watery eyes seemed to bulge out of their sockets. "I would like to teach you meekness. I would like you to become subservient to my will."

Her anger rose by degree. "How dare you think you can touch me in such an intimate way, sir!" She backed toward the door. "Know now that I will bow down to no man, you less than anyone."

Again his laughter surprised her. "I believe you will change your mind. I will wait for your answer for three days. If you decide against marriage to me, I think you will understand if I ask you to find another place for your mother to live . . . unless you can come up with the money."

She would have liked to have slapped the smile from his face. He did not think she could get the money. He expected her to come crawling back to him, asking for more time.

Hurriedly Valentina reached for the doorknob. When her hand wrapped around it, she jerked open the door and dashed outside, breathing in big gulps of fresh air. Shivering with disgust, she made her way back to the cabin. She did not know what she was going to do, but she would never marry that odious man. The touch of his hand had made her sick. She thought of Marquis Vincente and felt her heart ache.

Salamar met her at the door with a questioning look in her eyes. Valentina shook her head dejectedly. "He implied if I didn't come up with the rent money, I could either marry him or we would have to move. What will we do?"

Salamar stared at Valentina for a long time. At last she spoke in a whisper. "I believe you already know what you must do."

Valentina's eyes rounded in surprise. "You mean that I should dance?"

Salamar nodded. "It is the only way. If I could do it, I would. If you do not earn money quickly, you may be forced to marry Mr. Lawton for your mother's sake. I do not want this for you."

Valentina remembered her mother saying just that morning that if she were a dancer, she would be a sensation. Hadn't Salamar always told her that she was an exceptional dancer? But she did not want to be a sensation; she did not want to dance on stage before a mob of leering men. All she wanted was to take care of her mother and see that she got well.

"How can I do it, Salamar? If Mother were to find out, she would be horrified. Mother wouldn't like me to dance on stage. She would never approve of my dancing in the kinds of places they have here in San Francisco where men go to drink and gamble."

"You are right that your mother would disapprove,

but I have an idea that I think will work. If it does, no one will ever know your true identity."

Valentina tiptoed to the bedroom door and stared at her mother, whose face was pale even in sleep. "Tell me what I must do, Salamar," she whispered, turning back to the maid. "I know we are in dire need of money."

The office at the back of the Crystal Palace was cast in shadows. The owner, Tyree Garth, lit a cigar and lazily watched the smoke drift toward the open window. He then turned his attention back to the woman who sat across from his desk. When the woman had entered his office a few moments ago, he had noticed that she was of medium height. Other than that, he could not tell too much about her appearance because she was draped in black and wore a heavy veil. He had recognized the older woman who was with her as the one who had come to him a few days back asking to be employed as a dancer.

"I was told you wanted to see me, ma'am," Tyree said, straining his eyes to see past the black veil. The hand that reached up to pull the shimmering material more tightly across the lower half of the woman's face was small and delicate.

"I would like to work for you, Mr. Garth," a soft, feminine voice with a cultured English accent uttered from somewhere amid the veil.

"No disrespect intended, ma'am, but I have nothing suitable for a woman of your obvious genteel upbringing." He thought the woman was probably homely as sin or she would not have taken the trouble to cover her face. He did not have any objections to her being ugly. With the shortage of women in California, the men who drank and gambled in his establishment were not too particular. They were more concerned with a woman's body than the cut of her face anyway. The women who worked for him had to have a nice form, and this one was obviously shapeless.

Valentina studied the man through her veil. He was tall, broad shouldered, and dressed in a soft grey cutaway suit and yellow vest. His chestnut hair was curly and swept back from his forehead. His eyes were a deep blue and he had a mustache that was neatly trimmed. She found him handsome in a rakish sort of way.

"I can dance, Mr. Garth," Valentina said in a soft voice. "I can dance well."

Every time the woman in black moved, Tyree could hear a tinkling sound that aroused his curiosity. He flicked the ashes from his cigar and shook his head. "I don't have much use for a dancer, ma'am. This is a rough place. Why don't you just run along home now. I hear a woman can make a fair living as a laundress; leastwise, she could before the Chinese started arriving in San Francisco."

Valentina stood up. "I might consider your suggestion, Mr. Garth; but first allow me to dance for you. What have you to lose? If you don't like what I do, I will leave and never bother you again."

Tyree nodded at the older woman who stood near the door, her eyes alert, as if she were on guard. "Why not? I'm feeling in a generous mood today. Step outside and tell the head musician, Hubert Aims, what music you want him to play. The musicians at the Crystal Palace aren't fancy, but they have a good ear for music. I'll be out directly and watch."

Valentina walked to the door. "After I have danced for you, sir, there are some promises you must make before I will agree to work for you."

Tyree threw back his head and laughed. "You may or may not be able to dance, but you're not short on spunk. I'll see this dance and then you can leave and never bother me again. Is that a promise?"

137

"I promise, but I have very little doubt that you will ask me to stay. As I said, I am very good." The statement was not made in a bragging manner; rather it carried the earnest ring of the truth.

Tyree was becoming more intrigued by the moment. He walked to the door and waited for the two women to precede him. When they entered the massive barroom, it was empty but for the young boy who was sweeping the floor and the three musicians who played for the Crystal Palace. The leader, Hubert Aims, who was running his fingers over the piano, looked up with interest when they entered.

Tyree propped his elbow on the bar and motioned Hubert over to him. "This woman wants to dance for us, Hubert. Play something pretty for her."

"All right, boss," Hubert said, holding up his hands to catch the attention of the other two men. "What would you like us to play for you, ma'am?" he called out.

"Do you know 'Traveling Gypsy'?" Valentina asked.

"Yes, of course," Hubert answered, seating himself at the piano.

"I would like you to play it softly to begin with; keep the tempo slow, then gradually build up faster. When I give you the signal, I would then like you to play the rest of the melody at twice the tempo. I believe you will understand what I mean when I start dancing."

Hubert Aims was a man in his early sixties. Music had always been his life. At one time he had conducted an orchestra in Boston, Massachusetts. Too much drinking had shattered a promising career. He had sailed for California hoping to find himself again, which he had. At one time his talent had been heralded as promising. Now he played for rough men who cared nothing for fine music. He led three other musicians in bawdy songs for the amusement of the customers.

He had lived too long to be surprised by anything—

138

even the woman draped in black. "I'm not sure I understand what you want, ma'am, but I'll catch on."

"You will be able to follow me," Valentina said. "Please begin now." Salamar had insisted on accompanying Valentina and that left her mother alone. Valentina just wanted to get this whole degrading ordeal over with so she could return home as soon as possible.

Hubert looked at his boss, Tyree Garth, who shrugged his shoulders. Running his hands over the keys of the piano, the pianist instructed the other members to join in.

The young boy who was sweeping the floor leaned on his broom and watched the woman in black ascend the steps. When she was at center stage, the older woman seated herself on the steps, as if to discourage anyone from trying to approach too near.

Tyree almost choked on his cigar when the black drape fell away and landed at the dainty feet of a woman with the most sweetly curved body he had ever seen. She was wearing a bright red gypsy skirt with yards and yards of some kind of filmy material. Her young breasts were thrust against an off-the-shoulder peasant blouse. She was barefoot, with bangles about her ankles and wrists. Her identity was still concealed behind a veil, which covered the lower half of her face. Her hair was covered with a golden mesh net to which bangles were attached that hung across her forehead.

Hubert took his cue from the girl. She raised her arms and clicked the finger cymbals, causing a loud, rhythmic, ringing sound.

When she began to dance, she became grace and beauty. Everyone was mesmerized as she turned and whirled in time with the music. As the music shifted in tempo, she began moving her hips, tauntingly, enticingly.

Tyree had been watching her so intently that he let out

a loud oath as his cigar became a stump and burned his fingertips. His eyes were glued to the stage as he watched the most beautiful dance he had ever witnessed. As Valentina whirled around the stage, he felt joy in his heart. She was creating a lighthearted Gypsy feeling. She was the eternal woman; she was Venus come to earth to bless men with her loveliness.

As the tempo increased to a maddening pitch, the dancer dropped to the floor and bowed her head. For the space of several moments there wasn't a sound in the place. Then suddenly Hubert jumped to his feet and started clapping his hands vigorously. Soon he was joined by the other musicians. The cleaning boy was clapping and crying at the same time. He had never seen such a thing of beauty in all his sixteen years.

Tyree smiled to himself and called out, "You got the job, ma'am."

Valentina came to the edge of the stage, picked up her black drape, and pulled it back over her head.

"Not yet, Mr. Garth. As I told you before, I have some stipulations you must meet before I will work for you."

"I would advise you to take her at any price," Hubert advised. "I'll bet there isn't another dancer to rival her in this country, if indeed the whole world. She's talented; she's wonderful; she can put the Crystal Palace on top. Now we can introduce San Francisco to a little culture. We can have good music."

"Come with me," Tyree called out, making his way to his office. "If I don't hire you, I have a feeling Hubert will walk out on me."

As Tyree sat on the edge of the desk, he tried again without success to see the dancer's face. "What are your conditions, ma'am?" he asked, smiling.

"They are few and simple. I want the steps removed that lead up to the stage. I will want a dressing room large enough to practice my dancing in. Also there must be a back door leading to the dressing room so I can come and go as I wish."

"Agreed."

"I will always wear a veil. No one will know my true identity. You are not to try to find out who I am or where I live. In fact, if I am to dance for you, you must promise to protect my identity."

"Agreed."

"I will dance for only an hour a night and never on the Sabbath."

"I see no problem with that."

Valentina hesitated. ". . . I want to be paid a hundred dollars a week."

A slow smile spread over Tyree's face. "I was prepared to pay you a hundred and fifty."

"Not at first. Wait and see if I am worth more. The time may come when I must demand more money."

"May I know your name?" he asked.

"Let's just say that I am called Jordanna."

"All right, Jordanna. Is there anything else you wish to say?"

"Yes." Again she was hesitant. ". . . May I have the first week's salary in advance?"

Tyree's laughter filled the room as he pulled out a metal box, unlocked it, and counted out the money. "I have a feeling that if I'm not careful, you'll be running the Crystal Palace before long."

Soft laughter touched his ears. "I don't wish to run your saloon, Mr. Garth. I only wish to use it as a means to an end."

He watched her leave, followed by her strange foreign-looking maid. "I'll be damned," he said, lighting another cigar. "I'll be damned."

It was late in the evening when the knock came on the

front door. When Salamar opened it, Prudence Lawton entered. Looking about her, she took in every change that had been made in the cabin.

"Good evening, Miss Lawton," Valentina said politely. "May I offer you refreshments?"

"No, I just came to do you a good turn," the older woman said, lifting the curtains at the window and examining the material while Valentina waited for her to continue. "This place isn't half bad the way you have it fixed up."

"Thank you," Valentina replied demurely.

"Well, seeing that the hour is late, I'll come right to the point. Are you looking for employment?"

Valentina managed not to show her surprise at the blunt question. "Indeed I am, although I am finding I am not qualified for many things."

"Can you read?"

"Yes, of course."

Prudence reached into her drawstring bag, withdrew a slip of paper, and pressed it into Valentina's hand. "This is the address of Mrs. Windom. She is a widow. Her husband was a sea captain who lost his life coming around Cape Horn last year. The poor woman is suffering from some kind of stroke and can't speak. She requires someone to stay with her in the afternoons and read to her. I heard about her through Maddy Dillan at the fish market."

"I thank you very much, Miss Lawton. I shall go and see Mrs. Windom first thing in the morning."

Prudence nodded in approval. "I'm always willing to do my Christian duty. The poor woman likes to be read to, but there aren't many women who can read in San Francisco."

Valentina was surprised that Prudence Lawton would bother to help her. She knew the woman did not like her very well. "I suppose that's true, Miss Lawton. Thank

142

you for thinking of me."

"Think nothing of it. I just want to be a good Christian. I'll be going now."

Valentina accompanied Miss Lawton to the door and thanked her again for her kindness. After the woman had gone, Valentina shook her head in amazement. "Wouldn't it be wonderful if I were to get this job? If it paid enough, I wouldn't have to dance at the Crystal Palace."

Salamar said nothing. Removing the foot warmer from the fire, she wrapped it in a heavy cloth and carried it into Evonne Barrett's bedroom.

Marquis had been having dinner with the Estradas. After the meal, as if it had been planned, Isabel's parents had excused themselves and left their two daughters at the table to entertain their guest.

Across the table from Marquis, Isabel laughed and tossed her hair, trying to entice him. He felt her foot touch his boot and then slide up his leg. Toying with his wine glass, he did not even look up. When her foot moved up to rest on his thigh, his eyes flickered and locked with hers.

Isabel had expected her bold movements to cause passion to ignite in him, but it had not. She could tell he felt nothing by the dullness in his eyes. The look he gave her was one of bored indifference, and Isabel could not endure indifference—especially not from the man she was to marry. She jerked back her foot and glared at him.

"I am sure that if my hair were golden you would notice me, Marquis Vincente!" she hissed. As if a serpent were poisoning her mind, she felt hatred building deep within her. "Would you want to bed me if my eyes were the strange silver color of the English woman's?"

Through lowered lashes, he flicked an imaginary crumb from the table. No, he thought, in your case it wouldn't help. Aloud he said, "Are you not concerned that your sister can overhear your conversation?"

Isabel glanced at Eleanor, who was pretending not to hear. Seething inside, she realized she had just been spurned. Marquis was not attracted to her at all. "She cannot have you, you know," she said, lowering her voice.

His lips curled into a smile, though coldness laced his words. "Who cannot have me?"

"You know I speak of the English whore."

For the first time there was life in the depths of Marquis's eyes as anger turned them to slow-burning fire. The hand that grasped the wine glass tightened; the knuckles whitened. "Tread easy, Isabel. Do not say something you will regret."

"My God!" she declared, jumping to her feet. "I will not endure your defending that bitch to me. Am I not the woman you are going to marry? You have treated me as if I had some dread disease ever since we first met."

Marquis rose slowly to his feet, looking at her with an unreadable expression. "I believe it is time I took my leave. If you would not mind, please pay my respects to your mother and father." Walking across the room, he stopped at the door. "I am going to pretend tonight did not happen, Isabel. I suggest you do the same." With a slight smile to Eleanor, he quickly moved out the door and down the hallway.

Isabel stared after him in disbelief, her mouth hanging open. "How dare he!" she raged, her voice rising in volume. "How dare he treat me with such contempt! I will never allow Marquis Vincente to forget this night."

*　　　*　　　*

Marquis swung his leg over the saddle and, turning his mount, he cantered toward home. It would have angered Isabel still more had she known how easily Marquis had dismissed her from his mind. His thoughts had returned immediately to the golden-haired goddess who haunted him day and night.

Chapter Ten

As it turned out, Valentina's hopes for finding suitable employment were dashed. After gaining the approval of Mrs. Windom's housekeeper, Mrs. Gibbins, Valentina was led into the bedroom and introduced to the dour Mrs. Windom. The elderly woman showed her disapproval of Valentina immediately and, nodding toward the door, indicated that Valentina should leave at once.

The housekeeper ushered Valentina out the door and into the entryway. "I'm sorry, miss. My employer seems to have her heart set on a certain kind of young lady. She has a strong dislike for anything British. Perhaps that is why she sent you away. I hope you won't take the slight personally."

"I need this job desperately. Is there any chance that Mrs. Windom might change her mind?"

"No, ma'am, but then, you see, the position doesn't pay that much anyway. Mrs. Windom was only offering three dollars a week."

Valentina shook her head. "I need more money than that to take care of my mother. That would hardly be enough to put food on the table at the high prices in San Francisco." Valentina extended her hand to the housekeeper. "Thank you for your kindness, Mrs. Gibbins."

"For what it's worth, I think Mrs. Windom made a mistake in not hiring you, miss," the maid said, acting genuinely sorry. "You seem a very well-brought-up young lady."

"Thank you again. It is unfortunate for me that you don't have the last word in hiring me," Valentina said, taking her leave.

Her footsteps dragged on the way home. She had had high hopes for the job with Mrs. Windom. Now she would have to dance at the Crystal Palace for an indefinite period of time.

When Valentina arrived home, she sank down in a chair, feeling miserable. Salamar, with a concerned frown on her face, handed her a cup of tea. "I take it the interview did not go well?"

"No. It seems that the lady had an aversion to my being English. Perhaps I should have informed her I was half French."

"It may be for the best, Valentina. I doubt that the position would have paid all that well. Besides, who would want to work for a woman who condemns a whole race of people just because she does not like one or two of them?"

"You are right about the woman and the pay. We couldn't have survived on the meager amount, and I wouldn't have been happy working for her."

"What are you going to do?"

Valentina's shoulders drooped and she felt completely deflated. "I just don't know, Salamar."

"I believe you do."

"Yes, you are right. I will dance for Tyree Garth. I owe him a week of dancing anyway since he already paid me. I was just hoping a week was all I would have to dance. I do not know how we will keep Mother from finding out about what I'm doing."

Salamar stared into Valentina's eyes. "You could tell

148

your mother that you got the position with Mrs. Windom. That will lend respectability if anyone inquires about how you are earning money."

"I cannot tell an untruth, Salamar. You always taught me to be honest. If it was wrong in the past to be untruthful, it's still wrong."

"What you say is true. We must weigh carefully what the truth would do to your mother. I do not think we are prepared to take the chance." Salamar sat down beside Valentina and looked at her with sad eyes. "If I could take your unhappiness in my hands and crush it, I would do so. If you can believe this, then know that the road to true happiness is often strewn with stones."

Valentina smiled. "Are you trying to tell me that at the end of the rainbow is a pot of gold?"

"Yes, something like that."

Valentina laughed uncontrollably as the tears streamed down her face. "What cannot be cured must be endured, Salamar. I must flaunt myself on a stage where men will gawk at me. My mother would die of shame if she ever found out. I will try to remember that I am doing this for our survival; otherwise, I couldn't go through with it."

Salamar felt tears in her own eyes, knowing Valentina was suffering from shame and heartbreak. She knew Valentina was being torn apart inside because she was forced to dance in a place like the Crystal Palace. Taking the girl in her arms, Salamar held her tightly, allowing her to cry out her misery. "This too, shall pass, Valentina. I swear to you that you will one day see the gold at the end of the rainbow."

The Crystal Palace was noisy and smoke filled. The sound of the roulette wheel was swallowed up by the sounds of murmuring voices and loud laughter from the men at the gambling tables.

Tyree glanced up at the stage where new red velvet curtains hung. Looking about him at the rough-hewn faces of the customers who frequented his establishment, he wondered if he had made a mistake in hiring the girl who called herself simply Jordanna. These miners might not appreciate her talent. They might be just as happy if Dora and Sadie, the two women who served drinks for him, climbed on stage and tried to dance. They would only be interested in a show of legs or a low-cut bodice. It was evident that Jordanna would show neither.

Holding a cigar between his teeth, Tyree scraped a match across the edge of the bar, watching it ignite with the accompanying sulphur smell. Touching the match to his cigar, he heard Hubert run his fingers over the piano keys and fill the room with a soft melody. The song he was playing reminded Tyree of summer skies and bluebirds he had seen long ago in his boyhood. The music stopped and he knew it was time for Jordanna to appear.

The men who were drinking and gambling did not even glance up as the curtain opened and the slight figure of the woman glided forward. Tyree watched in shocked surprise and more than a little anger. Jordanna was not wearing the red gypsy skirt she had worn the day he had hired her. She was draped in filmy white material that hung down to her ankles. Her hair was covered with a white veil, which fell across the lower half of her face, concealing her identity. She was not barefoot, but wore the white satin toe shoes of a ballerina.

His teeth clamped down on the cigar, and he swore under his breath. He had gone to the expense of redoing the stage and having the dressing room decorated to the woman Salamar's specifications. He damned sure hadn't hired her to do some damned fancy toe dance. This was the West, not some luxurious salon in Europe. He was so angry he decided to go backstage and order Jordanna either to dance the Gypsy dance or leave the Crystal Palace at once.

Valentina eased up on her toes and began swirling around in a circle. Tyree was halfway to the stage when a strange sound met his ears—the sound of complete silence! The roulette wheel wasn't spinning, and there was no laughter or murmuring. Turning around, he glanced at the faces of the men only to find their eyes glued to the stage. Awe and reverence were written on the weathered faces of the old men. A look of adoration graced the faces of the younger men. Jordanna had them all completely under her spell.

Tyree leaned back against the wall, poked his hands in his pockets, and watched Jordanna with a smile on his face. The soft music filled the room and she whirled, she spun. She danced on her toes; she gracefully moved like poetry across the stage, her white gown always modestly hugging her ankles. As she danced, each man was reminded of eternal youth and beauty. Tyree watched one old, hard-bitten miner with a white beard dabbing at his eyes. Others were crying openly and unashamed. They were witnessing something so lovely, so unbelievable, they would never forget it.

The music built up in tempo and Jordanna leaped into the air as if she had taken wing. In her graceful broad leaps, her legs swept out into perfect splits. The music slowed and she spun around and then dropped into a deep curtsy.

With one last glance at the audience, she arose and disappeared backstage. For what seemed an eternity, silence reigned in the Crystal Palace. Then, all of a sudden, the men went crazy. Bedlam swept the crowd as they applauded and called for the dancer to return. Voices were raised in tribute to the goddess who had just blessed them with a glimpse of undeniable beauty.

Tyree felt a jolt at his elbow and smiled into the

laughing eyes of Julian Mathews, a reporter for the *Missouri Republican*, who had been sent to San Francisco to write articles about the gold rush.

"You have been holding out on me, Tyree. Who was that lovely angel?"

"Just that—an angel."

"Introduce me to her. Damnit, she is the most graceful and talented dancer I've ever seen, and I've seen plenty. It isn't fair to keep her for yourself; she's too beautiful for just one man."

"How could you tell she was beautiful when her face was covered?" Tyree asked lazily.

"I could just tell. Are you going to introduce me to her or not?"

"Not."

"Then I'll just go backstage and introduce myself."

Julian Mathews turned in the direction of the stage only to be yanked back by Tyree. "I can't let you do that, Julian. See Bob Taylor over there nursing that rifle? His orders are to allow no one backstage. As you know, Bob is a stickler for following orders."

"Why won't you allow anyone backstage?" Julian asked, his reporter's nose smelling a story. "What's the big mystery about this dancer?"

"The mystery is that this is the way she wants it. I don't know her story. I only know that if she keeps dancing for me, she'll make me a wealthy man. If she doesn't want anyone to see her face, that's the way it'll be. If she doesn't want anyone backstage, that's the way it will be too."

"What if I find a way to meet her?"

"I would ask you not to do that. If you succeeded, I believe she would disappear and none of us would ever see her dance again."

Julian ran a hand through his sandy curls as his eyes lit up with an idea. "I've had a change of heart. I don't want

152

anyone to know who she is. I am going to make that little lady famous. Everyone loves a mystery. I will fight as hard as you to protect her identity, because she is going to provide me with whopping news stories for a long time to come. The folks back East will eat this up."

Tyree nodded. "I'm glad you see it that way." To himself he murmured, "I wonder who she really is and what her story is."

The next morning's newspaper headlines hailed the mystery lady that graced the stage at the Crystal Palace. It mentioned something about her being the golden Venus, hiding her face because she was too beautiful for mortal man to look upon.

Marquis and one of his Indian vaqueros, Tomico, rode up the rocky slope toward Valentina's father's mine. Halting their mounts in front of the mine opening, Marquis called out in English, "Hello, is anyone here?"

When there was no answer, Marquis got off his horse and motioned for Tomico to draw his rifle and remain mounted. Walking cautiously toward the cabin that was just past the face of a cliff, he called out again.

This time he was rewarded by a grumbling voice and a man pulling up his suspenders came out of the door. He looked at Marquis suspiciously and would have drawn the gun he wore crammed into the waist of his trousers had he not spied Tomico's rifle aimed at him.

"What you want around here, stranger? If you came to rob me, you'll find poor pickings," Samuel Udell said, his eyes moving from the Indian to the dark-eyed Spaniard.

"I have come to inquire about a man named Ward Barrett." Marquis knew this man with his white beard and mustache and a distinct American accent could not

153

be Valentina's father. This man was too crude, too uneducated. Ward Barrett would be a much younger man who spoke English with a clipped British accent.

"Have you now? And just what in the world would be your interest in my partner?" Samuel Udell looked over the fancily dressed Spanish man carefully. His appearance proclaimed him to be of the landed gentry— probably some aristocratic grandee, he thought. He could not imagine why the man would be inquiring about Ward Barrett. "Why would you want to know about a dead man?" he questioned.

"I made Ward Barrett's daughter a promise that I would find out about her father. I am told that you were the last person to see him alive."

The old man scratched his head. "Now that would be a fact. We was digging down in the mine, and there was a fearsome cave-in. He were buried so deep in that there mine that they'll never find his body."

"I would like you to show me where the cave-in occurred so I can tell his daughter that I saw where her father was buried."

"Now I ain't likely letting no strangers go poking around in my mine. How do I know you haven't come to rob me? A man can't be too careful these days. There's plenty of claim jumping going on."

"But, señor, you have intimated to me that you have nothing to steal. Did you not tell Señora Barrett that the mine was nonproducing. As far as I can see, that would bring up another question to be answered. If you have not found gold, why do you continue to dig here?"

The old man's eyes became hooded and he laid his hand on the handle of his gun. When he heard the click of the Indian's rifle, he held out his hands. "I don't have nowhere else to go. I sunk all my money into this mine. I have to stay with it, come rain or hell."

"It would be wise for you to speak the truth, señor. I

154

would not want to believe that you have cheated the Barrett family," Marquis stated flatly, the merest hint of a threat hanging in the air.

Samuel Udell eyed the Spaniard, sensed he did not make idle threats, and saw he was a dangerous man to cross. There was something in those dark eyes that made his words ring with sincerity. "Now, I wouldn't go cheating a partner. How could you even think I would? Ward Barrett was my friend as well as my partner."

"If that is so, then you have nothing to fear. You will show me the place where Ward Barrett's body is buried. Then I will be on my way and you can go back to your digging."

"You can't see nothing back there but the cave-in. The air's so thin the lanterns won't burn."

"I was not born without a brain, señor. Take me to the place where you claim Ward Barrett died."

Samuel Udell licked his dry lips and glanced again at the Indian with the gun. "I'll take you in, but I ain't going in with no Indian."

"Tomico will do you no harm unless I tell him to. But no matter; I will go into the cave with you alone. However, I feel I should warn you not to try anything funny. If I don't come out in one piece, Tomico will slit your throat without thinking twice about it."

Samuel moved toward the mine opening, grumbling under his breath. Once inside, he waited for Marquis to join him. When they moved away from the front of the mine, it became pitch dark. Marquis waited for Samuel Udell to light the lantern. The old man then motioned for him to precede him into the dark interior. The flames from the lantern flickered across the cave wall, distorting their shadows. As they moved deep into the bowels of the mine, it was as quiet as a tomb, with only the occasional sound of dripping water breaking the silence.

As the tunnel veered off to the right, Marquis happened to glance up at Samuel's shadow and saw him raising a pickax over his head, ready to strike him down from behind. In one quick motion, Marquis jumped aside and at the same time grabbed the pick handle and easily wrestled it from Samuel's grip. Pushing the miner onto the ground, Marquis straddled him and pushed the pick handle against his windpipe. Applying pressure, he watched Samuel's face redden while he gasped for breath, clawing at Marquis's hands, trying to free himself.

"You had better talk, old man," Marquis hissed through gritted teeth. "What happened to Ward Barrett?"

Still Samuel clawed and groped at Marquis's hands, trying to push him away. By now his eyes were bulging, and blood was trickling from the corner of his mouth. Finally Marquis released the pressure and the miner grabbed his throat to draw in a deep breath.

"Are you ready to give me some straight answers? What happened to Ward Barrett?" Marquis asked, standing up and placing the heel of his boot against the frightened man's throat.

"I'll talk," Samuel whispered in a tight voice. "Move your foot and I'll tell you everything."

Marquis stepped back and leaned against the wall of the mine, casually folding his arms across his chest. "I am listening, Samuel Udell. Do not think I won't know it if you speak falsely."

The old man crawled across the cave floor, grabbing a loose beam and pulling himself up. Still gasping for breath, he leaned against the wall for support. "What if I was to tell the truth, and you don't like what I have to say? What would you do with me?"

"Your fate hangs entirely on what you did to Mr. Barrett," Marquis said in a deadly tone.

Samuel looked uneasy, and his eyes shifted away from Marquis's. "It wasn't none of my doing. I felt bad about

156

getting rid of Ward. He were a good man and a mighty fine partner."

"What did you do?" Marquis held his breath. He hoped for Valentina's sake that her father was still alive. "Speak up," he demanded. "Where is Ward Barrett?"

Samuel stared down at the toes of his scuffed brown boots. "I had heard tell that in San Francisco most ship captains was paying top dollar for sailors to man their ships and weren't asking any questions as to where they came from. It seems that there are so many seamen deserting their ships and lighting out for the gold fields that there ain't enough men to sail out of port."

"You mean you had Ward Barrett shanghaied? Is that what happened?"

"Yep, it pains me to say I did. I have since had regrets, but the deed was done. As far as I know, he ain't no worse for the wear."

Marquis wasn't convinced of the man's sincerity. "Why did you decide to shanghai your partner?"

"It weren't an easy thing to do. I guess greed got the better of me. When we struck gold, I guess I just went a little crazy. Suddenly half a gold mine wasn't enough. I wanted it all."

"What is the name of the ship that took Ward Barrett aboard?"

"The *Southern Cross*. She's a three-rigger ship out of Boston."

"This will take time to check. If I find you have not told me the truth, I will be back. You can depend on that. I'd better find Mr. Barrett unharmed, or you will pay dearly. I will see that you are placed behind bars for what you have done to the Barrett family."

"If you did that, what would happen to my mine?"

"You should have thought of that before you cheated your partner. When I return, Samuel Udell, it would be best if you were gone."

Marquis walked out of the mine into the bright sunlight feeling lighthearted. If Samuel Udell was telling the truth, there was a good chance that Valentina's father was still alive. He could hardly wait to reach San Francisco so he could find out if the *Southern Cross* was still in port. If it wasn't, there was nothing he could do but wait until she returned to California.

Marquis watched Samuel come limping out of the mine rubbing his throat. He turned away, hardly giving the old man a second thought. His heart was singing because he would soon see Valentina again. Perhaps he would have some hopeful news to tell her. "Remember, if you have lied, old man, it will not be long until you see me again," Marquis declared, despising the man who had caused Valentina such heartache.

As he and Tomico rode away from the mine, Marquis sent a prayer to heaven that Ward Barrett was still alive. He wanted to see Valentina's face light up with joy. He wanted to hand her something to make her happy.

Chapter Eleven

Salamar and Valentina had placed a daybed beneath the shade of a tall oak tree that stood majestically in the side yard. This enabled Valentina's mother to soak up the fresh air while giving her a change of scenery.

Evonne Barrett, wearing a soft pink dressing gown, reclined on the daybed. She watched the overhead branches sway in the gentle breeze while she listened to Valentina's voice as she read the words of Jane Austen's *Pride and Prejudice*. She was feeling stronger every day; the illness that had sapped her strength seemed to be lessening with the passing of time. Soothed by her daughter's voice, Evonne closed her eyes.

Valentina glanced down at her mother, noting that she had fallen asleep. Softly she closed the book and laid it aside. Tucking the coverlet about her mother's neck, she bent and kissed her cheek. Doctor Cline had said only today that her mother was much improved and would soon be able to lead a normal life. Of course Valentina knew her mother well enough to realize that she would not completely recover until she found out if her husband were alive or dead.

Moving across the yard, Valentina drank in the beauty of the sun-washed land. She felt good about everything these days. There was enough money so they did not have to worry about being able to pay for her mother's medicine, she and Salamar had made some much-needed improvements in the cabin, and her mother was so much better that she could now take short walks in the bright, healing California sun. There was now more color to her mother's face, and she was becoming more restless by the day, sometimes making it difficult for Valentina and Salamar to keep her in bed.

Valentina glanced at the house where Mr. Lawton and his sister lived. She was glad the reverend was away from home. She was not looking forward to another confrontation with him. He had been less than overjoyed when she had given him the rent money. Valentina knew he had wanted her to be dependent on him. If she continued to make money, she would never have to deal with that man again. If he bothered her in the future, she would just find another place to live.

Valentina flexed her tired muscles. She spent most afternoons reading to her mother. Later in the day, while her mother napped, she would slip away and enter the back door of the Crystal Palace that led to her dressing room. There she would practice the dance she would perform that night.

As it turned out, Valentina had not been forced to deceive her mother about her employment. Because Salamar, Valentina, and her mother had discussed her prospective interview with Mrs. Windom, Evonne Barrett had assumed her daughter had gotten the position. Valentina felt guilty for not setting her mother straight and allowing her to draw the wrong conclusions, but she and Salamar had decided it would be best not to raise her mother's suspicions. They wanted to avoid questions they did not want to answer.

It was always late at night when she arrived home

after her performance. She would be up early in the morning so she could practice her dancing before her mother awoke. Valentina did not know how much longer she could continue at this maddening pace. Constantly with her was the fear that someone would discover that she was the dancer at the Crystal Palace and inform her mother.

Valentina's mind moved to the dark Spaniard who seemed to occupy so much of her thoughts lately. Once in a while she would take the crumbling rose Marquis had given her and gently caress the now-dry petals. In her daydream she could almost see the way he had smiled at her, hear the tone of his deep voice, feel the touch of his hand. Now, she could almost hear the jingling sound of his spurs—

Jerking her head around, Valentina looked down the walkway. She had heard the sound of spurs! As if thinking about him had made him appear, Marquis Vincente was walking toward her. He was dressed in the Spanish fashion she loved so well. This time he was all in blue but for the silver strips that ran the outsides of his trouser legs. Removing his low-brimmed black hat, he bowed to Valentina. His dark eyes were so expressive, she could almost read his thoughts. Valentina ran her hand down her pale yellow gown, hoping she looked her best.

Her heart was beating so fast she could scarcely breathe as she met Marquis's bold eyes and saw that he was pleased with her appearance. When he stood before her, neither of them spoke until he smiled.

"I wondered if you were as beautiful as I remembered. I find you even more so," he said at last.

"I am pleased to see you, señor," she said, turning back to her mother and finding that she had awakened.

Evonne caught the eye of the stranger and, in that

161

moment, she knew he was the same man who had rescued her daughter. She smiled a warm welcome and he flashed her a disarming smile.

"Mother, I would like to introduce you to Señor Marquis Vincente. He and his family so graciously took me in when I was injured in the buggy accident."

Marquis glanced into the mother's silver eyes, thinking they were very like Valentina's. The woman, though ill, had a loveliness that reached to the soul. Marquis knew the daughter had that same kind of ageless beauty.

"I want to extend my gratitude to you, Señor Vincente," Evonne spoke in Spanish with a heavy French accent. "My daughter is very precious to me. I will forever be in your debt."

Marquis was amazed at Evonne's accent. "I can assure you it was our pleasure, Señora Barrett." He smiled politely to cover his astonishment. "I did not know you were French, madame. Your daughter did not tell me."

"But yes." Evonne laughed. "I am not surprised my daughter didn't tell you, señor. You see, she thinks of me as English."

Marquis took the delicate hand that was offered to him and raised it to his lips, then spoke to her in French. "My humble house was honored by your daughter's presence, Madame Barrett."

The smile that passed between Marquis and Evonne was one of mutual admiration. They had shown that each could speak the other's language. "You speak French very well, Señor Vincente," Evonne told him.

Marquis seated himself on the doorstep beside Valentina. "Your Spanish is as good as your daughter's, madame."

"Thank you. It should be. My husband taught us both."

162

Valentina watched as her mother and Marquis charmed each other. A smile tugged at her lips when they both lapsed into English.

Marquis turned and his eyes swept Valentina's face. "So your daughter is half French, madame? An astounding combination."

"My husband is always fond of saying that Valentina was born as a child of the world since she has traveled so extensively." Suddenly the sparkle went out of Evonne's eyes to be replaced with a glaze of sadness. "You have heard about my husband's disappearance, have you not, señor?"

Marquis saw Evonne Barrett's eyes moisten with tears, and he spoke softly to her. "Do not grieve, madame. I have reason to believe that your husband may still be alive."

"Have you found out anything about my father?" Valentina asked hopefully. Her eyes moved to her mother, noting the way her cheeks had paled. Valentina rushed to her side, fearing she might be having a relapse.

"I have been to the mine and talked to your father's partner, Samuel Udell," Marquis said, drawing both women's attention. "He told me just enough for me to believe your father may be alive."

Valentina turned to grasp Marquis's sleeve while her mother leaned back against the pillow, her face white and drained, her eyes filled with hope. "Tell me what you found out about my father," Valentina urged. "If there is the slightest hope that he is alive, I will find him."

"You will just have to trust that I will do everything in my power to find out if your father is alive. Do not ask me any more questions at this time. As I find out about him, I will come to you. Will you trust me on this?"

Valentina caught and held his glance. "With all my heart I will trust you. It seems this puts me in your debt

163

once more."

Marquis had the strongest urge to take Valentina into his arms. He wanted to protect her so nothing ugly or unpleasant would ever touch her life. More than anything he wanted to find her father safe and well. "Give me a little more time, Señorita Barrett. I am following a lead. It may not be too long until I have some word of your father."

"Will you not tell me what you found out?" Valentina asked.

"It would be better not to discuss the matter at this time. I will inform you of anything I discover."

Valentina nodded. "I will not press you further. Promise you will let me know the moment you hear anything."

His eyes softened. He wanted to touch her, but he dared not. "I promise," he whispered huskily.

"Tell me news of your family, Señor Vincente. How is your grandfather's health?"

Marquis shook his head sadly. "It is not good with my grandfather. His health is very fragile." He smiled down at Valentina. "My sister sends her love along with an invitation to visit Paraíso del Norte as soon as possible."

At that moment Salamar came out the door of the cabin carrying a tea tray. Marquis was astonished to find the maid so foreign looking. When her eyes met his, he immediately realized the intelligence of the woman. Her eyes were ageless, as if they could see right into a man's mind. In the space of an instant, Marquis realized that this strange woman knew of his confused feelings for Valentina.

"Señor Vincente, this is my maid and companion, Salamar," Valentina said, making the introduction.

Marquis stood up and nodded politely to Salamar. She inclined her head ever so slightly. There was no need for words between them. They each knew the other's thoughts. Salamar was the watchdog that guarded Valentina. She let Marquis know with the merest darkening of her eyes that she would be watching him.

Evonne, now emotionally drained, had closed her eyes and drifted into sleep. "Please do not be offended by my mother, Señor Vincente," Valentina said. "She is in ill health and falls asleep so easily."

"There is no reason to apologize. I find your mother utterly charming. It is easy to see why your father wanted to make her his wife."

Valentina smiled. "Yes, theirs was . . . is a very special love." Her eyes sought his, and he could see the uncertainty reflected there. "Please find my father as quickly as possible."

"I will do all in my power, little Silver Eyes," he assured her.

Valentina could feel the pull of Marquis's charm. She remembered the things he had said to her that night in his garden. Looking at him, she was silent for a moment. When she spoke, her voice trembled. "May I offer you a cup of tea, Señor Vincente?"

"No, I must leave. I have an appointment to see an old friend. I just wanted to tell you that I looked into your father's disappearance and found reason to hope. Keep good thoughts about your father."

Valentina wondered if the old friend Marquis was going to see could be a woman. "How can I ever thank you for all you have done for me and my mother?"

He flashed her a smile. "I have done nothing. It is a pleasure to be of service to two such lovely ladies. I have a very good friend who lives here in San Francisco. I will ask him to pay his respects to you so that if you ever need anything, he will contact me."

"That will not be necessary, but thank you all the same."

"I insist. His name is Tyree Garth. He is a man who can

be trusted."

Valentina glanced quickly at Salamar and noticed the smile on her lips. Dear Lord, she thought, I can't meet Tyree Garth as Valentina Barrett! He would know immediately that Jordanna and I are the same person. "No," she said quickly, feeling panic rising inside her. "I do not need your friend. We are able to take care of ourselves."

"I want someone here in San Francisco looking after your welfare. After all, you are three women alone. Tyree Garth can be trusted completely."

Valentina shook her head. "I appreciate all you have done for us, but we do not need your friend. We are not your concern." She could think of no further argument to offer against meeting Tyree Garth.

"You will always be my concern, Silver Eyes." His eyes swept hers, pulling, tugging at her heart. He was reaching for her, seeking to bring her under his spell. She lowered her eyelashes, knowing she must fight against the feelings he aroused within her young body.

With a jingle of spurs—a sound Valentina was sure she would never forget—he replaced his hat and moved down the path. Turning back to her, he touched his fingers to the brim of his hat in a salute. "Until we meet again, Silver Eyes."

Valentina stared after him feeling a loneliness that cut deep. She wanted to be with him. At that moment, she wanted to run after him, to declare that she loved him. Was she completely crazed! Marquis Vincente wouldn't welcome such a declaration from her.

She felt Salamar's eyes on her and turned around. "What has he discovered about your father?" Salamar asked.

"He said he had news that Father might be alive. I wish I had insisted he tell me all he knew." Valentina placed her hand over her heart to stop its drumming. Every time Marquis Vincente came into her life he left her feeling strangely alive and excited.

Valentina was startled when Salamar handed her a cup of tea and said, "He is the one you will love."

Valentina took a sip of the tea, not bothering to deny Salamar's prediction. "But will he love me, Salamar? He has promised to love another."

"This I do not know. You will have to find the future through the passing of time."

"I know that I love him. I am miserable because he will marry Isabel Estrada, a most unlovable person. Why did I have to love someone who can never love me?"

"Time, Valentina . . . allow time to pass." Salamar turned away, disappearing into the cabin.

Tyree studied the fifty-year-old brandy with appreciation before taking a sip. Rolling it around on his tongue, he smiled at his friend, Marquis Vincente. "I don't know how you came by this brandy, but I know men who would kill for just one taste."

Marquis placed his glass on Tyree's desk and rested his hand against his black boot. "I was given a case of the brandy by my future father-in-law. I believe he came by it in Spain."

"Well, wherever it came from, thank you for this bottle."

Tyree and Marquis had known each other for twenty years. Tyree had been a boy of twelve when he came to California with his trapper father. Marquis's father had been attacked by a bear, and Tyree's father had come along just in time to save his life. Despite the care the Vincente family gave Tyree's father, he died of his wounds. The Vincente family had taken young Tyree into their home and he and Marquis had become like brothers.

It had not mattered to the young boys that Marquis's family were aristocrats and Tyree's father had been only a trapper from Tennessee. It was Marquis's grandfather who had lent Tyree the money to build the Crystal Palace. The establishment had done so well that Tyree had been able to repay the loan within the first year.

"What brings you to town, Marquis? I had thought the arrival of your new bride-to-be would keep you closer to Paraíso del Norte."

Marquis frowned. "I came to San Francisco to aid a friend; I was hoping I might be able to enlist your help as well."

"You know if you want my help all you have to do is ask, Marquis."

"Are you acquainted with a ship called the *Southern Cross?*" Marquis inquired, taking another sip of the brandy.

"Yes, of course. She's a frigate that sails out of Boston. Her captain is a giant redhead, and as mean as they come. I have barred him from the Crystal Palace because he and his crew invariably start a fight and break the place up."

"Do you know when the *Southern Cross* is due to dock in San Francisco?"

"No, but I can find out." Tyree looked at his friend with a puzzled expression on his face. "Why do you need to know?"

"I fear the father of a friend of mine has been shanghaied by the crew of that vessel. I want to find out for sure."

Tyree's eyes danced. "Is this friend of yours male or female?"

Marquis smiled. "She is female."

"Friend or lover?"

168

"She is an angel. You have never seen a woman like her. Her hair is golden and her eyes are like quicksilver. Her face is so perfect. She is intelligent and witty and—"

"Enough," Tyree interrupted, laughingly holding up his hand. "You are whetting my appetite. You don't sound like a man who is about to be joined in blissful matrimony"—he arched an eyebrow—"unless the angel you are talking about happens to be your betrothed, Isabel Estrada."

Marquis looked grim for a moment, then he shrugged. "No, I was not speaking of Isabel. My friend is in trouble and I want to help. This has nothing to do with my betrothed," Marquis said indignantly.

"I see. . . ." Tyree laughed. "I will keep my eyes open. As soon as I have any news of the *Southern Cross*, I'll send word to you."

"This is very important to me, Tyree. I am afraid for this woman. She lives alone with an ailing mother and a strange, exotic-looking maid named Salamar."

Tyree's ears perked up at the mention of Salamar's name. He remembered that Jordanna had a maid named Salamar and decided there could not be two such women in San Francisco. The friend Marquis was talking about and his dancer, Jordanna, had to be the same person. "What is your friend's name and where does she live?" he asked. "Perhaps I can keep an eye on her for you."

"That is what I was hoping you would say, Tyree. But I want you to understand that this woman is a real lady. She is . . . different from the women you are usually associated with. I will expect you to treat her as a lady at all times."

Tyree lit his cigar and chuckled. "You can trust me to do the right thing. Regardless of what you believe to the contrary, I can be a perfect gentleman when the occasion calls for it."

169

"I'm counting on that. I told her your name and said you would be getting in touch with her."

"Tell me about this woman," Tyree pressed. He had honored Jordanna's wishes and had not allowed anyone near her. Nor had he taken it upon himself to find out who she was. But he couldn't be blamed if her identity happened to fall into his lap, could he?

"She came from England to join her mother and father. When she arrived, she found her father was missing and her mother ill. I do not know if she needs money, but I would like you to find out. If you discover she is in need of anything, make sure that she gets it, and I will see that you are repaid. She is proud, so I do not think she will take charity. Take care not to offend her in any way."

Tyree swirled the amber liquid around in his glass. So, he thought, that was the reason Jordanna had been so desperate for a job dancing for him. He smiled to himself. She needn't have worried. Even though he now knew her identity, the secret would be safe with him.

"How did you meet such an outstanding woman?" Tyree asked guardedly.

"I met her when she had an accident while searching for her father."

"I see." Tyree took another sip of brandy. "Tell me, have you heard about my new dancer?" Tyree watched Marquis's face carefully. He wondered if Jordanna had told Marquis about her dancing. He was almost certain she had not.

"No," Marquis answered with little interest. "But then I don't get much news from San Francisco. I hope she is more exciting than the last one you hired. She had the face of a horse and the legs of a hairy goat."

Tyree chuckled and shoved the newspaper across his desk toward Marquis. "Here, read what this reporter thinks about my new dancer."

Marquis scanned the paper, noting that the reporter's praise was high indeed. He went on and on about the woman being poetry in motion . . . too lovely to be believed . . . the toast of California—a mystery lady that no one knew.

"It says that the dancer wears a veil, so therefore she could still be hiding a horse face," Marquis remarked lazily, tossing the newspaper back on the desk. "Have you seen her unveiled?"

"No."

"I fail to see the attraction of a woman who hides her face and dances across the stage. I have very little liking for dancers anyway."

"As I recall, your sister dances a beautiful Spanish dance," Tyree reminded him. "Are you only scornful where dancing professionally is concerned?"

"Perhaps," he admitted. "But the Spanish dance is a thing of beauty—it is an art. Can your dancer master the Spanish dance?"

"I don't know. I will tell you this, though. She has worked for me for over a week and not once has she danced the same dance."

"I think I would be bored with your masked dancer. I would much rather spend the evening with Bonita."

Tyree knew that Marquis kept his mistress, Bonita, at the Madison Hotel. There had been a time when he had come to town once a week to see her. Lately, he hardly came at all. "Why don't you come and see my dancer tonight? Come and judge for yourself if you find her boring."

"Perhaps I will. What have I got to lose but time, Tyree?"

*   *   *

The men in the smoke-filled room seemed tense with excitement and anticipation as they waited for Jordanna to make her appearance. Marquis sat at a front table with his arm draped about Bonita's shoulder, a wine glass balanced between his fingers. He gave his mistress a smile that melted her heart. Bonita snuggled close to him, feeling happy for the first time in weeks. Marquis had finally come to see her.

"Why do I hardly ever see you anymore, Marquis?" she asked, almost afraid to press him. Marquis was not the kind of man that a woman could easily hold.

Marquis hugged her to him and laughed heartily. "You see more of me than any other woman does."

"I always knew when your betrothed arrived from Spain that my days would be numbered . . . but I had hoped—"

His eyes narrowed, reminding her that she was not to speak of his betrothed. When he saw her distress, he lifted her chin and smiled down at her. "Tonight is not the time for long faces. We are together, are we not?"

Bonita nodded, knowing she had already lost Marquis. She doubted he would ever come to see her after tonight. Oh, he would be generous, and he would be kind, but she would miss him so much.

The music filled the room, and all eyes became glued to the stage. A lively Spanish song was building in tempo and suddenly the curtains rose, revealing a woman dressed in red shimmering material. Her floor-length gown was tapered to a long, ruffled train in back. Her dazzling costume picked up the lights from the lanterns and gave her the appearance of motion, even though she was standing still. Around her hair was a shimmering red net that dropped down over her face. As always, the only part of her face that showed were her eyes, and no one could tell their color from such a distance.

The men were going crazy, hollering and whistling. She stood poised with her arms in the air, waiting for the right moment to begin her dance. Several bags of gold dust were tossed upon the stage in tribute to the mysterious beauty.

Tyree seated himself at Marquis's table, watching his friend's face. "Good evening, Bonita. It is good to see you again," Tyree said, raising her hand to his lips.

"Are we about to be entertained by your famous mystery lady that I have been hearing about, Tyree?" Bonita asked.

"That's her," he answered, laughing in amusement, his eyes locking with Marquis's. "It seems she will do a Spanish dance tonight."

"No doubt you told her to," Marquis sneered. "There is more to dancing than just drawing a man's eye."

"Just wait," Tyree said. His eyes suddenly lit up. "I'll tell you what I'm going to do. I will wager a hundred dollars that you will say after Jordanna's dance that she is the most talented dancer you have ever seen. I will expect you to be honest about it."

Marquis reached into his pocket and counted out the money while Tyree did the same. "We will let Bonita hold the bills until after the dance," Tyree said, chuckling. He knew the bet was as good as won. When he handed the money to Bonita, she giggled, pushing it down the front of her gown.

Marquis's shoulders shook with laughter. "So far all your Jordanna has done is stand there and allow these poor fools to go wild. I do not call that dancing. I am afraid you will lose, my friend."

"Just watch," Tyree said, nodding at the stage. "You haven't won yet."

Valentina moved her foot just the merest fraction of an inch and her fingers clicked the castanets as though

173

introducing herself to the audience. Slowly, enticingly, her hips began to move with the music, the movements smooth and sultry. All at once the music became faster and she began tapping her feet in rhythm. Faster and faster her feet tapped until the audience went wild. Marquis was not even aware that he was holding his breath.

The slim, shapely arm moved gracefully over the dancer's head while she spun around in a circle. Then there was a pause—as if her body was about to take flight—alerting the audience there would be a change in tempo. Gracefully she flowed across the stage, taking the heart of every man present with her. She danced, she whirled, she arched her back and moved her hips. She was pulling, stimulating, drawing the audience to her.

Marquis was stunned. He was sure he had never seen anything so beautiful. The fact that her face was hidden seemed to add to the beauty. Every man at the Crystal Palace could imagine her face as he wanted it to be.

Hearing a sulphur match grating against the bottom of Tyree's boot, Marquis watched Tyree light his cigar. His friend blew out a puff of smoke and smiled. They both knew that Tyree had won the bet.

The dancer's feet tapped out the tempo of the music like a drum roll, then she arched her back and crossed her lovely arms in front of her. Too soon, she raised a dainty hand into the air; she waved good-bye to the audience and hurried off the stage.

Marquis found himself jumping to his feet yelling *"Brava"* at the top of his voice. The din was deafening because over a hundred men chanted Jordanna's name, calling to her, begging her to return.

"Will she come back?" Marquis asked when the noise had finally died down.

"No, she will not be back tonight," Tyree told him.

"Do I win my bet?"

Marquis sank down in his chair feeling as if the dancer had drained him of his strength. She had put so much into her dance and she had taken it out of her audience. "You win," Marquis admitted, wishing the mysterious woman would return. "She is the best I have ever seen."

When Bonita made a move to withdraw the money from the bodice of her gown, Tyree caught her hand. "You keep it," he said with a laugh. "I just wanted the satisfaction of winning against Marquis. It isn't often I can prove him wrong."

Bonita blinked her eyes. She knew Tyree had won, but she had lost. Without being told, she knew Marquis would pursue the dancer. She had observed him while he had watched Jordanna. He had worshiped the woman with his eyes. Bonita had been so deep in thought she had not heard the ensuing conversation between Marquis and Tyree. All she knew was that now Marquis was leading her across the room. He was taking her home. She sensed in her heart that after tonight he might never come to her again.

Valentina leaned against the door of her dressing room. Her heart was pounding wildly and it had nothing to do with the fact that she had been dancing so fast. She had seen Marquis in the audience with his arm around a woman's shoulder. She had also seen the way he had watched her dance. Had he recognized her? "Please, no!" she cried, sinking down to her knees.

Salamar came to her and helped her to her feet. "What is wrong, little one?"

"Oh, Salamar, Marquis was in the audience tonight. If he ever finds out who I am, he will despise me. I couldn't stand that."

"It is better not to worry about something until it has happened. Turn around so I can help you undress."

Valentina did as she was told. All she could think about was Marquis watching her dance. Perhaps he hadn't guessed her true identity. But wouldn't Tyree Garth put two and two together and realize who she was? If he did, would he tell Marquis?

Sometime later, two lone figures slipped out the back door and down a side street. No one saw Valentina and Salamar go into the small cabin and close the door behind them.

Marquis stood at the window of Bonita's bedroom, looking down on San Francisco. He smiled when Bonita came up behind him and clasped her arms about his waist. "I'm glad you came to town today, Marquis. I have missed you so much."

He turned to her, a frown creasing his brow. "I do not want you sitting here alone waiting for me, Bonita. I do not demand that you be a hermit."

"You once told me you didn't want to share me with anyone, Marquis. I have not been with another man since I became your woman."

Marquis felt trapped. He always hated good-byes. Why did a woman always make parting so difficult? They always wanted to hold on to a man. He smiled at Bonita. She had given him many hours of pleasure; he would let her down gradually. Perhaps, he decided, it would be better to see her a few more times. "You must remember when we first met, Bonita, I told you there was no future for us. You agreed to my terms at that time."

Her arms went around his neck and she pressed her face to his. "I remember," she sobbed. "I will let you go when the time comes."

When Marquis lowered his head to kiss Bonita, he was

unmoved by her sigh. He was picturing silver-blue eyes and lips as soft as a rose petal. Suddenly his mind was invaded by thoughts of an uncommonly beautiful body dressed in shimmering red. As Bonita's hands moved through his hair, he recalled the dancer's hips moving enticingly.

Chapter Twelve

Percival Lawton was standing at his window watching Valentina. She had dropped down on her knees and was digging in the yard, obviously planting something. Picking up his hat, he clapped it on his head and hurried out the door and down the path to talk to her.

Valentina was deep in thought, planning the dance she would perform that night, and did not hear Reverend Lawton's approach. "Miss Barrett, I want to talk to you right now," he said in a booming voice that almost made her jump out of her skin.

Dropping the spade to the ground, Valentina stood up, trying to rub the dirt from her hands. "I didn't know you had returned, Mr. Lawton. Your sister said you were making the rounds of the gold fields."

A wisp of hair blew across Valentina's cheek and Percival had to resist the urge to reach out and touch it to see if it was as silky as it appeared. Troubled as he was by his confused thoughts about Valentina, he found that his voice had been louder than he had intended. "Just what in the world do you think you are doing, may I ask?"

"I am planting a garden. Your sister said it would be all right if I tended it and shared half of everything with you. There will be corn, peas—"

"I'm not talking about some fool arrangement you made with my sister," he interrupted, dabbing nervously at his face, then poking his handkerchief in his hip pocket. "I am talking about how you came to have money to pay the rent and can live such a frivolous lifestyle. My sister tells me that you have comforts in the cabin that are completely unnecessary."

Valentina was annoyed and wondered why she always allowed this man to tax her patience. She felt that a man of God should have more understanding and charity in his heart for his fellowmen. Percival Lawton always seemed to be looking at the sordid side of life, never at the good in people. Since houses were hard to come by in San Francisco, Valentina knew she must make an effort to stay on good terms with the reverend and his pious sister. But that did not mean she would allow either one of them to push her around.

"I had not thought that renting a house from you gave you the right to pry into my personal finances. You should only be concerned that I pay my rent on time. As for making the cabin more livable, that was done for my mother's sake. She likes being surrounded by beautiful things. I like being able to make her life a little brighter."

Reverend Lawton cleared his throat and his watery gaze wavered against Valentina's intense stare. "My sister says you are working for Mrs. Windom. I know she doesn't pay you enough to buy frivolities. It's only natural that me and my sister would wonder why you seem to be throwing money around. You will remember that before I was called away, you gave me the impression you couldn't meet your rent."

His eyes shifted and he stared at a tree branch just behind her. "I'm sure you will also recall, out of the goodness of my heart, I offered to make you my wife."

Valentina suddenly felt pity for the man. He could not be happy unless he found the bad in people. He was somehow pathetic and that made her speak to him in a kinder tone of voice. "I was deeply honored by your offer of marriage, Mr. Lawton. It was kind of you to want to marry me when you don't love me, and I don't know you well enough to love you. I know you will understand when I tell you I could never marry a man I don't love."

Before Reverend Lawton could answer, both he and Valentina heard someone coming down the path toward them. Valentina recognized Tyree Garth. She wondered if she dared disappear into the house. Dear Lord, she cried inwardly. I had hoped he wouldn't come. What will I do if he recognizes me? It's too late to flee.

As Tyree neared Valentina, he saw the frightened, questioning look in her eyes. Doffing his hat, he bowed gallantly to her.

Before he could say anything to her, however, Reverend Lawton spoke up. "If you have come to see me to protest the citizen group I'm raising to boycott your wicked establishment, Mr. Garth, you are wasting your time," Reverend Lawton announced, staring down the end of his nose in indignation.

Tyree's laughter stung Percival to the quick, and his face reddened with anger. "This is a free country, Reverend Lawton. You are free to pursue your righteous concerns. However, I think I should point out to you that you will have a devil of a time finding enough people to march with you. Most of them can be found inside the Crystal Palace, buried in what you would call vice and corruption."

Valentina saw the laughter dancing in Tyree's eyes. He was not in the last intimidated by the good reverend. She liked him in spite of the fact that he was a rascal and a rogue. He had been kind to her and had honored her wishes thus far. Looking into his eyes, she tried to decide if he had recognized her. All she saw was the twinkle of good humor. He was a man who never took life too

181

seriously and was not impressed when others did.

"Why have you come then? I'm sure Miss Barrett wants nothing to do with the likes of you." Percival Lawton moved in front of Valentina as if he were the flaming hand of the Lord trying to protect her from degradation.

Tyree chuckled and winked at Valentina. "As a matter of fact, it is Miss Barrett I came to see. I would be deeply grateful if you would make the formal introductions. You see, we have a mutual acquaintance who has asked me to look in on her for him."

Tyree's eyes ran quickly over Valentina. Marquis had been right; she was a lovely angel. It was hard to think of her as the girl who charmed hundreds of men every night on the stage of the Crystal Palace. He had expected her to be beautiful, and he was not disappointed. She was the fairest of the fair. He could see uncertainty in her eyes and knew she was wondering if he suspected who she was. He decided to feign ignorance of her identity for the time being.

"Who would you know who would be an acquaintance of Miss Barrett's?" Percival questioned doubtfully. "She wouldn't associate with you and your kind."

Valentina said nothing for the moment. She knew why Tyree had come. He was here because Marquis had asked him to look in on her.

"I say you are a liar and a scoundrel, sir," Reverend Lawton was saying. "Leave this property at once."

Tyree's eyes hardened for the briefest moment and then danced with mirth. Looking past Percival, he spoke directly to Valentina. "Miss Barrett, I am a friend of Marquis Vincente's, and he's the one who asked me to keep an eye on you. I see you already have a champion in Reverend Lawton. If you will excuse me, I will take my leave and apologize for troubling you."

As he turned to leave, Valentina made a quick

decision. How could she stand there and allow Tyree Garth to be treated badly by Reverend Lawton when he had been so kind to her? She could not just let him walk away—he deserved better from her. "Wait, Mr. Garth. If you were nice enough to call on me, the least I can do is offer you a cup of tea. Won't you come into the house and meet my mother?"

"Miss Barrett, what can you be thinking!" Percival declared in shocked surprise. "It's most unseemly for a woman of your breeding to entertain such an unsavory gentleman in your home. Most unseemly indeed."

Tyree laughed in amusement. "Don't get in a lather, Reverend. I am on my way down to the docks and will have to decline the invitation this time. I hope the offer will be extended at a later date, Miss Barrett."

"Indeed it will, sir," she said, caught by his infectious smile.

"I will look forward to it."

"Mr. Garth," Valentina spoke up hurriedly. "Do you know if señor Vincente has found out anything new about my father?"

"Nothing yet. That's why I'm on my way to the docks now. I want to make some inquiries. Let us hope that it won't be too long before we will know something."

Much to Percival's displeasure, Valentina reached out and placed her hand on Tyree's sleeve. "You are most kind, sir. I have met the most wonderful people since coming to California. On behalf of my mother and me, I want to thank you for trying to help locate my father, Mr. Garth. My mother has been ill and is resting at the moment. I know she will extend her gratitude to you on your next visit."

Tyree flashed her a rakish grin. "I have done nothing, so far. But I am looking forward to the next meeting, Miss Barrett." He nodded at the reverend, tipped his hat to Valentina, and strolled leisurely away, while Valentina and Reverend Lawton both stared after him.

"That man is not the kind you should associate yourself with, Miss Barrett. He owns that den of iniquity and shouldn't force his friendship on decent people."

"I saw nothing wrong in his offer of friendship, or his most generous offer to help me find my father."

Jealousy burned in Percival's watery eyes. "Why didn't you ask me to help you find your father instead of going to Marquis Vincente and Tyree Garth?"

"I didn't ask either of them for help—they offered on their own."

"I would have helped you."

"No, you wouldn't have, Mr. Lawton. You tried to convince me that my father was dead." All Valentina wanted to do was escape from this man who seemed to soil everything he came in contact with. Was there nothing, or no one, he approved of? She excused herself and made a hasty retreat.

Later in the evening, as Valentina poured hot water into the tea pot and set the cups on a tray, she pondered Tyree Garth's visit. Apparently he hadn't recognized her. But it was only a matter of time before he found out her true identity. If Tyree had accepted her invitation today, he would have seen Salamar, and he would have known she was Jordanna. Somehow she did not mind Tyree finding out who she was—she had the feeling he would understand—but, for some reason, she did not want Marquis to learn she was the dancer at the Crystal Palace. He would never understand . . . or forgive.

By now Jordanna's fame had spread the length and breadth of California. Men journeyed for hundreds of miles to see the woman who captured their hearts and imagination. Not one of the rough-hewn miners had ever attempted to touch her; they wanted only to worship her from afar. The usual bags of gold dust were tossed on the stage as a tribute to her; armloads of flowers were delivered to her dressing room.

The newspaper reporter, Julian Mathews, helped add to the legend of Jordanna. He wrote glowing reports of her graceful beauty. He wrote how astonishing it was that no man ever attempted to go backstage to see Jordanna— not that the two guards posted at the entrance would have allowed it had they tried.

Valentina was uneasy because of the publicity she was receiving. She considered quietly slipping away, allowing Jordanna to disappear, just as her mother had when she had left Paris, but not yet. If it turned out that her father was dead, she would need enough money to buy passage back to England for her mother, Salamar, and herself.

Each night Valentina searched the faces in the audience, looking for Marquis. He had yet to disappoint her; he was always there watching her dance. After her fear that he would recognize her diminished, she began to dance for him. The sensuous movements she made were to entice him. She felt no shame as she glided across the stage, knowing he was watching her every move. The irony was that, in her way, she was making love to him.

Now, as Valentina slipped the veil over her face, she hoped Marquis would be present tonight. She felt excitement building up deep inside. Tonight she would dance her best. She would dance for Marquis Vincente alone.

Marquis watched the curtains expectantly, waiting for them to open. He, like all the other men in the audience, had come to see Jordanna dance. He was hopelessly caught by her spell; she kept pulling at him, bringing him

185

back each night. Marquis had the feeling that she was dancing for him alone. He could not see her eyes, but he knew she was watching him. Tonight he would ask to meet her in person. He had not believed Tyree when he had said she did not mix with the male customers. She would not be flaunting her charms before the men if she did not like what she was doing. Jordanna's exotic movements suggested she was trying to entice rather than entertain.

Marquis's dark eyes blazed. She had been born for a man to make love to. Marquis intended to be that man— or perhaps he would be just one of many. Most probably Tyree had already had the woman in his bed.

At that moment the music began and the curtains slowly parted. The haunting melody grew louder as a soft light centered on a woman draped from head to foot in shimmering gold material. As Valentina rose to her feet, the golden fabric fell away and the audience gasped in awe. She wore golden-colored harem pants with just a hint of skin showing through. Across her face and covering her hair was a golden net with tiny bells attached so that each movement she made brought the most delightful tinkling sound.

The men were dazed by her beauty. When she reached to pick up a sword from the floor, they waited, scarcely breathing, to see what new, exciting dance she would perform for them this night.

Marquis felt his heart thunder against his chest, keeping time with the music. Faster and faster the tempo rose as the woman swung the sword over her head. Leaping into the air, her face hidden behind her veils of secrecy, she slashed the air with the blade. Grasping the sword in both hands, she raised it over her head, then, to everyone's amazement, threw it across the stage where it landed point first in a block of wood, hitting a bull's-eye. Softly the music drifted around the room, lending its beauty to Valentina's performance. She was so talented, she pulled every emotion from her audience. She amused, titillated; she made them feel sorrow, anger, passion. She drew all her strength from her audience, leaving them drained and completely under her spell.

The crowd roared their approval as she dramatically leapt into the air and came down in a soft curtsy. Silence followed. Then electricity seemed to charge the air, for her audience worshiped her talent, adored her feminine beauty.

When she stood up slowly, the crowd went wild, as always. Valentina's eyes were on Marquis. She saw him touch his lips to a single snow white rose before tossing it to her. It landed at her feet, and Marquis watched spellbound as she reached down and picked up the fragrant flower and touched it to her lips. Valentina knew she was flirting, but she could not seem to stop herself. The stage was littered with bags of gold dust, yet she had chosen to acknowledge him by picking up his rose. What he could not know was that she was remembering the crimson rose he had given her as Valentina.

Blowing a kiss to the audience, Valentina quickly ran across the stage and disappeared. Everyone knew she would not come back that night, but still they called for her long after she had gone.

Tyree sat down at the table beside his friend, eyeing him speculatively. "I have seen more of you in the past two weeks than I usually see of you in a year. Could it be that you are enchanted by my new dancer, Marquis?"

"I want to meet her, Tyree. We have been friends for a long time. Surely you would not deny me this one small favor. Introduce me to her."

"Sorry, Marquis. It is her wish not to meet anyone. I have sworn to keep everyone away from her."

"Since you won a hundred dollars from me, you have to give me a chance to win it back. How about a small wager, Tyree? You are a betting man. What do you say?"

Tyree chomped down on his cigar. "I'm listening. What do you have in mind?"

"I have a note that I want you to deliver to Jordanna. If she doesn't want to see me, I will owe you a hundred dollars."

"She won't see you," Tyree said with assurance. He found it amusing that Marquis had not yet discovered that Jordanna was Valentina.

"If you are so sure she won't see me, deliver this note to her."

Tyree took the extended piece of paper and stood. "I never could resist a sure thing. When I return, I'll expect to be paid."

Marquis watched Tyree walk away, not at all sure that Jordanna would see him. She had flirted with him, but that did not mean she would want him backstage. She was like a fever in his brain. He wanted her—he wanted her almost to the point of madness.

Tyree knocked on the dressing room door and waited for an answer. He had spent thousands of dollars having the dressing room furnished for Jordanna. The colors were soft blues and whites. There was a blue velvet settee and even a bed covered with a white satin spread. At her insistence he had had an outside door built so she could leave the Crystal Palace without being seen.

Tyree smiled when Jordanna opened the door to him. There was only one small candle burning, and he could see very little in the dimly lit room. Jordanna, still dressed in her costume, motioned for him to enter.

She looked at him questioningly. "It's payday," he said, smiling. "Of course your big money comes from what the men throw to you on stage. You should be doing very well now."

Tyree was a big man and seemed to fill the room with his presence. He was so kind, and Valentina was becoming very fond of him. "I will always be grateful to you for giving me this chance, Mr. Garth."

Tyree fingered an edge of the golden veil she wore and ran it through his fingers. "How do you happen to have so many different costumes? I would wager you didn't find this kind of material here in San Francisco."

"Many of my costumes belong to Salamar. I am merely borrowing them."

"You know you're making me a wealthy man, don't you? If your popularity continues, I may have to expand."

"No, don't do that," she said quickly. "I will not be here for any great length of time, Mr. Garth. I wouldn't want you to think you can depend on me much longer."

He seated himself on the blue settee. "How soon will you be leaving?"

"I don't know." Valentina then did something that took Tyree completely by surprise; she unfastened her veil and pushed it aside. "You knew all along who I was, didn't you?"

He smiled. "Yes, Valentina, I knew."

"Yet you still protected my identity."

"We made a deal."

"Does Marquis know who I am?"

Tyree saw the misery in her beautiful silver eyes. He wanted to pull her into his arms and pledge eternal love and devotion, but he knew she was not for him. He reached out for her hand, patting it affectionately before releasing it. "No, Marquis doesn't know. As a matter of fact, he has sent Jordanna a note. He wishes to see you."

"I don't understand."

Tyree laughed at the joke on his friend. "He is enchanted by you as the dancer, my dear. He wants to talk to you. I think you can guess why."

"I . . ." She lowered her head. "I don't want him to

189

find out who I am."

"He won't find out from me, Jordanna. Shall I send him away?"

She hesitated for just a moment before she answered. "No. I want to see him."

Tyree felt a twinge of jealousy tug at his heart. He also feared that Marquis would hurt Valentina if she were not careful. "You know what he wants, Valentina. He is of the Spanish nobility. His life has been laid out for him since the day he was born. You know you could never occupy more than a small corner of that life." Tyree knew he had to warn Valentina about what she would be facing with Marquis, though he had no desire to hurt her.

"Yes, I know." Her eyes were sad. "Even knowing he is pledged to another, I still want to see him. I know it's wrong to deceive him, but I can't let him know who I really am."

"Marquis is not like most men, Jordanna. He's from a proud breed. He may despise you when he learns you have deceived him. He thinks Valentina is an angel—I don't have to tell you what he thinks about Jordanna."

Tyree watched a tear roll down Valentina's cheek. "I will just see him this once. I will take care that he never finds out who I really am."

Not knowing how to answer her, Tyree stood up and walked to the door. "I would caution you not to feel too deeply about Marquis, Jordanna. He has broken many hearts. He wouldn't think twice about breaking yours."

She turned her back to him, knowing he spoke the truth. Had she not seen Marquis with a woman who was not his betrothed? Tyree had hinted that there were many women in Marquis's life.

Hearing the door click shut behind her, Valentina knew Tyree had gone and quickly picked up her veil and pulled it over her face.

*   *   *

Marquis did not hear Tyree come up behind him until he dropped money on the table in front of him. "You win this time, my friend. She will see you."

Marquis pushed the money aside. "You keep this. I will have something better to keep me warm."

Tyree grabbed Marquis's arm and spun him around. "Don't joke about her, Marquis. And don't hurt her. She isn't one of your doxies . . . she's special."

Marquis jerked his arm free and faced his friend with a smile on his lips. "I don't intend to hurt her. I will be very good to her. When I'm finished with her, I'll give her back to you, shall we say, more experienced."

Tyree clenched his fists together as Marquis walked away. It was all he could do to control his temper. Stalking across the room, he swore under his breath. All hell would break loose before too long. He intended to be around to pick up the pieces when Marquis tired of Jordanna. He hoped for Valentina's sake that Marquis never found out her true identity. Marquis would not like being made the fool. Sighing heavily, Tyree wished he had refused to deliver Marquis's note to Valentina.

Chapter Thirteen

Valentina heard the soft knock on the door and felt her heart leap with apprehension. Why had she agreed to see Marquis? Perhaps she should just tell him who she was and be done with it. A second rap caused her to swallow her fear. Thinking quickly, she disguised her voice and called out in French, then switched to English, imitating her mother's heavy French accent. "Enter."

Marquis swung the door open and narrowed his eyes in the darkened room. All he could see were vague shadows and outlines. When at last his eyes became accustomed to the dark, they rested on the woman still draped in gold. Smiling, he closed the door behind him.

"Thank you for seeing me."

She inclined her head.

"I was not sure how I should address you, señorita," he said in a deep voice.

"I answer to Jordanna," came the accented reply. "You may call me that."

"Jordanna is a lovely and unusual name," he remarked. "I do not believe I have heard it before."

"It is a family name," she answered, stepping away from the small circle of candlelight.

"I am Marquis Domingo Vincente, and I have been

watching you perform. You dance beautifully."

"I thank you." Valentina purposely made her voice deep and husky. Her knees began to tremble when she saw the undisguised look of admiration in Marquis's eyes. It was strange being alone with him, with him not knowing who she was. Valentina began to relax. Marquis had no notion of her true identity. She realized if he ever saw the color of her eyes he would immediately know she was Valentina. Therefore she stayed in the shadows, protecting herself from discovery.

"I brought wine. Will you have a drink with me?" He moved farther into the room, holding up a bottle and removing two glasses from his pocket.

"Yes," she whispered and motioned him to the settee. The candle was on the dressing table, and when Marquis moved forward, he blocked much of the light, throwing the room into darkness.

After Marquis poured her a glass of ruby wine and handed it to her, he moved over to make room on the settee. Valentina took a sip of the wine and felt its warmth spread through her body. She could not see Marquis's face very well and took comfort in the fact that he could not see hers either.

When Marquis touched his glass to hers, his laughter was warm. "I drink a toast to the most alluring, talented dancer in all California. You are hailed far and wide as a goddess. I see in you a real flesh-and-blood woman."

Even though he had not touched her, Valentina felt the heat of his body. When he set aside his glass and captured her face between his hands, she did not move away.

"I am enchanted with you, Jordanna. You know that, don't you?"

She did not bother denying his assertion. There was no need for false modesty between them. Each could sense how the other felt. The heat and excitement that ran between them was apparent in every fiber of their beings.

She watched as he reached his hand into his breast pocket and withdrew an oblong box. "This is for you, Jordanna. I wanted to give you something to enhance your beauty. I hope you will accept this small tribute to your talent."

"What is it?" she asked, refusing to take the box from him. Marquis smiled and flipped open the catch. There, dazzling, on a bed of black velvet, was a large ruby on a heavy golden chain.

Valentina shook her head and pushed his hand away. "I cannot accept this from you. I am insulted that you should think I would."

Puzzlement was written on his face. "I do not understand. Do you think the stone is too small? You do not turn away the gold dust that is thrown at your feet on stage each night."

"That is different."

"How is it different?"

"I—"

He smiled. "Don't bother. I know what you are trying to say. And, yes, I have insulted you. Forgive me?"

"I'm not sure. I don't know why you would think I would accept such a personal gift from a gentleman."

He arched a dark brow at her. "You are not going to tell me that men have never given you expensive baubles before. I am sure you have been showered with attention by men all over the world."

Valentina stood up and turned her back. "You are mistaken about me. I am not what you imply I am."

She felt him rise to stand behind her. "No, you are mistaken, Jordanna. I implied nothing but that I find you fascinating. Perhaps I am rushing you. Would you prefer that I leave now."

"I would prefer that you never come here again."

He turned her around slowly to face him. His shadow fell across her face and he could not see more than her outline. He was curious about her looks; he wondered what color her eyes were. Perhaps it was best not to know, he decided. Mystery was what had drawn him to her in the first place. He felt wildly alive with her. Jordanna drew many of the same emotions from him that Valentina Barrett had. Of course the dancer was not pure like his little Silver Eyes. But she could help ease the deep ache that Valentina had left inside him.

"Again I ask that you forgive my boldness. I started out all wrong. I can only say in my defense that I was overcome with admiration for you. Give me another chance, and you have my word that I will make it up to you."

His black lashes lowered to hide the dark eyes. "Allow me to be your friend, Jordanna."

"I . . . there are reasons why I cannot have you for a friend."

"Are you married?"

"No."

"Would you tell me what your reasons are?" He looked about the dimly lit room and the truth hit him. "No, don't tell me. You don't want me to know who you are, do you?"

"I don't want my identity known to anyone."

Marquis savored the moment. Excitement throbbed through his body like wildfire. His whole being had been seduced by the dancer—seduced by the mystery of her! He had to see her again! He had to! "If I promise not to press the issue, will you allow me to visit you again?"

Valentina was experiencing the same emotions Marquis was feeling. Her stomach was knotting and her hands were clasped tightly in her lap for fear that she would give in to the impulse to reach out and touch him. There was a deep longing brewing, stirring, bursting forth within her. "I don't know . . . I think it would not be proper," she stated, wanting desperately to say yes.

He laughed softly, exhilaration singing through his body. "You have my word that I will act with decorum at all times. Can I call on you at your home tomorrow night after your performance?"

"No. If you want to see me, it will have to be here in my dressing room."

He chuckled delightedly. "I will do as you say, but I still contend that you are hiding a husband somewhere. Why else would you go to the trouble of surrounding yourself with such secrecy?"

Valentina felt his hand brush against her arm. Her throat seemed to close off, and she wanted to melt against him. More than anything she wanted to put this farce aside and lift the veil of deception. She wanted to be held in his arms and kissed. It did not matter that he was betrothed to another and that he probably had dozens of mistresses. From the very beginning he had stirred something to life inside of her; now it had reached a boiling point.

"It is getting late. I think you should leave now," she managed to say, wishing she dared ask him to stay.

His hand slid up her veil and he brought her face close to his. Feeling her stiffen, he said, "Do not fear me, little dancer. I, like everyone else, am intrigued by your mystery. Until you give me permission, I will not lift your veil. Your secret is safe from me . . . and with me." His fingers trailed seductively along her cheek. "I will leave for now, but I will be back tomorrow night, Jordanna. Know that I will be in torment until I see you again."

Valentina felt as if she had fallen into a deep abyss as his lips brushed hers through the veil. Before she could react, he moved across the room and was out the door. Sinking onto the settee, she wondered if those who dared to play with fire really did get burned.

Marquis had been coming to every performance for over three weeks. Afterward he would come backstage to Valentina's dressing room. He was always the perfect gentleman, saying and doing everything correctly. Even so, the tension between the two of them mounted each time they were together.

To Valentina's surprise, Salamar had made no objection when she learned of Marquis's visits. She was always careful to leave before Marquis came, knowing he would realize who Valentina was if he saw her.

The first few times Marquis visited her, Valentina had been nervous and uneasy about being alone with him. She found that when he was not with her, she dreamed about him, awake or asleep. Soon she began to question why he did not try to kiss her. What was wrong with her? Didn't he like her? Night after night the strain between them was building. Valentina knew it was but a matter of time before everything came to a head.

Marquis had not gone back to Paraíso del Norte since he had met Jordanna. He knew he was neglecting his duty, but he could not seem to leave her. She was a fever in his brain as well as in his body. He had to have her. He did not delude himself into thinking he loved the dancer, but he desired her with a seething passion.

As the curtain rose there was no sound other than the music—exotic music that could have come straight from ancient Egypt.

Marquis caught his breath as Jordanna appeared on the stage draped in a shimmering silver veil. With a high leap she rushed across the stage, holding the veil so it billowed out in front of her. The audience gasped as she

198

allowed the veil to mold to her, outlining her beautiful body. Jordanna swirled and turned, soft and alluring, feminine and seductive.

As always, she held the audience in the palm of her hand. The Crystal Palace was so crowded it could not have accommodated another person.

Marquis looked at some of the faces of the men as they watched Jordanna dance. He was annoyed at the way they worshiped her. He wanted her to himself. He did not like the idea of sharing her with anyone. As he studied the faces, he wondered if any of the men had been Jordanna's lovers.

Tonight he would have a serious talk with her. He would offer to make her his mistress. He would set her up in a fine house on the hill and staff it with servants. She would want for nothing, and she would dance only for him.

Another gasp could be heard as Jordanna dropped the veil to the floor. She stood still as the silken material settled about her feet. She was dressed as Cleopatra, the queen of the Nile. A thin silver veil covered the lower half of her face. A shoulder-length black wig framed her head and silver slippers adorned her feet. The sparkling material crossed over her breasts, revealing a creamy white shoulder. The gown was molded to her body like a second skin.

Her hips started moving, and the audience adored her with their eyes. The music became louder and louder, the tempo faster and faster. She whirled and danced, carrying the heart of every man across the stage with her. The audience belonged to her—she held them enraptured. There wasn't a man who wouldn't have died for her at that moment.

The tempo slowed and Jordanna blew a kiss and ran off the stage, disappearing behind the curtains. The noise was deafening as the men jumped to their feet crying for more.

Tyree Garth watched Marquis make his way through the crowd, annoyed that he was going to Valentina's dressing room. Tyree foresaw heartbreak ahead for his little dancer. He wished he had the means to protect her. Marquis was his best friend, but he could be cruel and unfeeling where women's hearts were concerned.

Tossing his cigar on the floor, Tyree ground it beneath his boot. Why should he care what happened to Valentina? he asked himself. She was nothing to him—she worked for him like all the other women he'd hired. No, she wasn't like the others. For some reason unknown to him, he cared very much what happened to her.

Marquis tossed his hat on a vacant chair and propped his booted foot on the rung while his dark eyes surveyed Jordanna. As usual, there was a single candle burning, and it gave off very little light. Jordanna's face was still hidden by a thin veil that fit over the lower half of her face. Her hair was covered with a green turban so it was impossible to determine its color.

"Do you still insist on remaining my mysterious little dancer?" Marquis asked with a twinkle in his eyes. "Do you not know by now you can trust me to keep a secret, Jordanna?"

Sitting before the mirror, her back to Marquis, Valentina pulled the light green brocaded robe about her neck, all the while drawing away from the light. "You gave your word you wouldn't question me about my identity."

His laughter was warm. "Never fear, I am a man of my word. I find you very intriguing. Perhaps if I knew who you were, I would lose some of the fascination I feel for you."

Valentina could not help but smile at his observation. She was excited by his mere presence. A warmth spread through her body every time he was near. She had the advantage of knowing what it was like to be kissed by him. But the kisses he had given Valentina had been chaste and sweet; she wondered what his kiss for Jordanna would be like.

"What if you were to learn I am nothing more than a respectable matron, with a husband and six children waiting for me at home," she teased.

He walked slowly toward her, and his hands landed heavily on her shoulders. Through the mirror they stared at each other. Marquis's eyes searched the shadows of her face, seeking her eyes. As always, her features were cleverly disguised. "Jordanna, I do not care who you are when you walk out that door. While you are in this room, you are exciting and intriguing. I should not have to tell you that I"—he paused for effect—"enjoy being with you. I look forward to getting to know you better . . . much better."

She dropped her head to avoid his eyes. "I don't know what you mean."

He moved so he was facing her. His hand touched her cheek, and he tilted her face up to him. "Yes, you do. Do not play coy with me. A woman does not reach your position without having her share of lovers. I know you must feel something for me or you wouldn't allow me access to your dressing room. I am in a position to know you have turned all other men away. I want to make love to you and you know it, Jordanna. Why do you turn me inside out? But I suppose you have taken lessons on how to torture men and make them want you."

Valentina felt her face burn with shame and indignation. How could Marquis believe such a thing of her? Before she could voice her anger, he lowered his head and brushed his lips against her forehead.

"I want you, Jordanna. You know it, and I know it. I believe we both also know I will have you before too much time has passed." He spoke without arrogance, as if merely stating a fact.

She opened her mouth to protest, but he silenced her. "Shh. Don't say anything, Jordanna. I know I am a beast. I sometimes speak too bluntly, but I like to lay my cards on the table. If I have offended . . . will you forgive me?"

She did not hesitate. "Yes."

He toyed with the fringe on her turban. "Perhaps I have been pushing you too hard. I have decided to give you some breathing space so you can consider what I have said to you. I am going to be away for awhile. When I return, I want to have a serious talk about you and me."

"You are going away?" Her heart sank.

"Yes. Nothing but duty could keep me away from you. I should be back within a week."

"Where are you going?" she queried, unable to keep herself from asking.

"I have a favor to perform for a friend." His smile was infectious, and Valentina felt a smile tugging at her lips. "I will be bored the whole time I am away. Will you manage to miss me?"

Valentina pushed his hand away and stared at him once more through the mirror. "I shall be too busy to think of anything but my dancing."

He chuckled and walked to the door. "You are not entirely truthful. I know you will think of me."

Before Valentina could reply, Marquis had disappeared out the door. Yes, she would miss him. He had told her he had a boring task. She wondered what it was.

Chapter Fourteen

Prudence Lawton rapped on the cabin door and waited for it to open. She had been dying of curiosity ever since she had seen the workmen leaving the day before. She had listened to the hammering and sawing with anticipation. Valentina had asked permission to make a few improvements in the cabin, and Prudence had gladly agreed, knowing any repairs would be beneficial to her and her brother.

Prudence drew back as the foreign-looking woman stood in the open doorway staring at her with cold eyes. "I want to see your mistress," Prudence declared, pushing past Salamar and giving her no chance to object.

Prudence stopped short, gawking at the luxury of the cabin interior. Brightly colored yellow and blue rugs lay on the polished wooden floor. The cracks in the rough log walls had been filled in and whitewashed. Fragile porcelain figurines decorated the mantel above the fireplace. Copper pots and pans glistened on the wall above the table. Her eyes fell on the frail woman sitting on the lounge, amid satin covers.

"I do declare, Miss Barrett," Prudence stated, "this is far nicer than my house. Where did the money come from to fix this place up so grand?" Envy burned in the woman's eyes. "I can see we don't charge you enough rent. I'm sure my brother will correct that little matter as soon as he returns from the mountains."

Evonne took a deep breath. Now that she was feeling better, she was ready to tilt with her landlord's sister. "Can I offer you tea, Miss Lawton?" she asked, more out of politeness than any need to be social.

Prudence dragged over a chair beside the lounge and plopped down on it. "I don't mind if I do. If that's stew cooking in the pot, I wouldn't say no to a bowl full of it." She looked at Salamar suspiciously. "Your woman there wouldn't put anything unseemly in the pot, would she? I've heard it said that those heathen women sometimes cook dogs, lizards, and other unmentionables."

Evonne had always had a sense of humor, and now she found that humor rising to the surface, egged on by a streak of mischief. "I didn't know that, Miss Lawton. Could that be the reason the stew has had a peculiar taste to it lately?"

Prudence's eyes seemed to bulge out of her head. "On second thought, I don't think I'll have anything. I had lunch just a while ago." Her eyes fastened on the lacy blue shawl that was draped across Evonne's shoulders. She had always been partial to that color blue. Greed and envy caused her voice to rise to a high-pitched tone. "You never did say where the money came from that paid for all this. I know it wasn't long ago that you and your daughter was without means, and she came to my brother asking for help."

"I wasn't aware that my daughter asked your brother for help," Evonne said, glancing at Salamar for denial, but Salamar seemed not to be listening to the conversation.

"Well, she did. My brother felt so sorry about your plight that he even offered to marry her, thinking it was the Christian thing to do."

Evonne's eyes blazed as she thought of the poison that escaped this woman's lips in the name of Christianity. "My daughter will never have to marry anyone because he feels pity for her. As to where our money comes from, you should know. After all, it was you who helped Valentina get the position with Mrs. Windom. The woman is very wealthy and pays my daughter quite well."

Prudence leaned toward Evonne and lowered her voice. "I know of no one in this town who would pay the kind of money it would take to fix this place up so grandly." Prudence's colorless eyes seemed to take on a glow. "If I was you, I'd get to the bottom of this. Your daughter is making money all right, but I doubt she gets it from that sick old woman."

Salamar saw Evonne's face whiten, and she quickly picked up a tray she had been preparing and approached Prudence Lawton. "I have your lunch, madame," she said, smiling. "The meat is a bit tough, but I hope you will find it tasty. I prepared it like we do in my country. I added some special ingredients . . . I hope you will find it to your liking."

Prudence jumped immediately to her feet and headed toward the door. "I can't stay. I just remembered something that I have to do," she called over her shoulder.

Salamar caught Evonne's eye, and they both burst into laughter. "I'll take my food now, Salamar," Evonne said at last, holding out her hand. "I thought you always used my mother-in-law's recipe when you made stew."

Salamar sat down in the chair just vacated by Miss Lawton. "So I lied when I said it was a recipe from my homeland. What can you expect from a heathen?"

Evonne's eyes were dancing with mirth. "Loyalty and friendship," she said, taking a bite of Salamar's delicious stew. "I don't find it tough, but it needs more salt."

Again the cabin rang with laughter, and Salamar was

able to make Evonne forget all about Prudence Lawton's visit for the time being.

When Valentina came in later, she was glad to find her mother in such good spirits. She asked the reason for it and was surprised to hear that the cause of her mother's gay mood was none other than Reverend Lawton's sister.

It was a mild Sunday afternoon, and Valentina stood brushing her mother's hair away from her face, then fastened it behind her ear with ivory combs. Evonne laid back against the pillow and smiled at her daughter.

"I am feeling stronger each day, dear. My spirits have been lifted since you and Salamar arrived. You have made this dreary cabin into a warm and cheerful home and given purpose to my life."

"I'm afraid that Salamar deserves most of the credit. She is the one who turned this drab place into a home."

"What would we do without her, Valentina?"

"I hope we never have to find out. She is as much a part of this family as any of us."

"Yes, she was always a part of your life. When you were born, she became devoted to you." Evonne's eyes moved over the room. "Where is Salamar?"

"She has gone to the dock to buy fish. She doesn't like the fish that comes from the market."

Evonne plucked at the coverlet in her lap. "I suppose we have to watch our money and spend wisely. I know it must have cost a great deal to have this cabin made livable."

Valentina avoided her mother's eyes, feeling guilty. She and Salamar had taken every precaution to keep from her mother the fact that she danced at the Crystal Palace. "You aren't to worry about money. I am paid very well. In fact, if there is anything special you want, you have only to say the word and I will get it for you."

"I didn't think taking care of an eccentric old woman would be your lot in life, Valentina. I want the best of everything for you. When your father comes home, you will stop working immediately."

Valentina felt her heart plunge, for she despised the lies that stood between her and her mother. She hated keeping the truth from her, but the truth, in this case, would probably bring on a relapse, and Valentina could never allow that to happen.

Evonne squeezed her daughter's hand. "We will all be happy when your father returns. I wonder if your Señor Vincente has heard anything new about your father?"

"He isn't *my* Señor Vincente, Mother . . . and I'm sure if he had found out anything new, he would have let us know immediately."

"I suppose, my dearest." Evonne's eyes drifted to the window, and she stared outside with a wistful expression. "I miss your father more and more each day. I know he's alive, just as I know he will come home to me. If only . . . if only. . . ."

Valentina barely heard her mother, for her mind was far away. Although she appreciated Marquis's help in searching for her father, she regretted not having demanded more information from him. She could not continue to depend on him and Tyree. She would have to find out for herself what had happened to her father.

"I have decided to make another trip to the mines and talk to Mr. Udell, Mother," she said at last. "I thought if I could get away that I would go next week."

"It's dangerous, Valentina," her mother protested. "You know what happened the last time you tried that."

"I can take care of myself. I want to hear about my father right from Mr. Udell's own mouth. I want him to look me in the eye and tell me what happened to Father."

"I will worry about you, Valentina. If only there were something else we could do. I feel so lost without your father's guidance."

Valentina did not want her mother to become depressed and decided it was time to distract her. She reached behind her and picked up a package. With a smile, she placed the parcel in her mother's lap. "I have two surprises for you today. This is the first one."

Evonne looked puzzled. "What can this be?"

"Why don't you open it and find out."

Evonne excitedly ripped the paper aside and held her breath at what she saw. The soft pink gown was embroidered with tiny white roses, and there was a satin sash for the waist. The neck was cut high with a white lace collar. "This is lovely. I'm sure you spent too much money on me. How did you ever come by such a gown in San Francisco?"

Valentina held the gown against her mother, noting the way the soft color complimented her skin tone. "I found a woman who is a wonder with a needle. Her husband is off searching for gold, and she sews to feed their three children."

Evonne's eyes sparkled with delight. Standing up, she held out the gown to her daughter. "Do you think I could try it on?"

Valentina was aware that since discovering her mother's illness, it had been she who had become the strong one. Where her mother had once looked to her father for guidance, now she looked to her daughter. Sometimes Valentina longed for someone strong to lean on herself. She was new at making decisions, for her life had always been ordered for her.

Pushing her troubles aside, she smiled at her mother. "Indeed you can try it on. That brings me to the second part of my surprise. Doctor Cline said you were well enough to get out of the house for a short time, if you don't overdo. I am taking you out to lunch tomorrow at the San Francisco Hotel."

Evonne's eyes lit up with happiness. "That will be wonderful. I haven't been out since . . . since—"

"Tomorrow you are going to be the center of attention. Everyone who sees you will wonder who the beautiful woman wearing the pink gown could be."

Evonne giggled girlishly. "My darling daughter, no one will notice me with you at my side. You have grown into a lovely young woman. You look very much like I did at your age, but with one exception—you are much more beautiful."

"Nonsense, Mother. You are the original model that can't be improved upon. I am merely the copy."

"I have been twice blessed in my life, Valentina. I have the best husband any woman could ever want, and together we produced an exceptional daughter." Valentina noticed that the sadness was back in her mother's voice, and she vowed that tomorrow would be special for her. Nothing was going to spoil it.

"I suggest that you rest this evening. Tomorrow will be a big day, and I want you to have fun, Mother."

"What mode of transportation will we use?" her mother inquired as her spirits rose once again.

"Nothing less than the best," Valentina told her. "Before Salamar went to the dock, she was to find Santiago and engage his services for tomorrow."

"As I recall, the last time you used Santiago's services, you ended up with the buggy on top of you," Evonne reminded her daughter.

Valentina laughed. "Let us hope this time it will end differently."

A serious expression caused Evonne's brow to furrow. "Valentina, why did you never tell me that the Reverend Lawton asked you to marry him?"

Valentina, on her knees brushing the dust from her mother's pink leather shoes, dropped her head so her mother could not see her face. "I didn't say anything to you about it because it wasn't important. I never for one moment considered his offer."

"There's something else. Why didn't you mention that we were having money problems?"

"You were ill and I didn't want to trouble you."

"I see. One more question and we can close the book on this discussion. I know that everything in San Francisco costs six times what it would anywhere else. How can we afford to live so well? Surely we don't have much money to live on."

Valentina had known that as soon as her mother grew stronger she would start asking questions. Evonne Barrett was an intelligent woman and not easily fooled. At the same time, she enjoyed the luxury and care Valentina and Salamar were providing. Never a realist, Evonne had always hidden any kind of unpleasantness from herself. She did not want to delve too deeply into the matter of Valentina's employment. She did not really want to learn where all the money had come from.

Valentina knew if she were going to tell her mother the truth, now was the time to do it. For the first time, Valentina noticed that Salamar had come in. Her eyes were telling Valentina to tread lightly where her mother's feelings were concerned. Valentina realized she wanted to confess in order to ease her own guilt, but if she did it might be at her mother's expense.

"There is no reason for you to worry about money. We are doing fine," she said at last. "I . . . feel that I earn the money I am paid, Mother." Her heart was aching over the half truth that had come so easily to her lips. She hoped God would forgive her for deceiving her own mother.

Evonne's next words made Valentina feel even worse. There was blind trust in the silver-blue eyes that shimmered with tears. "As I said, the subject is now closed. I just had to hear it from your own mouth."

* * *

Santiago helped Valentina and her mother into the buggy, beaming all the while. As they arranged their skirts, he climbed aboard the buggy and guided the horses onto the dusty roadway.

Evonne glanced about her excitedly, her impressions coming in quick snatches. It was so good to be out of the house. The streets were filled with wagons and carts, and people of all nationalities milled about. It seemed there had been a great influx of Chinese laborers lately, giving a strange, foreign appearance to the town. There were shanties, tents, and shacks—everything made of either wood or canvas—all crowded to overflowing. The storefront windows were stacked with colorful merchandise, and, as they rode, the constant sound of the hammer and saw could be heard.

The community was thriving—bursting at the seams. Gold fever ran rampant, and men were getting rich off human misery. Even so, there was an excitement in the air. This was a new land, and both women were confident that San Francisco would survive the growing pains to one day become a great city.

Valentina noticed that she and her mother were stirring up a great deal of interest from the passersby. They received more than passing glances from many of the gentlemen, who did not often get a chance to see two lovely ladies dressed in such finery.

When the buggy stopped before the San Francisco Hotel, Santiago jumped to the ground and helped both ladies down. After Valentina told him to return for them in an hour and a half, he hopped in the buggy and disappeared down the street.

The inside of the dining room was surprisingly elegant. The walls were filled with reproductions of old masterpieces, and the tables were covered with snowy white tablecloths and laid with silver and crystal. The clientele was obviously upper-class—the men and women of the elite San Francisco society.

All eyes followed Valentina and her mother across the room as a stiff headwaiter showed them to a table. Valentina could feel everyone staring at her, so she looked neither to the left nor the right.

After they had ordered lobster with butter sauce, Valentina observed the excited flush on her mother's cheeks. The doctor had been right—this outing was doing her a world of good. As Valentina scanned her mother's lovely face, she was glad to see the illness had left no mark. She was as pretty as ever.

"This room reminds me of a hotel your father and I stayed at in India."

"Are you having fun, Mother?" Valentina asked, changing the subject, fearing her mother would become sad again.

"Oh, yes, dear. The only thing that would make this day complete would be if your father walked in that door right this moment."

Valentina instinctively glanced up at the door and her eyes collided with a man who had just entered. It was Marquis Vincente! When she saw he was with the same woman he had brought to the Crystal Palace that first night, Valentina licked her dry lips and quickly turned away. Confusion and hurt waged a battle within her. Marquis had lied to her. He had said he would be out of town for at least a week. Valentina stared down at her gloved hand, realizing he did not even know she had caught him in a lie, because he did not know she was Jordanna.

Daring another peek in Marquis's direction, Valentina watched the waiter lead him and the woman across the room. To her horror, she saw that the waiter was taking them to the table next to hers.

Out of politeness, Marquis paused at their table and bowed stiffly before moving away.

Valentina nodded slightly then turned away herself.

She knew Marquis could hardly engage her and her mother in conversation while he had his mistress with him. She felt an ache in her heart, as if he had betrayed her, yet she did not know if it was Valentina or Jordanna he had betrayed.

"Valentina, isn't that Marquis Vincente?" her mother asked, moving forward and lowering her voice.

"Yes, it is," Valentina answered. Her mind was in a turmoil. Apparently Marquis preferred to be with that woman rather than with her.

When a shadow fell across the table, Valentina glanced up to see Tyree standing over them. "Pardon me for the intrusion, Miss Barrett, but I wanted to pay my respects."

Valentina smiled cheerfully, grateful for Tyree's distraction. "I am pleased that you did, Mr. Garth. May I present my mother to you. Mother, this is the man who has been so kind to me. He has made several inquiries about Father for us."

Evonne offered her hand to Tyree. "If what my daughter says is true, Mr. Garth, you have my eternal gratitude."

Tyree glanced from one woman to the other, thinking that San Francisco had rarely had two such beautiful women to grace her shores. While Valentina's beauty was blossoming with youth, her mother had the radiance of the full-grown flower. Each had a classic beauty that would only be enhanced with age.

"I can assure you I have done nothing, Mrs. Barrett. However, I would like you both to think of me as a friend."

"Won't you join us for dinner, Mr. Garth?" Evonne offered.

Tyree smiled at Valentina. "Perhaps you should tell your mother that it isn't considered wise for a woman to be seen in my company."

Valentina's eyes were warm with laughter. "What Mr. Garth wants me to tell you, Mother, is that he is the proprietor of the Crystal Palace."

Evonne looked shock for just a moment, but she quickly recovered. "I can assure you, Mr. Garth, that my daughter and I will never snub one who has so graciously offered his help to us. That would be the epitome of hypocrisy. My offer still stands if you would like to join us. If you but knew it, I have a past that might shock you."

Tyree chuckled and seated himself at the table. "How can I refuse such an intriguing invitation. I wonder, would you consider telling me about your secret past, Mrs. Barrett? I can assure you I am a man who knows how to keep a secret." His eyes met Valentina's. "Do you trust me, Miss Barrett?"

Valentina stared into laughing eyes. "With my life," she answered.

Tyree felt the warmth of Valentina's gaze. Feeling almost light-headed, he quickly turned to the mother. "Will you share your secret with me? As you can see, your daughter trusts me."

Evonne took a sip of wine and smiled at the young man. She could tell he was thoroughly enchanted with her daughter. He looked something of a rake, but that made him all the more charming in her eyes. Lowering her voice, she motioned for him to lean closer. "I was once a dancer," she admitted. "On the stage."

Tyree's eyes moved to Valentina, and he saw shock register on her face. Smiling to himself, he nodded. "I can well imagine you were a wonderful dancer."

Valentina was completely surprised that her mother would admit to having been a dancer in the past. She felt the need to defend her mother's reputation. She did not want Tyree to think her mother had danced in a saloon. "My mother was once a very famous dancer in Europe.

214

She was a prima ballerina."

Tyree caught the guarded look on Valentina's face. "I have only recently seen a ballerina dance, Mrs. Barrett. I can assure you it is by far my favorite dance." He leaned back and studied the mother. "Tell me about your dancing career."

As her mother continued, Valentina could feel Marquis's eyes burning into her. Looking past Tyree's shoulder, she saw what appeared to be anger on his face. The woman beside him had leaned across the table and had taken his hand, but he was not listening to her. He did not seem at all pleased that Tyree had joined Valentina and her mother. Valentina wondered why.

"How much of San Francisco have you ladies seen?" Tyree asked, disrupting Valentina's thoughts.

"Not very much, I'm afraid," Evonne admitted. "I have been ill, and my daughter has a job as companion to an elderly woman."

Tyree raised his brow at Valentina, and, as usual, the humor danced in his eyes. "Indeed. What a fortunate lady to have your daughter as a companion." Suppressed laughter curved his lips. "I will have to show you my city after we have eaten."

Lunch was an uncomfortable affair for Valentina. She was aware of Marquis's brooding silence, and she tried to pretend indifference, for she could not let him discover she was wise to his lies. Despite her efforts, her anger rose so near the surface that she was afraid to look at him.

After they had eaten, Valentina and her mother moved across the room while Tyree stopped briefly to speak to Marquis and Bonita. "Well, I'm off to show two very charming ladies San Francisco, Marquis. I trust you two will fare well without my company."

Marquis ground his teeth. "I am sure you will make the most of it, Tyree. As I recall, you were supposed to have lunch with Bonita and me."

215

"I apologize, but I couldn't turn down such a charming invitation, my friend." Tyree grinned. "You can't have every lovely lady that crosses your path. You have to save a few for the rest of us poor devils." Chuckling to himself, Tyree winked at Bonita and strolled away to join Valentina and Evonne Barrett.

Tyree's horse trotted along beside the buggy driven by Santiago. After they had climbed a steep grade, he instructed Santiago to halt the buggy so he could show Valentina and her mother the spectacular view of San Francisco. Steering the ladies to the edge of the hill, Tyree pointed out the places of interest.

"The town grew almost overnight from the sleepy little village of eight hundred people that it was in 1847 to the thriving beehive you see now. There are more than a thousand people and only two hundred buildings. You guess where they all live, because I assure you I don't know. Most of the buildings are wood and, in my estimation, too close together. It doesn't take much imagination to realize the fire hazard they represent. It would be advantageous to all concerned if they built with fire safety in mind."

"I hadn't thought of that," Evonne said, allowing her eyes to move over the town. "I know that London was almost wiped out by fire at one time."

"That is just one aspect of the town. If you will look toward the waterfront, you will notice the many deserted ships that ride at anchor. Their captains and crews have deserted for the lure of the gold fields. Some lie low in the water and will eventually sink. Notice how some of the ships are listing at crazy angles with their masts and riggings entangled with nearby ships."

Valentina watched one ship riding at anchor, rolled half on her side and dipping drunkenly with the motion of the waves. She caught Tyree's eye, listening with interest as he continued.

"In the holds of many of the ships is rotting cargo that will never be unloaded. It's been estimated that over two hundred empty ships strain at their anchors since their captains and crews have abandoned them."

"I'm sure there is nowhere on earth like California," Evonne speculated. "And believe me I know, because Ward and I have seen most of the world. This is a paradise, or could be. My husband told me of great waterfalls and giant trees that are wider than a house. Man is a great spoiler. If he isn't careful, he will spoil this lovely land."

Tyree smiled at Valentina's mother. "You're right. I have loved this land ever since I came here with my father. To my way of thinking, when God was creating the earth, he paid particular attention to California."

"Yes, this is a land where children could grow and thrive. It makes one wonder how it would have developed if gold hadn't been discovered," Evonne speculated.

"We'll never know," Tyree answered. "One of the saddest sights I've seen is the many families torn apart because of the greed for gold. The husband can't afford to keep his wife with him, so he sends her packing, back East to the kids, who wait for them both to return. There is always a spectacle when the ships arrive. You can stand on the wharf and catch a glimpse of husband and wife being united, their hearts full, thinking they will find gold and go home wealthy. There is also the disappointment when an expected loved one doesn't disembark from the ship."

Tyree gazed out to sea as if searching for something before he continued. "You can read the unspeakable grief on the face of a young husband waiting for his wife, only to discover she has succumbed to some disaster or sickness at sea. On the other side there is the wife who

217

searches the faces of the crowd for her husband, only to find her journey was a fruitless pilgrimage, for her husband has already been claimed by death. Some arrive sick and feeble, unable to work. Theirs is the saddest plight of all. In a land of plenty, there are those who are starving."

Tyree's eyes moved to the city, automatically seeking the Crystal Palace. "San Francisco is a pesthole. The streets become a sea of mud in the rainy season. Animals, as well as men, have been known to drown in the mire. Many horses have sunk into the mud and have to be shot because they couldn't be pulled out. There is a great need for sewers and pure water. There is no real law here, and the dregs of the world have descended on us."

"I thought you loved San Francisco, yet you sound like you hate it here," Valentina observed.

He smiled at her. "To the contrary, I love San Francisco. I just don't like what's happening to her."

"Did you never try your hand at mining, Mr. Garth?" Evonne wanted to know.

"No. I decided right away that the real money would be made right here in San Francisco. I borrowed money from Marquis's grandfather and built the Crystal Palace." His eyes sought Valentina's and he smiled. "I have never been sorry. Lately I have been blessed with a talent that has made me a very wealthy man. No, I do not want to break my heart or my back in the gold fields."

Valentina glanced at her mother and saw the tired lines etched on her face; her eyes were misty and her hand trembled as Valentina took it in hers. The sun was going down, and the lights of the town reflected against the clouds in a soft yellow hue. "I believe we should go home now, Mother. You have had a full day," Valentina said, protectively sliding her arm about her mother's shoulder.

Tyree gathered up his horse's reins and swung himself

218

into the saddle. "I want to thank both you ladies for a most enjoyable afternoon. It was a pleasure to show you my city."

Evonne gave him her winning smile. "Thank you, Mr. Garth. If you ever feel like a home-cooked meal, come by the house. My daughter and I would welcome you."

He tipped his hat, nudged his horse forward, and was soon lost from sight over the rise. "What an extraordinary man," Evonne observed. "I like him."

"So do I," Valentina agreed. "I have found him to be a good man."

"Yes, but with him your eyes don't light up as they do with the other one. Being your mother, I was well aware that you were upset because Señor Vincente was with that tawdrily dressed woman. I could tell you not to worry about her kind, but you wouldn't understand."

Valentina led her mother toward the buggy. "I don't know what you are talking about," she said just above a whisper. "What Marquis Vincente does, or doesn't do, is no concern of mine."

Chapter Fifteen

On the ride home Evonne slipped into silence. Valentina became concerned when her mother leaned her head back against the carriage seat and closed her eyes. Gripping her hand, she found it cold.

"I fear we kept you out too long, Mother. We should have gone home after lunch."

"No, I enjoyed every moment of this day. It's just that"—she hesitated—"when Mr. Garth was talking about the families who had lost loved ones, I couldn't help thinking about your father. I am desperate for word of him, Valentina. I need my husband."

Valentina touched her mother's face softly, feeling a burning ache in her heart. "If there is any clue that can be found about Father, I will find it, Mother. You have my solemn oath on that."

By the time they had reached home, Evonne had slipped into complete silence. Salamar and Valentina quickly undressed her and put her to bed. Valentina sat beside her mother, holding her hand, helplessly watching her fight against tears.

Feeling her mother's forehead, Valentina was glad to find that her fever had not returned, relieved that she was not having a relapse. Valentina realized, as her mother clung to her, that her spirit was crushed. In the dimly lit room, Valentina could see the tears on her mother's cheeks. She began to understand that it would not be enough to take care of Evonne's physical wants; she would have to see to her mental needs as well.

The cold hand of reason closed over Valentina's heart; her mother would die if she did not find out what had happened to her father.

Long after Evonne had fallen asleep, Valentina stayed at her bedside. When she quietly left the room, she found Salamar waiting for her. Handing her a cup of tea, Salamar motioned for her to be seated.

"The outing did not go as you expected, Valentina. You are not to blame yourself. This would have happened anytime your mother went out among people. It will make her remember your father."

"Everything was fine until Mother started thinking about Father." Valentina glanced at Salamar. "She isn't going to get well if I don't find Father, Salamar. I have decided I will start out for the mines on Monday."

Valentina expected Salamar to object, but she only nodded her head in agreement. "You must do what your heart tells you to do. There is more bothering you than just your mother," Salamar observed with her usual perceptiveness.

"I discovered that Marquis lied to me."

"In what way?"

"He doesn't know I found out about his lie. He told me as Jordanna that he was leaving San Francisco for a few days. Mother and I saw him today. He was with this woman I believe to be his . . ."

"Mistress," Salamar finished for her.

"Yes, or whatever she is called. I don't know how many women it takes to satisfy Marquis Vincente. He's betrothed to one woman, has a mistress, and flirts with me on the side. I never want to see him again. Today at the hotel dining room, he was hardly civil to me and my mother."

"You said he was with his mistress. You hardly could have expected him to introduce her to you and your mother, now could you? What did you expect?"

"I am so mixed up, Salamar. I could feel him staring at me this afternoon. If I didn't know better, I would say he was jealous of Tyree's attentions to me."

Salamar smiled that mysterious smile of hers. "When Valentina and Jordanna merge into one woman, perhaps Marquis Vincente will need no one but you. Until that time, he will battle within himself to understand the feelings he has for both of you. Beware that you do not let him discover who you are too soon. If you do, you will lose him."

"I can't lose him because I don't have him."

Salamar moved to the fire and placed another log on the flames. Valentina drew in a tired breath. At the moment she was feeling unequal to the task before her. "Why does God sometimes make life so complicated, Salamar?"

Salamar's wise eyes seemed to gaze inwardly as though searching for answers. "God doesn't make the complications. Man makes his own trouble without God's help or approval."

"You are right, Salamar. I suppose I was just feeling a bit sorry for myself."

"Not a weakness you often give in to. You are a survivor, Valentina. Your mother has never had your strength, and she now depends on you. I know the burdens that have been placed on your small shoulders have weighed heavily. I have tried to help you in this all I can, but you must carry the heaviest load alone."

Valentina smiled at the woman who had been the greatest influence in her life. "If I am strong, it is because you taught me to be. I love my mother, but yours is the

223

face I remember from childhood. Yours were the hands that soothed my fevered brow when I was ill as a child. It is from you that I have always tapped my strength."

Salamar's glance was warm, and her dark eyes seemed to sparkle with what Valentina knew to be tears. "I could never have a daughter of my own, Valentina. God, in his infinite mercy, allowed me to borrow you. There will soon be another who will step into your life and give you strength . . . that is as it should be."

Valentina was too weary to listen closely to Salamar's words. Already her eyelids were drooping. Salamar took the teacup from her and helped her to stand. As she led her charge to the bed, Valentina shook her head. "I can't go to sleep now; I have too much to do. If I am going to the mines, I have plans to make."

"The plans will wait until tomorrow," Salamar insisted as she slipped Valentina's dress over her head and helped her into her nightgown. "You are weary now, so go to sleep. I will see to the details of the journey for you."

Already Valentina's eyes were drifting shut and her body was relaxing into the soft mattress. "There is so much to do. I must contact Santiago so he can get supplies together. Mr. Garth needs to be informed that tomorrow night will be my last performance for awhile."

"Sleep," Salamar soothed. "I will do this for you."

Salamar gazed upon the face of the daughter she had never had. Valentina was the most important person in her life. She wished there were some way she could ease the pain she was going through, but pain was a necessary part of life. Salamar knew she could only deal with the little details in Valentina's life, making sure everything ran smoothly. She could not help her with the big problems. Since they had landed on the shores of California, Valentina had been forced to grow up quickly and face heavy responsibilities. Salamar was proud to see she had done so with determination and courage.

Salamar slipped through Valentina's dressing room into the hallway to Tyree Garth's office. She took every precaution not to be discovered. After rapping lightly on the door, she heard Tyree call out for her to enter.

There was a look of surprise when Tyree saw Salamar. Since the day he had hired Valentina as a dancer, Salamar had kept herself hidden, knowing that if anyone saw her, he would connect Jordanna with Valentina.

Tyree motioned for Salamar to be seated, but she stubbornly chose to remain standing. Draped in a black fringed shawl, Salamar could not be seen very well. "Your mistress isn't ill, is she?" Tyree asked at once.

Salamar took a step closer. "No, but her mother is grieving for her husband. It seems the outing today stirred up memories for her. Valentina wants you to know she will be going to her father's mine to see if she can find a clue to his disappearance."

Tyree stood up slowly. "What can she be thinking about, Salamar? It wouldn't be wise for her to go to the mine. She knows Marquis is doing everything he can to find Mr. Barrett."

"Valentina will do what she feels she has to." Salamar liked Tyree Garth because he had been good to Valentina. He was a man of great worth, and she knew he loved Valentina.

Tyree swore under his breath. "What in the hell does she think she can do alone? The last time she tried that little stunt, it almost ended in disaster for her."

"She will not be stopped," Salamar assured him.

"Damnit, if I can't stop her, I'll have to go with her. I don't intend to let her go alone."

Salamar bowed her head. "You must do what you feel is right. I only came to tell you that after tomorrow night,

225

Jordanna will not be dancing for a while."

Tyree gazed hard into Salamar's face. "When does she plan to take this foolhardy excursion?"

"Monday."

"Does your mistress ride?"

"She is a good horsewoman."

"Good. Go back and tell her I'll make all the arrangements. I will bring horses. Tell her to expect me at six o'clock Monday morning. If she's bent on doing this, we need to get an early start."

"I will tell her. It may be that she will not want you going with her. You are not the proper escort for a young woman."

Tyree grinned, showing his charm. "I can be trusted, Salamar—at least where Valentina is concerned."

"I know this. If it were not so, I would not allow you near Valentina."

Tyree's amused laughter was interrupted when the door was pushed open and Marquis entered. Tyree turned his attention to his friend. "You sure took your time about getting here," he said in an amused voice. "I expected you much sooner." Tyree knew that Marquis had not been pleased to see him with Valentina today. He had known Marquis would come sooner or later to voice his disapproval.

Marquis's eyes swept the room and at last came to rest on Salamar. For the briefest moment he was startled as he recognized Valentina's maid.

"You know Salamar, don't you, Marquis," Tyree stated.

Marquis's eyes narrowed. "Yes, I know her." He looked into Salamar's eyes and found the same disturbing light he had seen there before. "What I don't know is why she has come to you."

Salamar smiled to herself, knowing Marquis was jealous of Tyree. "I will be leaving now, Mr. Garth. It

226

will be up to you whether or not to inform Mr. Vincente of the reason for my visit." Salamar turned away, soundlessly crossing the room and slipping out the door.

"What in the hell was that all about?" Marquis demanded to know. "Have you taken to courting older women—or does she bring you love notes from Valentina?"

"Alas, Salamar doesn't fancy me as a suitor, and, unfortunately, Valentina isn't pining with love for me either," Tyree answered with his usual humor.

"I am in no mood for your little jests, Tyree," Marquis said sourly. "You don't have to tell me what Salamar wanted if you don't want to."

"Oh, I don't mind. She was delivering a message from Valentina. She wanted me to know she is going to her father's mine. I volunteered to go with her."

Marquis moved slowly across the room. "*No*, you aren't going with her . . . are you crazed? She was injured the last time she tried to reach her father's mine. You are not going to take her there." Marquis's face was a mask of fury. "Have you lost your mind completely?"

Tyree laughed in amusement. "What's the matter? Do you want all the beautiful women for yourself?" Suddenly the laughter left his eyes and he searched his friend's face. "If you want Valentina for yourself, what makes you think I will give her over to you without a fight?"

"Because we are friends, and you know I have deep feelings for her."

"Marquis"—Tyree's voice vibrated through the room—"put a name to those feelings!"

"I can't."

"Try."

"I . . . love her," Marquis admitted, as if the confession had been forced from his lips. "I . . . adore her. I cannot get her out of my mind."

"Like you can't get Jordanna out of your mind?"

"No. Valentina Barrett is an angel; Jordanna fires my blood. Valentina is the kind of woman a man marries; Jordanna is the kind he beds."

"Do you have both earmarked for yourself?"

"No, not Valentina Barrett. She isn't for either of us, my friend. She is too good for us both."

"I never thought I'd see the day you would admit any woman was too good for the great Marquis Vincente. What brought all this on?"

"She is a real lady."

Tyree smiled to himself, thinking that the situation was getting to be a real tangle. What would Marquis do when he discovered Jordanna and Valentina were one and the same? "I have watched you move from one woman to another over the years. You don't want Valentina Barrett, yet you don't want me to have her. You want Jordanna, yet you will never make a commitment to her. You must have an insatiable appetite, my friend. What will you do with all the women who are cluttering your life at the moment?"

"I will make Jordanna my mistress and try to forget about Valentina Barrett. I will marry Isabel, and Valentina will probably return to England and marry someone there who is not worthy of her."

"I'd say you very definitely have a problem." Tyree knew that Marquis had always been of a passionate nature, but he had never before given his heart to a woman. He hoped his friend would not put honor ahead of love. If he did, he would spend the rest of his life regretting it. "I'm your friend, and I feel it my duty to advise you either to marry Valentina or stop seeing her altogether."

"I have tried that. Out of honor I stayed away from her. That's why I spend so much time with Jordanna. She helps me forget. Do you have any notion how it tore me

228

apart inside to see you with Valentina today?"

"You are a fool, Marquis. I do not respect your kind of honor. Where is the honor in denying love?" At that moment Tyree would have told Marquis that Valentina and Jordanna were one and the same if he had thought it would make any difference, but he knew it would not, so he kept his counsel. "You are a blind fool," he reiterated.

Marquis's dark eyes blazed with unleashed anger. "No one calls me a fool, and I have let you get by with it twice tonight, Tyree."

"Marquis, damnit, if you love Valentina, why don't you just tell Isabel that you can't marry her and marry Valentina?"

"It isn't that simple. I am committed. Once a Vincente gives his word, he cannot withdraw it." Tyree could almost hear don Alonso speaking through his grandson. "You lived with my family long enough to know how we feel about honor, Tyree."

"Well, let's see how long it will take you to change your mind. If you really love Valentina, as you say you do, nothing could keep you from taking her as your wife."

Marquis waved Tyree aside. "You will never understand my kind of commitment in a hundred years, Tyree, so let us drop the subject. I do not understand how you can humor Valentina in this madness. You know that Udell said her father had been shanghaied. When is she supposed to leave for the mine?"

"Monday morning at six. I also told her I would bring a horse for the journey."

"You must go to her and tell her that we suspect her father is a prisoner on the *Southern Cross*. Make her see it would be foolish for her to go to the mine at this time."

"I thought you didn't want her to know that her father may have been shanghaied," Tyree stated flatly.

"You're right. Knowing how headstrong and impulsive she is, I feared she might begin frequenting the docks and get herself into trouble. Now she wants to go to her father's mine. Last time it almost cost her her life. I do not want her to go." Marquis watched his friend's face, waiting for his reaction.

Tyree hesitated. ". . . I agree."

Marquis nodded. "I feared you were going to fight me on this. Valentina Barrett has us both running around in circles, does she not?"

Tyree merely shrugged his shoulders. "You have never run around in circles for any woman in your life, but you will for this one before long, Marquis. The day may soon come when you will have to choose between love and honor. I know you well enough to realize that if you don't bend, you will break."

"I don't think so, my friend. A Vincente must always do what is expected of him, no matter what his feelings are to the contrary."

Suddenly Tyree started laughing. "I thought you would blow up today when I saw you with Bonita and you realized you couldn't stop to talk to Valentina and her mother. I wonder how you explained your ill humor to Bonita."

Marquis was not amused. He was still brooding about the afternoon. "I didn't. Bonita has seen that I have changed. She knows we are finished. I must say she has been a lady about the whole thing."

"Did she have any choice?"

"No, none."

"I thought you had gone home for a week. What happened to change your mind?"

"I needed time to think. I decided I didn't want to see Isabel. It is hard to face her, knowing I love Valentina."

"Marquis, you should be glad that you have found love at last. Why don't you reach out for it with both hands? Why can't you be happy about this?"

Tyree could not know the torment that raged inside his friend. He fought a battle in which he was being forced to marry a woman who left him cold, a battle against his desire to possess Jordanna, and—the hardest battle of all—the one he fought against loving Valentina.

Marquis crossed the room to the door. "The truth of the matter is, I have never been less happy about anything in my entire life."

Chapter Sixteen

Monday morning arrived with the bright rays of sunshine lighting up the muddy streets of San Francisco with a golden glow, disguising the shabbiness with an illusion of a make-believe wonderland. Pulling the curtains aside, Valentina glanced out, dreading the trip that was ahead of her. She was weary to the very depths of her being. Dancing at the Crystal Palace and trying to keep her mother from finding out about it was taking its toll on her nerves.

When she heard Salamar coming up behind her, Valentina turned to observe the frown of concern on her maid's face.

"I have a bad feeling about this journey, Valentina. I cannot explain it, but I sense disaster if you go to the mines," Salamar said, meeting Valentina's eyes. "I wish you would not go."

Valentina felt momentary fear, knowing Salamar would not speak lightly about her feelings. "I have no choice in the matter, Salamar. You know Mother will not get well until she knows about Father. I can't just do nothing while she broods over his disappearance."

"It would be better not to go at this time," Salamar stated, taking Valentina by the shoulders and making her meet her eyes. "Do not go to that mine, Valentina. Listen to me . . . heed my warning."

Valentina felt a chill touch the back of her neck. Salamar would never have shared such a dark foreboding unless she felt it deep inside. "What should I do, Salamar? Tyree should be here any moment. What can I tell him?"

"Tell him you have changed your mind about going," Salamar stated simply.

"I can't do that." Valentina frowned. "I have to make every possible effort to find Father."

Salamar shook her head. "You are determined to do this thing?"

"Yes. Tell me what you feel, Salamar."

"Nothing I can put my finger on. Just a coldness inside when I think of your going to your father's mine."

"Would you feel better if I postponed the journey and went at a later time?"

"It would only be postponing the inevitable. I do not want you to go at all."

Before Valentina could answer, she heard a heavy rap on the door. Tyree removed his hat and smiled. "Good morning, Valentina," he said as she welcomed him into the house. "The fog was heavy last night, but it turned out to be a glorious morning."

"Would you like a cup of coffee before we leave?" Valentina asked, trying to delay their departure. Although she wanted to find her father, Salamar had made her fearful about some unknown danger.

"I wouldn't say no to a cup of coffee, but I came to try to convince you to postpone this journey to your father's mine."

Valentina looked at him in puzzlement. "Why?"

Tyree seated himself at the table while Salamar placed a cup of steaming coffee in front of him. He took a drink of the hot brew before answering. "Marquis and I talked it over and we believe you should wait a bit." As Tyree spoke, his eyes moved around the room, taking in the warmth and homeyness of the cabin. Looking back at Valentina, he continued. "What I'm about to tell you now is something Marquis didn't want you to know before because he didn't want to raise your hopes, perhaps to have them later dashed. Marquis has reason to believe that your father has been shanghaied aboard a ship."

The color drained from Valentina's face as she sank down on a wooden chair. She did not know whether to be happy or more upset. "What are you saying?"

"When Marquis went to the mine and talked to your father's partner, Sam Udell, the man told him that your father had been shanghaied and placed aboard a ship called the *Southern Cross*."

"I don't understand. Why didn't Marquis tell me this before?"

"As I told you, Marquis didn't want you to live on false hope. There was no proof that what Sam Udell told him was based on fact. Also Marquis feared you and your mother would be more upset if you thought your father had been forced into slave labor."

Valentina covered her eyes with her hands. "I don't know what to think. Is there no way to prove whether or not my father has been kidnapped?"

"Shanghaied," Tyree corrected. "Mr. Udell told Marquis that your father was taken aboard the *Southern Cross* and we have been waiting for her to return to San Francisco so we can find out the truth."

Valentina's hands trembled as she reached across the table to have Tyree clasp her hand in his. "Men die when they are shanghaied, don't they, Tyree? Aren't they treated cruelly and beaten if they don't obey orders?"

"I won't lie to you, Valentina. It is a cruel fate for any man to suffer. You can see now why Marquis wanted to keep this from you."

He saw the worried frown on her beautiful face and the hint of tears in her silver-blue eyes. "Try not to worry," he said, patting her hand comfortingly. "If your father is strong, and if he follows orders, he could come out of this unharmed."

"I don't know what to feel. I fear for my father's fate at the hands of unscrupulous men. My father is a proud and stubborn man. He will not take well to being forced to do anything against his will."

"I hope you are wrong. If he is aboard the *Southern Cross*, I hope he will be wise enough to follow orders."

Valentina rubbed her temples with her fingertips. "I cannot tell my mother about this. It would set her back if she thought my father were being mistreated."

"Don't tell her. Just say that every effort is being made to locate your father."

"When will the *Southern Cross* again sail into San Francisco harbor?"

Tyree took another sip of coffee before answering. "In about three or four weeks," he replied, placing the cup on the table.

"I will postpone the trip to my father's mine until the ship returns. If my father isn't on board, I will then go to the mine. If I don't find him within six months . . ." Her voice momentarily faded. ". . . I will think about taking my mother back to England."

Not wanting to discuss the possibility of her leaving San Francisco, Tyree stood up. "Rest assured that Marquis and I will continue to do everything within our power to help you find your father."

Valentina looked into soft eyes that did not dance with their usual humor but instead held a light of sincerity. "You are my friend, Tyree. I don't know what I would have done without you." She did not mention Marquis, for she was not too clear on how she felt about him at the moment.

In a flash, the dancing light was back in Tyree's eyes and he lowered his rich voice so that only Valentina could hear. "I will always stand ready to help my little dancer in any way I can."

Valentina's smile was warm as she looked up at him. "I believe you would always stand ready to help any lady in trouble, Tyree. In my estimation you are a gentleman in every sense of the word."

He chuckled as he moved to the door. Placing his hat on his head, he bowed slightly. "Don't allow that rumor to circulate—I fear it might ruin my reputation around San Francisco."

When he left, Valentina turned to Salamar. "I don't know whether or not to be happy about the possibility that my father is the prisoner of some unsavory sea captain who may mistreat him."

Salamar placed the dirty coffee cups on a tray. "Time will reveal all her secrets. For now, I am happy that you did not go to the mine, Valentina. I hope you will never go, because I feel that if you do something bad will happen."

As Valentina turned away, Salamar's warning hung heavily in the air. Valentina, too, hoped she would never have to go to her father's mine.

Over the next week, Valentina's mother seemed to slip into a silent, passive mood. She ate if she was fed and answered yes or no when spoken to. The doctor declared her fever was much improved. He admitted to Valentina that her mother was suffering from a broken heart. He cautioned Valentina against taking the situation lightly and stated that treating a broken heart went far beyond his medical expertise. He urged Valentina to find out what had happened to her father, feeling Evonne Barrett would be far better off if she were to know the truth of her husband's fate.

Valentina and Salamar kept troubled eyes on Evonne, fearing she would waste away to nothing. Valentina tried to cheer her mother by purchasing new gowns, bonnets, and shoes. They did not seem to help. Evonne would only glance at the expensive gowns with little interest, showing no enthusiasm about trying them on.

In desperation Valentina haunted the docks, waiting for the first sight of the *Southern Cross*, knowing that if it did not come soon, her mother might become another casualty of the California gold rush.

Valentina had just finished a difficult performance. The crowd had been enthusiastic as usual, but their response had left little impression on her. In her dressing room, she glanced in the mirror, noting the faint shadows beneath her eyes. She had to get some rest or she might collapse. If that should happen, what would become of her mother and Salamar? she wondered desperately. They were both dependent on her for their survival.

Hearing the soft knock on her dressing room door, Valentina called, "Come in," expecting to see Tyree enter. When she saw Marquis Vincente, she took a deep breath, hoping to still her thundering heart. She wondered why his presence always affected her so strongly. All Marquis had to do was look at her with those dark eyes and she melted inside.

His eyes were soft and grew even softer as they ran the length of her gently curved body. She had just performed her Cleopatra dance and was grateful that she still wore the black wig and the silver veil. "I didn't see you in the audience tonight, so I did not know you would be coming," she said in her exaggerated French accent.

"I was detained by business, but you should have

known I would come, Jordanna." He pushed the door lock into place before advancing a step closer, making Valentina feel uneasy. "You know I could not stay away from you." His dark eyes were sending her a message that was unmistakable. He wanted her and intended to have her tonight!

Valentina licked her dry lips, wishing she could stop her heart from pounding in her ears. When his hand reached out to her, instead of pushing him away, she gave him her hand and it trembled as he raised it to his lips.

"It's time, Jordanna. Thoughts of you keep swirling around in my brain and I cannot get rid of them. Do not turn me away tonight. Have I not courted you long enough?"

"What of the woman I saw you with the first nigh—"

He laid his finger against her lips. "I no longer see her. She could only pour water on the fire you started in my body. Only you can stoke that fire." His dark eyes caressed her, pulled at her, excited her.

"Marquis, do not force me into anything. Do not ask that which I cannot—"

His eyes sparkled as he ran a finger along the edge of the silver veil. "Force you? I would never force you to submit to my will, Jordanna. I would not want you that way. Nothing but your complete surrender will satisfy me." Lowering his head, his lips brushed her eyelids one by one, teasing and playing with her long, silken lashes.

As he raised his head, his eyes were like a physical touch. She watched his hands, fascinated as he toyed absently with the hook on her veil. Conflicting emotions battled inside of her. A part of her feared he would remove the veil and discover her identity; another part of her hoped he would do just that.

Glancing into his face, she could almost read his thoughts. He believed her to be his by way of conquest, by right of possession.

Marquis pulled her against his well-defined muscular chest. With each breath he took, his skin brushed her breasts. His thigh was pressed against hers. She could sense the throbbing, pulsing life of him against her quaking body. His eyes were a velvety darkness, and the sound of his voice vibrated through Valentina, making her quiver all over.

"I want there to be honesty between us from the first, so no question will arise later. You can expect my devotion and attentiveness."

Valentina knew he was telling her there could be no future for them and, still, she wanted to be with him.

"What is it to be, little queen of the Nile? Do you come to me tonight . . . or send me away in torment?"

Valentina was fighting a battle within herself and sensed she was losing. She knew what Marquis was suggesting was wrong, but her body craved the pleasure his eyes promised. Shaken to the very core of her womanhood, Valentina stepped out of the circle of Marquis's arms.

He watched her snuff out the candle, throwing the room into darkness. He understood it would have to be this way the first time. Perhaps later she would allow him to see her face—perhaps not. The mystery of Jordanna fascinated him as much as the idea of making love to her. He waited in the dark for her to come to him. As he held his breath, she softly took his hand.

Inflamed thoughts of what was to come blocked out everything else in Marquis's mind. Valentina guided him across the room to the satin-covered bed. Marquis scooped her up in his arms, placed her on the bed, and dropped down beside her.

His blood was on fire. He had waited a long time for this little dancer. He somehow knew she would prove worth the wait. If she wanted to protect her identity, it did not matter to him; he would play her little game. It would not bother him to discover she was hiding a horribly scarred face—all that mattered was that she surrender to his demands tonight; otherwise he would go out of his mind.

In the darkness Marquis reached out and slowly removed the veil that covered her face. Cupping her chin, he pulled her forward to receive his burning lips. "Kiss me, my little dancer," he breathed against her lips. "Kiss me and stoke the fire that already burns within my body. Later we will put out the fire together."

Valentina was an innocent. She did not fully know what Marquis expected of her, but whatever he demanded she would give to him freely. She could never have him as Valentina, but as the dancer Jordanna she would be allowed to hold on to him for a time. Hers was a hopeless love—one that had no happy ending. She would only borrow a little happiness from the beautiful Isabel tonight. She was cheating no one but herself.

Valentina knew from some of the remarks Marquis had made that he believed she had been free with her favors. Would he be angry when he discovered she had never been with a man? she wondered.

His hands were becoming acquainted with her soft body while artfully removing articles of clothing one by one. The hooks on her gown did not slow his progress— Marquis had performed this task many times in the dark. As his lips brushed her earlobe, Valentina melted against him, wishing she could stay in his arms forever. His lips gently moved across her face, touching each point, moving on to the next, finding her perfectly formed. There were no disfiguring scars on this face, he noted feverishly.

A sweet aroma, like flowers in a meadow after a soft rain, assaulted Marquis's senses when Valentina turned her head, trying to find his lips. Valentina was aching for his lips to touch hers. It was as if he were teasing and

241

taunting, holding off the final pleasure to torment her. Again he had inspired this strange bittersweet excitement inside her body. Did Marquis know about the dull, empty feeling inside her that ached for fulfillment? she wondered.

When Marquis at last covered her lips with his, Valentina drew in a shuddering breath. Softly his tongue glided across her mouth, awakening even deeper, more disturbing emotions. He gently probed her lips apart and thrust his tongue inside, causing her to groan in pleasure.

Valentina's hands moved inside his shirt, and she began tugging at it, wanting to remove any barrier that stood between her body and this masculine body that was pulsing with passion and life. He was stoking the fire, encouraging it higher and higher.

He chuckled softly. "Patience, little tigress. Pull in your claws. We have plenty of time to explore each other's bodies." His hand drifted across her breasts and moved to rest against her quivering stomach. He could tell she was aroused by the touch of his hand, just as he was by hers. "You are experienced in pleasing a man, Jordanna. I can tell it is an art that you have been taught well," he breathed hotly in her ear. "You will please only me tonight, little dancer."

Valentina did not bother to deny his accusations or correct his assumption that she was accustomed to being with men. Soon Marquis would discover she knew nothing about pleasing a man; he would find out he was her first and only lover. She feared when he learned the truth he might be disappointed in her, or perhaps he would even be angry.

Marquis moved away, and Valentina reached out for him to discover he was removing his clothing. It seemed like an eternity until he took her in his arms and gathered her tightly against his hot, naked body. Valentina felt a heat that almost choked her as his male hardness pressed against her thigh. His hands ran up and down her spine, circling, caressing, pulling her closer to paradise.

Valentina's heart was beating so fast she thought it would burst. Even if he did no more than hold her like this, it would be enough for her to live on forever. Raising her head, her lips brushed against his cheek; reaching higher, she touched his lips with her tongue. Shyly at first, wanting to give him pleasure as he had given it to her, Valentina allowed her tongue to slide across his lower lip, then slip into his hot, moist mouth.

Marquis groaned. His head pounded and his body cried out at the sensuous feelings that rushed through every pore of his body. His hand glided down to move between her thighs. Gently he pried her legs apart and his finger slipped into the wet, velvet softness.

At first Valentina gasped in surprise. When his finger began moving in and out, she bit her lip to keep from crying out in pleasure. Marquis had awakened a part of her body that had never been aroused. She squirmed, trying to find relief from the feeling that was building up deep inside. Her responsive movements triggered a fevered awareness in Marquis. He could not wait—he had to take her now. Never had a woman reached inside of him and demanded so many emotions of him.

Rolling Valentina to her back, Marquis positioned himself above her and drove deeply into the core of her body. Valentina felt a sharp, stinging pain, as if she were being ripped apart. Pressing her lips against his shoulder, she tried not to cry out in pain. As she felt Marquis's uttered oath, the pain began to abate.

Marquis fought his way back from a raging plane of euphoria to stark reality. "My God, Jordanna, you have never been with a man before me!" he said harshly. "Why did you not tell me? What have I done?"

She reached up and drew his head down to hers. He had filled the inside of her, and her flesh was a quivering mass. She needed him to soothe the ache that burned and twisted in her stomach. "I saved myself for just the right man," she said breathlessly, remembering just in time to speak with a French accent.

Still Marquis paused. His manhood throbbed and ached from the feel of the wet silkiness in which it was embedded. "It is not my practice to deflower virgins, Jordanna. You should have told me you were untouched."

"We both wanted this, Marquis. Do not feel guilty on my account." Valentina listened to the words she boldly spoke. It was as if she were two people—one the dancer, Jordanna, who would give Marquis all he wanted, and the other the confused and muddled Valentina. It was Jordanna who spoke now. "Do you not want me, Marquis?"

He needed no more encouragement. In the soft, warm world of darkness, on a bed of cool satin, Marquis introduced the dancer Jordanna to the pleasures that a man can give a woman and, in so doing, took Valentina to heights she had never dreamed possible. No matter what happened after tonight, Valentina knew her heart would always belong to Marquis Vincente.

Marquis instructed her on each movement. His tongue aroused and teased the nipples on her breasts. Valentina, so willing to please, so excited by each new feeling he awoke in her, gave herself over to Marquis's tutelage eagerly. She was now a complete woman, reaching plateaus of glorious new sensation, floating on a tide of passion. Her skin was sensitive to his every touch, her mouth ready for his heated kisses.

When the storm of their passion had subsided, Valentina sighed contentedly and curled up in Marquis's arms. He hugged her tightly, knowing she had given more than any woman had ever given him. Always before when he had made love to a woman, he had wanted to leave immediately afterward. With Jordanna, he still wanted to touch her, to caress her, to hold her close to him. There was something different this time, and he did not want to analyze his feelings. Somewhere in the back of his mind he knew he could find the answer, but he did not want to try.

Jordanna's lips brushed his cheek and she spoke softly. "Did I please you, Marquis? Were you disappointed with me?"

He smiled at her completely feminine question. "Never have I been more pleased." He shifted her weight so her head was resting against his chest. "However, I should be angry at you for not telling me you had never been with a man."

"You are not angry at me, are you?"

"No." He chuckled. "How can I be angry with you when you have given me more than a mortal man should expect from his lady love."

She was silent for a moment before she asked in a soft voice, "Are you saying that you love me?"

His hesitation was obvious. "Jordanna, love is an emotion I have had little experience with. I admire your talent; you excite me. Tonight you gave me the greatest pleasure I have ever experienced with a woman . . . but love . . . no, I do not love you or any other woman."

"Do you love the woman you are to marry?"

When she felt Marquis stiffen, Valentina realized she had committed a blunder—the unpardonable sin.

"Jordanna, the one subject that you and I will never discuss is my betrothed. You are new at being a mistress so you could not know that you have committed an error."

Valentina felt her heart break at his cruel words. He had just reminded her that she had lost her right to speak

245

as a decent woman. Already he thought of her as his mistress. She thought of the woman who had been sitting with Marquis in the audience the first night he had seen her dance. Last night, at the hotel, Marquis had been with the same woman. At those times Valentina had thought herself better than that woman, but now she was in the same class as Marquis's mistress. So deep was her hurt that Valentina wanted to cry out in pain.

Moving away from Marquis, Valentina rose up on her elbow. "No, I am not your mistress, Marquis—nor will I ever be. I can assure you I will never bring up your betrothed again because I don't ever intend to see you again. What happened tonight will never be repeated."

He only laughed and pulled her back against him. "Oh, yes, it will happen again, my sweet dancer. You are only angry with me because I scolded you. You will get over it."

"In other words, I should know my place and keep to it?" she asked heatedly.

"I would not have put it so harshly, but yes, something like that."

Valentina wanted to strike out at him, to hurt him as he had wounded her, but already his hands were working magic on her naked body. His lips brushed against her breasts, and she groaned in surrender. His soft, amused chuckle was lost against the loud pounding of her heart.

This time Marquis made love to her lingeringly. He was gentle with her, and he seduced her mind as well as her body. Valentina knew she was lost when her body trembled beneath his masterful hands. She felt him move inside her, filling her heart with the joy and beauty of the joining of body and soul. Marquis was the perfect lover— he was her other half. With him, she found total fulfillment.

Even at the moment of her ultimate surrender, Valentina realized she could never be Marquis's mistress.

This night must be all they would ever have together. Her pride would not allow her to lose control again.

His hands curved around her waist and he raised her up, kissing her long and leisurely. After Valentina could catch her breath, she spoke in an uneven voice. "I want you to leave now, Marquis."

He kissed her and chuckled. "All right, I will leave for now, but I'll be back."

Valentina felt him move off the bed and she could hear him pulling on his clothing. "This won't happen again, Marquis," she said, feeling she had to make him understand that she was not his to command. "I do not ever want you to come backstage to see me again."

His laughter was warm as he moved across the room and opened the door. "Do not think you can keep me away now that I have felt the joys of your body, Jordanna. You would miss me and you know it."

She heard the door close softly and buried her face in the satin covers to stifle the deep, wrenching sobs that were building within her. Her body felt strangely alive and different. Marquis had awakened her passions—he had made her a woman—but he did not own her mind. She would fight against him with every ounce of strength she possessed.

Marquis Vincente was arrogant in his belief that he could control her. She would prove him wrong!

Chapter Seventeen

As if moving through a dream, Valentina managed to get through the next few weeks. She had condemned herself over and over for weakening and having allowed Marquis to make love to her. How could she have been such a fool? She remembered with shame the words he had spoken when he had taken it for granted that she would become his mistress. She also remembered how defensive he had become when she had mentioned Isabel. Even though Valentina would never consent to becoming his mistress, in Marquis's mind he had already marked her as such. He believed himself better than she—to him she was no more than a strumpet.

Valentina found some relief when she was working, for only then could she escape Salamar's probing glances. Valentina tried to elude Salamar's eyes, fearing the all-knowing Salamar would be able to read the guilt on her face.

Valentina remembered periods when she had been a child and had been upset about something. Salamar had always told her then that time was the great healer of spirit and soul. Now Valentina wished that time would pass quickly so that she could put her shame and guilt behind her.

She feared in her heart that if Marquis came to her again she might weaken and allow him to make love to her. She had to avoid being alone with him at all cost. He had not come to her since she had demanded that he leave her alone. Perhaps, she mused, after his conquest he had lost interest in her. She told herself that she was glad he stayed away. And yet, every time she heard a knock on her dressing room door, her heart would thunder within her, and she would rush to open it, hoping it would be Marquis. It never was.

Valentina moved through the ensuing days and weeks with a watchful eye toward the sea. Each afternoon she would go to the docks and inquire if there had been any word about the *Southern Cross*.

In the sad course of events, Evonne Barrett's fever returned and she lay weakly on the bed, wasting away before Valentina's eyes. Valentina and Salamar huddled near Evonne's bed, trying to make her as comfortable as possible. Again Doctor Cline pressed Valentina to find out some news of her father's whereabouts.

The one thing that Valentina no longer had to worry about was money. She could pay for any comfort her mother required. She had been able to pay off all the debts her father had incurred and had been able as well to put money in the bank.

Lately, the only time Valentina was truly happy was when she was on stage, losing herself in her dance, giving all of herself to her audience. Time passed slowly and each day marked renewed heartache for her.

Valentina knew she should be glad that Marquis had taken her seriously when she had told him to stay away from her, but she was not. She longed for the sight of his face, for the touch of his hand, for the sound of his voice.

Tyree had told her that Marquis had returned to Paraíso del Norte to prepare for his forthcoming wedding. Valentina sorely felt the helplessness of her situation. Perhaps it would be best if she never saw Marquis again, she tried to tell herself. She had enough problems in her life without the kind of trouble he represented.

It was the nights that were the hardest for her to get through. Sometimes Valentina would lie on her bed and stare into the dark, remembering the touch of Marquis's hand on her body. Sometimes she would dream they were together and wake up with an emptiness that ached like an open wound. She did not know where the future would take her and, tired and weary of heart, she sometimes did not know where she would get the strength to make it through the coming weeks. She, her mother, and Salamar were living in a strange kind of limbo, waiting . . . waiting . . . waiting.

Marquis dismounted and walked up the steps of the Estradas' house. At his grandfather's insistence, he had decided to pay a call on Isabel. As he glanced around the Estrada ranch, Marquis's lips curled in disgust at the neglect he saw. The barn door was falling down and the corral was in disrepair. The garden was overgrown with weeds and the house was in great need of paint. He had never had a particular like for any of the Estradas. Señor Estrada was lazy and undependable, while his wife was a simpering gossip. To Marquis's way of thinking, the only one of any worth was Eleanor.

In response to Marquis's knock, an Indian maid opened the door. Smiling in welcome, she spoke to him in Spanish. "If you have come to see Señor Estrada, he is away from home at this time."

Marquis sighed heavily. "I have not come to see him, but to pay my respects to Señorita Isabel. Will you inform her that I am here?"

The maid cast him a troubled look. She had seen Isabel walk in the direction of the barn, but she did not know if it would be proper to send Señor Vincente to the señorita. Looking into smiling dark eyes, she made up her mind. It would do no harm for the lovers to have some time alone, she thought.

"You will find Señorita Isabel in the barn, señor. I am sure she will be happy to see you."

Marquis nodded his head and, turning, he moved down the steps. His mind was not on Isabel as he walked in the direction of the barn; he was remembering the touch of silken skin beneath his fingertips. He was thinking of the pleasure Jordanna had given him. No woman had ignited so bright a flame in his body—it had been an all-consuming fire that had threatened to burn down his defenses, to make him forget his honor and obligations. Marquis had purposely stayed away from Jordanna, fearing he would be drawn so deeply under her spell that he would never be able to face his obligations— to face Isabel, whom he must wed.

Marquis had also thought of Valentina Barrett. She and the dancer had come into his life at a time when he had needed them both. Each of them, in her own way, had left a lasting impression on his heart. His memories of them would help to sustain him through the years of a loveless marriage.

As he approached the barn, he saw that the door was open and he stepped inside. It was a bright, sunny day, and Marquis had to wait a moment until his eyes adjusted to the darkened interior. Hearing a girlish giggle, he decided not to call out, but instead walked toward the back stall where the sound had come from.

His eyes swept past the railing to the pile of hay where Señor Estrada's *gran vaquero*, Petra, lay astride a woman, pounding away at her. Marquis intended to leave quietly, thinking he was interrupting Petra and one of the Estradas' housemaids. Turning away, Marquis's eyes fell on the face of the woman, and he was shocked to find it was Isabel. Her gown was pushed up to her waist, and the man was thrusting back and forth between her legs. Isabel's eyes were glazed with passion, and she made little purring noises deep inside her throat.

Marquis's jaws clamped tightly together at the sickening sight that met his eyes. Stepping back into the shadows, he decided not to interrupt them. Let Isabel hang herself by her own deeds, he thought angrily. Suddenly Marquis's scowl turned to a smile; this little incident would free him from any obligation he felt toward Isabel. Almost lightheartedly he leaned against a post and waited for his betrothed to have her fill of the *gran vaquero*.

"Oh, yes, Petra," Isabel purred. "Each time you take me is better than the last. Faster, faster—go deep," she cried out in a breathless voice.

The man said something in reply, but Marquis did not hear him. His lips curled in contempt and disgust. It was most fortunate that he had come here today. Otherwise he might never have known about Isabel's faithlessness. He would have been trapped in a marriage with no escape.

Marquis did not have very long to wait before the man walked out of the stall, fastening his trousers. When he saw Marquis, he stopped dead in his tracks, his face draining of all color. He could see his death written on the wall. No one crossed Marquis Vincente and lived to tell about it. He edged himself along the stall. No woman was worth his death, especially not the whore, Isabel Estrada.

"It is not what you think, Señor Vincente." The man licked his dry lips, tasting the acid tang of fear. "I did not seek out Señorita Isabel. She came to me."

"Petra, are you talking to me?" Isabel called. She came out of the stall and the smile died on her lips. "Marquis, what . . . who . . . ?"

Petra backed closer to the door, all the while keeping his eyes on Marquis. When he reached the door, he lost no time in disappearing beyond it.

Marquis turned calm eyes on Isabel. "I believe we can safely say your father's *gran vaquero* will not stop until he is at least a hundred miles from here." Not even raising his voice, Marquis sounded deadly calm. "Pity you will lose your lover, Isabel."

By now Isabel had found her voice. "Marquis, surely you do not think I gave myself to Petra. He is nothing but a hired hand. I would never—"

Marquis held up his hand. "Spare me the lies, Isabel. I saw the two of you."

She pushed a lock of black hair out of her face and held out her hand in a pleading gesture. "Marquis, it is not what you think—he raped me!"

Marquis's laughter was so sinister that it sent waves of prickling chills through Isabel's body. "Poor Petra," Marquis stated dryly. "More than likely, you raped him. I heard what you said about each time he had you, Isabel; today was not the first time he has rolled you in the hay."

Isabel raised her head, giving Marquis a haughty look, while her eyes took on a calculating light. "All right, I admit Petra has been my lover. He is not the first and he will not be the last. Do not expect me to beg on my knees for your forgiveness. I am sure you have had your whores—why is it all right for a man to take a lover and not a woman?"

Marquis felt his stomach heave. He doubted he would

ever have been able to make love to this woman. "I will leave you to wonder what is right and wrong for the sexes, Isabel. I have only one request to make of you."

Isabel looked into dark eyes that were icy cold. "You are the one with the bargaining power, Marquis. I am at your mercy, for the moment."

Marquis reached out and plucked a bit of straw from Isabel's hair. Smiling slightly, he pressed it into her hand. "I want you to go to my grandfather today and tell him you have decided you do not want to marry me. Make up any excuse you want to, but do it today."

She did not miss the silent threat that laced his words. "And if I refuse?" she asked in a final act of bravado—a bravado she did not feel.

"If you refuse," he began slowly, "I shall tell my grandfather what I saw here today. It is my belief that he will not be amused by my little story of today's happenings."

Isabel could feel the trap door slamming in her face. She was losing Marquis and there was nothing she could do to prevent it. "What if your grandfather does not believe you, Marquis?"

"It is highly unlikely that my grandfather would dispute my words. But in the event that he might question your virginity, I could always call in our family doctor. His examination should prove you are not a maiden."

Isabel could feel Marquis slipping away from her. She had ached for months for him to bed her. She had dreamed of the paradise a woman would find in his arms. Since their first meeting, Marquis had been arrogant and elusive. He had all but ignored her, forcing her to take a lover to soothe her passions. She was defeated and she knew it. She would have to back down for now, but Isabel was not a quitter; she would live to fight another day. She did not easily let go of something she desired, and she desired Marquis Vincente with all her being. Now that he was so distant, he was even more appealing to her.

"Must I go to your grandfather today?" she asked in a breathless voice.

Marquis's eyes turned hard. "I insist that it be done as soon as possible. I do not want the sundown to find you still betrothed to me."

"You are a cruel, cold man, Marquis. I know you have every right to be disgusted with me. I can understand your not wanting to marry me, but what I do not understand is why you have been so distant right from the start. I sensed in you a reluctance long before today."

He was leaning back against a partition with his arm propped against a saddle that hung over the top. "I suppose I felt we were incompatible from the beginning. Perhaps I detected some of your true nature," he suggested airily.

Isabel's eyes blazed with anger. "This is not over, Marquis. I think we will play out other scenes before we are through with each other."

He looked down his nose at her and spoke in a bored tone. "As far as I am concerned, you do not exist. I will always carry within my mind the sight of you rutting in the hay with one of your father's underlings."

Isabel's face reddened, and she reached for a leather whip that hung on the wall. Before Marquis guessed her intention, it snaked through the air and, with a loud snap, licked at Marquis's face. At the last second he crossed his arms in front of him, and the lash cut into his black leather jacket.

"I will kill you," Isabel screamed as hatred and rage distorted her face. "If it is the last thing I ever do, I will destroy you or something you love!"

Marquis jerked the whip from her hand, tossing it

aside. "Just see that you talk to my grandfather today. If you do not, you will rue the day you ever heard the Vincente name." His warning hung heavily in the air. Marquis's eyes were so cold, and his superior air deflated Isabel.

She watched helplessly as Marquis turned and walked away. She had never loved a man before, but she came as close to loving Marquis in that moment as she had ever come in her life. "I will have you back," she whispered, raising her fist and shaking it in the air. "I will have you back or I shall see you dead!"

Valentina heard the knock on the door of her dressing room and pulled her veil into place. When she saw it was Tyree, she motioned him into a chair.

"You were exceptionally good tonight, Jordanna. I never saw you dance better. You had the audience in the palm of your hand."

She sank down in a chair and took the pins from her hair so that the golden curtain spilled down her shoulders. "I thought I was clumsy and missed a step several times."

"If that is so, no one knew it but you." His eyes sought hers in the mirror. "The *Southern Cross* came into port this afternoon."

She spun around to face him. "Was my father on board her?" She hardly dared to breathe as she waited for Tyree's answer.

"No. I found out from a reliable source that your father was never taken aboard her."

Valentina felt her hopes dashed into nothingness. For so long she had convinced herself that she would find her father aboard the *Southern Cross*. "Are you very sure, Tyree? Can there be no mistake?"

257

Tyree's heart went out to her. He wished with all his heart that he could give her a grain of hope. "There is no mistake." He watched her eyes cloud over. "I wish I could have brought you good news, Valentina." He had forgotten his resolve always to call her Jordanna when she was at the Crystal Palace. "I do not want you to give up hope. I will continue to search for your father until I find out something."

Valentina felt tears of hopelessness sting her eyes. "This is the worst day of my life. I do not know what I will do. There is nowhere to turn. Everything seems to be going wrong."

In a flash, Tyree was across the room and down on his knees before Valentina. When he raised her chin, forcing her to look at him, the sight of her tears caused his heart to ache. "There is more here than not finding your father, Valentina. What has caused your tears?"

"I . . . can't talk about it. Not with you, not with anyone."

"Honey, don't cry," he said, wiping her eyes with his handkerchief and handing it to her to blow her nose. "Don't you know you can tell me anything? Don't you know by now that you can trust me?"

"You will hate me if you know my guilty secret, Tyree." Again the tears spilled down her cheeks. "I . . . don't want you to hate me," she sobbed.

He gathered her close to him and stroked her hair as if she were a baby. "I think I know, or at least I can guess." He felt a knife twist in his gut. "Does this concern Marquis, Valentina?"

She nodded her head as sobs shook her slight body. "Are you going to have a baby?"

He felt her stiffen. "How . . . did you know?"

His face was grim as his arms tightened about her. "Just a lucky guess," he murmured. "Cry it out and then

258

we will decide what to do about your situation. You are not alone in this. I will stand as your friend."

Valentina's shoulders shook as dry sobs racked her body. She had suspected for weeks that she was carrying Marquis's child. Now, with her getting sick to her stomach every morning, she was sure of it. She did not know where to turn. She could not even bring herself to tell Salamar about her predicament.

When her tears had subsided, Tyree gazed at her kindly, noting the look of shame on her face. "No, Valentina, never be ashamed with me." His smile brought a slight answering smile from her. "Marquis doesn't know, does he?"

Valentina shook her head. "No. I could never tell him."

"What if I tell him so he can do the right thing by you? Don't you think it's time you put a stop to this deception? Let him know that Jordanna and Valentina are one and the same. It's my guess he will want to marry you and give the child his name."

"No!" Her eyes took on a look of silvery fire. "Marquis made it clear from the beginning what I could expect from him. Marriage wasn't a condition. I do not want you to tell him that I am Jordanna; let him believe that Jordanna just disappeared."

His voice was soothing, his eyes sparkling with sympathy. "I think you are making a mistake. Marquis would never offer Jordanna marriage, but he would Valentina."

"No, Tyree, no." She shook her head. "I'll never tell him I'm Jordanna. And as for making a mistake, it won't be the first one I have made. Knowing me, it probably won't be the last."

His eyes suddenly softened as he looked at her. Standing up, he spoke almost hesitantly. ". . . I'll see you through this, Valentina. If you don't want to tell Marquis about the baby, would you consider marrying me?"

Her eyes brimmed with tears as she stood up. Reaching out, she touched his face. "My dearest, sweet friend, I would never place my burden on you. How dear of you to offer to make a respectable woman of me, but I would never lay my shame at your feet."

"Suppose I told you I wanted to marry you?"

"Then I would say that you give too much to a friendship. I will always remember your unselfish offer of marriage. I love you too much as a friend to accept such a sacrifice from you."

Tyree wanted to hold her and let the words of love roll off his tongue, but somehow he could not confess his love—it would leave him too vulnerable, strip him naked. "I care deeply about you, Valentina. I would do anything to make you happy."

She pressed her cheek to his, and he felt the wetness of her tears. "Leave me this one shred of decency, Tyree. I love Marquis, but I know he will never love me. I cherish your friendship and would never find a solution to my problems at the expense of your feelings."

"Valentina, I—"

She laid her hand over his mouth. "I will always remember that you are the dearest friend I could ever have, Tyree. Your friendship means more to me than you will ever know."

He moved back a step, carrying her with him. He realized Valentina would never change her mind. She loved Marquis, not him. "Have you seen a doctor?"

Valentina's face reddened. "No!"

"Then how can you be sure?"

"I'm sure."

"Do you have any plans?"

"Not past finding my father. I don't have time to dwell

on my problems. If I don't find out something about my father soon, I may have to bury my mother."

He frowned for a moment, then gave her a lopsided smile. "I stand ready to help you in any way I can."

Tears blinded her as she touched the face of this dear friend. "I know you do, Tyree. That's why I'm asking you if you will accompany me to my father's mine. Will your friendship stretch that far?"

He hugged her to him, knowing she would never consider him anything other than her friend. "I have this craving to see the countryside. When would you want to leave?"

Smiling brightly through her tears, Valentina spoke. "In the morning, bright and early."

"I'll be there."

Valentina stood on tiptoe and kissed his cheek. "Thank you, my dear, dear friend. I fear I have used you sorely."

Again he smiled, never letting her know his heart was hers for the asking. "What is a boss for if not to help his little dancer when she needs it?"

Valentina pulled a heavy black scarf over her face and walked toward the outside door. "I'll be waiting for you tomorrow morning."

Tyree stared at the door long after Valentina had gone. Taking a deep breath, he stalked out of the room, knowing he must face Marquis. Valentina had asked him not to tell Marquis that she was Jordanna, but she had not said anything about telling Marquis that the dancer was carrying his child.

As luck would have it, Tyree did not have long to wait to face Marquis. When he entered his bedroom to pack his saddlebags for the trip to the mine, Marquis was sitting on his bed, waiting for him.

"I thought you were bored with town living, Marquis," Tyree said by way of greeting.

"Not entirely. I just had some unfinished business to settle. You might be interested to know that I no longer have a betrothed."

Tyree was not feeling very charitable toward his friend. Cramming an extra shirt into his bag, he raised his eyebrows. "How awful for the poor lady. How did you manage to detach her?"

Marquis caught the sarcasm in his friend's voice but took it for teasing. "Well, I would not want to go into the details, not wanting to damage the woman's reputation. Suffice it to say I saved myself just in time."

Tyree turned to Marquis. "Good. This will work out better than I thought. You can marry Jordanna and make a respectable matron of her."

Marquis frowned. "How did you find out I had been to bed with Jordanna? Did she tell you?"

"She didn't want to, but she has a little problem and needed a friend, since you impregnated then deserted her."

Marquis's eyes narrowed to slits. "What in the hell are you talking about?" he demanded to know.

"You heard me. I said Jordanna is carrying your child. What are you going to do about it?"

Marquis stood up slowly, not once taking his eyes off his friend. "Whatever I decide to do about it is no damned business of yours. I just escaped one designing female. I do not intend to be caught by another."

"You don't have a very high opinion of the fair sex, do you?" Sarcasm laced Tyree's words. "I wonder what happened to make you so suspicious and cynical."

"Call it caution."

"Well, you can mark Jordanna off your list of

designing women. She doesn't even know I'm talking to you about her. She was just going to disappear and let you guess what happened to her. She's asking nothing from you."

Marquis glanced at Tyree. "Why do you feel you must defend Jordanna to me? Did she go right from my bed to yours?"

Tyree's anger had reached the boiling point. With rage in his heart, he swung his fist at Marquis, grazing him on the lower jaw. Marquis caught Tyree's arm and spun him around, pinning the limb behind him. "What in the hell has brought all this on? I intend to see that your dancer has money to ensure her and the child's comfort for the rest of their lives. Surely you cannot be implying that I should marry her? A Vincente does not marry soiled goods."

"Damn you, Marquis!" Tyree shouted, trying to wrestle his arm free but finding Marquis the stronger.

"Tyree, do not let some woman come between us," Marquis pleaded. "We have been like brothers." Marquis was puzzled by his friend's attitude until he realized that Tyree must love the dancer. "Perhaps you will want to marry her yourself?" he asked, releasing the arm at last.

Tyree rubbed his shoulder to restore the circulation. "I already asked her to marry me—she turned me down."

Marquis was still reeling from Tyree's announcement that he had fathered a baby by the dancer. His feelings were still too raw to examine. "I will go to the bank tomorrow morning and withdraw a substantial sum, and you can turn it over to Jordanna. You might hint to her that the climate in San Jose is most healthy and enjoyable this time of year."

"To hell with you, Marquis. You are a coldhearted bastard. One day you will meet your match, and I will laugh as she brings you down off your lofty perch. The Vincentes aren't gods, and they don't own the world. You think yourself too good for Jordanna—in my estimation she is a better person than you will ever be."

Marquis shook his head, knowing Tyree was speaking out of anger. He did not want to fight with him. "Watch out what you say, Tyree," Marquis warned. "I would not want to lose your friendship."

"One day you will meet the woman who will turn you inside out. I pray that I will be around to witness your tumble from sainthood."

"I would not wait until that happened, Tyree. I have no intention of allowing some scheming female to get her hooks into me."

"I have heard that even the mighty can fall from grace. You may just prove that one day, Marquis." Tyree pulled his holster and gun out of a drawer and pushed it into his saddlebag.

It now occurred to Marquis that Tyree was packing. "Are you going somewhere?" he asked curiously, hoping to move on to a safer subject.

"Yes, I am going to take Valentina to her father's mine."

"I thought we agreed I would take her and only if the lead on the *Southern Cross* turned out to be false."

"I didn't agree to anything like that, but for your information, the *Southern Cross* story turned out to be a hoax. Valentina insists on going to her father's mine to talk with his partner, and I'm going with her."

"You do not know how to get there," Marquis challenged.

"I'll find it. You forget I know this country as well as you do."

Marquis was beginning to tire of Tyree's sarcasm. Moving across the room, he spoke. "Tyree, for some

264

reason you think I have wronged Jordanna. I may have made mistakes with her, but I will make it right. I do not want you to think this excuses you where Valentina is concerned. I will never allow you to ruin Valentina's reputation."

Tyree's lip curled. "I leave the ruining of young ladies' reputations to you."

"I will take Valentina to her father's mine. If you want to come along, I have no objections, but you cannot keep me from going."

Tyree was thoughtful for a moment. Perhaps Valentina and Marquis needed this time together. Valentina loved Marquis and Marquis also loved her. He damned sure didn't want to get in their way. Perhaps if they were alone, Valentina would tell Marquis she was carrying his baby.

He tossed his saddlebag on the bed. "Yes, perhaps it would be best if you took her to the mine instead of me. I find that I am very busy at this time and need to stay around the Crystal Palace."

Marquis looked puzzled. It was out of character for Tyree to give in without a fight. "What are you up to?" Marquis asked suspiciously. "Are you thinking you can have Jordanna to yourself with me out of the way?"

"Let's just say that one of us needs to look after Jordanna's interests."

Marquis felt a prickle of jealousy. There was a painful ache in his chest and a dryness in his throat. He had spent one unforgettable night with the dancer. He did not like the thought of Tyree bedding Jordanna. "Will you take her for yourself?" he could not help but ask. Marquis was disillusioned by women at the moment; the sight of Isabel rolling in the hay with her father's *gran vaquero* was still painfully fresh in his mind.

"I believe I'll let you stew on that one for awhile."

Marquis was further puzzled when Tyree laughed deeply. "Yes, indeed, I think I'll let you wonder about that."

Later, when Marquis entered the hotel room where he would spend what was left of the night, he was overcome by guilt. After all, he had been the first man to bed Jordanna. There was no doubt that the child was his. He felt a moral obligation to Jordanna and the child, and he would see that they wanted for nothing. But he would not be forced into marriage. Dear God, he cried inwardly, hadn't he just extricated himself from marriage with Isabel? Why would he want to marry a woman whose face he had never seen? No longer wanting to be involved with Jordanna, he would let Tyree handle the transaction between them as discreetly as possible.

He lay down on the bed, pleased with himself and the simple solution. As soon as he returned to town, he would tie together all the loose ends of his life.

Closing his eyes, Marquis could see Jordanna whirling gracefully around the stage. Her beauty had touched his heart. In some strange way, he ached because she would never belong to him. Opening his eyes, Marquis listened to the sounds rising from the street below; San Francisco was alive, even at this late hour.

Marquis was thinking of the two extraordinary ladies who had touched his life. There was Jordanna, who had stirred his blood, and Valentina, who had stolen his heart.

He was now free to offer Valentina his name. She had an undeniably fine background, whereas Jordanna—who would bear his child—could never marry into his family.

Why could he not make Tyree see that he owed it to his family to marry well. His mind was tortured. Jordanna may have been a saloon dancer, but she had been untouched when he had taken her—she was an enigma. He tried to remind himself that a Vincente could never marry beneath him. Even if Jordanna had his baby, he could never recognize her or the child, and that thought continued to haunt him.

Chapter Eighteen

The morning mist hung heavily in the air, shrouding the land, making it hard to see more than a few feet ahead. Valentina glanced out the window. She could hear horses neighing and assumed Tyree had arrived.

"He's here, Salamar. I have to go."

"I still feel this thing is not right, Valentina. Do not go," Salamar pleaded.

"I must, Salamar. I promise I will be careful. You know Tyree will take care of me."

"What will I say if your mother asks where you are?"

"In the state she's in, I doubt she will notice. If she does, tell her I am searching for Father."

Kissing Salamar on the cheek, Valentina moved quickly across the room and dashed out the front door, fearing she might change her mind. Her nerves were unsettled because of Salamar's warning. It would take very little persuasion on Salamar's part to make her give up the venture. Yet Valentina knew this might be her last hope of finding out about her father.

There was a chill in the air and she was glad for the long sleeves on her wine-colored riding habit. As she rushed along the path that led to the road, she saw a man standing beside two horses. Since the mist was so heavy, she could not see him very well, and not wanting to attract the attention of Reverend Lawton and his sister, she did not call out a greeting until she was near him.

"Good morning, Tyree. I hope I didn't keep you waiting."

Marquis swung around to face Valentina in time to see the shock that registered on her face.

"What are you doing here? I was expecting Tyree," she gasped out past the lump in her throat.

"Tyree was unexpectedly detained. He asked if I would extend his regrets to you and he hopes you will accept me as his substitute."

Valentina felt her stomach muscles tighten and a wild excitement rush hotly through her veins. "I . . . don't know. I wouldn't want to impose—"

"You did not seem to feel it was an imposition for Tyree—why should you think it would be for me?"

"I don't know you as well as I know Tyree," she replied lamely.

A guarded look moved over Marquis's face. "Do you know Tyree so well?"

"I . . . not all that well," she stuttered, feeling like a young schoolgirl. Her mind was in a whirl and she wished she dared turn and walk away, but she stood rooted to the spot, listening to the pounding of her heart.

"You should have known I would take you to your father's mine if you wanted to go. Did you not know I would never allow you to go alone? I warned you that your father's partner is a dangerous man."

"I wasn't going alone. Tyree was going with me," she reminded him.

Without another word, Marquis placed his hands around Valentina's waist, lifting her onto the back of the sorrel mare. Turning away in grim silence, he mounted his own horse.

As they rode away, neither of them saw the face

pressed against the window watching them. Percival Lawton stared resentfully after the two on horseback. Miss Valentina Barrett was not as good as she would have people believe. She was beginning to show her true colors with all the men hanging around her like dogs in heat. She was not the prim and proper miss she pretended to be.

Envy and anguish burned in Percival's heart. He wanted Valentina for himself, but he wanted her pure, virginal. He had decided that he would keep a close watch on Valentina's activities. He had learned only yesterday that the widow, Mrs. Windom, for whom Valentina claimed she worked, had died three weeks earlier. That left him to wonder where Valentina went each afternoon when she claimed to be going off to work. He would soon find out how she still managed to have money after her former employer's demise.

After Marquis and Valentina had ridden hard all morning, he called a halt to rest the horses. They were now in the mountains and had left the heavy mist far below them. The bright sun promised a warm, golden afternoon.

Valentina took a drink from the canteen and watched Marquis move up the steep incline. His body was hard and muscled, and he moved with an easy grace, each step announced by the jingling of his spurs. There was something almost primitive in the way he stood with his legs apart, his hands resting on his hips, as he stared across to the next valley.

Suddenly, without warning, he swung around to look at her, and Valentina felt her breathing cease. His dark eyes moved across her face, almost questioningly.

When he looked away, she felt as if he were seeking something in her, but what?

Valentina did not look up as he rejoined her, until his

271

shadow fell across her face. His hand was extended to her, and she placed hers in its grasp. With strong fingers, he helped her to her feet.

"Do you feel up to riding on now?" he asked.

He was so near that she could see the beads of sweat on his upper lip. Wildly, her heart beat against her ribs, reminding her of the night she had lain in this man's arms and he had taken her to heights of glory. "Yes," she managed to say. "I am ready to continue."

Just before sundown, Marquis halted his horse. Looking around, Valentina discovered that they had arrived at the spot where she and Santiago had made camp the last time she had been in these mountains.

Silently, Marquis tended to the horses while Valentina moved about gathering wood for a fire.

The tension mounted during the meal of beans and dried beef. Valentina could feel Marquis staring at her, pulling her to him. Steeling herself against his magnetism, she tried to remember why she was here. She had come to find some clue about her father and nothing must deter her from her course. She could sense in Marquis a deep brooding. Was he thinking about the lovely Isabel? she wondered.

Finally she could stand the silence no longer. Standing up, she moved away from the campfire to where her bedroll had been spread beneath the wide branches of a tall oak tree. Without a word, Valentina sat down, removed her boots, then slipped beneath the blanket.

Drawing in a deep breath, she filled her lungs with fresh, cleansing air. The moon played hide-and-seek between the branches of the tree as her mind went to the man who filled her heart with love. Marquis could not know that at this very moment she was carrying his baby, and Valentina could not understand why Marquis was helping her. Why had he decided to take her to the mine instead of Tyree?

Hearing a twig snap, Valentina watched Marquis move to his bedroll and sit down. She noticed the rifle he placed close at hand. As the silvery moon touched his dark face, he turned to look at her.

"Sleep unafraid, Silver Eyes; nothing will harm you tonight."

The next morning their luck held. A bright sun chased rain clouds away, leaving a brilliant blue sky. As they had the day before, they rode hard.

Valentina appreciated the fine horseflesh, knowing the animals they rode had been bred for their endurance. She had never seen finer horses anywhere. When they stopped to rest, Valentina turned to Marquis. "Where did you ever find these horses? They are extraordinary. Most horses would never have kept up the steady pace we have been setting."

Marquis seemed preoccupied and answered her in a sharp tone. "They were raised on Paraíso del Norte." Seeing the hurt in Valentina's eyes, he explained more kindly. "They are a special breed that owe their origin to my grandfather's genius in crossbreeding. They are his greatest pride and joy."

Valentina could have said that Marquis, himself, was most probably Don Alonso's greatest pride and joy, but she did not. Instead she asked, "Is it much farther to my father's mine?"

"No."

"Will we be there before sunset?"

Marquis tightened the girth on his horse and answered without looking at Valentina, "Yes."

Valentina drew a breath in vexation. If Marquis was going to answer in monosyllables, she would not waste

273

her time talking to him at all. What right did he have treating her so high-handedly? She had not done anything wrong . . . unless . . . unless he knew that she was Jordanna!

Walking around her horse, she decided to find out. But when Marquis turned his dark eyes on her, she felt the words she was about to speak stick in her throat.

"Are you hungry?" he asked.

"No."

"Are you ready to go on, or do you need to rest a bit longer?"

Taking her courage in hand, she spoke. "I am not tired, but I want to ask you something."

He uncapped the canteen and handed it to her. "I am listening."

"I . . . you seem to be put out with me, and I don't understand why. Have I done something to make you angry?"

His dark eyes softened as they swept her face. Taking a step toward her, he shook his head. "I cannot think of anything you could ever do to make me angry with you, Valentina. I am angry, but not with you—with myself. I have done some things lately that I am not very proud of. I suppose I am riddled with guilt."

Valentina caught the troubled expression in his dark eyes and wondered what could be bothering him. "Are you sure you aren't angry with me?" she pressed, hoping she was not the reason for his guilt. But no, she told herself, he could not know about the baby, no more than he could know that she was Jordanna.

He smiled and softly touched her cheek. "Yes, very sure. You would not know about the jealousy that can burn in a man's heart when he cannot have the woman he wants. You cannot guess what demons haunt a man when he sees that woman with another man, knowing he has no right to object."

Valentina blinked her eyes, glancing across the valley. Why would Marquis tell her about his love for another woman? He could not know that hearing about his love for someone else ripped her heart apart. "I'm sorry," she said for want of a better reply.

"Are you?"

"Yes, of course."

Marquis looked as if he would like to say more, but he clamped his lips tightly together. Reaching for Valentina, he hoisted her into the air, set her on the horse, and soon they were making slow progress up the steep mountainside.

Long after they left the valley behind, Marquis's words stayed with Valentina. Glancing over at Marquis, Valentina wondered again why he was the one who had come with her in Tyree's place. Was this a ploy of Tyree's to try to get them together? If it was, it would never work.

Valentina looked quickly away when Marquis glanced at her. As the trail narrowed, he moved ahead of her and called back, "Stay close to the face of the cliff and do not look down."

The words had no sooner left his mouth than she did just what he had warned against and glanced below. Her stomach tightened into knots, and she felt her head swimming dizzily. Fastening her eyes on Marquis's back, she did not again look down.

It was almost sundown when they rode up to the mine entrance. Marquis unhooked the flap on his holster so he would have easy access to his gun. Scanning the area, he finally dismounted and walked over to Valentina. He circled her waist with strong hands and lifted her to the ground.

"The place seems to be deserted," Marquis observed, glancing beyond the mine to the cabin that stood some

275

hundred yards away. "If I were to guess, I would say your father's partner left soon after my last visit."

Valentina looked toward the cabin. "I had hoped Mr. Udell would be here so I could question him."

"I do not think the man knows how to tell the truth. I believed him when he said your father had been shanghaied. Apparently he lied about that."

"What do we do now?" Valentina asked, looking about her with an air of hopelessness. "Now that I am here, I no longer know what steps to take."

Marquis unfastened his saddlebag and a large leather satchel, then slung them over his shoulder. "I would suggest that you bring your bedroll so we can make ourselves as comfortable as possible in that cabin." He nodded skyward. "From the looks of those clouds, it appears it might rain during the night. In the morning we will start back to San Francisco."

Valentina loosened the straps on her bedroll, gathered it in her arms, and followed Marquis toward the cabin. Passing the entrance of the mine, she paused and stared into its dark recesses. A shiver ran the length of her spine, and she remembered Salamar's grim prediction. Hurrying her pace, she caught up with Marquis.

"I want to go into the mine tomorrow," she stated, more to herself than to Marquis. "Perhaps there will be a clue to my father's disappearance there."

"I do not believe you will find anything. I went into the mine with Mr. Udell but found nothing."

She looked into his face and saw the smile that curved his lips. "It was a good thing that I was suspicious of him or I might never have come out alive."

"You aren't saying that he tried to . . . that he—"

"That is exactly what I am saying. Mr. Udell took an instant dislike to my questions about your father."

They had entered the cabin, and Valentina set down her bedroll on the dirt floor. "If Mr. Udell is that unscrupulous, he could have harmed my father. I am going into that mine tomorrow, and you can't stop me. I want to know for certain if my father . . . died here, or if I have reason to go on searching for him."

Marquis turned his attention to the open hearth. "I will find wood to build a fire."

"I'll help you," Valentina volunteered, not wanting to be left alone. The sun had already dropped behind the mountain, and the cabin was bathed in an eerie light.

"No, you can spread our bedrolls before the fire. I will be back before you know it, and I will cook you a meal tonight that you will never forget."

For long moments they stood gazing into each other's eyes. Valentina forgot Jordanna's grievances against Marquis. All hurts and disappointments faded away and she felt her knees go weak at the softness in his eyes. Finally, when she thought she could stand it no longer, he turned and went out the door, leaving Valentina staring after him.

Going down on her knees, she spread out his bedroll, then moved across the room and unrolled hers. What was this strange magic that Marquis wove about her? All he had to do was look at her and she fell apart on the inside. Her hand stole up to her stomach, which was still flat and firm. For the first time, she thought of the baby she was carrying as a real person. Would her child have flashing brown eyes like Marquis's, eyes that could soften to velvet in an instant? Pushing her troubled thoughts aside, she sat down on her bedroll, hugging her legs to her, waiting for Marquis's return.

Moments later, Marquis entered the cabin carrying an armload of wood. Dropping down on his knees, he soon had a fire blazing in the hearth, which helped considerably to dispell the dreariness of the cabin. Valentina moved closer and watched with interest while Marquis took an iron pan and dropped some kind of flat bread into

277

it. In another pan he heated a quantity of dark-colored beans. Once the bread was steaming, he removed it, placing it on tin plates. Spreading the warmed beans over the top, he sprinkled them with ground peppers, dried tomatoes, and slices of cheese. He then rolled one up and handed it to Valentina.

She bit into the bean roll and smiled with delight at the taste of melted cheese and spices. "This is delicious," she declared. "What is it?"

"I was taught to make these by an Indian from Texas who now works for me. He called them *frijoles tortillas*. He would be delighted to know that a lovely lady approves of his secret recipe. Mine has hot peppers on it, but I did not think you would want yours hot. I was careful to bring the mild *chilis* for you."

Valentina could not help but be pleased that Marquis would take such care about her food. "I once tried a hot pepper in India. I found the taste wonderful, but I never became accustomed to it burning my mouth."

"I believe one has to be born eating hot *chilis* to be able to endure the pain. It is hard to understand why most *gringos* find *chilis* hot. I have never felt the burning that your race speaks about."

"Marquis, you have a wonderful command of the English language. Did you learn to speak it from Tyree?"

He chuckled. "That, among other things, I learned from Tyree. He is the best friend I have. Did you know that?"

"Yes, I thought as much."

"My grandfather insists that I speak in English as much as possible. He believes the Spaniards who do not look to the future will die with the past."

"He may be right," Valentina agreed sadly. "What a pity."

When Marquis turned away to eat, Valentina allowed her eyes to roam hungrily over his body. How she had missed seeing him. If he were to discover how much she loved him, he would be shocked. But if he were to find out about the baby, he probably would never want to see her again.

"Tell me, how is your family, Marquis?" she asked, trying to change the direction of her thoughts. "I have very pleasant memories of my time with them. They were so kind to me when I stayed in your home."

"When my grandfather knows that I am going to San Francisco, he always asks about you. You charmed him when you were Paraíso del Norte. My sister often mentions you and wants to know how you are doing."

Valentina noticed that he did not mention his mother, but she was not surprised. Doña Anna had not been as open and friendly as Marquis's grandfather and sister had been. Valentina would have liked to have asked what his mother's feelings were for her, but she did not dare. Trying to keep the conversation light, she thought it would be only polite to ask about his wife-to-be. "How is Isabel and her sister Eleanor?"

Marquis stiffened. "I am sure they are fine." His face was turned away from her, so she could not see the frown that touched his forehead. Marquis did not like to think about Isabel; it was too much of a reminder of how close he had come to making the biggest mistake of his life. "I have not seen much of them lately."

Valentina had finished her food and shook her head no when Marquis offered her more. She busied herself with cleaning the pans with water from the large canteen, then stored them in the leather satchel.

The fire flickered low and Marquis added more wood. Seeing that Valentina had placed her bedroll across the room from his, he gave her a slight smile and brought it over to the fire beside his. "You do not have to be afraid of me. I will not bite," he said, laughing at her decorum but delighted all the same. How refreshing her modesty was, he mused silently.

"I am not afraid of you." Feeling mischievous, she smiled. "Perhaps I bite, and I was trying to protect you from me."

His smile was warm, and he reached out his hand to brush a tumbled curl off her face. "I would not mind being bitten by you, Silver Eyes." Valentina drew back from his touch, leaving him to shrug and remark, "I believe you do fear me a bit."

"No, I do not," she denied, thinking that her worst fear was her reaction to his touch.

A heavy silence followed until Valentina spoke. "I don't feel my father's presence here," she observed, looking around the deserted cabin. "I believe I would feel it if he had ever lived here."

"Perhaps it was built after your father . . . left. Most of the miners use a tent while they build a cabin. Many of them never build a cabin at all."

"I feel the answer to my father's disappearance lies with Samuel Udell. I wish he were here."

The sound of the wind moaning down the mountain made Valentina shiver and she curled up on her bedroll. "What do you suppose happened to Mr. Udell, Marquis?"

He was not sure if Valentina realized she had been calling him by his first name all day. The sound of his name on her lips pleased him very much. His eyes moved over her soft curves, up her smooth back, to fasten on her beautiful face. The flames cast a glow on Valentina's golden hair, and it seemed alive with amber and red highlights.

"We may never know what Fate dealt to Mr. Udell, Valentina. But if it is at all possible, we will find out about your father."

She rose up on her elbow and caught his eye. "I am going into the mine tomorrow, Marquis. You don't have to come with me if you don't want to."

He smiled. "I will chance it if you will."

Sinking back on her bedroll and closing her eyes, she felt the tiredness wash over her body. "I still don't know why you came with me," she remarked, hiding a yawn behind her hand.

His voice was deep. "Do you not?"

"No," she murmured before drifting off to sleep.

Marquis stared at her for a long time. He watched the steady rise and fall of her breasts and felt an ache in his heart. What if Fate had meant this woman for him? Dare he ask her to be his wife? He thought of Jordanna and felt shame over what he had done to her. Had loving Valentina made him aware of the pain he had caused Jordanna? Was his new-found heart going to remind him of his guilt for the rest of his life? For the first time in his life, Marquis was frightened—frightened that Valentina would not return his feelings, thus sentencing him to a loveless life.

Leaning back with his arms folded behind his head, Marquis tried to decide what to do. He should do the right thing and marry Jordanna. How could he when every part of his being cried out to possess Valentina? But what about the child? he asked himself. He would see that the baby and Jordanna never wanted for anything, he assured himself. If the child turned out to be a boy, he would see to it that he was well educated. If it was a girl . . . he could not bear to think of a little girl who had come from his body being shamed before the world because she had no name.

Staring at the flickering light of the fireplace, he swore softly. "Damnit, I had no guilt before. Why should I have developed a heart at this time in my life?" No, he was not going to allow guilt to make him offer marriage to Jordanna. As he had already decided, he would give her money, but that was all she could expect from him. He did not want to see the child after it was born. His eyes moved to Valentina. She was the woman who would bear the next generation of Vincentes. He loved her—he always would. Now that Isabel was out of his life, he could reach for his heart's desire. Valentina would be his. Surely he could convince her to marry him.

His heart felt light. Had this thought been in the back of his mind all the time? Was that why he had been so glad to be rid of Isabel? Closing his eyes, he thought of how he would woo and win Valentina Barrett. He would have to treat her gently. After all, she was of superior breeding, and as skittish as a blooded mare.

As he drifted off to sleep, his mind was filled with pleasant thoughts of the future.

Valentina awoke to the delicious aroma of coffee. Glancing about the cabin, she noticed that Marquis was nowhere to be seen. She stretched her arms over her head, feeling strangely rested and refreshed. She had slept the whole night through without waking.

Hearing a sound, she turned to watch Marquis enter the room. His smile was bright as he bent down to pour her a cup of coffee. "You will spoil me by waiting on me," she said, taking the cup and raising it to her lips.

"I believe a man would take pleasure in spoiling you," he said lightly. "Would you like breakfast now?"

Valentina remembered her morning sickness and shook her head no. "I only want coffee."

"What kind of a breakfast is that? You will soon waste away to nothing unless you eat," he scolded, finding that her health was most important to him.

"Have you eaten?" she wanted to know.

"Yes, hours ago. I have already been abroad scouting out the land. It appears that no one has been around here in some time."

Valentina stood up and walked outside. The air was crisp and clean and the sky was so blue it almost hurt her eyes to look at it. Her gaze wandered over to the mine, and once again Salamar's warning came back to haunt her. Pushing her fear aside, she squared her shoulders. She had to go into the mine because there might be some sign or clue that had been left by her father.

Feeling Marquis standing beside her, she nodded at the mine. "I'm going in now."

He picked up a torch he had made earlier and lit it. "Let's go," he said. "I have learned, during our short acquaintance, that it does not pay to oppose you in anything."

Her laughter bubbled out. "No man learns such a valuable lesson about a lady in such a short space of time. You are but humoring me."

His laughter joined hers. "Perhaps I am."

As Valentina neared the mine, a dark foreboding seemed to engulf her. She had the strongest desire to flee from this place, for she sensed evil here. She could feel it with every step she took—in every breath she inhaled. Refusing to give in to panic, she entered the mine behind Marquis.

A dank, musty smell assaulted her nostrils, and the torch did little to dispel the gloom of the shadows. In the distance, she could hear the scurrying of tiny feet and she shivered visibly.

Marquis turned to face her. "How deep do you want to go?"

"To the end."

He led the way past the main cavern. As they progressed deeper, they often had to stoop to make it through a small archway. Deeper and deeper they went. When Valentina glanced back toward the entrance, all she could see was darkness. Drawing a deep breath, she trudged on behind Marquis, searching for any sign of her father, finding nothing but emptiness.

Suddenly Marquis stopped and held his torch high. "There is a small cavern off to the right," he observed. Reaching up and testing the timbers that braced the entrance, he found them loose. "I am not sure we should go in there—the beams appear to be unsound."

"I won't be satisfied until I have explored every inch of this mine," she declared stubbornly. To prove her point, she walked over to the arch, ducked her head, and entered. It was dark and she could not see anything until Marquis joined her with the torch.

As the light flickered across the recesses of the dark chamber, Valentina saw something on the ground that made her breath catch in her throat. Her piercing scream filled the chamber as she stared at the dead body of a man who lay face down on the floor of the cave.

"Oh, God, no!" she cried. "Don't let that be my father!"

Marquis pushed her back and handed her the torch. Going down on his knees, he turned the body over and stared at the dead man. Standing up, he moved over to Valentina. She was leaning against the wall with a look of horror and disbelief on her face.

"This is not your father, Valentina. It's Sam Udell."

Valentina dragged her eyes away from the hideous sight and buried her face against Marquis's shoulder as tremors shook her body. She was overcome with relief that the dead man was not her father.

"Wh—what happened to him?"

Marquis shrugged. "There is no mark on him. He appears to have died of natural causes. Pity he was so greedy and had to die alone."

She suddenly felt the bile rising in her throat and knew she was going to be sick.

Rushing toward the archway, she felt her foot land on a rock and she lost her balance. Grabbing at thin air, she tried to catch herself. As she fell forward, she clutched the boards that had been used to shore up the walls. A splintering sound split the air, followed by a loud, rumbling noise. Marquis gripped Valentina and pushed her behind him just as the whole mine seemed to pour down upon them. Valentina reached out frantically to Marquis, but already the torch had been smothered out, leaving them in total darkness.

"Marquis, where are you?" she screamed just before something hard slammed into her head and she fell into unconsciousness.

Marquis knew what was happening but was helpless to prevent it. He heard Valentina scream and tried to reach her. With a loud rumble, the heavy timber collapsed, crushing Marquis's leg beneath it. Pain shot through his limb and he moaned in agony. A whirling tide of pain pinned him to the ground. In a desperate effort, he reached out again for Valentina. Why was she so silent? he wondered frantically.

Marquis's last conscious thought was to wonder if Valentina had been injured.

Chapter Nineteen

Valentina regained consciousness in a haze of fear. She was in a pitch black hole, feeling as if she were in the very bowels of the earth. She had landed hard and she tested her arms and legs to see if they had been injured. Suddenly she remembered the baby she was carrying and her hand instinctively moved down to her stomach. She hoped with all her heart that the fall had not harmed her unborn child. When she tried to rise, a shower of rocks and dirt sifted down around her, cautioning her that there could be another cave-in if she were not more careful.

After slowly lifting herself onto hands and knees, Valentina rose shakily to her feet. With her back pressed against the wall of the mine, she edged her way forward, an inch at a time.

"Marquis, are you hurt? Answer me if you can." When there was no immediate response, she feared Marquis had been badly hurt.

If only she could see, she thought wildly. The only sound that penetrated the darkness was dripping water somewhere in the distance.

"Marquis, where are you?" she called out in a panic-stricken voice.

Stopping her progress to listen, Valentina heard a soft moan somewhere ahead of her in the darkness. Dropping down to her knees once more, she crawled along in the inky blackness, reaching out in front of her, trying to locate Marquis. Suddenly her hand came in contact with his body. Quickly feeling for his face, Valentina found that Marquis's eyes were closed. Another soft moan convinced her that he was not dead. Tenderly she touched his face again, feeling gratitude in her heart that his life had been spared.

"Marquis, are you all right?" Now she was wild with grief, fearing he had been badly injured. Feeling his breath on her hand, she realized he was unconscious.

Tentatively, she began examining his arms and legs to see if he had any broken bones. Her heart sank when she discovered that his legs were pinned beneath a large section of wood that had been used to shore up the mine. Valentina grabbed the timber with both hands, lifted with all her might, and felt it give a little. With desperation, she thrust her shoulder against the timber and used it as a lever. After pushing and straining, she was at last rewarded when the wood slid off Marquis.

Valentina quickly examined him and breathed more easily when she felt his steady heartbeat. Then she ran her fingers over his legs. Although he was unconscious, she felt him flinch in pain. The probing continued, but she was more gentle, feeling first the left leg, then the right one. As her hand slid down the right thigh, she felt something warm and sticky and knew it was blood.

"Marquis, speak to me," she urged desperately. "Please tell me what to do."

Again there was no answer. Knowing she must take quick action, Valentina ripped a strip of cloth from her petticoat and bound it securely about the leg that was bleeding. In frustration, she wished for water to cleanse the wound and a knife to cut his trouser leg away.

Finally, not knowing what else to do, Valentina lifted his head onto her lap, praying all the while that his wound was not too serious and he would be all right.

Time had no meaning for Valentina as she stared into the hellish blackness. She kept one hand on Marquis's chest, comforted by the steady rise and fall of his breathing. Once in a while a soft moan would escape his lips, but he did not regain consciousness.

In her despair, Valentina cried out Marquis's name, only to hear the muffled sound echo off the walls of the mine. How long she sat there with Marquis's head in her lap she had no way of knowing. Soon her head nodded, and she drifted off to sleep.

Valentina was jarred out of her sleep by the sound of a muttered oath. "What in the hell is happening?" Marquis swore. When he tried to sit up, pain shot through his legs and he fell back, trying to catch his breath. "What has happened?" he questioned in confusion.

Valentina touched his face, forcing him to lie back on her lap. "We were in a cave-in. Lie still. I fear your legs have been badly hurt."

In the dark he groped for her hand. "Yes, I remember now." His voice was filled with all the uncertainty Valentina was feeling. "How long have we been here?"

"I have no way of knowing because it's so dark. Is your injury very painful?"

Marquis tried again to rise. Valentina felt him straining before he collapsed and his head fell back onto her lap. "I do not believe my legs are broken, but I cannot seem to move them."

"Marquis, both your legs were hurt, but your right one was bleeding a great deal, so I bound it with my petticoat. They . . . they may have been crushed. You must lie still."

He was silent for a moment, as if he were assessing the situation. Finally he spoke. "Have you heard any sound that might indicate someone might be digging us out?"

"No, nothing," she answered.

"I thought not, but we shall," he stated with confidence. "Tyree will discover us missing and be up here before too long." Marquis reached for her hand and gripped it reassuringly. "Help me stand, Valentina. We cannot just sit here doing nothing."

She heard him groan when he moved forward. Scrambling to her feet, she took his arm and tried to help him stand.

"It is no use," he told her, falling back. "See if you can find two pieces of wood. I am going to need splints on my legs or I will not be able to walk."

"Don't, Marquis," Valentina begged. "Both your legs are injured. You should not try to stand."

"I must try," he said. "If you do not help me, I will have to do it myself."

"Wait," she agreed, knowing that if she did not help him he might hurt his legs more. Already she was moving along the wall to reach the place where the cave-in had occurred. "I will find boards that were used to shore up the doorway. You just lie still until I return."

Reaching around in the dark, Valentina finally found several splintered pieces of wood. Tucking them under her arm, she made her way back to Marquis. Going down to the ground, she began tearing more strips from her petticoat and attached the splints to both his legs. Marquis gritted his teeth in pain when Valentina tightened the splint.

"You had better rest, Marquis. I am going to make my way back to the mine entrance. It might be that I can dig us out."

"Help me stand, Valentina. I want to go with you."

290

"No, Marquis. You must stay off your legs as much as possible. We don't know how badly you are hurt or how much blood you have lost."

He reached out and caught her arm. Clamping his lips tightly together to keep from crying out in pain, he stood up slowly. Leaning against the wall, he waited for the wave of pain to pass and fought against the nausea that threatened to engulf him.

Knowing what a proud man he was, Valentina said nothing else about him staying off his injured legs. She knew she would only be wasting her breath.

She clasped his hand in hers, and they both made their way slowly toward the mine entrance. It seemed to take forever to make it a few yards. Every so often, they would pause to allow Marquis to catch his breath. At one point Valentina's foot caught on the edge of a rock and she pitched forward, landing on her stomach. For a moment she was too stunned to move. She could hear Marquis calling out to her, but she could not answer until the pain in her stomach subsided. Fearing she surely had injured the baby this time, her hand stole protectively to her abdomen.

"Valentina, are you hurt?" Marquis asked frantically, flailing out for her in the darkness.

"I don't think so. I just tripped. This is where the entrance caved in, and the floor is littered with debris. Be careful that you do not fall," Valentina cautioned.

"Are you sure you are unhurt?"

"Yes, I was no more than winded," she assured him.

"Find me a good sized piece of wood, Valentina. I want to make a torch."

After she felt around in the dark and found what Marquis required, she crawled over to him and pulled herself up beside him.

"Let me have a strip of your petticoat, Valentina," he urged. He was having difficulty balancing his weight on his injured legs while he dug into his pocket for his flint.

Valentina ripped a strip of her now tattered petticoat and handed it to Marquis. Wrapping the cotton material around the stick, he finally succeeded in lighting it.

The darkness of the cave gave way to flickering shadows of light. Valentina stood transfixed, staring at the rock-strewn litter that stood between them and freedom. There was no way she and Marquis could dig their way out past the unmovable mountain of rock.

Her eyes sought Marquis's, and she saw her own conclusion reflected there. "Are we to die here?" she asked in an uneven voice.

His smile did not quite reach his eyes. "Of course not. If we are not back in a day or two, Tyree will raise a hue and cry. All we have to do is wait."

Valentina suspected that Marquis was only trying to make her feel better. He knew, as she did, that no one would miss them for several days. By that time, it would be too late.

Knowing it was futile to put her thoughts into words, Valentina knelt down to examine Marquis's legs in the light. Already the white rag that was wrapped around his right leg was blood soaked. She had to do something immediately to stop the bleeding.

"Put your arm around my shoulder and allow me to help you move away from here. I need to apply a tourniquet to your wound," she said, taking the torch from him and guiding his arm about her shoulder. Beads of sweat dotted Marquis's forehead. Even though his expression was unyielding, Valentina knew he was in agonizing pain.

Marquis accepted her help grimly, thinking it did not matter if he bled to death, died of hunger, or suffocated when the air ran out. More than likely, this would be his and Valentina's final resting place. He was astounded by her courage. Most women would be crying and carrying on by now. Her silver-blue eyes held no hint of panic in their brimming depths; they held only a sad acceptance of the situation.

Valentina planted the torch in the soft dirt and turned her attention to Marquis. A quick examination showed that the left leg did not appear to be as seriously injured as his right one.

"I should cut your pant leg to apply the tourniquet, Marquis."

"No, just tie it around the upper leg, Valentina," Marquis gritted out. The pain was so acute that his head swam drunkenly.

Valentina modestly turned around before ripping strips from her petticoat. Marquis lay with his back braced against the cavern wall while she tied a strip of material above his right thigh and tightened it to stop the flow of blood. Valentina's heart was heavy as she watched Marquis clamp his lips together so he would not cry out in pain.

She saw the beads of sweat pop out on his forehead and knew he was in agony. After she was satisfied that the flow of blood had stopped, she sat down beside him, watching for any sign that he might be losing consciousness.

"Why not lay your head in my lap," she suggested. "You don't have to put on a brave front for me. I can see that your legs are badly injured." She added softly. "I will make sure the torch keeps burning if you wish to sleep."

His lips quirked into a smile. "You are something very special, Valentina Barrett. I should be taking care of you. What do you intend to keep the fire going with when you have no undergarments left to burn?" Marquis could have told her that the torch was using up precious oxygen they should be conserving for their own use, but he did not. He did not want to cause her undue distress.

293

Her face eased into a frown. "This is all my fault. If I hadn't insisted on coming here to the mine, neither of us would be in this predicament. Before too long, we will be out of oxygen. Already the air feels heavy, and it's hard to breathe." Her eyes sought his. "I am truly remorseful that I involved you in my problems, Marquis."

He reached out and clasped her hand in his. "Nonsense, Valentina. I will always want you to come to me when you need help."

She smiled slightly. "You talk like there will be a next time. You know, as well as I, that we will never get out of here alive."

"I know nothing of the kind. I think we should both sit as quietly as possible to conserve what little oxygen we have left. I feel help will arrive before long."

"In the event that no one comes . . . what then?"

He raised her hand to his lips and kissed it softly. "In that case there is no one I would rather share the hereafter with than you, Silver Eyes."

Looking deeply into Marquis's eyes, Valentina was startled by the warmth she saw there. "I don't suppose this will endear me to Isabel, and who can blame her."

Marquis looked past her and focused his eyes on the torch. She could see the flame reflected in the dark depths of his eyes. "I am no longer pledged to Isabel. Even if we are rescued, she will never be my wife."

Valentina heard the bitterness in his voice. She knew that he was having a hard time focusing his eyes and that he was on the verge of losing consciousness again. Taking his head between her hands, she pulled it down to rest against her lap.

"Don't talk, just rest," she cautioned, moving her hand across his forehead soothingly.

"Do you not want to hear why I am not going to marry Isabel?" he asked in a faint voice.

Oh yes, she wanted to know, but she dared not act too interested. "It is not my concern."

"Is it not?" His voice trailed off and his eyes fluttered closed. Feeling his uneven breath against her hand, Valentina knew he had either fallen asleep or had passed out again. The grimace on his face told Valentina that Marquis was in pain even in his sleep, and it cut into her heart. She felt anguish at the thought of his agony. No matter how gallant Marquis had been in not allowing her to take the blame, it was her fault that they were trapped in this mine—she and she alone was responsible for this disaster.

Softly touching his face, she remembered she was carrying his child within her body. If they were going to die, should she not confess to him that she and Jordanna were one and the same? Should she tell Marquis that she was having his baby? Would it make a difference to him?

The torch flickered low, and Valentina knew it was but a matter of time before it went out, casting them into darkness. She decided it was not important to keep the torch lit. She no longer had any fear of the dark. There was only a deep sadness that she and Marquis would die here in this hole in the ground, never to feel the sunshine on their faces again. The child that was a part of them both would never draw its first breath of life. What would happen to her mother? She was not strong. Who would take care of her?

Leaning her head back, she closed her eyes, feeling the warmth of Marquis's skin as she touched his cheek. She loved him more than her own life. She wished with all her heart that it had not been her persistence that would ultimately cause his death.

Too weary and exhausted to think, Valentina tried to close her mind to her surroundings. She thought of the man who lay with his head in her lap and his baby that she carried within her body.

Valentina came full awake with a start. It took her

moments of staring into the blackness of hell to realize where she was. A moan escaped her lips when she remembered her hopeless situation. She did not know how long she had been asleep, but it was apparent that the air was much thinner now. It was difficult to breathe. Valentina felt as if a heavy weight were pressing on her chest.

She groped in the darkness, trying to find Marquis, but he was not there. Terror finally overtook her reasoning. She was going to die and Marquis wasn't with her!

A scream was building up inside, and it came out as she yelled out his name. *"Marquis!"*

"Do not panic, Silver Eyes," she heard Marquis say just beside her.

With tears streaming down her face and sobs racking her body, she groped in his direction.

"Do not cry, Valentina, I am here," he soothed, taking her tightly in his arms. "I would not have left you, even if I had had the chance."

"I don't want to die," she moaned. "I have so much to live for now."

His lips brushed her cheek, and his arms tightened like bands about her. He wished he could keep her safe—he wished she did not have to die in this dark hole—but he held out very little hope for a rescue. Valentina had been so brave until now. He cradled her head on his shoulder, wanting to protect her from anything that threatened to harm her. But how did one fight against certain death? There was no way he could protect her, so he decided to make the end as painless and easy as possible for Valentina.

"Where were you?" she sobbed. "I awoke and couldn't find you."

He gently stroked her face. "I was trying to dig us out." He rested his cheek against hers. "You must not give up hope. It is possible that at this very moment my men are on their way to rescue us."

Valentina shuddered. She knew deep inside that Marquis was only trying to calm her. He knew as well as she did that help would not come in time to save them. "Shouldn't we both try to dig our way out?" she asked in a shaky voice, remembering the pile of rubble that blocked their path to freedom.

"No, Silver Eyes. It is impossible, even for the two of us, to move all that rock. We should conserve as much energy as we can."

He leaned back against the cold wall of the cave, clutching her to him. For long moments neither of them moved. Marquis was thinking of the nights he had longed to hold Valentina in his arms. Now he might hold her forever. This was not the way he would have planned it. Thoughts of Jordanna moved through his mind. Both she and Valentina had touched his life as no other women ever had. He had planned to take care of Jordanna and the child. If he died, what would happen to them? he wondered. Perhaps Tyree would see that she and the child were looked after.

Valentina spoke, breaking into his thoughts. "I am sorry I got us into this, Marquis. It's all my fault."

He pushed her tumbled hair out of her face. "I came with you to the mine because I wanted to. I am not sorry I am with you now." He smiled against her face, trying to make light of their situation. "It is true, however, that I wish we were both somewhere else at the moment."

Valentina was silent as she digested his words. He had to be the bravest man she had ever known. He knew they were going to die, and still he tried to keep hope alive for her. Suddenly she wanted to end this pretense between them—she wanted him to know that she was Jordanna, to tell him that she was carrying his baby.

Wiping the tears away, Valentina raised her face to his. "I have a confession to make. I don't know what you will think of me after you hear my guilty secret, but I don't want to die with this lie between us."

He smiled, thinking he was going to hear some trivial little confession that had been weighing heavily on her soul. She was goodness and light, everything a woman should be. She could never do anything to be really ashamed of. "Do you want to tell me that you are responsible for all the gold shipment robberies that have been plaguing California lately?"

"No. If only that were my crime. I have done something far worse than robbery. I have been untruthful and deceitful. I have been a . . . I cannot say the word."

She felt him shake with laughter. "Have you been listening to the Reverend Percival Lawton? Has he told you that your soul was blackened with sin?"

"Marquis, this is serious and you refuse to listen to me." She could feel her shame burning her face. He thought her to be a good person. She ached inside because she was about to change his opinion of her. "I am Jo . . . Jor . . ." she began, but the words would not come. She could not bear the thought of his rejecting her because she was Jordanna, whom he considered unworthy of his love—certainly not worthy of giving life to a Vincente. All he had ever offered her was the prospect of becoming his mistress.

"Silver Eyes, nothing you confess would make me think any less of you."

Before she lost courage again, Valentina said, "Not even . . . not . . . even if I told you that I . . . was . . . I'm . . . going to have a . . . baby!"

The silence that ensued was as ominous as the darkness that surrounded them. "You . . . what? I had better have misunderstood you." Valentina felt him stiffen; his hand tightened on her shoulder. He was mentally pulling away from her. He sounded every inch the Spanish grandee. What Valentina had feared had happened. Marquis had turned hard and cold. He was unapproachable. Did he hate her?

"I do not find that a very funny jest, Valentina. As you may have guessed, I am not laughing."

Tears now streamed down her cheeks. She forgot that she was in the bowels of hell and probably would not live more than a few more hours. She forgot that there was a world beyond the darkness where the sun shone and the birds sang.

"This is no jest, Marquis. Are you not wise enough to understand?"

His fingers bit into her shoulders. He shook her so hard that the pins flew out of her hair and the silky curtain came tumbling down about her face. "You were raped! I will kill the bastard who dared to touch you!" he gritted through clenched teeth. "Tell me who has committed this atrocity and I will see him dead!"

Valentina shook her head. He had completely misunderstood her. How could he be so blind? "I wasn't raped, Marquis," she said in a dull voice.

His grip became even tighter and more painful. "You would never allow a man to . . . no . . . damnit, no—I will never accept that. You are pure and good. You are an angel." She could hear the disbelief in his voice. In his despair he cried out, "You were raped!"

"No, Marquis, I was not raped," she admitted again. Never had she wanted so badly to take the easy way out. She knew she would be in his arms again if she were to let him believe she had been attacked. Disregarding the lie, she gathered her courage to speak the truth. "I gave myself to the man I love. I gave myself to you."

In Marquis's pain-stunned mind, he did not hear the words of her confession. At that very moment a battle raged inside him. The woman he had worshiped as pure and untouchable had been touched by some bastard! he

299

silently agonized.

Not knowing he had not understood her, not understanding the battle he fought within himself, Valentina believed he was rejecting her and his baby.

She could not see the pain that filled his eyes. Even though Marquis reeled from confusion, he suddenly realized the truth of Tyree's words. He had fallen in love for the first time in his life and it felt like hell. Tyree would be pleased if he knew. Always before Marquis had used women, but now he found himself wanting to hold and love this woman. She was precious to him, and it ripped him apart to know that another man had held her in his arms and had loved her as he had dreamed of doing. He wanted to tear the child from her body and remove the memory of the man who had planted that child in her.

Marquis could feel the fever building in his mind. The pain ripped through his body and he knew he wasn't thinking clearly. He only knew that he wanted Valentina. "If we get out of this alive, you will marry me. I will give your child a name."

She choked on a sob. He wasn't making any sense. Couldn't he understand that she was telling him he was the father of her child? Couldn't he draw the conclusion that she was Jordanna? "Even if we do escape from here, Marquis, I will not marry you. Neither me nor my baby are your responsibility." Hurt made her add, "You must have many bastard children running around California."

He grabbed her and pressed her tightly against him, almost crying out from the pain in his legs. Anger was coiled in his stomach like a snake ready to strike. "Damn you, do not ever say that! I will not hear such harshness coming from your lips."

She had come too close to the truth. In his fever-tortured mind, he remembered Jordanna—Jordanna, who stole men's hearts while she danced; Jordanna, who was going to have his child. There was no doubt in his mind that it was his baby Jordanna carried. If he and Valentina got out of this alive, he would do the right thing by Jordanna; he would take care of her needs and see that she had money. But he would marry Valentina. Suddenly a troubling thought came to him. What if the man who had fathered Valentina's baby wanted to marry her?

"Does the father know about the baby, Valentina?"

It was getting harder to breathe all the time and Valentina took in a shallow breath. "Yes, he knows," Valentina choked out.

"Will he marry you?"

"No."

"Then, like I said, you will marry me. Forget about the other man. I will hear no argument against my proposal." Inside he was shaking. Dear God, he would have Valentina for his own. She would belong to him and no one else. That thought swept through him like a cleansing breath of air. Yes, he had the solution to his problems. It was so simple. He would marry Valentina, whom he loved, and take care of Jordanna, whom he desired.

Valentina knew in that moment that her pride would never allow her to admit that she was Jordanna. She would die with the lie on her lips, and pain in her heart.

"No, Marquis. I will never marry you."

His arms tightened around her. "Yes, by God, you will. You will be my wife!"

"Are you not shocked by my wanton behavior?" she taunted with tears washing down her cheeks. He must think she was being ungracious by not accepting his sacrifice, she reflected. He couldn't know he was tearing her apart inside. "I know all about your aristocratic race. You think you have the God-given right to populate the country with your seed."

Her barb had hit too close to home and Marquis shifted

uncomfortably. "Even if I did have a bastard child on the way, unlike the man who planted his seed in you, I would offer to take care of the child's future."

"By marrying the mother?" Valentina was breathing deeply, waiting for his reply, knowing she would again try to make him understand who she was if he gave the right answer.

"No, not by marrying the mother. I am a Vincente and I owe it to my ancestors and future generations to honor the name." Marquis was half delirious and did not know what he was saying. "I could not offer my name to one who was unworthy."

"Are you saying that even if you loved a woman and she was having your baby, you wouldn't marry her if she weren't good enough to bear your name?"

"That is a fair assumption," he admitted, wishing the pain in his legs would lessen.

"I don't understand you, Marquis. Why then would you offer to marry me, thinking I'm carrying another man's child?"

She was unable to see the grim expression on his face, but she could hear the irony in his voice. "I offer you my name because you come from a good family background. I would never want you to be shamed before the whole world."

Marquis could have said that he loved her and could not bear the thought of any man's dishonoring her. He wanted to confess his undying love for her, but he kept his silence. It was getting difficult to breathe, he was weak from loss of blood, and his leg ached painfully. He knew there was only enough air to last a few hours more.

"Do not talk about your baby, Silver Eyes," he said in a soft voice while his hand moved up her arm to cup her breast. "Just let me hold you for the time we have left."

Valentina forgot that she was angry with Marquis when his lips sought hers. She knew she should push his

302

hand away, but she did not. Love, so precious and sweet, washed over her as his hands moved across her leg, pushing her gown upward. "I want no more than to hold and touch you," he breathed in a husky voice. "I can never have you for my own, but I will die touching you."

Valentina tried to breathe as his hand moved her undergarments aside and found her hot flesh. With soft, stroking motions, he moved his hands between her thighs. It was crazy; it was madness—it was so right. Her lips quivered beneath his hot mouth. Valentina did not know if her head was spinning from lack of oxygen or from the maddening feelings Marquis stirred to life in her body.

After a while his hand became still and she felt him relax. He did not move his hand but allowed it to rest against her stomach. "The end is near, isn't it, Marquis?" she whispered.

"Try not to think about it, Valentina. For the time we have left, let us play a pretend game. Did you ever do that as a child?" Marquis knew in a short time he would lose consciousness. He did not want to leave Valentina alone. If only she would go before him, he agonized. Dear God, don't let her be left alone in this hellhole, he prayed.

"Yes, many times. What shall we pretend?"

His lips rested against her temple. "Let's pretend that you are not going to have another man's child. Let us imagine that we are madly and passionately in love with each other, and know we are about to die. Do you think you can pretend that?"

Valentina's heart cried out that there was no reason for her to pretend. As her lips brushed Marquis's, she felt the heat from his body and knew he was burning up with fever. He was delirious and did not know what he was saying. She supposed he thought dying would be easier if he pretended to be with someone he loved, and who loved him.

303

"Yes, I love you with all my heart, Marquis. I would die alone if I could wish you to safety. I have loved you for a very long time. There has never been another man in my heart but you."

His hand tangled in her hair. "Damn you for how easy the lies come to your lips," he said weakly. The anger suddenly drained out of him to be replaced with sorrow. He was giddy from pain. Fresh blood oozed through the bandage from the gash on his leg and trickled down his calf. "Do you remember the day you walked into my courtyard for the first time, Valentina?"

"Yes, I remember," she admitted. How could she forget the day she first lost her heart to this dark, handsome Spaniard.

"I fell in love with you at that very moment, Valentina. I knew that the woman my heart had always sought was standing before me. As I came to know you, I realized you were dangerous to my peace of mind—to my way of life. I had to stay away from you or risk not doing what was expected of me by marrying Isabel."

Valentina's head was pounding and she gasped for breath. How deeply his words wounded her—how well he played the game of deception. "It would seem lies come easily to your lips also, Marquis," she told him. He was saying the words that she had wanted to hear, but she had to remind herself that it was only a pretend game, to keep death's sting at bay.

"If we get out of this alive, Valentina, you will marry me," he said again. With great difficulty, he sat up, moving to adjust her clothing. He did not want whoever found their bodies to see her with her skirt pulled up. The movement took every ounce of his strength.

Falling back against the hard wall of the cave, he spoke in a voice that was no more than a whisper. "Come into my arms, Valentina. I have not the strength to come to you."

304

Moving to his side, she swallowed a sob. Lying beside him, she pulled his head to rest against her shoulder. "My dearest love," she whispered, while tears of grief rolled down her cheeks. "Rest, my love. I will be beside you throughout all eternity."

"Yes," he said through trembling lips, his eyes blurring with tears. "If we are to die, let no man disturb our grave so we can be together until the end of time." Marquis thought of all the things he would have liked to have shown Valentina, the things he would have liked to have shared with her. They would never grow old together—they would remain eternally young together, lost in the space of time.

"Valentina, Silver Ey—"

Valentina felt Marquis go limp and knew he had lost consciousness. Never had there been such a silence— never had she felt so alone. In panic, she touched Marquis's lips and felt his faint breath against her hand. She closed her eyes and prayed that she would die before Marquis. She could never live in a world without him. Perhaps this had been her destiny all along, to die with Marquis. Was this what Salamar had tried to warn her against?

"My love, my only love," she cried through hysterical sobs, clutching his limp head to her heart. "I would never have been able to live with you as your wife—but I can die with you, as the woman you pretended to love!"

Chapter Twenty

Valentina felt a pressure on her chest, as if something heavy was crushing against her. Clawing at the air, she tried to rise, only to find she did not have the strength.

Slowly her eyes opened and she saw only darkness. A groan escaped her lips when she realized she had not been having a nightmare but was really trapped in a mine with the oxygen running out.

Reaching out in desperation, she felt Marquis's arm and was relieved to find he was still alive. With her last bit of strength, she dragged herself the short distance to lay in his arms. Valentina was cold and found comfort in the warmth of his body.

Valentina knew she and Marquis were slowly suffocating. She was somehow glad that Marquis was still unconscious, because he would not have to know the end was near. Thank God he would be spared that agony, she told herself.

From a distance, she could hear a faint noise, as if someone were chipping at stone. In a haze of pain, she wondered if help had come at last, or if her tortured mind was merely conjuring up a rescue attempt. Groping in the darkness, she found Marquis's hand and held it up to her lips.

"I . . . love you. . . ." she gasped with a last precious breath. "I . . . don't want you to die."

It hurt to breathe. Each breath she took felt like sand rubbed across her throat. Attempting to draw in a deep gulp of air, she felt her head swimming drunkenly. Slowly her head slumped to the side. The last sound she heard was that of picks chipping away at stone. In her hazy world, she believed she was only imagining that the sound of digging was growing louder.

Tyree leaned into the heavy boulder, pushing it out of the way. Grabbing up the lantern, he entered the small cavern, his eyes searching the shadows. Almost immediately his eyes fell on Valentina and Marquis, who were lying on the ground wrapped in each other's arms.

"I found them!" he cried to the half-dozen men who had helped him with the digging. He handed the lantern to one of the men and bent down to touch Valentina. Her body was still warm, but he could not detect any breathing.

"Carry her out of here quickly," Tyree told the man just behind him. Reaching across to Marquis, Tyree shuddered when he saw the blood-soaked rag on his leg. He felt Marquis's face and found it cold. Fearing Marquis might be dead, Tyree carefully lifted his limp body in his arms, taking every precaution to brace the injured leg. As he walked out into the sunshine, Tyree saw that Salamar was already bending over Valentina.

Tyree laid Marquis down beside Valentina and began working over him. Leaning forward, he placed his head against Marquis's chest, listening. Tense moments passed as he waited to hear a heartbeat. Faintly at first, then louder and stronger, he heard the sounds that brought joy to his heart. Marquis's heartbeat was steady, and a groan escaped his lips. Tyree told several of the men to carry Marquis into the cabin and make him comfortable.

As they lifted Marquis in their arms, Tyree quickly moved his eyes to Valentina. He watched in amazement as Salamar blew into Valentina's mouth while simultaneously pinching her nostrils together. "Is she all right?" he asked, moving to assist Salamar, fearing to hear the truth. To him, Valentina looked dead.

Sad, all-knowing eyes fastened on Tyree's. "Right now the breath of life has left her body." Salamar's eyes suddenly sparkled with the fire of determination. "I will not accept this death. I will breathe the breath of life back into Valentina."

Tyree felt tears in his eyes as he picked up Valentina's limp hand, lifted it to his lips, and placed a kiss on the palm. "I have never heard of anyone breathing life into a dead person, Salamar. It is medically impossible." He felt the hopelessness and heartache of acceptance. "I'm afraid we will both have to accept the fact that Valentina is . . . gone."

Salamar roughly shoved him aside. "You do not know everything, Tyree Garth," she declared. "You can accept what your eyes see, if you want, I have no time to waste on doubters. I *will* bring Valentina back to life!" Bending forward, Salamar again demonstrated her skills. With short puffs, she blew air into Valentina's mouth.

Tyree was tense, waiting for some sign of life, hoping Salamar knew some magic cure to save Valentina. Sitting down cross-legged, he lifted Valentina's head onto his lap and gently brushed the sand from her face. Salamar gave him a mystifying glance and again blew the breath of life into Valentina's lungs.

Distraught, Tyree raised his head to the heavens, speaking the first prayer he had uttered in years. Unashamed of the tears that fell down his face, he whispered softly, "God, I haven't talked to you in a long

309

time. I don't even know if I remember how. If you have the time—if you are listening—just let me ask you for one thing and I'll never trouble you again." The tears glistened on Tyree's face. "Please, God, let Valentina live . . . please give her back. I don't know if you are a betting man, but I would wager, if you give her life back . . . I'd build you the grandest church, on the highest hillside, overlooking the bay in San Francisco. You have my word on it. If you know anything about me, God, you know my word's good."

Tyree wiped his eyes and glanced down at Valentina. She was not breathing. Desperately he raised his face to the sun and closed his eyes.

"All right, God, you seem to demand more of me. I guess you're right. Valentina's life is worth more than one church. You drive a hard bargain, God, but I'll make a deal with you. If you let Valentina live and also throw in Marquis's life as well, I'll not only build you that church . . . I'll attend that church every Sunday—come hell or high water—for the rest of my life."

Bowing his head, Tyree clutched Valentina's still-limp hand. Glancing at Salamar, he saw tears in the woman's eyes. Again and again she breathed into Valentina's mouth. Precious moments were slipping away. There was no sign of life on Valentina's pale face.

Tyree clutched Valentina's cold hand in his, watching for any movement, any sign that she was breathing. Suddenly the small hand moved ever so slightly—so slightly that Tyree was sure he had only imagined it. Staring at the dainty fingers that rested in his hand, he watched with joy in his heart as they twitched. Catching Salamar's eyes, he saw the joy on her face.

"She lives," Salamar stated matter-of-factly. "Valentina breathes."

"Dear God," Tyree cried, clutching Valentina in his arms. "Thank you, God—thank you!" As an afterthought, he asked, "What about the child?"

"The child is unharmed," Salamar replied in her all-knowing way. "Valentina was not unconscious long enough to harm the child."

Valentina felt as if she were floating in oblivion. There was no light and no feeling. She was contented and strangely detached from everything. Suddenly bright lights and loud noises exploded in her head. A strong rush of air filled her lungs; the force of it jarred her eyes open. Wonderful, cool, refreshing air filled her starving lungs, creeping into her chest cavity. She took a deep, cleansing breath and then another.

Against the sunlight, Valentina saw the outline of several people, but they were faceless—vague shadows. Turning her head away from the bright light, she closed her eyes. She did not know if she was alive or dead. She only knew she was at peace. Sleep claimed her in its gentle arms—restful sleep, the sleep of healing.

Tyree had sent a man for the doctor at a nearby mining camp. When he had examined both Valentina and Marquis, he talked to Salamar and Tyree. He was sure that Valentina would recover completely, but he was concerned about Marquis's legs. Both had been badly crushed and the gash on the right one was infected. He refused to comment on whether or not he thought Marquis would ever walk again.

When evening fell, most of the men had gone back to San Francisco. Three remained behind to stand guard outside the cabin. Marquis and Valentina had been made comfortable on their bedrolls, while Tyree and Salamar sat before the fire, talking in low voices.

"You are truly an amazing woman, Salamar. When you first came to me with the crazy tale that you had seen Marquis and Valentina in a cave-in, I thought you had to

311

be out of your mind."

Salamar smiled brightly. "Yet you humored me. You gathered the men together and lost no time in getting here to the mine."

He flashed her a crooked smile. "You can be very persuasive. I can still see you telling me that if I didn't come up here with you, I would live in hell for the rest of my life. You convinced me that I would be saving Valentina and Marquis from death. How could I not come?"

Again Salamar smiled. "I have found that when all else fails, the best way to get my point across is by using dramatics."

He chuckled. "You did get your point across. I still don't know how you knew about the cave-in."

"There are some things that do not need explaining," she said, bending forward and placing more wood on the fire. "Some things one must take on faith."

Tyree watched Salamar's face closely. "I would like to know how you brought Valentina back to life. I know for a fact that she was dead."

Salamar's dark eyes seemed to look inwardly as she spoke. "I was born into a harem—in a faraway place—in another lifetime. While growing up in the palace, I learned many strange and wondrous things from many parts of the world. The breathing of life was taught to me by my father's concubine from Siam."

"Valentina was dead, wasn't she?" He was having a hard time dealing with the miracle he had witnessed. Tyree knew he would never be the same after today. His faith had been tested to the limit, his belief in God restored.

"Yes, Valentina was dead. But who of us can say if it was I who returned life to Valentina's body by the ancient healing . . . or you who brought her to life with your loving prayer to the one true God? I do not know

312

the answer to this. Perhaps I was merely the instrument God used to answer your prayer."

Tyree's eyes moved across the room to settle on the warm glow of health on Valentina's beautiful face. "You won't tell her what I did, will you?"

Salamar shook her head. "I will not tell her that your love reached out to her from the grave, bringing her back to life. You are a good man, Tyree Garth, but you know she will never belong to you. I am somehow unhappy about this."

He smiled sadly. "Have you seen into the future and know this for a fact?"

"I have seen this."

"I was only jesting, but I believe you really do have the sight." There was pain in his gentle eyes. "I will always love Valentina and want her happiness above all else."

Salamar nodded. "Valentina belongs to the man whose baby she carries. Her life will not know peace for a time. She must suffer still more before she finds the real meaning of happiness."

At that moment Valentina started mumbling and turned her head. Salamar quickly went to her and held her hand tightly. "My baby . . . please don't let my baby die," Valentina begged.

Salamar placed her hand on Valentina's abdomen. "All is well with your baby, Valentina. Sleep and grow stronger."

After that, Valentina seemed to settle into a peaceful sleep, so Salamar returned to the fire.

"Did Valentina tell you about the baby, Salamar?" Tyree asked.

"No, but she did not have to. I have known for a long time that she would not resist Marquis Vincente. She was destined to walk beside him in this new land."

Tyree had learned that Salamar often talked in riddles that he could not fully understand. She was strange and mysterious, performing deeds that most men would find hard to believe or accept. Tyree liked her a great deal. Although he was curious about her strange powers, he decided not to question her further. Some things were better left unknown, or left to chance.

"You have a church to build," Salamar reminded him with a mischievous glint in her eyes. "When will you lay the cornerstone?"

His laughter filled the room. "As quickly as possible. I can just see the clergy of San Francisco, not wanting to take tainted money to build a church."

"Nothing you touch will ever be tainted, Tyree Garth. You have a heart of gold, and the woman who taps that heart will be rich indeed."

His grin was wide, showing his flashing teeth. "What if I set my sights on you, Salamar?" he teased.

She giggled girlishly. "If I were twenty years younger, you would not get away from me, Tyree Garth. I would catch you in my web, and we would live happily ever after."

Both of them were caught up in happy laughter, until suddenly Tyree's mood became serious. "I am worried about Marquis's legs," he said grimly.

"It is very bad," Salamar agreed. "I pray that he will regain all his strength. He will need it in the days ahead."

"He doesn't even know Valentina is having his baby. I don't know how she will ever tell him of her other identity," Tyree said with a troubled frown on his face.

"It is not good to weave a web of lies. One can get tangled in them. Of course, in Valentina's case, she had no choice. She had to do what she could to earn money to buy food and medicine for her mother. Her mother would have died without the costly medicine."

Tyree leaned forward, picking up a burning twig from the hearth and applying it to the tip of his cigar. It had begun to rain and the droplets splattered and hissed down the chimney onto the burning embers.

Salamar was silently gazing into the flames, as if she saw that which no one else could see. Tyree lay on his bedroll, and soon he extinguished the cigar and fell into an exhausted sleep.

Marquis's eyes fluttered open. For a moment he was in a state of confusion as he tried to remember where he was. He was as weak as a babe, and found it took all his effort just to turn his head. Strange and frightening memories danced through his mind as his eyes adjusted and skirted across the room. How had he gotten back here to the cabin? he wondered. The last thing he remembered was being trapped . . .

As he tried to rise, pain nailed Marquis down. Striving to speak, he murmured painfully, "Valentina?" His voice rose higher as panic saturated his brain. "Valentina's dead!" he cried out in agony.

From out of nowhere, Tyree dropped down beside Marquis, smiling that crazy, crooked smile of his, bringing comfort and some substance of reality to Marquis's tortured mind.

Reaching out, Marquis grasped Tyree's shirt front. "Valentina?" he questioned in a strangled voice. "Is she dead?"

Tyree pulled the blanket about Marquis's shoulders and grinned reassuringly. "No, she is very much alive. Like yourself, she is going to recover. I consider you both damned fortunate to be alive at all."

"How did you find us?"

"It's a long story, which I'll tell you when you have the time."

"This is another one I owe you, Tyree." Their eyes met. "I owe you so much."

"Nonsense. Friendship doesn't mean owing. I hap-

315

pened to be in the right place at the right time."

Marquis's eyelashes lowered over his eyes, as if holding them open was too much effort. "Get me a priest, Tyree," Marquis demanded. "Have him here as quickly as possible."

Tyree laughed. "I said you and Valentina were going to be all right. Neither of you needs a priest to administer the last rites at this time. You will probably grow to be a very old man—fuming and hell raising."

"I want the priest to marry me and Valentina," Marquis said, wishing his throat did not hurt so badly. He was grateful when Tyree lifted his head and gave him a drink of water.

"I'll be damned," Tyree exclaimed at last. "You come into town and leave with the catch of the season. Don't think I'll ever let you forget you captured Valentina right from under my nose." Tyree felt pain in his heart, but he hid it well behind the face of a jester.

"My leg?" Marquis questioned, touching his right thigh. "It hurts like hell."

"Give it time to heal, my friend," Tyree assured him.

"How did you"—Marquis licked his dry lips—"how did you find us?"

"I had a lady with me who was better than any tracking dog you'll ever see."

"Salamar?" Marquis questioned.

"Yes, that's right."

"You are sure Valentina is well?"

"The doctor seems to think she weathered the ordeal better than you. He wants you to stay off that leg for a long time."

The shutters at the window had been thrown open and now admitted the cool evening breeze. Marquis could see the stars twinkling overhead. He had thought never to see the sky again. "I cannot stay off my leg, Tyree. I am to be wed tomorrow. I will stand on my feet to marry Valentina."

"I don't think so, Marquis. You will follow the doctor's orders. You may have to be wed from a horizontal position," Tyree declared crisply.

Tyree wondered if Valentina had told Marquis about the baby. Was that why he wanted to marry her so quickly? "How did you convince the lady to marry you? You aren't good enough for her, you know."

Marquis managed a tight smile. "She has not said yes . . . yet. I will have to use my fatal charm on her, will I not?"

Tyree shook his head while his eyes danced merrily. "You'd better not do that; you would only chase her away." A grin spread over his face. "Now, if you really want to sweep her off her feet, you'll let me do the asking for you. You would only end up telling the lady how lucky she is to get you."

Marquis laughed so hard it sent pain shooting through his leg. Catching his breath and gritting his teeth, he spoke. "Not a chance, thank you all the same, Tyree. I will do my own asking. I live or die on my own. I do not want you stealing the lady from under my nose."

Tyree was perplexed. Marquis had said nothing about the baby. Had Valentina admitted to Marquis that she was also Jordanna? He decided it was best to change the subject. "As soon as you feel stronger, I will take you to Paraíso del Norte. I have already sent word to your grandfather about the accident and asked him to send a wagon."

"Where is Valentina?" Marquis asked, scanning the room. He trusted Tyree to have spoken the truth when he said she was all right, but he just wanted to see her for himself.

"She is lying near the fireplace. See, she is there with

317

Salamar. Valentina is but resting," Tyree assured him.

Marquis was weary and his strength was waning fast. He urgently wanted to talk to Tyree about the baby Valentina was carrying. "I owe you an apology, Tyree," he said in a whisper. "At one point I thought you were the father of Valentina's baby, and I wanted to kill you for it."

A look of amazement passed over Tyree's face. "I don't understand how you could have drawn that conclusion, my friend." He paused and then asked, "You do not know who the father is?"

"Hell, no, but it does not really matter. I may never know, but I will marry Valentina anyway." Marquis glanced at Valentina. "Do you have any notion who the father is, Tyree?"

Tyree felt as if everyone but him was crazed. Nothing made any sense. "I may have some idea, but I am not at liberty to say." He glanced across the room to where Valentina lay sleeping. "I'll be damned. If I live to be a hundred, I'll never understand you, Marquis."

Tyree bent down and lowered his voice. "You won't marry the woman who is carrying your baby, but you'll offer to marry a woman you believe to be having another man's child! I would say you are more than a little confused. Are you sure you didn't suffer a blow to the head? Do you perchance have your priorities misplaced?"

He saw that Marquis's eyes had narrowed, and he knew that stubborn clamp of his jaw so well. "Who is the father, Tyree!" Marquis demanded. It wasn't a question. It was a command to know.

"We have often spoken of honor, Marquis. I am honor-bound not to say," he said cryptically. "You can understand honor, Marquis."

"I do not want to talk anymore, Tyree," Marquis whispered. Tyree had trapped him with his own words. "I need sleep." Marquis closed his eyes, dismissing everything from his mind.

Tyree rose to his feet and stared down at his friend. This thing was getting out of hand and turning into a real tangle. None of it made sense. Why had Valentina let Marquis believe another man had planted his seed in her? What in hell had happened in the mine?

Moving across the room as quietly as possible, Tyree walked outside and stood staring up at the night sky.

"It would be so simple if people would just communicate with each other. Life in general is one damn big joke after another," he said to no one in particular. "And not a very funny joke at that. Most of the time the joke's on me."

Chapter Twenty-One

Valentina awoke feeling slightly disoriented. She heard a soft noise and found Salamar seated beside her. Valentina weakly reached out her hand, but before she could speak, Salamar raised a cup of water to her lips. The cool liquid soothed the burning in her throat, easing some of the pain.

"How . . . did . . ." Valentina's mouth was dry and it hurt to breathe. "Marquis?" Her painful whisper was a plea to know the fate of the man she loved.

"Marquis is well," Salamar replied. "He has also been asking about you."

"You wouldn't keep anything from me, would you, Salamar? If Marquis were . . . dead, you would tell me, wouldn't you?"

"You have my word he is alive." Valentina had to be assured over and over that Marquis was alive. "He was moved to a tent so you could have the privacy of the cabin," Salamar told Valentina.

Valentina pressed her hands across her brow, wishing the pounding ache in her head would go away. "I cannot seem to remember much of what happened. I vaguely recall the sounds of digging. I know nothing about being rescued."

"That is not surprising since you were unconscious the whole time. You and Marquis had been trapped in the mine for two days when we found you. Since the rescue, you have slept for two more days."

It was hard for her to grasp the fact that the cave-in had occurred four days before. Her hand reached out for Salamar's, for she needed the comfort only she could offer. There were many things that demanded her attention—many questions that plagued her—but now, she needed sleep. . . .

Salamar lifted the heavy bucket and poured water into a pan. Picking up the pan, she moved over to where Valentina lay and seated herself beside her. First she washed the grime from Valentina's face and hands. Later, she began brushing the tangles from Valentina's hair.

"Salamar, who is staying with Mother?" Valentina wanted to know.

The maid smiled slightly. "Tyree asked Maggie Payne from the Crystal Palace to take care of her. I left instructions about the medicine, and the woman seemed very capable."

"Are you sure Maggie will take good care of Mother?" Valentina had never spoken to the plump woman who spun the roulette wheel and served drinks, but she remembered her as always happy and laughing. "Will Mother not think it strange that she is left alone with someone she does not know?"

"Your mother seemed to accept Maggie very well. Maggie was eager to help."

"I hope Mother doesn't discover what occupation Maggie pursues. She would never understand."

"I cautioned Maggie not to talk too much. She seemed a sensible woman." Salamar glanced away from Valentina. "I told your mother that you and I were looking for your father, which, in a way, is true. She did not question me more."

Valentina's eyes glistened with tears. "I don't know where to look for my father. It will be difficult to tell Mother that I have no clue to Father's disappearance. We found Sam Udell dead in the mine. I have no hope left."

Salamar brushed Valentina's hair away from her face and tied it with a yellow ribbon. "We are never without hope, Valentina. As long as there is life, there is reason to hope."

Valentina smiled sadly. "Of course you are right. How soon can we go home?"

Salamar avoided her eyes. "I do not know that you will be going home—at least not to San Francisco."

"I don't know what you mean. I am going with you. Why should you think otherwise?"

Salamar dropped the hairbrush in a satin bag before turning her eyes to Valentina. "I have something to say to you and I want you to listen carefully. Listen with your head and not your heart. Think of the baby you carry and not yourself."

Valentina's hand moved up to her abdomen. She dropped her eyes, feeling too ashamed to look at Salamar. "How did you know about the baby?"

"That is not important. The important thing is that the baby have a father."

Slowly raising her head, Valentina met Salamar's eyes, finding no condemnation in the dark depths. Always the realist, Salamar spoke her mind. "At times, when you were asleep, you would cry out for your unborn child. I believe you feared it might have been injured by your ordeal."

"Do you think the child is all right?" Valentina looked for hope in Salamar's eyes.

"I do not know. Time will answer that question." Seeing the concern written on Valentina's face, Salamar quickly added, "Since the child has survived this long, the chances are good it was not harmed."

Valentina plucked at a raveled edge on the blanket. "I don't know what to do. If Mother finds out about the baby, it will kill her for sure. I feel remorse for being so weak and stupid—I have managed to further complicate my already complicated life."

"It was never weakness, nor stupidity, that drove you into Marquis Vincente's arms. You have loved him for a long time. I knew if he continued to press you, he would tear down your resistance. Now you must think not of yourself, or of Marquis, but of the child and your mother."

Valentina felt her body tremble. "Marquis asked me to marry him when he thought we were going to die in the mine. I have doubts he will feel the same way now that we have been rescued."

Salamar tilted up Valentina's chin and stared into her silver-blue eyes. She read uncertainty and heartache there. "Marquis is determined to marry you. He sent for a priest and has been waiting for you to awaken."

Valentina pressed shaky hands over her face. "What am I going to do, Salamar? Marquis doesn't know this is his baby. Why is he doing this? I don't want his charity— I will not marry him under these circumstances."

"I told you earlier to think with your head—you are not doing that, Valentina. You know Marquis is the father of this child. Confess the truth to him. Tell him about Jordanna. Then, if he still wants to marry you, you will have been honest with him."

"I tried to confess," Valentina said, shaking her head. "He completely misunderstood me. He believes my baby was fathered by someone else."

"Perhaps you should try again . . . or give him a little more time," Salamar wisely responded.

"I haven't got time," Valentina reminded her. "As you

324

said, I have to make plans for the baby. At the moment I don't know what to do."

"Tyree Garth would be willing to be your husband and the baby's father," Salamar suggested, observing Valentina's reaction to her words.

"No. I confess I am sorely tempted to take Tyree's offer, but I like him too much to ruin his life. He deserves much better than raising another man's child. Besides, he is Marquis's best friend. How would he feel being the father of his friend's child. No, I can't do that to him."

"You have to decide quickly what you are going to do. I must get back to your mother before too long," Salamar said, helping Valentina to stand and proceeding to fold the bedding. "Marquis wanted to see you as soon as you were able."

"I am not going to see him," Valentina replied, thinking that if she and Salamar left right away she could avoid making a decision about her future. Valentina was a proud woman, and now that she knew Marquis was going to live, she remembered the unpleasant remarks he had made concerning the baby. How dare he offer her marriage, believing she carried another man's child? Her chin jutted out and that obstinate gleam that Salamar knew so well was reflected in her eyes.

"No, I will not go to Marquis on his command. I will not beg for his attention. I do not need his name or his charity for my baby. I didn't go to him as Jordanna. I most certainly won't go to him as myself."

Salamar shrugged her shoulders. She knew only too well the hurt to her pride Valentina had suffered. She also knew that Valentina had been forced to carry heavy burdens on her small shoulders. She had been strong, and Salamar was proud of her. Now was the time for Valentina to lean on Marquis. He would help her with the burden of the child.

"Marquis cannot come to you, Valentina. He cannot

325

walk because of his leg injuries. The doctor does not know at this point if he will ever walk again."

Valentina's face paled, and she shook her head in disbelief. "Dear God, no," she whispered, unable to bear the thought of Marquis, so vitally alive, being crippled. Tears wet her cheeks and she cried out, "It's all my fault. He wouldn't be hurt if it weren't for me."

"All rests in the hands of God. No man can be so prideful as to think he can turn the future away from God's plan. This is no one's fault."

Valentina leaned her head against the rough cabin wall, feeling it would take very little to push her over the brink of total mental exhaustion. "I don't care what you say, Salamar. I will always feel responsible for Marquis's being hurt."

"What do you propose to do about it?"

She turned to face Salamar. "I don't know."

The look of despair in Valentina's eyes reminded Salamar of times when Valentina had been a child and had sought guidance or needed advice. "I think you know what you have to do. It does not matter now if Marquis thinks the child you carry belongs to another man. All that matters is that you give this daughter a name—her real father's name. Later, after Marquis has healed in body and spirit, you can tell him the truth about the baby."

An incredulous spark reflected in Valentina's eyes. "You said daughter! Do you know this for a fact?"

Salamar nodded. "I had not meant to tell you this, knowing that it might upset you. I dreamed of the daughter that would come from you and Marquis. I saw her not as a child, but as she will one day be. She will be the one to return to England and settle an old dispute over Morgan's Folly."

Valentina whirled away from Salamar. "I don't like it when you do that. I don't want to think of this baby as a person right now," she shouted. "Just once, I'd like to do what I want to do and not what others expect of me."

Valentina was crying hysterically, and Salamar knew she had reached the breaking point. There were too many demands being made on her, too many people depending on her and draining her strength.

Moving across the room, Salamar enfolded Valentina in her arms. Cooing to her as if she were a child, she allowed her to cry until her tears were spent.

"I'm sorry, Salamar. You must think I am selfish and unfeeling. I can be a real trial at times, can't I?" Valentina said, smiling through her tears. "Forgive me?"

"There is nothing to forgive. You are never a trial to me, Valentina," Salamar stated loyally. "If it is your wish, we will return to San Francisco today. No one will force you to do anything you do not want to do."

Valentina drew in a long, deep breath and let it out slowly. "I will go to Marquis. I will swallow my pride and take what he offers. It is the only way to protect the child from being shunned and my mother from shame."

"Will you tell Marquis the child belongs to him?"

"Yes. I want there to be no more lies between us."

As Valentina moved across the room and out the door, a smile tugged at Salamar's mouth. "Life is going to be exciting from here on out," she said aloud to herself. "A new beginning in the golden land of California. A new generation will be born with proud Vincente blood flowing through its veins—a new generation with the stamina and endurance that Valentina will pass on to her children." Acting totally out of character, Salamar clapped her hands and chuckled delightedly. She hoped she would be around to watch Valentina and Marquis's children blossom and grow.

The sweltering noonday heat seemed to radiate

through the tent in which Marquis lay on a soft mattress. A splint held his right leg in place, while the other was bandaged from calf to knee, yet nothing seemed to alleviate the agonizing pain that ripped through his thigh.

He was not taking well to languishing on a sickbed, waiting for Valentina to awaken and come to him. Tyree had tried to convince him that home was the best place for him, but Marquis stubbornly refused to be moved until Valentina came to him. He had the priest waiting at a nearby mission, ready to perform the ceremony should Valentina agree to wed him. Not that Marquis would accept her refusal. Hell, if he had to, he would force her into marriage, he silently swore.

Fleetingly, Marquis wondered about himself. Why had he tried to block out Jordanna's baby, only to insist on marrying Valentina. Never had his Spanish heritage felt so binding to him; never had he been pulled in so many directions. His conscience was so heavy!

He would take care of Jordanna and his child. In time he might even seek custody of it, but he would not ever give up Valentina. He wanted her as his wife. He needed her so desperately.

The tent flap was thrown aside and Tyree stooped to enter. Seeing that his friend was awake, he dropped down on a stool, stretching his long legs out in front of him. "Your grandfather sent word that he wants you home today. He wants the family doctor to tend your injuries."

"I will not go until I can take Valentina home with me as my bride." A light flickered in the depths of Marquis's dark eyes. "Only then will I go home."

"What if she won't have you?"

"She will have me."

Tyree chuckled. "You are very sure of yourself, my friend. I wouldn't be planning the future just yet if I were you. Ole gentleman, Fate has a way of tossing rocks on our paths. Just when we think our lives are all neat and orderly, we find another obstacle."

"I can deal with whatever Fate throws at me," Marquis stated with an assurance he was far from feeling. "What I cannot deal with is lying here doing nothing."

Neither of them heard the soft footsteps outside the tent. Tyree smiled when he heard Valentina call out in a small voice. "Marquis, may I enter?"

"Here's your chance to test Fate," Tyree stated, rising to his full height and moving across the tent. "I'll let her in on my way out." Giving Marquis a quick smile, he added. "Good luck, my friend. I sincerely hope she'll have you."

As Tyree swept out of the tent, he greeted Valentina with a long, searching look. "You don't look any worse from your ordeal. Are you feeling well?"

"Yes, thank you. Salamar tells me I have you to thank for the rescue. I stand in your debt once again."

He shrugged off her gratitude and nodded toward the tent. "You had better go in. He's chomping at the bit to see you."

Valentina lowered her voice so it would not reach the inside of the tent. "How is he, Tyree?"

"Mending. We still don't know about his legs. Even though he tries to hide it, I believe they give him a great deal of pain." Pulling the tent flap aside, he smiled. "Go in. He's waiting for you."

Valentina gathered up her courage and raised her head, feeling as if she were Daniel walking into the lion's den. The heat in the tent was oppressive, but it was the heat of Marquis's glance that sent shivers down Valentina's spine. His eyes were so intense she had to lower hers.

"Do you know I have waited all day for you?" he stated sourly.

She seated herself on the stool Tyree had just vacated.

"How are you feeling? Do your legs pain you much?" she asked, concern written all over her beautiful face. He was dressed in dark blue, tight-fitting trousers, the legs of which had been slit to accommodate the splint and bandages. She wanted to reach out and soothe away the pain she saw on his face.

"Do you recall that I asked you to marry me while we were trapped in the mine?" Marquis had gotten right to the point. He was impatient and in no mood to play games. She was unaware of the yearning that caused Marquis's heart to beat wildly. She did not see the fear, the uncertainty, in his dark eyes.

Valentina managed to smile tightly. "I will not hold you to any proposal I extracted from you under duress."

He waved her stab at humor aside. "I am waiting for your answer." His voice was clipped and he sounded as if he had just issued a command.

"I told you I won't hold you to—"

"Your answer," he demanded as his eyes collided with hers. "What is your answer?"

Valentina could not know that his insides were drawn up into a tight knot as he tensely waited for her to reply. Fear gnawed at his insides, for he believed she might laugh at his offer of marriage. He had spoken brave words to Tyree when he had said he would never take Valentina's no for an answer. He realized with a sinking heart that if she refused him there would be no way he could force her to reconsider.

Valentina dropped her eyes from his probing gaze. "Tell me the reason you are doing this. Are you just being kind?" She waited for his answer, hoping against hope that he would say he loved her. She wanted to hear him say his life would not be complete without her. If he said he loved her, she would tell him about his baby.

Marquis was thoughtful for a moment as he pondered how to answer Valentina. To confess his love would leave

330

him open to hurt and rejection. He already knew she loved another man. He was nothing if not a prideful man, and so he said instead, "I have been thinking for some months now—actually since the Americans took over California—that the time may come when the gringos might not honor the land grant handed down to my family by a Spanish king many years ago. I believe if I were to marry into your race, Paraíso del Norte would be safe for the generations to come."

Valentina felt her hopes dashed into nothingness. Proudly holding her head high, she replied, "I cannot help you in this. You would do well to look elsewhere for the salvation of Paraíso del Norte. As you very well know, I am not American—I'm English."

He watched her face closely. "It amounts to the same thing. You are of the same race. Marry me and we will both gain from the endeavor. I will gain assurance that my land will be in my family for future generations; you will have a name for your baby."

Valentina met his eyes, trying to make some sense out of what he was saying. "You have a poor reason for wanting me as your wife, Marquis. I do not believe that you fear the Americans will eventually take your land. What is the real reason you want me to marry you?"

He hesitated, wondering if he should confess his feelings for her. Never one to speak rashly, he weighed his words carefully. "I would be less than honest with you if I did not admit to being drawn to you. You have known for some time that I have feelings for you. I admitted as much while we were trapped in the mine. I find the thought of having a beautiful, silver-eyed wife very appealing. I believe I would like to awaken each day and find you seated across the breakfast table from me."

Valentina blushed, remembering Marquis's bold caresses while they had been trapped in the cave. The look he gave her proved he was remembering too.

Quickly she looked away from him. "What about my baby?" she asked boldly.

His eyes never wavered. "The child will have my name. But there is one point I must stress to you, so there will be no misunderstanding later. Should you bear a son, he could never inherit Paraíso del Norte."

"What do you mean?" she asked, feeling an ache deep inside.

"Only a son that is fathered by me will inherit my land. I want this understood right now."

Valentina remembered Salamar's telling her that she would have a daughter. She wondered what Marquis's reaction would be if she were to tell him he had fathered her baby. He had admitted that he was drawn to her, but was that the true reason he wanted to marry her? So many questions nagged at her, and she needed some answers.

"Will you marry me, Valentina?" he asked softly.

"I . . . don't understand why you would want me and my baby. The only reasons you have given me, thus far, are not very convincing."

Marquis frowned slightly, wondering how he could persuade Valentina to marry him without revealing his love for her. "Let us say that my planned marriage to Isabel ended abruptly, leaving me with no suitable bride. My grandfather is getting no younger and would see me married. You will grace my table and make an admirable wife to show off to my friends and neighbors."

Valentina felt the sting of his words like the twisting of a knife in her heart. Had he been in love with Isabel, and had she refused to marry him? Was he asking her to marry him so he could save face before his friends?

Pushing her hurt aside, she asked the most obvious question. "Have you thought how your friends will react when I deliver a child two months earlier than the accepted nine-month period?"

"That will be no problem. My doctor is a good friend. He will swear the baby was born prematurely. Even if some friends do not believe the lie, they will only think I loved you so much I could not wait to be married to you before I bedded you."

Suddenly the truth hit Valentina full force. She wondered why it had taken her so long to see it. "You want everyone to think that you and I . . . that we . . . that this baby is yours, and it was conceived before we were married. You were shamed when Isabel refused to marry you, and you want everyone to think that you were already . . . that you—"

"That I was in love with you all along," he finished for her. "Yes, that would save face, would it not?" His eyes sparkled as he smiled at her. "What do you say? Do we seal a bargain that will be beneficial to us both?"

Valentina tried to think of a hundred reasons to say no. Point by point, arguments against marrying Marquis started clicking off in Valentina's mind. He would probably trample on her heart, for she loved him so much and he did not love her at all. They came from different worlds, worlds that were far apart in language and customs. At one time Spain and England had warred over those differences. Marquis believed she loved another man, and she believed he still loved Isabel. He was arrogant, haughty, prideful, and demanding. How could she marry this man?

Marquis watched the different emotions playing across her face. He knew she was weighing her decision carefully. "Tell me, Valentina, do you hesitate because I may become a cripple? If so, you are wise to think on this. I do not imagine it would be too pleasant being married to a cripple."

Valentina shook her head and looked into his eyes. She wanted to go down on her knees and gather him to her. She wanted to assure him that she would love him even if he were to lose both legs. "It is my fault that you were injured, Marquis," she admitted through trembling lips. "I would never turn you away because you suffered from my stubbornness. How can you think I would be so heartless?"

He smiled and reached for her hand. "It would seem we have cleared away all your objections, does it not? Say you will become my wife, Valentina?" Slowly she gave him her hand and felt his grip tighten about her fingers. "Do we make a pact, Valentina?"

". . . You may regret it later."

"Nothing is certain in this life. I believe we are well suited to each other. Say . . . yes," he whispered, causing an ache deep inside of Valentina.

She closed her eyes for just a moment. There were many reasons she should say no, but her heart cried out for her to accept him on any terms. Opening her eyes, she found him staring intently at her. ". . . Yes, I will marry you."

Joy leapt into Marquis's eyes, and his heart soared like a bird on wing before his lashes half covered those glorious dark eyes and he was able to hide his jubilance behind a mask of casual indifference. "Good. I was sure you would be sensible. Go and prepare yourself for travel. I have plans to make."

Valentina was stunned. She had just agreed to marry Marquis. He had accepted her answer with as little enthusiasm as if she had agreed to bring him a drink of water. Should he not at the very least have said something about being happy that she had accepted his proposal? Did he have to say she was being *sensible?* When was he going to take her in his arms and kiss her?

Standing up, she hid her disappointment. "When would you want the wedding to take place, Marquis?"

"We will be married today. There is a small mission

that lies between here and Paraíso del Norte. We will be married there."

"I cannot marry you this soon. I have to get home to my mother. She will have to be told that I could find nothing about my father."

"I will send Salamar and six of my vaqueros to transport your mother to Paraíso del Norte. They will be advised to take the greatest care of her health."

"It seems that you have everything planned, with one exception. What will your family think of our marriage? I cannot believe that they will agree wholeheartedly."

"My sister will be delighted. My grandfather will think I am most fortunate, and my mother will accept you in the course of time. Now go and send Tyree to me."

Valentina took a hesitant step toward the exit, wishing she dared ask if he was happy that she would be his wife. Raising her head and squaring her shoulders, she moved through the opening into the bright sunlight. The sky was its usual brilliant blue, and the same sun shed its light down on the golden land. Everything was the same, except Valentina. She had committed herself to a life of torment. She would be married to the man she loved, but he would never love her. How could she compete with the love he had for the beautiful fiery-tempered Isabel?

Seeing Salamar standing in front of the cabin, Valentina hastened toward her. Salamar would give her the comfort she needed. She would give her the assurance that Marquis had failed to offer.

Marquis gritted his teeth, feeling pain as if it were a red-hot poker being jabbed into his legs. It had taken considerable effort to hide his agony from Valentina. He had never wanted her pity, although he suspected that was why she had agreed to marry him. He had used her

335

guilty feelings—played on her sympathy—to gain her hand in marriage. But it mattered little what her reasons were for marrying him. He felt no qualms about capitalizing on her guilt.

Marquis had to have Valentina, and soon she would be his. No one—not even the man who had fathered her child—could take her away from him now.

Chapter Twenty-Two

In spite of the agonizing pain, Marquis refused to ride in the back of the wagon his grandfather had sent to transport him home. He insisted on riding his own horse, even though each step the animal took made him feel as if nettles were stabbing into his legs and back.

Still in command of the situation, he had sent six of his vaqueros with Salamar to make arrangements for transporting Valentina's mother to Paraíso del Norte. One of his men had gone ahead to inform his grandfather that he would be bringing Valentina Barrett home as his bride.

Valentina rode between Marquis and Tyree, staring straight ahead. Now that the heat of the moment had subsided, she was having second thoughts about her hasty decision to marry Marquis. What did she really know about him, aside from the fact that she loved him? She knew nothing about his customs and everyday life. What duties would she be expected to perform as the wife of a Vincente? She hoped he would treat her differently after they were married. Thus far, he had all but ignored her.

Tyree could feel her uneasiness and drew her into conversation. "I haven't had the chance to wish you well, Valentina. Marquis already knows how I feel, but I want you to know that I wish you both every happiness. You are two of my best friends, and I will glory in your happiness."

She smiled over at him. "I hope you know that I will always be your friend, Tyree. You have proven time and time again that you are mine."

Marquis's leg was throbbing, and he was in no mood to watch Valentina flirt with Tyree. "I thought we agreed you would ride ahead and tell the priest that we are on our way, Tyree," Marquis said sourly.

Tyree's lusty laugh caught Valentina's ear, and he cast Marquis an all-knowing glance, having realized his friend was jealous. He spurred his horse forward, wondering if Valentina knew how possessive her future husband was going to be. "I'll see you in church," he called back over his shoulder, and soon he was lost in a cloud of dust.

Without Tyree's comforting presence, silence and gloom hung heavily over the wedding couple. Looking across at Marquis, Valentina saw the beads of perspiration on his brow and the whiteness around his mouth.

"Are you in pain?" she asked quickly. "You shouldn't be riding so great a distance on horseback. Would it not be better for you to ride in the—"

He cast her a glance that froze her next words into silence. "I am in a better position to judge what I should and should not do. I am not like your puny Englishmen, who cannot endure a little discomfort."

Valentina choked back her hurt and her angry reply. She wished that Salamar could have stayed with her until after the wedding. Even though she was surrounded by more than a dozen vaqueros, she felt alone and deserted. Training her eyes on the landscape, she tried not to look at Marquis. If he was going to be rude to her just because she was concerned about his well-being, he could just suffer for all she cared. Her eyes misted at the thought of him being in pain. God help her, where was this all going to end?

Marquis knew he had hurt Valentina and that was the last thing he had wanted to do. He wanted to take care of her—to cherish her as she deserved to be cherished. But this was made impossible because of the weakness brought on by his injury and his bitter feelings about the child she carried. He would have liked to have forgotten about the child, but it stood between them like a wall of stone. He hoped that as time passed he would accept the child as his own. Yet Marquis dreaded the time to come when Valentina's stomach would swell from the baby.

Today was his wedding day. Already, in the distance, Marquis could hear the mission bells pealing in his honor. As his eyes skipped across Valentina's golden hair, which had come loose from the ribbon and was blowing freely in the soft wind, his heart overflowed with love. How beautiful she was—almost too beautiful. She was wearing the same riding habit she had worn in the cave-in. Salamar must have cleaned it because, even though it was tattered and torn, no dust or soil remained.

Marquis felt guilty for the way he had been treating Valentina. She was a bride today, and yet he had done nothing to make this day special for her. Holding up his hand for everyone to halt, he instructed one of his vaqueros to pick a bouquet of wildflowers from those growing beside the roadway.

The small meadow was dotted with golden flowers, and their aroma sweetly danced on the wind. The vaquero gathered an armload of the blossoms and approached Valentina, smiling broadly, honored that he had been chosen to pick the flowers for his *patrón's* lady. Doffing his wide-brimmed *sombrero*, the man held out the brightly colored flowers to her.

"Your wedding bouquet, Valentina," Marquis said softly, losing himself for the moment in the shimmering depths of her silver eyes.

Lowering her head, Valentina breathed in the strangely sweet aroma. "These are lovely. What are they called?" she asked.

"We Spaniards call them *'copas de oro'*—cups of gold. There is a legend that says these flowers grow nowhere but in California."

Valentina smiled up into his dark eyes. "This is a most appropriate bouquet for my wedding then, Marquis. I will become a Californian by marriage."

Marquis felt warmth in his heart as the blood went throbbing through his body. He wanted to take Valentina in his arms and wipe away the doubts he saw on her face. Instead, he moved forward in the saddle and gave the signal for them to proceed.

Clutching the sweet-scented flowers, Valentina turned her head to hide the tears that fell on the petals. She remembered that it had been Marquis's style to give a single rose. She wished with all her heart that she could turn back the sands of time to when Marquis had teased her and offered her his friendship. At least then he had respected her and called her Silver Eyes.

They rode on in silence, each lost in his own thought, both painfully aware that this was not the wedding day they had envisioned.

As the wedding party topped a hill, Valentina saw the green valley below. Nestled in a grove of oak trees was a small, insignificant-looking mission, its crumbling adobe walls in need of repair, its bells beckoning Marquis and Valentina to the welcome they would find there. As they drew near, the bells fell silent and a small, white-haired *padre* wearing a plain brown robe and crude leather sandals came rushing out to them.

While Tyree came forward and helped Valentina from her mount, two vaqueros assisted Marquis from his horse. When Marquis was placed on his feet, he felt the world tilt and stabbing pain left him breathless. Pride was pushed aside as he gripped the vaquero who stood nearby.

"José, you and Enrique carry me up the steps," he ground out, hoping he could make it through the ceremony standing on his own two feet.

Valentina rushed to his side and took his hand. "Marquis, you are in a great deal of pain. The wedding can wait until another day."

"It will take place now," he managed to say. "Everything is in readiness."

Valentina watched helplessly as he turned away from her to lean heavily on Enrique's shoulder.

The *padre* walked behind Marquis, assuring him how honored the mission was to have been chosen as the site for a Vincente wedding. He blessed the day, he blessed the wedding party, he blessed Providence for having sent him the grandson of Don Alonso Vincente.

Tyree took Valentina's arm and led her up the steps, giving her a reassuring smile. When they entered the mission, they were greeted with welcome coolness provided by the thick walls. A musty odor proclaimed the adobe structure to be very old. The walls, which had been painted with scenes from the book of Genesis, were chipped and peeling. Valentina could not help but be saddened that the art work of another time was being lost from either neglect or lack of money for repairs.

"Smile. You don't look like a bride is supposed to," Tyree gently warned.

Valentina stared down at the crumpled wildflowers clutched in her hand. "I don't feel like a bride. I fear I am making a terrible mistake, Tyree. I have the strangest urge to leap on a horse and ride for my life."

Tyree looked deeply into her eyes. "Do you love Marquis?"

"Yes. That seems to be the one thing that hasn't

341

changed. At least I think it's love."

"Marry him then, Valentina. Put your doubts aside and smile. I am about to have the great honor of giving you away to my best friend."

Valentina felt overwhelming pity as she watched the two men helping Marquis to walk. Although his back was to her, she could tell he was in pain. She could only imagine what that walk down the aisle was costing him. "He is a strange, stubborn man, Tyree. I don't really know him at all."

"He is a man who is bound by honor and tradition. He has a great capacity for loving and giving. I believe you will bring out his best qualities. Give him time, Valentina."

By now they had drawn even with Marquis, and Valentina had no time to reply. One of the men still stood beside Marquis, and he leaned heavily on him. When Tyree handed Valentina over to Marquis, she felt his warm grasp and knew he was feverish. She felt frantic, knowing Marquis was ill and needed to be in bed.

Marquis drew her closer to him and, for the first time, smiled at her. "You cannot get away from me now, Valentina," he whispered next to her ear. "I will never let you go."

The *padre* had opened his tattered black Bible and began to recite the wedding rites. At one point Valentina felt Marquis sway and her hand tightened on his. Tyree, seeing that Marquis was weakening, moved forward and stood behind to brace him.

When the *padre* asked if Marquis would take Valentina as his wife, Marquis could do no more than nod his head. Valentina was so concerned for Marquis that she hardly remembered replying to the *padre's* words. There, in the quaint old mission, with the blessing of the kind little *padre,* Valentina became the wife of Marquis Domingo Vincente.

At the precise moment that they were pronounced husband and wife, Marquis collapsed. If Tyree and Enrique had not grabbed him, he would have fallen. Tyree lifted his unconscious friend in his arms and told Enrique to run ahead and make the wagon ready.

Valentina cried out when she saw how pale Marquis was. Leaving a startled *padre* to wonder what was happening, she dashed down the aisle and outside. Climbing into the wagon, she helped Enrique arrange the feather mattress so there would be no lumps. When Tyree gently placed Marquis in the wagon, Valentina took his head in her lap and tucked a blanket about him. She softly pushed the dark hair, wet from perspiration, from his forehead.

"Is he going to live, Tyree?" she asked frantically. "He is just weak from the journey, isn't he?" she questioned, needing assurance.

The *padre* was saying a prayer for Marquis's recovery, as well as bestowing a blessing on the newlyweds. Valentina could only imagine what the little man would be thinking about the strange wedding he had just performed.

Her eyes sought Tyree's. "Marquis is a strong man. It will take more than a little accident to lay him low," Tyree told her. "He needs a few weeks—perhaps a couple of months—to heal properly." Tyree knew he was telling Valentina what she needed to hear. Nothing would be gained if he told her of his own fears. If the infection was not cured, Marquis could lose his legs, or even his life.

Valentina grabbed Tyree's hand as she searched his face. "Have I done the right thing, Tyree? Will Marquis forgive me when he learns that I have tricked him?"

"I don't know, Valentina, but you will have to tell him sometime."

He shifted his eyes, feeling guilty for having gone against Valentina's wishes and telling Marquis that

343

Jordanna was having his baby. He decided to warn Valentina about what Marquis's reaction toward the baby had been. "Valentina, bide your time and choose the right moment to tell Marquis that you are Jordanna."

"Why?" she questioned, looking down at her new husband.

Tyree had trouble meeting her gaze. "Because I told him that Jordanna was having his baby."

Her face whitened. "You didn't . . . he doesn't know that—"

"No, he does not know that you are Jordanna."

"What was his reaction when you told him, Tyree?"

This time he met her gaze squarely. "I won't lie to you, Valentina. He wanted me to give money to Jordanna to take care of her and the baby. He suggested she might move away from San Francisco."

Her silver-blue eyes darkened with pain. "I see," she said in a dull voice. "I see, but I don't understand. Why would Marquis turn his back on Jordanna and offer me marriage?"

"I believe you know the answer to that, Valentina."

Her eyes burned as she glanced down at Marquis. "Yes, I do understand. He is Marquis Vincente, Spanish blue blood; therefore, Jordanna was not good enough for him."

"Knowing that, handle the situation with care, Valentina. Tell Marquis the truth, but choose the time wisely," he warned. Turning to Enrique, Tyree told him to drive the wagon slowly and to avoid bumps whenever possible. Reaching out and grasping Valentina's hand, he smiled at her softly. "I will remain behind and settle everything with the *padre*."

"Aren't you coming with us?" Valentina asked with panic rising in her voice.

"No, you don't need me any longer. You are only a few hours from Paraíso del Norte. You will be there shortly

344

after dark. Don Alonso has the doctor waiting." Stepping back, Tyree waved the wagon forward. As they moved away from the mission, Valentina felt as if a door had just slammed shut on her past life. She was going into a frightening new world with no friend or family member to stand beside her.

As the mission faded in the distance, Valentina glanced down at the face of her husband. He was so pale and haggard looking. Closing her eyes, she gripped his hand, praying for his recovery. She willed her strength to pass from her body to his. She could not lose Marquis to death. He was a part of her. She carried the proof in the baby he had fathered.

Placing a cool hand on Marquis's forehead, Valentina found it much hotter than before. She yelled for the driver to stop, realizing she had to get Marquis's fever down. Once the wagon came to a halt, she spoke to Enrique in Spanish.

"I want a cloth and cool water. Your *patrón* is burning up with fever."

The vaquero lost no time in obeying her order. Several grim-faced men gathered about the wagon as Valentina washed Marquis's face from the canteen Enrique held for her.

"Should we stop and make camp for the night, Señora Vincente?" Enrique asked, concern on his wrinkled face.

It was the first time Valentina had thought of herself as a Vincente. Since Marquis was unconscious, it was natural the vaqueros would look to her for guidance. "No, we must go on. He needs a doctor. How much farther is it?"

"At the slow pace we are going, about three hours," one of the men answered.

"Let us get started then," Valentina said, trying to remain calm. "One of you ride ahead and inform Don Alonso that his grandson is gravely ill. Tell him we will be

345

there as soon as we can. We dare not drive the wagon very fast, for fear it might further harm your *patrón's* legs."

Slowly the wagon moved forward as the sound of hoof beats faded in the distance. Valentina kept her vigil, wetting the rag and applying it to Marquis's forehead. Her legs were cramped and she was stiff and sore, but she did not feel the discomfort. All that mattered was that they get Marquis home as quickly as possible.

Once in a while, she would place her hand on his chest to make sure he was still breathing. Looking at his right leg, she saw that blood was seeping through the bandages, staining them bright red. There was no time to stop and reapply bandages. Even if there had been time, Valentina would have been hesitant to remove the splint, fearing she could not redress the wound as well as the doctor had.

The sun had gone down, and a bright moon was riding high in the sky. After what seemed an eternity, Valentina saw lights in the distance. When the wagon drew nearer, she could see the Vincente house lit up like one of the lighthouses of Cornwall sending its beacon out to a floundering ship. Feeling Marquis's pulse, Valentina found it to be very faint.

"Hurry, Enrique, drive faster," she urged fearfully. Never had she felt so helpless. The man she loved was dying in her arms and there was nothing she could do to save him. Was it possible that she would become a wife and a widow in the space of one day? No, she would not allow Marquis to die. He was her husband—the father of her baby. She would will him to live.

As soon as the jostling wagon came to a halt before the huge Vincente house, an army of servants descended on them. Marquis was lifted into gentle arms as two of the vaqueros carried him into the house. Don Alonso hobbled up the stairs after them, leaning heavily on his cane, while Marquis's mother followed, wringing her hands in distress.

Valentina was dazed for the moment. No one had paid the slightest attention to her. It was as if she had been invisible. Standing up, she stretched her cramped muscles and climbed out of the wagon. When Valentina reached for her crumpled wedding bouquet, she caught a glimpse of Marquis's sister, Rosalia, walking slowly down the steps toward her. The young girl's face was streaked with tears as she held out her arms to Valentina.

"Welcome home," Rosalia sobbed as the two of them cried on each other's shoulders. When at last their tears were spent, Valentina turned to the house. "I must be with Marquis now. Show me where they have taken him."

Rosalia slipped her arm around Valentina's waist. "You will not be able to see him just now. The doctor is with him. I will show you to your room."

"I cannot go to my room until I know how Marquis is. Take me to him," Valentina demanded.

Rosalia nodded. "You are his wife. It is right that you should see him."

Leading Valentina past a large arched hallway, Rosalia took her up a winding stairway. "Marquis sent word that this wing should be made ready because he was bringing you home as his bride. The servants have been working all day to make it comfortable."

"I never knew about this wing," Valentina said, only half noticing the richness of her surroundings. She paid little attention to the thick red rug into which the heels of her riding boots were sinking.

"This wing was built so the heir of Paraíso del Norte and his bride could have privacy. It has been a custom in my family that when a man is newly married, he and his bride will live for one year apart from the rest of his family. Grandfather says it has been a tradition in the

Vincente family for over four hundred years. No one knows why the tradition was first begun."

When Valentina had last stayed there, her room had been on the opposite side of the house. She reasoned that since the house was built in a square, with the courtyard garden in the center, this wing made up the whole north side of the house.

As they moved forward, Valentina was aware that the hallway was larger than most rooms she had seen in other homes. There were heavy wood couches and chairs covered with white velvet, and the tables, which had been carved by a master's hand, gleamed from polishing. Brightly colored exotic flowers were arranged in heavy crystal bowls that had probably been in the Vincente family for generations. Valentina paid no attention to the sweet scent of the flowers that wafted through the air. Her eyes were fixed on the line of servants who stood anxiously before a thick double door. She did not have to be told that this was Marquis's room.

The servants moved aside, making a path for Valentina and Rosalia. Pausing at the door, Valentina was uncertain how to proceed. Rosalia, sensing her confusion, opened the door and waited for her to enter.

Valentina saw Don Alonso sitting quietly in a corner chair, while Marquis's mother stood beside the bed, assisting a man she recognized as the doctor who had treated her ankle. Hesitating only a moment, she moved across the room. Her eyes fell first on Marquis's face, and with a sinking heart, she noticed that he had not regained consciousness.

Doña Anna was holding a pan of bloody water, while the doctor bent over Marquis's leg. Valentina gathered her courage and moved forward. This was her husband, and she had no intention of being shut out of his life. "I will hold the pan," she said with more authority than she actually felt.

Doña Anna's eyes suddenly filled with resentment. Her grip tightened on the pan. "No, I will hold the pan," she answered defiantly.

Knowing this was no time to argue the point, Valentina glanced at the doctor. "I am sure you remember me, Doctor Anza. I am now Marquis's wife. What can I do to assist you?"

If the doctor was startled by her announcement, it did not show on his face. Without looking up, he spoke to her. "You are not one of those ladies who faint at the sight of blood, are you?"

"I can assure you I am not," she answered with confidence.

"Then you can hold your husband's leg. It wouldn't do if he were to regain consciousness and move while I am stitching him up."

To demonstrate that she would never faint at the sight of blood, Valentina moved around the bed. She felt her stomach churn when she saw the angry red gash that ran from Marquis's knee to the calf of his leg. It was easy to see that the jagged cut was inflamed and infected. Firmly gathering her courage, Valentina gripped Marquis's leg, holding it as tightly as she could.

Feeling Doña Anna's eyes burning into her and not wanting to watch the doctor stitch up Marquis's leg, Valentina kept her eyes trained on her husband's face. She wondered if he was dreaming. What was he thinking of as he floated in a world of limbo? She prayed he felt no pain.

After the doctor had finished stitching his leg, he wrapped it in clean bandages. "I do not believe this leg is broken, so I am not going to replace the splint," he said to Valentina and Doña Anna. "Since the leg is infected, I want to elevate it above his heart. Bring me several pillows so I can prop it up."

Doña Anna sailed out of the room to bring pillows, and

Valentina turned to the doctor with inquiring eyes. "How bad is the infection?" she wanted to know.

"It is too soon to tell." Then he turned his attention to the other leg. "This one was badly crushed. I don't know if it will heal properly or if there was nerve damage. It could be that he will never be able to walk again. I just don't know. I will stay here tonight in case he takes a turn for the worse."

Valentina felt herself swaying and gripped the bedpost. "Dear God, no," she whispered. "Don't punish Marquis for my willfulness."

Now Don Alonso joined them beside Marquis's bed. His tired old eyes were not as bright as they had been the last time Valentina had seen him. His hand, resting on the cane, trembled. "Do you foresee any complications?" Don Alonso inquired.

"I just cannot speculate. Marquis has lost a good deal of blood, his leg is infected, and he is unconscious. I will not give you false hope . . . this is serious."

Valentina felt Don Alonso's hand on her shoulder, and she reached up, gripping it for courage. "I will not believe that Marquis will never walk, Doctor Anza. He must walk!" Valentina cried.

"I am saying I do not know," the doctor repeated. "I have noticed there is no feeling in Marquis's legs now. This is a very critical sign."

"He has been in a great deal of pain, Doctor. How can it be that he has lost the feeling in his legs?" Valentina asked.

"Who can say? This is a wait-and-see game."

Don Alonso seemed to have aged ten years in a short space of time. "Is his life in danger?"

"Perhaps," the doctor answered grimly.

Don Alonso lowered his head, and Valentina turned to him. He seemed to go limp against her, and she helped him into a nearby chair. Going down on her knees, she patted his hand. "Do not worry, Don Alonso, Marquis will not die, and he *will* walk. I know this in my heart, and I believe you do too."

The old grandee's eyes searched her face, and he suddenly smiled. "This is not much of a welcome for you, is it, child?"

"It was a far less happy homecoming for Marquis," she told Don Alonso.

Marquis's grandfather glanced in the doctor's direction. "Doctor Agustin Anza, you know this young lady. Welcome her now as my new granddaughter-in-law, Valentina Vincente. Valentina, I am sure you know that Agustin is not only our doctor, but a good friend as well."

Valentina looked into the soft, kind eyes of the doctor. Since Valentina had seen him last, he had grown a trim little mustache. He had been washing his hands, and he turned around to pick up a towel. Moving forward, he took Valentina by the shoulders and raised her to her feet. He then surprised her by squeezing her in a tight hug.

"Sorry that we became reacquainted under such sad circumstances, but it allowed me to see what you were made of. You handled yourself very well a while ago." His eyes were twinkling, and Valentina knew he was referring to her standing up to Doña Anna as well as assisting him. "Tell me, Valentina, does your ankle ever bother you?" he asked.

She smiled. "No, I had a good doctor tending me. I have never had a moment's pain from it."

Doctor Agustin turned to Don Alonso. "This beautiful lady is too good for Marquis. I should have seen her first."

"That is what I think too, but she's probably too good for you and me also."

Valentina was only half listening to the conversation. Her eyes kept drifting back to Marquis. Walking over to him, she touched his forehead and found he still had fever. Her attention was drawn away from her husband as Doña Anna entered carrying an armload of pillows.

Doctor Anza arranged the pillows to his satisfaction and then turned back to the others. "Marquis will need someone with him all night to make sure he does not thrash about and reopen his stitches."

"I will stay with my son," Doña Anna spoke up, her dark eyes daring Valentina to object.

Valentina knew she had asserted her claim as Marquis's wife; now she could afford to be charitable to his mother. More than anything, she wanted to be beside Marquis throughout this critical night, but she also realized what his mother must be feeling.

"I will relieve you about six," Valentina said. "If you need me before then, I will not be sleeping."

Doña Anna turned away, saying nothing further to her new daughter-in-law. Valentina realized at that moment that she would have to win the older woman's respect before she gained her friendship. After the way the woman had treated her today, she was not at all sure if it would be worth the effort.

Feeling tired and drained, Valentina turned to Don Alonso. "I would like to bathe and rest for awhile, if someone will show me to my room."

The old grandee cast a look at Doña Anna, knowing she was deliberately snubbing Marquis's wife. It was not like her to be so uncharitable, but then her position had never before been challenged by an outsider—an English woman. "Forgive us all for not making you welcome in your new home," he said, raising his voice so it would reach the ears of his dead son's wife. "I am sure you will find Rosalia waiting outside the door to assist you. She will be happy to show you to your room."

Valentina bent down and placed a kiss on Marquis's brow. He was so still. Her heart ached for what he had suffered, and for what he might yet have to endure. She did not want to leave him. Suppose he were to die! she cried inwardly. Raising her head, she allowed the others to see the tears that were running down her face.

"Forgive me," she sobbed aloud, rushing across the room and out the door. Finding the hallway empty, she collapsed onto a sofa and let the tears flow freely. What would she do if she lost Marquis? He might not love her, but he was her husband and the father of her unborn baby. Her place was beside him, but she knew his mother would never allow her to take that place without a fight. For now, Valentina was fresh out of fight. She was ready to crumple.

Feeling comforting arms go around her, Valentina heard Rosalia's voice. "Come, you are weary. I will see that you have all you require."

Valentina allowed Rosalia to lead her to the room next door to Marquis's. The day had been endless, and she was emotionally drained and physically exhausted. She dropped down on the yellow-draped bed, feeling her body conform to the soft mattress.

"I must take a bath," she said, trying to rise but finding it too much effort.

Rosalia removed Valentina's shoes and pulled a light coverlet over her. "You rest; the bath can wait."

"I want to be awakened in an hour. I want to be awake in case Marquis regains consciousness."

"If you are needed, I will wake you," Rosalia promised, quietly leaving the room and closing the door softly behind her.

Doña Anna looked at her father-in-law, knowing he was displeased with her. "Do not tell me you were taken in by the girl's tears? She does not care for my son or she would never have allowed him to endanger his life. It is

353

her fault that my Marquis may die or become a cripple."

Don Alonso cared deeply for his dead son's wife, but he knew she could sometimes be a hard, unbending woman—especially where her son was concerned. "I do not think it was out of the ordinary for Valentina to cry, Anna. After all, today was her wedding, her husband is gravely ill, and she is spending her wedding night alone."

"I will not leave Marquis tonight," Doña Anna declared. "If he dies, the English woman will become a very wealthy widow. Have you thought of that?"

Don Alonso stood up and slowly walked to the door. "No, I had not thought of that and I do not believe Valentina has either. I saw love in her eyes as she stood over Marquis. One day I may tell you how fortunate you are that your son married this English woman and not Isabel Estrada."

"Isabel is of our kind. She would have made a far better wife for Marquis," Doña Anna stated airily.

"Why belabor the point. That will never happen now. I suggest you look to your son, señora. Leave his personal life for him to settle when he recovers."

Doña Anna ignored the opening and closing of the door. Only when she was alone with her son did she allow the tears to fall. Her son, her precious son, had betrayed his heritage by taking the English woman as his bride. She touched his face, fearing she would lose him—if not to death, then to Valentina. She had the feeling that Marquis's new wife would try to cut her out of her son's life completely.

In the room next door to Valentina, Marquis thrashed on his bed of pain, his body burning as if it were on fire.

"Silver Eyes," he cried out, needing to feel the soothing hand of his beloved cooling his fevered brow. "I love you," he whispered. In his nightmare world, he yearned for the touch of Valentina's hand, the sound of her voice.

"Sleep, my son," Doña Anna told him, not understanding his rambling or the name he mumbled. "I will stay with you," she promised.

The bright California moon moved across the ebony sky, shining down on Valentina's wedding night, spreading its light into her bedroom. The gentle glow fell across her face without disturbing her sleep. It was a lover's moon, hung in the sky as though a gift for the newly married couple.

As the moonlight filtered across the darkened shadows of the room, Valentina moaned in her sleep, trying to wake, knowing there was something she had to do, somewhere she had to be. Fighting against the drugged sleep that claimed her as its victim, Valentina called out Marquis's name to the silent room.

On the floor, beside Valentina's bed, lay the crumpled wedding bouquet—its sweet aroma fading, the blossoms wilted and dying.

Chapter Twenty-Three

Valentina tossed and turned on the bed as her dream turned into a nightmare. She was running from something, but she could not see what it was. The more frightened she became, the more her legs felt like heavy weights and the more difficult it was to run. Suddenly her back was against a wall, and she could go no farther. A swirling mist clung to the air, and whatever it was that had been pursuing her was hiding there. Moaning, she turned over in her sleep.

The dream continued as she glanced down at her feet to see Marquis lying wounded and unconscious. That was when she realized that the horrible thing that had been chasing her was not after her at all—it wanted Marquis! From out of nowhere a sword came sailing through the air to land in Valentina's hand. Gripping the handle, she wielded the sword over her head, determined she would defend Marquis with her last breath. Thrusting the sword forward, she heard a hideous roar and knew she had mortally wounded the faceless, nameless demon.

Going down on her knees, she hugged Marquis to her. He was all right; she had saved him. "You haven't saved him," a deep, raspy voice told her. "It is because of you that he must die: You are the instrument of his death!"

"No," Valentina moaned. "No, I would never harm Marquis; I love him."

Fighting her way out of the nightmare, she jerked upright in bed, coming fully awake. It took several moments for her thundering heart to return to normal. The bedroom was illuminated by the bright moonlight, and she remembered that she was at Paraíso del Norte.

Valentina feared the nightmare might very well become true, and Marquis might die. Finding she was fully clothed, she slipped out of bed, pushed into her shoes, and hurried out the bedroom door.

The hallway was aglow with several candelabra, arranged on low tables. Valentina paused for just a moment before Marquis's bedroom before opening the door. His room was mostly in shadows, with only the light of a single candle burning. Valentina did not see Doña Anna until she heard the whispered prayer. Marquis's mother was on her knees, her folded hands clasping a rosary.

For a moment, Valentina stood silently, not wanting to disturb Doña Anna at her prayer. Looking at Marquis, she thought his condition appeared the same as when she had left earlier. Needing to feel close to Marquis's mother so they could share their fear, she walked soundlessly across the room. Touching Marquis's face, she thought he felt cooler.

Doña Anna finally realized she was not alone and tossed Valentina a heated glance. "I do not need you to relieve me. Go back to bed. I will stay with my son," the older woman declared.

Valentina dropped down on her knees, taking Marquis's hand in hers. "I do not want to relieve you, Doña Anna. I merely want to pray with you. Perhaps God will hear us better if we both ask him to save Marquis."

Marquis's mother nodded slowly, willing to accept any spiritual help to save her son. Turning back to her prayer, she paid little attention to her new daughter-in-law. It was not in her nature to send someone away when she wanted to pray—not even the English woman.

Hours slipped by, and still the two women remained on their knees, praying for Marquis's recovery. After awhile, Valentina noticed that Doña Anna had fallen asleep with her head resting on the bed, her hands still clasped in prayer. She did not know what time it was, but her body was stiff and cold, and her back ached painfully.

Valentina was about to release Marquis's hand so she could rub her aching neck muscles when she felt his fingers tighten on hers. Slowly she stood up, fearing she had only imagined his firm grip. When she found his eyes open, Valentina's joy and relief showed on her face.

Bending over him, she laid her hand on his brow. "Are you in pain, Marquis?" she asked softly, hoping he would have some kind of feeling in his legs.

"How did I get here?" he wanted to know. "The last thing I remember was standing before the priest. Are we man and wife?"

Valentina brushed her tears away and nodded, realizing Marquis still clutched her hand. "Yes, I am your wife. You have been very ill, but you will get better now." She nodded toward his mother, who still slept with her head resting on the bed. "Your mother's prayers probably went as far as the doctor's medicine in healing you."

Marquis closed his eyes—he could rest now. Valentina belonged to him; she was his wife. He did not want to think about anything just yet; he was too tired. He only wanted to sleep. He was not even aware that there was no longer any pain in his legs. He did not realize that there was no feeling at all. He obediently allowed Valentina to lift his head and give him a cooling drink of water.

"How long has it been since we left the mission?" he asked.

"Only yesterday," she answered. "You have been asleep most of the time."

"This should have been your wedding night," he replied in a drowsy whisper. Already a calming, peaceful sleep was overtaking him, and he did not see Valentina's tears as they fell freely down her face.

"Silver eyes that haunt my dreams," Marquis whispered sleepily. "Silver eyes . . . silver eyes," he muttered over and over.

Valentina's heart was singing with happiness. Marquis was going to live!

Going down on her knees, she gently shook Doña Anna. When the older woman's eyes snapped open, she quickly started murmuring a prayer. "It's going to be all right, Doña Anna," Valentina said. "Marquis woke for just a moment. He is cooler and sleeps the sleep of healing."

The older woman tried to stand, but her legs gave way under her and she grabbed the bedpost, unable to move. Valentina placed her hand around Doña Anna's waist and helped her to her feet, thinking how devotedly Marquis's mother had watched over her son.

Doña Anna stumbled forward and touched her son's face to satisfy herself that his fever had broken. Her cheeks were glistening with tears as she picked up Marquis's hand and kissed it. "God has been merciful," she said. "He has given my son back to me."

Valentina could see Doña Anna swaying on her feet and knew she must get her to bed or she would collapse. Placing a guiding arm about her shoulder, she spoke kindly. "I will stay with Marquis now. Allow me to take you to your room. I promise I will let you know the moment there is any change in Marquis's condition."

"I cannot leave him," Doña Anna argued. "He may wake up and need me."

"He will always need you, Doña Anna, but he will need

you more in the days to come. Right now, he is sleeping peacefully and I doubt that he will wake for hours. Get some rest so you can be with him later."

Doña Anna's eyes searched Valentina's face. Seeing no malice there but rather genuine concern, she let her shoulders droop and she nodded her acceptance of Valentina's statement. "I will go to my room now. As you have done, I will only sleep for a short time."

Valentina saw the fire that snapped briefly in Doña Anna's eyes and realized she still had not accepted her as Marquis's wife. She dreaded the confrontations that were yet to come. She vowed for Marquis's sake that she would make every effort to maintain peace with his mother.

"Will you allow me to help you to your room, Doña Anna?" Valentina asked.

"No, you stay with my son. Do not fall asleep in case he needs you, and do not leave this room. I hope you are capable of tending someone who is ill."

Valentina could have reminded Doña Anna that she, herself, had fallen asleep moments ago. She could also have reminded her that she had tended her mother who was ill, but she saw nothing to be gained by prolonging the conversation. Doña Anna's voice carried the ring of a commanding officer. Valentina had never before met anyone like Doña Anna, but she was determined not to lose her temper with the woman. At the moment they were both tired and under a great deal of strain. Their tempers were frayed.

"I will not fall asleep, Doña Anna," she promised. "Rest, with the assurance that I will send for you if I need help."

Marquis's mother moved slowly across the room, as if she were reluctant to leave her son alone with Valentina. After she had gone, Valentina pulled up a chair beside the bed and sat down. She did not know what time it was, but the moon was riding low and the morning star was fading in the ebony skies.

Taking Marquis's hand in hers, Valentina stared into his sleeping face. His features were not rugged like Tyree's, but finely chiseled. His eyebrows arched over his eyes. Long lashes lay like shadows against his cheeks, covering those wonderful dark eyes that always disturbed her peace of mind. His nose was in perfect proportion to his firm lips—lips that could ease into a smile or clamp tightly together when he was displeased about something.

Hair as dark as a raven's wing was swept across his forehead. Gently, so she would not disturb his rest, she touched his hair, finding it soft and silky. There was nothing soft about the man, she thought. He was a man who was made to lead, to command other men—and to break women's hearts.

Her hand drifted down his face. This moment belonged to her alone. This was the first time she had been able to watch Marquis—to touch him—to allow her love to shine in her eyes. His olive complexion was not as pale as it had been earlier. Dark stubble covered his lower jaw, for it had been almost a full day since he had shaved.

Valentina's eyes moved lower. Since Marquis wore no nightshirt, she could see his smooth, bare chest. Unable to resist the urge to touch him, she laid her hand against his chest, thankful to feel the rise and fall of his breathing beneath her fingertips. He was the handsomest man she had ever known, and probably the most complicated. She wondered if she would ever understand Marquis or his mood changes.

Leaning back, Valentina lifted her legs into the chair and curled up, still watching her sleeping husband. Everything had happened so quickly, and she was dazed and bewildered. She was a wife, but she did not feel like one. She would soon be a mother, but she did not want to be one. Her own mother would be shocked at the

362

suddenness of her marriage. How would she ever make her mother understand why she had married Marquis without consulting her?

When Marquis groaned in his sleep, Valentina reached for his hand and spoke to him in a soothing voice. "Sleep, Marquis. I will stay beside you."

After that, Marquis seemed to settle down and Valentina began her long vigil through the remainder of the night. When he became restless and threw off the covers, she would hold his injured legs and talk to him quietly until he became calm again.

When the doctor came a few hours later, he found Valentina still at Marquis's bedside watching over him. "What a pretty nurse you make," he said, placing his black bag on the foot of the bed. Moving past Valentina, he picked up Marquis's hand, taking his pulse.

Valentina gave the doctor a tired smile as she watched him check Marquis's eyes to make sure he was sleeping and not unconscious. "What time is it?" she asked, standing up and stretching her aching muscles.

"The sun is not yet up. It must be near six o'clock. How did our patient fare during the night?"

"He was restless at times, but for the most part he slept peacefully. His fever seems to be gone."

"What about yourself? Did you rest?"

"Yes, some."

"Do you feel up to assisting me while I redress the bandages on Marquis's legs?"

"Of course. Just tell me what you want me to do."

"Good girl. I am going to remove the bandage and see if the infection is better or worse. Since he has no fever, my guess is that he is on the way to recovery."

Valentina was quick to follow orders as the doctor issued them. She helped him unwrap the bandages and held Marquis's leg while he examined it carefully. She could see that the wound still appeared to be inflamed, but it did not look as bad as it had the night before; some of the swelling had gone down. Marquis did not even stir or open his eyes when the doctor cleansed the wound.

"He is better, isn't he?" she asked the doctor as he applied ointment and rewrapped his legs.

"Considering all he has been through, I'd say he was making a remarkable recovery."

Valentina was afraid to ask, but she had to know. "Is it too soon to tell if he has lost the use of his legs?"

"Yes, much too soon to tell"—Doctor Agustin studied her over the rim of his glasses—"unless you noticed any movement in them last night that was not in conjunction with his body movements. Did you see the legs move on their own?"

"When he was restless last night, I held his legs on the pillow. I got the feeling all the movement came from his body, not his legs."

"Give it time, Valentina." He snapped his black bag together and smiled at her. "You do not mind if I call you Valentina, do you?"

"No, of course not . . . please do."

"Walk with me to the door. I have a few things to say to you and I would rather not risk being overheard." Without waiting for her to comply, he took her arm and steered her away from Marquis's bed. When he thought they were out of earshot, he released her arm and smiled.

"You are feeling bewildered by this family, are you not?"

". . . Yes," she admitted reluctantly.

"I have known the Vincente family for longer than I care to remember. I brought Marquis and Rosalia into this world. I even brought Marquis's father into the world. God be willing, I will be on hand when your and Marquis's son comes into this world. There is love in this family. Don Alonso and Rosalia give it willingly, while Doña Anna is much more reserved with her feelings. She has a kind nature, and, if you are patient, she will soon warm to you."

"I have guessed that already. I know Marquis's sudden marriage to me came as a shock to his family. It will be an equal shock for my mother when she finds out. I will try to be patient, knowing how important Marquis's family is to him."

Agustin's eyes danced. "Oh, how you are going to liven up this old house. You have brought new blood to this family. Whether or not they realize it, you are just what they needed. Even though I am Spanish, I never approved of an arranged marriage. Marquis is very fortunate indeed to have found you."

Valentina was surprised by his words. When he bent and kissed her on the cheek, she smiled.

"Fight for what you want, Valentina," he urged, "but only after you have discovered who is your true enemy. Watch for trouble and be ready for it."

Without further explanation, Doctor Anza opened the door and disappeared. Valentina tried to make sense out of his conversation. First he told her to be patient; then he advised her to fight for what she wanted. Who was the enemy he had tried to warn her of? He had issued her a warning—that she knew.

Moving back to Marquis's bed, she stood over him for a long moment. Would she fight to hold him? They were man and wife, but he did not truly belong to her and probably never would. Could she fight against the love he felt for Isabel? Turning away, she walked over to the window, quietly slipping between the heavy green velvet window hangings. She discovered a wide door, with two windows on each side running from floor to ceiling.

Valentina pushed open the door, moved out onto the balcony, and stepped into another world. The master suite balcony connected Marquis's bedroom and her room next door. There were stairs leading into the courtyard. Valentina wished she dared go down into the garden.

She watched fascinated as the first golden rays of morning sunlight chased the last remaining night shadows across the courtyard. The birds were singing and the scent of flowers filled the air while the fountain sparkled and shimmered.

The beauty of this gentle world took Valentina's breath away now, just as it had the first time she had viewed it. This was Marquis's home. This was where the Vincentes had reigned supreme for generations. She could see why Marquis was proud of his home and wanted it to remain in his family.

Hearing voices below, Valentina watched two brightly dressed Indian women carrying trays of food. When the delicious aroma reached Valentina, she remembered she had not eaten since the morning before, and her stomach growled in protest. When the two women moved out of view, Valentina glanced at the long table below her, which was covered with the snowy white cloth. It was laden with several different kinds of fruit, meat, eggs, and many dishes she did not recognize. It was a table fit for a king, and Valentina reminded herself that on their land the Vincentes *were* kings.

There was a vine next to her that climbed up the iron grillwork to the balcony. She smiled, reached out, and plucked a bright red flower. Raising it to her nose, she smelled its sweet fragrance. Casting a last glance below, she wondered if this would ever seem like home to her. She remembered that on first seeing Paraíso del Norte she had felt as if she had somehow belonged, yet now that she was married to the son of the house, she no longer felt that belonging.

Reentering Marquis's bedroom, Valentina saw that

Doña Anna was standing beside her son, her eyes blazing, her hands resting on her hips in a sign of agitation. "You said you would stay with my son. Why have you left him alone?"

"I only went out—"

"I knew you were not to be trusted," Doña Anna broke in. "I should never have left him with you."

Valentina felt her temper rising, but remembering Doctor Anza's words, she kept it under control. "I was only on the balcony a moment. I would never—"

"You are free to leave now. I do not need your help to look after Marquis."

Valentina saw the anger burning in Doña Anna's eyes and knew the woman was being unfair and unreasonable. She had done nothing wrong, but now was not the time to defend herself. Looking at Marquis's sleeping form, Valentina walked toward the door. "I will be back later in the day," she announced in a soft whisper. "At that time I will sit with my husband."

Once in the hall, Valentina leaned against the door, feeling completely drained. Was she going to be forced to battle Marquis's mother every day for the rest of her life? Valentina had never before dealt with anyone who so blatantly disliked her.

Gathering her thoughts, she walked slowly toward her bedroom. She wished for her own mother and Salamar, and she longed for peace of mind and spirit.

The night before, Valentina had paid little heed to the bedroom that had been given her. Now her eyes moved over the room and she realized it was only half furnished. There were no curtains for the windows, and the wooden floor had no rug. The only furniture in the room was the bed and a chair, and against the wall stood a tall wardrobe.

Valentina knew at once that this was to have been Isabel's bedroom. Apparently the decorating had stopped when the wedding had been canceled. Walking over to the wardrobe, she opened the door and stared at the gowns that hung there. She did not need to be told that the flamboyantly colored gowns belonged to Isabel Estrada.

An ache started in her throat and spread throughout her body. She closed the wardrobe door and turned away from the grim reminder of the woman Marquis loved. She wondered if she would ever learn why the wedding had been called off.

Walking stiff legged to the bed, she lay back and closed her eyes. It took too much effort to think about anything. All she wanted to do was sleep.

Isabel Estrada picked up the vase of flowers and threw it across the room, where it smashed against the wall. "How dare Marquis replace me with that puny English woman!" she screamed. "I will not take this kind of treatment from anyone. Who does he think he is!"

The Estrada family had been having breakfast when Doña Carmela Lopez, a neighbor known for her malicious gossip, brought them the news of Marquis's marriage to Valentina. Isabel had quietly smoldered as Carmela suggested that Marquis must have fallen in love with the English woman when she had stayed at his home.

After Carmela had finally gone, Isabel flew into a rage, venting her anger on anyone who was within earshot.

"I am ruined. Everyone will think—like that idiot old woman, Carmela—that Marquis got rid of me so he could marry the English woman. I will not stand for anyone pitying me."

"Now, now, Isabel," her mother spoke up. Her eyes darted nervously to her husband at the head of the table, hoping he would help her handle their daughter. "You know it was you who broke off the betrothal, Isabel.

Everyone knows it was you who did not want to marry Marquis."

Isabel turned angry eyes on her mother, and the woman cringed. "You are as simpleminded as Carmela. Surely you did not believe me when I told you that I threw Marquis over?" An evil laugh escaped Isabel's red lips. "Marquis is the one who did not want me. He despises me." In a burst of anger, Isabel whirled around, raking her arm across the table and scattering dishes and food on the floor. Broken glass flew everywhere; food ran down the walls, staining the green rug on the dining room floor.

Eleanor was the only one who seemed unaffected by her sister's rampage. She had often seen Isabel fly into rages. She had learned long ago that if she kept her mouth shut, her sister's anger was less likely to be directed at her. Eleanor picked up her tea, now tepid, and took a sip. She acted as if she were detached from the frenzy going on around her.

"But Isabel," her father said, trying to assert his authority as head of the house, "you told me and your mother, right here in this room, that you did not want to marry Marquis Vincente. Had I known that it was he who did not honor our agreement, I would have demanded that he make things right—immediately. I will go at once to Don Alonso. I will demand satisfaction."

A sneer curled Isabel's lips. "You do that, Father, but be prepared to face the consequences. Marquis will tell the world how he found me in the hay with one of your vaqueros."

Señora Estrada licked her dry lips. "What were you doing in the hay?"

Isabel glared at her mother. "You are a simpleton." Leaning into her mother's face, bracing her hands on the table, she spoke slowly and distinctly. "To put it in simple language, so even you can understand it, Mother,

I was coupling with one of the hired hands."

Señora Estrada's face whitened in disbelief, and she dropped her eyes. She had never known how to talk to her daughters, least of all Isabel. Perhaps it was because they had been reared only by her and an old-maid aunt in Spain.

Turning burning eyes on her father, Isabel dared him to say anything against her behavior. Pretending he did not hear, he took a bite of food and concentrated on chewing it. One by one, Isabel looked down into the faces of each family member, daring any of them to speak. At last her eyes fell on her sister, and she moved slowly toward her.

"You are glad about this, Eleanor, and do not deny it. You like to see me degraded and humiliated. You are happy that Marquis married someone else."

Eleanor moved off her chair to face her sister. She took courage in hand, ready to voice her opinion, knowing it would bring her sister's anger down on her head. "No one degrades you but yourself, Isabel. I do not blame Marquis for choosing the English woman—she is a lady, and he knows a lady when he sees one."

Isabel screamed out in her rage. Rushing at her sister, she hit her across the face countless times. Eleanor cried out in pain, which brought her father to her rescue. When he tried to stop Isabel, she vented all her anger in one final blow that sent her sister flying across the room, as if she had been a tiny rag doll.

Seeing Eleanor lying in a heap against the wall, Isabel stormed out of the room, vowing she would have her revenge on Marquis and his slut of a wife.

Eleanor felt her father lift her in his arms and heard him tell her mother to send for the doctor. Through the pain, she smiled. Isabel had finally found a man she could not manipulate. Marquis had seen through her right from the start. She was happy that he had taken the English woman as his wife. They would be happy together.

When her father laid her on the bed, she turned her face toward the window so she could see the bright sunlight. "Isabel will have to be watched," she said in a weak voice. "She is quite mad and extremely dangerous!"

Chapter Twenty-Four

Valentina had been married to Marquis for four days. In that time, she had seen him awake only once. His mother was determined to keep Valentina away from him. Every day she would go to Marquis's bedroom, only to find the door locked and to be told by servants that Marquis's mother was with him. Not wanting to cause trouble at a time like this, Valentina did not insist on her rights as Marquis's wife.

She kept hoping Marquis would ask for her, but apparently he had not. Each day, Valentina waited in the hallway, all but forgotten by the Vincente family.

Doctor Anza kept Valentina informed about Marquis's progress. He told her that the wound was healing nicely, but still he would not commit himself as to whether or not Marquis would ever be able to walk again.

As time passed, Valentina began to scan the western horizon, looking for some sign of her mother and Salamar. Valentina needed someone around her that belonged to her—a friend in an otherwise hostile camp.

Never invited to dine with the family, Valentina ate her meals alone in her room. She had been told that Don Alonso was ill and spent most of the day in his bed; otherwise, she knew she would have had a friend in him.

Valentina wondered where Rosalia could be spending her time, because she rarely saw her at all.

Doña Anna had been spoon-feeding Marquis a portion of *puchero,* when he pushed her hand away. "I do not want any more; take it away," Marquis said in a tired voice, turning his head to the wall.

"Doctor Anza says you should eat to keep up your strength, my son. Eat just a bit more to please me. I will tell you all that is going on with our neighbors."

"I do not want any more." Now his voice sounded irritated. "Do not mistake me for Rosalia, Mother. I am not your baby who needs constant attention."

"You are just tired of this bed, my son," doña Anna speculated. "You will get used to it after awhile. It is only natural that you should find this life dull at first."

He turned his head sharply and his eyes met hers. "What do you mean, I will get used to it? Are you saying that I will be confined to this bed?" Disbelief clouded his mind. "Are you saying I will never walk?"

His mother lowered her gaze. "I do not wish to take hope from you. Doctor Anza does not know if your legs will again be of use to you."

"My legs?" Marquis looked deeply into her eyes, trying to find answers. "What do you mean?"

"Now, Marquis, do not upset yourself. Doctor Anza says—"

"Yes, Mother, what does he say?" Marquis's mind was in a frenzy. It was true that he was unable to move his legs. When the legs had first been injured, there had been excruciating pain; now he felt nothing. For the first time, it occurred to him that his legs might be paralyzed.

In a panic, he strained, trying to move his injured legs. Again and again, he tried to raise them, first one and then the other, while his mother looked on helplessly. Finally, he fell back weakly against the pillows, gasping for breath, facing defeat for the first time in his life. "My God, no," he moaned. "I am a cripple."

Doña Anna's eyes filled with tears, and she threw herself across his chest. "You are not to worry about anything. I will always look after you. Every day I will read to you. The kitchen will be instructed to make only your favorite meals. I will never leave you alone."

Marquis gripped his mother's shoulders and pushed her away. His mind would not accept what she was trying to tell him. She was implying that he would be an invalid confined to his bed! He shook his head. "I will walk again. I will not stay in this bed one day longer than I have to."

Doña Anna feared that if Marquis recovered enough to get out of bed, she would lose him to the English woman. As long as she could keep him dependent on her, she could hold onto him. "After awhile you will be able to be carried to the garden. Perhaps one day you can even ride in a carriage. For now, just let me take care of your needs."

Marquis could see nothing but bleakness and emptiness in his future. His thoughts turned to his wife, the only bright spot in his life. Before today, he had been too ill to question Valentina's absence. He could not remember her coming to his room at all. Why was she not here with him now?

"How is Valentina taking to her new home, Mother?"

"I have had no time to see to her comforts." Doña Anna's eyes narrowed. "I was busy taking care of you."

"Has she been to see me?"

Doña Anna ducked her head. "Not since the first night you were brought home."

Marquis glanced down at the legs that kept him prisoner in his own room and would probably make him a cripple. Who could blame Valentina if she did not want to spend time with him? he thought bitterly. She was young and beautiful. She did not want to be tied down to half a man. The one thing he could never accept from her was sympathy. He could not stand to see those beautiful silver-blue eyes looking at him with pity.

"If Valentina tries to see me, tell her I do not want her in my room. Is that clear?"

Doña Anna nodded, her eyes gleaming with delight. "I will see that she does not disturb you."

"Leave me now." He needed to think about what his mother had just told him. "I want to be alone."

Doña Anna gathered up the tray and paused. "Word has come that the English woman's mother and servant will arrive today. Where shall I put them?"

"Put them in this wing. I believe her mother is ill. Valentina will want her nearby."

"And the servant?"

Marquis's lips curled into a smile. "I believe Salamar will put herself where she wants to be. I doubt that anyone will tell her what to do."

Marquis's mother brushed a kiss across his cheek, saddened by the dull look in his eyes. "I will be back soon. Rosalia will come to sit with you after awhile."

Marquis was not even aware that his mother had left the room. He was thinking how horrified Valentina must be at finding herself married to half a man. There was no will in him to get out of bed. He felt as weak as a babe. He had lost his strength, his pride. He would not allow Valentina to see him this way. It had been a mistake to marry her. He could never be a husband to her now. As his wife, she would be a prisoner the same as he—a prisoner of a cripple.

Doubling his hands into fists, he clamped his jaws tightly together. Would he have to be carried everywhere he went? Could he never hold Valentina in his arms, never give her a child of his body?

Closing his eyes, he saw visions of her beautiful face.

He also saw another face, the veiled face of Jordanna—
Jordanna, the woman who was having his baby, the
woman and the child he had rejected. He could never sort
out his feelings where Jordanna was concerned. Perhaps
if he could put a face to her, it would help.

Marquis pounded his clenched fists against his legs,
feeling no pain, feeling nothing. This must be his
punishment for having denied his own flesh, he
reasoned. He had to see Tyree and tell him to find
Jordanna. Something had to be done for her. She had to
know he hadn't deliberately deserted her.

Lying quietly on the bed, lulled by the soft musical
sound of the fountain in the courtyard below his balcony,
Marquis fell in a troubled sleep.

Since there was no mirror in Valentina's bedroom, she
could not see whether or not her hair was parted straight.
Brushing the golden tresses until they crackled, she
wrapped them around into a coil and secured it to the top
of her head.

Rosalia had brought Valentina several of her gowns to
wear, but since Rosalia was not as tall as Valentina, the
gowns were too short. Valentina preferred to wear her
own wine-colored riding habit, now that the tears from
the cave-in had been mended.

Valentina could feel herself being drawn up like a fish
in a net. She had no rights in this house. She did not
really belong here and probably never would. She
realized if she were not careful, she could be swallowed
up by the traditions of the Vincente family and lose her
own identity.

Sitting on the edge of the bed, Valentina pushed her
feet into her riding boots. Time lay heavily on her hands,
and she did not know what to do with herself. As always,
her eyes traveled to the wardrobe, where Isabel's gowns

still hung. They were a constant reminder to Valentina that she had not been Marquis's first choice as a wife.

Pacing back and forth restlessly like a caged animal, Valentina noticed something on the wall that made her stop in her tracks. There had once been a connecting door between this bedroom and Marquis's. It had been sealed up and painted over, but she could still see where the hinges of a door had been.

Her shoulders sagged as the meaning of what she saw became clear. If Marquis had married Isabel, the door would not have been removed. After he decided to marry her, he must have sent word ahead that he wanted the door sealed.

"No," she told herself, "I will not cry. I will not let anything Marquis does make me cry again." Valentina thought saying it out loud would give her courage, but it did little to stop the tears that spilled down her face. Having a door removed might seem a small thing to some people, but to Valentina it had great significance. Marquis was showing her her place in his life. They might have a private wing to themselves, but the only access to his bedroom would be through the hall or across the balcony.

In that moment, Valentina made a firm decision. She would no longer humiliate herself by trying to see Marquis. If he had wanted her, he would have sent for her by now. She could feel the gap between them widening. Marquis was proving to her that he wanted nothing to do with her. Even from his sickbed, he was making it clear that she had no place in his life—neither she nor her baby.

Hearing a rap on the door, Valentina smoothed her gown and moved across the room to admit whoever it was. As the door swung wide, Valentina cried out with joy. Salamar smiled brightly before wrapping Valentina in her arms.

"Salamar, you are here! I thought you would never arrive." She glanced over Salamar's shoulder expectantly. "Where is Mother? Didn't she come? Was she too ill to make the journey?"

Salamar laughed and moved into the room, turning around and assessing the scant furnishings with disapproval before she answered Valentina. "Your mother has been tucked into bed just down the hallway and has already fallen asleep. She took the journey well and will be anxious to see you when she wakes."

"Do you have a room yet?"

"There is a small room just off your mother's. I have told a servant to put a bed in there so I can be near her."

Valentina clasped Salamar's hand. "You just cannot know how glad I am that you and Mother are here. I have been so . . . everything is different here."

"Tell me all about what is going on," Salamar said, removing her brown leather gloves and tossing them on the bed. "How is Marquis?"

"I only know what the doctor has told me. It isn't known if he will regain the use of his legs," Valentina admitted sadly. "He may not be able to walk."

"Nonsense. It is probably an injured nerve."

"It's serious, Salamar."

"I would not lose heart yet. There are many things we can do to help him."

"I haven't been allowed to see Marquis since the first day. He hasn't sent for me. His mother stands guard over him, as though he were the family jewels, and I the thief."

Salamar heard the hurt in Valentina's voice. "Have you accepted his mother's word as law? The Valentina I know would never allow anyone to dictate to her."

Valentina made a hopeless gesture. "What can I do? I am an unwanted stranger here."

"Have faith, Valentina. You can be instrumental in

helping him heal."

"How could—"

Valentina was interrupted by another rap on the door. "We will talk later," Salamar said, opening the door to admit several servants carrying Valentina's trunks. She directed them as to where to place the heavy pieces. After the men had gone, she walked over to the wardrobe and opened it, giving Valentina a questioning glance.

"These are not quite your style. Besides being too big, you would never wear the bright colors."

"They belong to Isabel, the woman Marquis was supposed to marry."

Without ceremony, Salamar pulled the gowns out of the wardrobe and walked across the room like a woman with a purpose. Opening the door, she tossed the gowns into the hallway. "I am surprised you did not do that yourself. Has marriage made you soft in the head, or did you lose your courage somewhere between here and San Francisco?" Salamar inquired with a gesture of dusting her hands.

Valentina smiled brightly, feeling better than she had in days. "You are my courage," she admitted with tears in her eyes. "You give me the strength to stand up and battle the world."

Salamar nodded. "Good! That's the Valentina I know. But your courage does not come from me. You have always stood up for what you believed in. You just forgot for the moment what it was that needed defending."

"I don't know where to start, Salamar."

"You can start by throwing away that rag you are wearing and slipping into one of your lovely gowns. You are wearing your hair in the style of a woman twice your age. A woman needs to look her best in order to be armed with courage when she faces the enemy."

Valentina could feel the blood pumping through her veins as her courage returned. She was ready to do battle, to meet life head-on. "Oh, Salamar, you are incorrigible," Valentina cried happily. "I'm so glad you are here at last."

Not bothering to knock on Marquis's bedroom door, Valentina pushed past the startled servant who was on guard. She sailed into the room with banners flying, ready to take on the world. Her golden hair was caught up in a violet velvet ribbon and fell down her back in a mass of curls. Her white gown with tiny violets embroidered on the skirt swayed over the wide hoop. Salamar had been right—being properly dressed did give one courage. As Valentina met Doña Anna's hostile eyes, she prayed it was not false courage.

Marquis's mother jumped to her feet, objecting loudly. "You cannot come in this room! My son has asked that you be kept out of here."

Valentina paid little heed to Doña Anna's ranting. Her eyes went to her husband, who stared at her in disbelief. She almost lost her courage when his eyes burned into hers. He looked so different. He had the beginnings of a beard and mustache. His face was ashen against the stark white pillow. His injured leg rested on three pillows, and his arms were folded across his chest in stubborn defiance. The room was dark and stuffy, smelling strongly of medicines.

"I do not want you here," he said in a raspy whisper. "Get out of my bedroom."

Valentina felt the sting of his cruel words, but she would not give up yet. "You should have thought of that when you asked me to be your wife. If you believed you could place me in some obscure corner of your life and forget about me, you were mistaken." She raised her chin proudly. "I am your wife, and I have every right to be here."

Valentina had spoken in English and Doña Anna could not understand what she was saying, but she gathered from the tone that Valentina was trying to take over her son. "I will call the servants and have her thrown out," Doña Anna snapped, moving toward the door. "This English woman does not know when she is not wanted."

"Stop!" Valentina called out. "You had better know, before you try to have me thrown out of my husband's room, that I will not go without a fight. Do you want the servants to spread gossip to the neighbors that we do not love one another?"

Valentina's challenge hung in the air, halting Doña Anna in her tracks and forcing the woman to look to her son for guidance. She did not want her family to be the subject of curious gossip around her neighbors' dining tables.

Marquis thought Valentina was like a breath of spring. How beautiful she was as she stood her ground, defying him and his mother. Never had he admired her more than he did at that moment. He knew he would never be able to push Valentina out of his life and heart. He had thought by keeping her away he could forget about her. He was wrong. There had not been a waking minute she had not dominated his thinking.

"Let her stay if it pleases her to be where she is not wanted," he said sourly, turning away from her as if he could shut her out of his mind by not looking at her.

"I will just go for your grandfather," Doña Anna declared. "He will handle this English woman."

Valentina heard her mother-in-law leave, slamming the door behind her. Walking around the bed, she forced Marquis to look at her. "Is that how your mother refers to me? As 'that English woman?'"

Marquis almost smiled. "It seems to please her to call you that."

"You need a shave," she observed in a soft voice.

"If you do not like the way I look, then why not shave me yourself?" he asked, avoiding her gaze.

"All right, I will," she said, picking up the challenge. "First of all, you need light and fresh air in here. It's a glorious day outside. The gloom in this room is enough to make anyone feel ill."

"If you do not like it here, you can leave." His dark pupils were smoldering embers. "You were not invited in anyway." He turned his head away from her, fearing she would read the joy in his eyes. Yes, his heart sang when she was near. Her presence in his room was bringing him back to life. He could feel the blood pumping throughout his body, reviving his spirits. He dared not look into her eyes lest he see pity there.

Valentina moved to the window and pushed the heavy drapery aside. She opened the door to let in fresh air. Placing her hands on her hips, she turned to Marquis and found him staring at her. "Where do you keep your razor?" she asked.

"You are not going to shave me, Valentina," he said with bitter rage.

"Oh, yes, I am," she insisted. Looking about the room, trying to decide the most likely place he would keep his shaving kit, she finally decided on a tall chest near the window.

Opening the top drawer, she found just what she sought. Marquis watched her sullenly as she poured water into a pan and approached him with a drying cloth across her arm. "The water is still warm," she said cheerfully. "Your mother must have just bathed you."

"I do not need my mother to bathe me, nor do I need you to shave me." His eyes were boring into her, daring her to come near him.

Placing the pan on the bedside table, she draped the cloth across his chest. She searched her memory, trying to remember how her father shaved. Valentina prayed she would not cut Marquis, or he would have her thrown out for sure.

Wetting the brush, she whipped up a thick lather. "I never cared for a beard on a man," she said, trying to make light conversation.

"What do you like on your men?" he snarled.

"On you, I like the leather trousers and the *bolero* jacket." She laughed to hide her nervousness. "A good sense of humor is always nice to wear."

She saw his lips twitch and knew he was trying not to smile. "I can shave myself," he said, grabbing her hand.

"You said if I didn't like the way you looked, I could shave you. That's what I intend to do," she announced, jerking her hand free.

Meeting his eyes, Valentina refused to look away. She could not allow him to discover she was shaking inside. What she really wanted to do was ask him if he was in pain. She wanted to have him hold her and tell her he was glad she was his wife. She wanted to smooth out the frown lines that creased his forehead. Instead, she lathered his face, while he appeared to suffer in silence.

When it came time for the razor, she felt her hand shake. Mentally schooling her fear, she held his chin and dragged the razor down the side of his face. Taking an easy breath, she saw that she could be pleased with the results. Gathering courage, she repeated the stroke.

When the door suddenly opened, Don Alonso entered. He was taken aback when he saw Valentina shaving his grandson. Moving to the side of the bed, he watched in silence while Marquis cast him a withering glance that warned the older man not to make fun of him.

"When I was first married, my wife would shave me on occasion. I found it very relaxing," Don Alonso said, watching Valentina's smooth movements. "You have a light touch, my dear. I can see you have done this before."

384

Valentina wiped the razor on the drying cloth before gliding it across the lower half of Marquis's face. "No, this is the first time I have ever shaved a man," she announced with confidence. "It is good to know I am doing it correctly."

Marquis's eyebrows quirked briefly, and his grandfather fell into stunned silence. When Valentina applied the razor to Marquis's face again, both men flinched.

"There," Valentina declared, wiping Marquis's face with the cloth. "You look much better now. It wouldn't surprise me in the least if you felt better."

Don Alonso laughed with delight. "She may be right, Marquis. If I had just been shaved by a beautiful woman, I would certainly be feeling on the mend."

Marquis was not even remotely amused. His eyes were cold as he looked at Valentina. "If you are finished ordering my life, you can leave. I told you before I do not want you here."

Valentina's eyes dulled with hurt. "I . . . my mother will be waking soon, and I haven't seen her yet. I will just clean this away," she said, reaching for the pan.

Marquis grabbed her wrist, causing the pan to crash to the floor, splashing Valentina's lovely gown. She was bending to retrieve the pan when Marquis shouted at her, "Just leave it alone. My mother will clean it up. Do not come back to this room unless I send for you."

Valentina backed toward the door, not daring to look at Don Alonso, knowing she would see pity in his eyes. Turning, she ran from the room. Marquis had completely humiliated her. She would never again make the mistake of trying to be a wife to him. Salamar had been wrong. There were some things one could not fight against—and Marquis's coldness was one of those things.

When she reached her bedroom, Valentina found Salamar waiting for her. When she saw the wet streak down the front of Valentina's gown and the stricken look on her face, she did not ask what happened. She just nodded. "To lose the first battle means one must plan for the next, Valentina."

"I lost this one, Salamar. I do not want to fight anymore."

"You do not need to think about it today. It is time to see your mother. Let me help you change your gown."

Evonne, propped up against pink lace pillows, clasped her daughter's hands. "Are you happy, my love?" she inquired brightly. "I want your happiness more than anything."

Valentina tried to avoid answering her mother's question. "I am married to the man I love," she explained. Valentina noticed the faint shadows under her mother's eyes and knew she was exhausted. "You are to rest for the next few days, Mother. I want you to recover from the journey."

"All I do is rest," Evonne pouted. "I am so weary of staying in bed."

"There is a lovely courtyard garden here. Perhaps you can spend some time there when you are feeling stronger," Valentina suggested.

"Yes, that would be nice," Evonne said in a tired voice. "I want to hear all about your wedding, and why you were so impatient to become Mrs. Vincente that you couldn't wait for me to be with you."

"Rest now, Mother. We will talk tomorrow, when you have recovered from your long journey."

Valentina watched her mother's eyes close, then waited quietly until she had fallen asleep. What a tangled mess she had made of her life. How would she ever be able to tell her mother about the baby? She hoped with all her heart that she would not have to. Her mother would never understand.

Salamar motioned Valentina into the hallway. "I will

stay with your mother now. Go out into the garden and take in the fresh air."

Valentina nodded, needing to get out of the house. She felt the walls closing in around her, and she could not breathe. Many generations of Vincentes were probably turning over in their graves because one of their sons had married an English woman, she thought bitterly.

Stopping in her tracks, she remembered something Salamar had told her when they were still living in Cornwall. She had said that Valentina would be worshiped by many men. That had actually happened. As Jordanna, she had received adoration. She also remembered Salamar telling her she would love only one man. He would love her as two women and reject her as both! How could Salamar have known that Marquis would reject her as Valentina and Jordanna?

She tried to clear her mind of Salamar's predictions. They were too troubling to think about now when she was so weary.

As she walked alone in the lovely garden, drinking in its beauty, it came to her that this lovely old house should be a house filled with happiness. She was struck by the thought that California was a land that seemed to abound with food, plants, and wild life. This was an old world that should embrace new thoughts and ideas. As a shadow moved away from the sun, she raised her face to bask in the warmth. If this land would accept her, she would embrace it with open arms.

Chapter Twenty-Five

The days passed in a similar pattern. Valentina stayed close by her mother, making sure she was comfortable, reading to her each afternoon. Since the day Marquis had ordered Valentina out of his bedroom, she had not attempted to go near him. Sometimes Valentina would go into the garden and sit by the fountain, daydreaming about how happy she could have been in this house.

Valentina knew Marquis's mother was still trying to ignore her. Three times a day meals were delivered to Evonne Barrett's room for the three of them. They were never asked to the main dining room, and Doña Anna had not come to see them.

The only Vincente family member Valentina ever saw was Don Alonso. Twice he had sent for her, and she had gone to his study to play chess. He was always kind to her, but the two of them never spoke about Marquis's or Doña Anna's treatment of Valentina and her mother.

In addition to Valentina's other worries, her concern for her mother was growing. Evonne Barrett had no desire to get out of bed. No matter how many times Valentina and Salamar tried to interest her in going into the lovely garden, she kept putting them off.

This particular day was warm, and high, fluffy clouds floated in a lazy blue sky. As Valentina walked in the garden, she paused at the huge bird cage and watched a colorful parrot flex its wings. "He can talk. Did you know that?"

Hearing Don Alonso's voice, Valentina turned to him and smiled, glad he was well enough to walk about. She had been worried about his health. "Who talks, the parrot?" she asked, looking into his laughing eyes.

"Of course, the parrot. His name is Beau—named after your long dead Beau Brummell, because they both strut like peacocks."

Valentina laughed at the old grandee. "What can he say?"

Don Alonso tapped on the cage with his cane, and multicolored birds scattered everywhere—all except Beau. Perched on one leg, he blinked his eyes and preened his feathers. "I cannot make him talk, though I have tried on numerous occasions," Don Alonso said. "Beau will only talk to Rosalia."

Valentina had not seen Rosalia in days. She had thought the young girl might be avoiding her so she had not sought her out. "I will have to ask her to make Beau talk for me sometime, Don Alonso."

"Why do you not ask her now?" He scanned her face as if looking for something. "Rosalia would be glad to see you."

A sad smile touched Valentina's lips. "Your granddaughter seems to be avoiding me."

Don Alonso's shaggy white brows met across his nose in a frown. "Is that what you think?"

"Yes."

"You could not be more mistaken. Rosalia spends her days down on her knees in the chapel praying for you and her brother. You see, she loves her brother very dearly, and she has come to love you too. She thinks if she fasts and prays, perhaps God will reward her by bringing happiness to you and Marquis. Rosalia has always been very devout."

Valentina shook her head, realizing she had been mistaken about her young sister-in-law. "Where is the chapel?"

The old grandee nodded to a small archway all but hidden by climbing vines. "If you will go through there, then follow that path, you will find the chapel."

"Thank you, Don Alonso. I will go to Rosalia right away."

"How are you, Valentina?" he asked suddenly, his tired old eyes registering concern.

"I am well."

His gaze was probing. "Are you?"

"Yes."

He leaned heavily on his cane. "I want to say to you that I am aware of the insult you and your mother have suffered since coming to my home."

"I—"

"No," he interrupted, "allow me to finish. I may be confined to my bed most of the time, but I still know what is going on in my own house." He smiled slightly, reminding Valentina of Marquis. "I suppose what I am trying to say is, as far as I am concerned, you are like a breath of spring in this old house. I am glad you have come."

She smiled brightly, and the old man was touched by her delicate beauty. "I think you are special," she said, standing on tiptoe and kissing his cheek.

Don Alonso took her hand and raised it to his lips. "You flatter an old man. But I like you too."

Valentina would have moved away, but his hand stayed her movement. "I do not see you in my grandson's room anymore. Are you not his wife?"

"Yes, but that is a fact he chooses to overlook. He prefers his mother's company to mine."

Don Alonso shook his head. "You are mistaken. He only allows his mother in his room for a short time each day. He lays there in the dark, day after day, brooding—

about what, God only knows. You see, Agustin Anza told Marquis three days ago that he will never be able to walk."

Valentina shook her head in disbelief. Tears tipped her lashes and her throat tightened in grief. "No, it cannot be!" Never to see him walk again, she thought frantically. Never to see the graceful movement of that whipcord body. Never to hear the jingle of his silver spurs.

"Agustin says he cannot walk," the old man continued. "I say he *will* not, and do you know why? Because he feels like a cripple. Nothing anyone says can make him believe otherwise." His old eyes misted over. "My grandson will never walk because he does not believe he can."

"I will not accept that," Valentina declared. "I will make him walk!"

Hope flared in the old man's eyes. "Do that, Valentina. Only you can bring him back to his family." He paused and looked her over. ". . . If you dare to try."

She wiped the tears away and raised her head. "If daring would make it so, he would already be walking. I am going to the chapel right now. I hope when I come out, I will be better able to face Marquis."

His eyes narrowed. "He will fight you," he warned.

She tossed her golden hair and raised her chin. "I never ran from a fight until I came here. I believe I am ready to take on your grandson in battle."

"There may be battle scars."

"I'm sure there will be. I expect Marquis to fight me every step of the way. I am weary of acting the scared rabbit—I am his wife, and it's time I acted the part."

"Brava!" Don Alonso declared encouragingly. "I applaud you and stand ready to lend you my support."

Her smile showed a hint of doubt, as if she were looking ahead to a battle she might lose. "I am going to find Rosalia now, Don Alonso. I may very well call for your support later."

The grandee watched Valentina walk quickly beneath the archway. When she was out of sight, he called out without turning, "You can come out now, Doña Anna. I know you are there because I saw your shadow."

"She cannot make him walk," Marquis's mother said spitefully, stepping from behind a thick hedge and wiping her eyes on a delicate lace handkerchief.

"Perhaps you want to keep your son a cripple. Perhaps you think to keep him dependent on you. Señora, do you want a whining son who clings to his mother's skirts—or do you want the man Marquis once was and could be again?"

"If the English woman could help my son, I would give her my blessing," Doña Anna sobbed. "Doctor Anza has said Marquis will never regain his strength in the one leg, and the other leg is useless."

"It may be that he will never walk because he has given up. That does not mean he has to live his life in darkness. This woman can bring him back into the light."

Doña Anna moved away, calling on the saints to punish her for interfering in her son's life. She had pushed Marquis too far, and now he believed he was a cripple. She could no longer reach him; he had become bitter and brooding.

The chapel was almost in darkness, with three candles as the only light. Valentina walked down the aisle, serenely aware of the feeling of peace that settled over her. This was the place where generations of Vincentes had been christened and later buried. When she saw Rosalia on her knees with her head bowed, she moved to her side and dropped to her knees.

Rosalia glanced up, staring at Valentina in amazement. Her hand trembled as she reached out to her. "You will be the one to help my brother walk," she whispered. "I should have known it would be you." Tears washed down the young girl's face as she clasped Valentina's hand.

393

"No one can help Marquis walk, Rosalia. He has to do that for himself. We have to face the fact that he may never have the will to get out of bed."

"No, you do not understand," Rosalia declared. "I have prayed here in the chapel for days and nights on end. Only moments ago I had a vision. An angel came to me and told me that the next person to kneel beside me would save my brother!"

Valentina stared in disbelief at the angelic face of Marquis's sister. A halo of light seemed to surround her head. She appeared more spiritual than human. Valentina was not Catholic, but at that moment she and Rosalia shared the same faith—the same God. "When you say it, you make me believe it, Rosalia. Let us pray together that even if Marquis never walks again, he will find peace in his torment, and his spirit will not be crippled."

Rosalia smiled joyfully, jumping to her feet. "No, let us raise our voices and rejoice. God has answered my prayers!"

Under the shadow of night, Valentina stood on the balcony that connected her bedroom with Marquis's. As usual, his curtains were drawn. She wondered if he were awake or asleep. Did he ever think of her? Tomorrow she would gather all her courage and enter his room. She had stood in church and exchanged wedding vows with him; that made her his wife, whether he acknowledged the fact or not.

Salamar moved onto the balcony. Placing her hands on the railing, she peered down at the garden, which was awash with silvery light. "This reminds me of the garden of my childhood. There are many similarities."

"Salamar, do you ever miss your home—your family?"

"Where you are is my home. Your family is my family."

"But you had a mother. Surely you miss her."

"My mother loved only the sultan, my father. She paid little attention to me. She died when I was very young."

Valentina placed her hand on Salamar's. "Have we been selfish with you? Have we depended too heavily on you and demanded too much of you?"

"Is this the night for searching the soul?" She smiled. "I am where I always wanted to be. You and your mother are all that matters to me."

Valentina sighed inwardly. "I have a task ahead of me that I am not looking forward to."

"Let me guess . . . you are going back into the lion's den."

"Yes. Marquis is wasting away, and I can't allow that to happen. He was injured trying to help me. The least I can do is see him through this ordeal."

"Are you ready to go all the way? Can you stand up to him when he throws abuse at you and orders you out of his room?"

". . . Yes," she answered slowly. Valentina had lost some of the confidence she had felt earlier in the day.

"This is what I have been waiting to hear from you," Salamar declared. "How would you like to make your husband walk?"

Valentina clasped her hands together. "If only that were possible."

"It is possible . . . but not if you are fainthearted. You will rue the day you took on this task. Your back will ache, you will drop from weariness, you will have to close your ears to Marquis's pain. He will abuse you with words and order you from his room. Many times you will want to give up, but once you have started there is no turning back."

"Do you know how to cure Marquis?" Valentina asked hopefully. Salamar had many strange and wonderful powers, but could she make Marquis walk when the doctor had given up hope?

"There is no certainty, but I know a way that may help him. It will not be easy."

"When do we start?"

"In the morning before sunup."

Valentina nodded. "I will do anything to help Marquis. If there is the slightest chance that he can walk, I will take it."

That night Valentina's sleep was deeper and her dreams were a little sweeter. She had a purpose—a goal to reach for.

Marquis stared angrily at the servants who marched into his room uninvited, wondering what they were doing and whose orders they were following. He knew they would never take it upon themselves to come to his room.

His curiosity was piqued when two men placed a large hip tub by the window and several women began filling it with hot water. "What in the hell is going on in here?" he yelled.

His anger grew when the servants ignored his ravings, placidly going about their appointed tasks. Some were moving furniture, while others placed folded sheets beside the tub. Marquis was fuming by the time Valentina entered, wearing a simple brown gown and with her hair tied away from her face. "Good morning, Marquis. It's a glorious day, isn't it?" she remarked cheerfully.

His brows arched in a frown. "I might have known you would be behind this." He waved at the tub. "Are you out of your mind?"

"Perhaps I am. You may not like what is about to happen, but Salamar and I are going to make you walk."

Marquis glared at Valentina, wishing he could get out of bed and physically shove her out the door. "Get out of my room, Valentina!" he demanded.

"When you are able to get up and throw me out, I'll leave, and not a moment before," she declared, hands on hips, eyes spitting fire.

He struggled up on his pillows. "Damn you, I'll have the servants throw you out. I told you before I do not want you here."

"You can't have the servants throw me out," she said, moving over to the window and pushing the curtains open. "Your grandfather is still in command here, and he has told the servants to obey me in all things." Valentina remembered the talk she had had with Don Alonso just moments ago. He had been delighted with her plan and had given her his full support. "You see, Marquis, if anyone is going to evict me from your room, it will have to be you."

"What are you going to do?" he asked suspiciously. "You are not going to get me into that tub."

Valentina pushed her sleeves up past her elbows. "Yes, you will be put in that tub. If it is at all possible, you are soon going to stand on your own two feet. When that day comes, I will walk out of this room on my own—you won't have to throw me out."

His eyes were dark storm centers. "Damn you to hell, Valentina. You cannot come into my room and order me about. No woman can order my life for me."

"You can get mad at me—you can yell until they hear you all the way to San Francisco—but as God is my judge, if it is at all possible, you are going to walk!"

Marquis stared openmouthed at the little slip of a girl, whom he could break with his bare hands. How dare she push her way into his room making impossible demands! She had to know that she was torturing him. The doctor had said he would never be able to walk.

397

Moving to the bed, Valentina picked up a pair of scissors that lay on the bedside table. "Juan, hold his leg while I cut the bandages off." Immediately the servant complied.

"You are not a doctor, damn you, Valentina. What are you doing? Are you insane?" Marquis raged at her.

"Perhaps I am insane," she answered, tossing the dirty bandages in a heap on the floor. Examining his leg, she almost felt her resolve slip. It was healing well, though the angry red scar was still inflamed and his thigh was swollen. She was reminded that it was her fault he was now suffering so tremendously.

Marquis wore faded black trousers that had had the right leg cut away to accommodate his bandages. Stepping back, Valentina pointed to the tub. "Juan, you and Carlo pick up your *patrón* and place him in the tub. Do it gently and take care not to bend his legs."

As Marquis was lifted into the air, his loud protests filled the room. "Damnation, Valentina, I will not be treated like a baby. Who in the hell do you think you are?"

As he was lowered into the tub, she dropped down beside him. Marquis had never known anger such as he now directed at Valentina. "You will pay for this," he said through clenched teeth. "I'll see that you do."

Marquis had not seen Salamar until she stood over him. "You may not like what we do to you, Marquis Vincente, but, as Valentina said, we will leave when you can throw us out."

His jaw tightened and he leaned back, staring at the ceiling. He would never give Valentina or her strange-looking maid the satisfaction of humiliating him. He just would not talk to them.

Salamar dropped to her knees, gently picked up his leg, and began kneading and massaging it at the calf. Marquis could not feel Salamar's touch since his leg had no feeling in it, but he could feel the tension draining slowly out of him. Her fingertips worked like a healing balm, magically relaxing his whole body.

Closing his eyes, he felt the water wash over him with a soothing warmth. He was unaware that his bedroom was undergoing a transformation while he relaxed. His bed was moved in front of the window. His bed covers were changed, and fresh flowers were placed on several tables about the room.

Soothing hands lathered his hair and massaged his scalp. Opening his eyes, he saw that Valentina was bathing him while Salamar was massaging his leg. His anger was still there, but it had cooled considerably.

"I have not had my breakfast yet," he said testily, fighting against defeat.

Valentina was near his ear when she spoke. "You will eat as soon as the exercise is completed."

Suddenly and unexpectedly, a prickling sensation moved through Marquis's injured leg. He gripped the side of the tub to keep from crying out. Salamar was bending his leg back and forth. The prickling sensation turned to ravaging pain that stabbed like hot knives into his flesh.

Groaning, he turned his head from side to side. Agony such as he had never known assaulted his senses. He clamped his lips tightly together so he would not cry out in pain.

Salamar saw the beads of perspiration that popped out on his upper lip. "You are a proud devil," she said, clasping his leg firmly and bending it downward. "You would not ask me to stop if it killed you, would you, Marquis Vincente?"

His eyes opened and he stared into Salamar's strange eyes, which seemed to search out his deepest thoughts. "You must enjoy torturing me," he gasped.

Valentina gripped Marquis's shoulders, feeling his pain as if it were her own. She wanted to tell Salamar to stop, that she was tormenting him. She wanted to give him strength, to assure him that Salamar knew what she was doing.

"What kind of a wife are you that you want to see me suffer?" Marquis's voice was accusing.

"Tell your wife where you hurt," Salamar said softly.

His eyes bounced off Valentina to stare at Salamar. "You know damned well you are hurting my . . . leg!" His face registered surprise. "My legs!"

"Yes, the leg that has no feeling in it," Salamar confirmed with a smile. "If you can feel what I am doing to you, then you will regain the use of this leg."

Marquis looked uncertain for a moment. "I can feel pain!" He was almost afraid to hope. "Could I be mistaken? I did feel pain, did I not?" he questioned.

To demonstrate that the sensation he had felt had indeed been pain, Salamar moved the leg to one side and then the other, satisfied when Marquis's face whitened. His face was colorless as she smiled at him. "You felt pain, Marquis Vincente."

Valentina felt joy sing through her body. Marquis was going to recover!

"That is enough of this for today," Salamar declared, standing up. "After you have had a good breakfast, we will try something new."

Valentina stood up and called out to Juan and Carlos, who had been waiting by the door. "Place your patrón in a chair, dry him off well, and put dry trousers on him. When that is done, tell Maria to bring his breakfast. Empty the tub, but do not put it away. We will do this same exercise every day."

Marquis hated the fact that Valentina was in charge of his life. He had not wanted her to see him this way. Still, he had felt pain in his leg. Even now it was throbbing. Hope nipped at his mind. The door of doubt had been cracked, and perhaps it would soon open all the way.

400

Valentina left without saying another word, but Salamar smiled at Marquis on her way out. "This morning did not go too badly. Let us hope the afternoon goes equally well."

Marquis ate a hearty breakfast. He was exhausted but excited. He would soon be a whole man again! He found himself looking forward to the afternoon.

Marquis was not asleep but resting with his eyes closed when Valentina and Salamar entered his room. He was aware of their presence when he smelled the soft scent of roses that he always associated with Valentina. Slowly his lashes opened and his eyes locked with soft, silver-blue eyes.

Seeing the wistfulness in Valentina's gaze, Marquis realized that he had been deliberately punishing her. He had married her, then deserted her in his own home. He could only imagine what she thought about him. So many things were unsaid between them. Probably they would never be said.

"It is time for your afternoon exercise," Salamar stated in a tone that said she would brook no argument. "This will be worse than the morning session," she warned, "but only because the feeling is coming to your leg. We are going to work with both legs this time."

Marquis looked at her with complete resignation. "I do not suppose there is anything I can do that will get rid of both of you?"

"Not unless you can kiss your elbow," Salamar mocked. Giving Marquis no time to consider, she jerked the cover off him and tossed it on the floor. "The sooner we get started, the sooner we will finish," Salamar told him.

How he got through the next hour, Marquis would never know. Pain was his constant companion as Salamar forced him to push his heel against the foot of the bed. Then Salamar massaged his leg, twisting it right and left. Just when he thought he could stand it no longer, she started on the other leg. When Salamar finally announced he had had enough for one day, he was weak with relief.

Marquis lay back against his pillow, trying to breathe past the pain in his leg. It was a wonderful feeling—the pain—because it meant his legs were not dead.

Valentina placed the cover over him, looking at him with wide, sympathetic eyes. "Do not pity me," he whispered, too weary to think clearly. "Do not ever feel sorry for me."

"Why should I pity you, Marquis? You are going to recover completely," she told him, turning away.

Slipping out of the room, Valentina knew she did indeed feel pity for him. If only he knew how difficult it had been for her to watch his suffering. She knew he would have to do the same tomorrow, and the next day, and as many days as it took for him to walk.

Every day for a week, Valentina and Salamar went to Marquis's room in the morning and afternoon. Marquis would never have admitted it, but he found himself looking forward to those times. He could feel himself growing stronger, and the pain in his legs lessened with each treatment.

Valentina closed the book she had been reading to her mother, bent, and kissed her cheek. Standing up, she flexed her tired muscles. Salamar was seated by the candle, mending a gown. Valentina whispered, not wanting to disturb her mother. "I'm going to bed now."

Salamar put her mending aside and walked Valentina to the door. "You cannot go to bed yet. There is still something you must do for Marquis. The treatment I have started must be followed exactly."

"But we have done the exercises for today," Valentina

402

said in bewilderment.

"Tonight we begin a new treatment. Did I forget to tell you?"

"Yes. You said nothing about our going to Marquis's room tonight."

"Not we, Valentina—you." Salamar pressed a jar into Valentina's hand. "This must be rubbed into Marquis's legs, taking care not to get it on the wound. You must softly massage his thighs and calves. When that is done, have him turn to his stomach and massage his arms and back. Then have him turn over and rub his chest and stomach. Do this in the sequence I tell you, and do it very carefully, caressingly. It will stimulate the flow of blood in his body."

"But—"

"No buts. If Marquis can fulfill his part and endure the pain, then surely you can do yours."

"I must get dressed first." Valentina was still confused. "I am wearing my nightgown and robe."

"Do not be silly. Marquis is your husband. Go as you are."

Valentina nodded, wishing she did not have to go to Marquis's room alone. "What if he is sleeping," she asked hopefully.

"If he is asleep, you will awaken him."

"What is this for, Salamar?" Valentina inquired, lifting the lid off the jar and smelling the pleasant scent of wild honey and some hauntingly exotic spices.

"It is one of my own creams. If it is applied properly, it will do what it is intended to do for Marquis. Remember, you must rub the cream into the skin, softly."

Valentina was resigned to her fate, but walking slowly down the hallway toward Marquis's room, she dreaded what she must do.

*   *   *

The maid's face eased into a smile—she was rather pleased with herself. "Yes, indeed, Salamar"—she clapped her hands delightedly—"you are a genius! If Valentina applies the cream correctly, it will have the desired effect on her as well as on Marquis."

Salamar knew that the cream had no healing substance, nor was it a magic potion. It was nothing more than her own body cream. The magic would come when Valentina's hands moved over Marquis's body. The two young people loved each other. She would merely give them the opportunity to admit that love. What could be more intimate than Marquis and Valentina alone in his bedroom while Valentina stroked his skin?

Valentina found Marquis's room in darkness but for the faint moonlight that streamed through the open windows.

"Marquis, are you asleep?" she called softly.

He had been sleeping, but at the sound of her voice he stirred and opened his eyes. He had been dreaming about Valentina and was not sure if she was truly there or if he was still dreaming.

"Marquis," she called again, reaching out to touch his shoulder.

"No more exercise," he groaned. "Let me sleep."

"This will not be bad, Marquis. I must apply this cream to your body. You can even close your eyes while I massage it in."

"I do not suppose you will go away until I agree," he bit out in an irritated voice.

"Salamar says this is very important."

"Very well, get it over with," he said grudgingly. "Do what you will."

Valentina did not bother to light a candle. She was just as happy performing this task in the half-light.

Pulling the covers aside, she dipped her fingers in the cool cream and spread it lightly across one leg. Softly she rubbed until it was absorbed into the skin.

"You have magic fingers," he whispered, beginning to come fully awake.

"You must lie still and don't talk," Valentina said, moving her hands up the back of his legs, rubbing softly. When her fingers moved across his upper thigh, Marquis could not have uttered a word if his life had depended on it. His blood was beginning to stir. He was becoming more aware of Valentina with every sweep of her hand.

"Help me turn you on your side, Marquis," Valentina said. With her help, he was able to turn over. She was feeling strangely alive when her fingers moved across his hard-muscled back. Valentina was not aware that her movements had become caressing. She did not know that her breath had caught in her throat and that she was having a hard time swallowing. Bittersweet memories tugged at her mind. How well she remembered the strength of this body.

Trembling slightly, Valentina wondered if she would be able to continue. She was thinking of the night Marquis had made love to her in the dressing room. It had been dark then also.

"Can you turn to your back?" she asked in a breathless whisper.

After he was resting on his back, Marquis closed his eyes as her hands moved across his chest. She was stroking, circling, massaging, moving lower, lower, across his stomach. His muscles tensed, and he felt his manhood stiffen to a throbbing, pulsating ache. He wanted her—he had to have her. What could be more right? After all, she was his wife.

Valentina felt her heart hammering in her ears. Her breath was heavy and waves of passion melted her resistance. She wanted desperately to run from the room, but she stayed.

Valentina did not pull away when Marquis's strong arms went around her, dragging her onto the bed beside him. He expected her to protest, but she melted against him with a gentle sigh.

Frantically he sought her lips as a man seeks water on the desert. He emitted a groan and his tongue darted into her mouth, plunging and plundering. Hot blood was drumming in his pulses, and his hands moved aside Valentina's offending clothing so he could find the soft, creamy flesh beneath.

Her aching need was almost painful as Valentina felt his hands slide up her thigh and plunge into her moist body. Gasping for breath, she allowed her hand to drift across his hips, pulling him closer. Lowering his head, he settled his mouth on her breasts. First he tasted and circled one with his tongue, then did the same with the other.

Valentina was in agony as his wonderful hands worked magic on her body. Softly his finger moved in and out of her body, arousing, teasing, promising things to come. When he withdrew his hand, she moaned in protest, but he only laughed. Pulling her on top of him, he thrust upward and buried himself deep inside her.

A thousand candles seemed to burst forth with light as Valentina's body shuddered. With each forward thrust, he took her breath away, filling her body with his throbbing desire.

"Your legs," she managed to whisper. "We mustn't hurt—"

He pulled her head down to him, and his warm breath fanned her mouth. "Shhh," he whispered against her lips. "So sweet," he groaned in a breathless voice. "You have been eating away at my brain, Silver Eyes. I have had to watch you without touching for so long. Tonight I will have you—all of you."

With a swift upward thrust, Marquis drove all the way into her body. Valentina threw her head back and cried out in sensuous pleasure.

"Marquis," she whispered as his body became as one with hers.

With one final thrust, he brought them both to a shuddering climax. Valentina collapsed against Marquis while the whole world trembled. Slowly they both came out of the soft spell that had been woven about them. Marquis's hand moved lovingly across her face, and he pushed the curtain of gold aside, finding her lips.

"I will never let another man touch you," he declared possessively. "Swear you will never—"

Her lips touched his, stopping whatever he had been about to ask of her. Soft kisses and gentle sighs filled her mind and heart. "Have I hurt your leg?" she asked at last, breathless from his kisses.

He chuckled. "It is too late to think of that now. Probably if your Salamar knew what happened here tonight, she would say it was good exercise."

Valentina smiled, feeling happiness in the very depths of her being. "It would not surprise me if this was what Salamar had planned all along," Valentina stated. "Most probably it was her plan."

"Stay with me tonight," Marquis murmured against her ear. "You dazzle me with your sweet fire. You make me feel more alive than I have ever before felt. I need you."

Nothing he could have said would have made her happier. "Suppose someone comes in and finds us together?" she asked.

He laughed in delight and hugged her to him. "They will just think I could not resist my wife's charms any longer and finally took her to my bed. Besides, no one would dare barge into my room without knocking, with the exception of you and Salamar."

"I have been bossy and pushy, haven't I?"

He smiled against her lips. "I cannot tell you how you badgered and bullied me, and me laid up in bed."

Moving over so she could lay beside him, Valentina rested her head on his shoulder. Marquis might love Isabel, she mused, but Isabel would never experience the special bond she had shared with him tonight. She did not have to be told that their lovemaking was special.

"What are you thinking?" she asked suddenly.

His hand drifted across her arm. "I was thinking how my life has changed since I met an obstinate, opinionated, silver-eyed vixen."

"I have been a lot of trouble to you, haven't I, Marquis?"

He wrapped a silken curl around his finger and raised it to his lips. Her sweet face was drawn up in a questioning frown. "No one would believe what you have put me through, Valentina Barrett Vincente. Are you always going to complicate my life?"

"I'm afraid so," she answered earnestly. "I just always seem to get into trouble. You will be put out with me many times."

He laughed deeply, hugging his precious burden to him. "I can hardly wait to see what new trouble you will get me into. You will have to go far and try hard to find something to match the cave-in."

"Don't say you haven't been warned, Marquis," she whispered. "I always get into trouble."

His hand moved down to her stomach, and he pulled it away quick, as if he had been burned. Valentina knew he had just remembered the baby. Would he turn from her because of the child she carried?

She waited tensely to see what he would do. "I forgot about the child. I did not hurt you, did I?"

"No, you didn't hurt me."

He still held her in his arms, but she could feel him

408

withdraw from her. What if she were to tell him that she was Jordanna? she wondered. Would she lose him completely?

Gathering up her courage, she spoke. "Marquis, I have something I must tell you."

"No, not tonight. Let us just pretend that there is only you and I, and that this is our wedding night. Your body was made perfectly to accommodate mine," he whispered. "Have you noticed?"

Oh, yes, she had noticed. His hands were again working magic on her body and she had no will to resist. With the same frenzied ecstasy as before, the two of them sailed across the silver skies of passion, lost in the wonder that they brought to each other.

Chapter Twenty-Six

Valentina was awake to welcome the first golden streaks of morning that touched the room with its shimmering light. She had been watching Marquis sleep for a long time. She lightly touched the dark hair curled about his ear. Her lips brushed against his long lashes. For the moment, he belonged to her alone. She could allow her eyes to roam over the face she loved so much, without being seen. Softly, almost timidly, she touched her lips to his.

Carefully she traced a birthmark that was on his right shoulder. It was perfectly heart shaped, and red in color.

Valentina could not seem to touch Marquis enough. Lightly her finger traced the outline of his lips. She jumped guiltily as he caught her finger in his teeth. Slowly that wonderful smile of his spread over his face, causing her breath to catch in her throat.

Glancing into his eyes, she could read his thoughts. The brown depths did not speak of love but rather of possession. She was his by way of mastery—by right of conquest.

"You have a birthmark," she said, feeling foolish and coy.

He smiled. "Yes, it is a Vincente trait that shows up

411

from time to time. Sometimes it will skip whole generations. It is said that a Vincente who has the red heart is blessed. I never believed that before . . . but I do now."

She drew in her breath. "Do you feel yourself blessed, Marquis?"

His dark eyes swept her face, taking in the golden hair that curled across her forehead, moving to the softly curved lips. "After last night, I feel blessed." His bold eyes sparkled when he touched her cheek. "You were wonderful, you know. So alluring and breathtaking."

Valentina felt joy ringing in her heart. "I thought I dreamed last night," she said almost shyly. "When I awoke and discovered I was in your bed, I realized it was no dream."

"I have been in a dreamworld since I first met you, Valentina. If this is dreaming, let me never wake up. Will you stay with me, Valentina?"

She did not fully understand his meaning. "I must get up soon. There is much to do."

His smile was warm. "I do not mean now, although that is not a bad idea. We could bar the door and not admit anyone. Last night was our official wedding night. You made me your slave, little Silver Eyes."

A light flush tinted her cheeks, and she lowered her eyes. She liked it when he called her Silver Eyes. There was hope in her heart. Perhaps before long she would make him forget Isabel.

She moved away from him, glancing down at his leg. "Are you feeling any pain this morning?" she asked with a troubled frown on her face.

"Come here, Silver Eyes." He chuckled. "I do not want to talk."

Her smile was like the sunshine, dazzling and bright. Taking Marquis's offered hand, she allowed him to pull her against his chest. With each breath he took, his skin

412

brushed her breasts. His thigh was pressed against hers so tightly she could scarcely breathe. She could sense the throbbing, pulsing life of him against her skin. His eyes were a soft, velvety darkness. The sound of his voice vibrated through her, making her quiver all over.

Time was forgotten as his soft eyes beckoned to her. His lips spoke of sensuous feelings rekindled, and she slipped under his spell once more. Their bodies merged into one hot, searing flesh.

Valentina felt a sob building up deep inside; she was moved to tears because of the beauty of their lovemaking. Everything else was forgotten but the man who drove his life-giving shaft into her body.

Valentina had been living in a dream for over a week. Each day she would work with Marquis under Salamar's instructions. At night she would lie in his arms and feel the thrill of his kisses and the magic of his hands. She was sure no one had ever loved a man as deeply as she loved Marquis. She held out hope that he would one day return her love. She knew she brought joy to his body; she lived for the day she would bring joy to his heart.

Salamar watched delightedly as young love blossomed. She saw the way Valentina and Marquis would touch when they thought no one was looking. She gloried in the tender looks that passed between them when they were across the room from each other. Valentina was glowing with happines, and Salamar's world was content.

Each day Salamar urged Valentina to tell Marquis the truth about being Jordanna. She assured Valentina that their love was strong enough to survive Marquis's first bitter anger at being made to look the fool. After the initial shock, he would be glad that the child Valentina carried belonged to him, Salamar insisted. But Valentina refused to consider telling Marquis the truth, fearing it would spoil what they had together. Salamar feared if Valentina waited too long, it could prove disastrous.

Marquis was steadily improving. He had not yet taken that first step, but Salamar was confident it would not be long before he would be ready.

Valentina had just finished reading to her mother and decided to check on Marquis to see if he would like to have Carlos and Juan carry him down to the garden. When she opened the bedroom door, she stopped in her tracks. There, standing in the middle of the floor, was Marquis.

"You walked!" she cried, taking a step toward him. "My God, Marquis, you can walk!"

His laughter was deep as he took a guarded step toward her. "I have been practicing for days. I did not want to tell you about it until I was walking normally."

"Oh, Marquis, you did it!" Their hands touched and he pulled her to him. "I knew you would do it, Marquis. I'm so proud of you."

She watched him take a hesitant step. He stopped to catch his breath. "You and Salamar deserve all the credit, Valentina. Without the two of you bullying and prodding me, I might never have found the courage to walk."

Her eyes were tear bright when he pushed her away to take several more faltering steps. Going to him, she took his hand and he leaned against her for support. As she helped him to the bed, she could tell by the way he leaned against her that he was tiring.

Lying back on his pillows, he smiled. "You and Salamar helped me prove the doctor wrong. I do not know what magic the two of you wove about me. I only know that my leg had no feeling in it until you and Salamar started working with it."

Valentina fluffed up the pillows, giving him a warm smile. "I know no magic, but I'm not too sure about

Salamar. She has amazing abilities."

"In what way?"

"She once saw in a vision that we were coming to California. This was the day before I received the letter from my mother, telling me to come."

"What else does she see?" he asked with interest.

"She says my baby will be a daughter." Valentina had spoken without thinking. When she saw the frown on Marquis's face, she regretted her words, wishing she could take them back. "Would you like something cool to drink?" she asked, quickly changing the subject.

Marquis had lost his good humor. His dark eyes were dull, and he turned his head away from Valentina. "No, I just want to rest now."

Valentina walked to the door and left quietly. Going to the bedroom next door, she moved out onto the balcony. Her hand strayed to her abdomen, which was now slightly rounded, and she felt the tiny flutter of the child inside her body. She had been feeling its movements for a week now. Soon everyone would have to be told that she was with child. She wondered how Marquis would handle all the congratulations from his family. She was so confused. Perhaps she would soon gather the courage to tell Marquis everything, as Salamar had suggested.

Every day Valentina had more reason to rejoice. Her mother was growing stronger, and Marquis continued to improve.

Marquis's mother and grandfather were delighted that he was able to walk again. Don Alonso was quick to give Valentina praise, while Doña Anna credited the miracle to her prayers and her son's courage.

Marquis still walked with a decided limp, and Valentina knew he was often in pain. He stubbornly turned away from any show of sympathy. Most of his

415

days were spent in the garden. Even though Valentina begged him to rest for at least an hour each day, he refused. With his recovery came his impatience to take his place as patrón of Paraíso del Norte.

One morning Valentina awoke to find Marquis already dressed and standing over her. "If you want to go riding with me, wife, you had better get up and dressed."

She stared at him for a moment. "Do you think you are well enough to ride?"

"Indeed I am. I am almost as good as new," he assured her. "Now if you do not want to be left behind, you had better be dressed in ten minutes."

She scrambled out of bed and pulled on her robe. "Give me five minutes," she called, running out the door and into her bedroom where her clothing was kept.

Valentina felt reborn as she and Marquis galloped across the soft, rolling hills. Happiness made her heart take wing when he turned and smiled at her. "Where are we going?" she asked breathlessly.

"I want to show you a place I have never taken anyone else—not even Tyree has been there. When I was a boy and I was troubled about something, this was where I would go."

Marquis spurred his horse on, and Valentina followed his lead. Was it possible that Marquis was beginning to love her just a little? she wondered. Her heart was beating so fast it was keeping time with her horse's thundering hooves.

They crossed a shallow stream and rode up a hill. In the distance Valentina could see a wide river running swift and strong. Their horses moved down a steep incline that led to the river. Soon Marquis pulled up his mount and motioned for Valentina to dismount. Fearing he would hurt his leg, she held her breath as Marquis

416

dismounted. But he threw his leg over the saddle and dropped to the ground with ease.

Valentina shaded her eyes, watching a hawk circle above them. Opening its wings, it appeared to be suspended on the wind. There was nowhere on earth Valentina would rather have been than there on Paraíso del Norte with Marquis at her side. Filled with the beauty around her, and her love for this land, she listened quietly and heard the sound of rushing water. "Marquis, is there a waterfall nearby?" she inquired, looping her horse's reins around a tree trunk.

"That is exactly what it is. Come with me. I will show you."

Taking her hand, Marquis led her around a bend in the river. There, in stunning glory, filtering over the side of a cliff, was a magnificent waterfall. Water plunged some forty feet to the river below, swirling and bubbling musically.

"This is lovely," Valentina exclaimed, smiling up into Marquis's face. "So this is where you came to be alone as a boy?" She tried to imagine him as a boy, but the vision eluded her completely. He was so strong, so proud, she could not see him as a child.

"We have not come to my secret place yet." He led Valentina straight to the waterfall. The water rose like a mist and showered down on them. Valentina was puzzled when Marquis took her hand and pulled her upon a ledge that jutted out to the side of the river. She held her breath, fearing he would slide off the slick rock and hurt his leg.

Lifting Valentina's hand and clinging to the cliff, Marquis edged his way forward. They were actually behind the waterfall now and Valentina could see a cave just ahead.

Fear gnawed at her insides as they neared the cave. It brought back memories of her father's mine and the cave-

417

in. Marquis stepped down to the cave and held his arms up to her. Seeing her pale face and the fear that lit her eyes, he pulled her forward, knowing what she was thinking.

"You need have no fear of this cave, Valentina. It is very shallow and the sun shines through the falls to light every corner of it."

Valentina called on her courage and allowed Marquis to lift her off the rock. Laughing, he grabbed her about the waist and set her down in the cave.

Glancing around with awe, Valentina saw that it was indeed a shallow cave, no more than twenty feet deep. The walls looked like shiny white marble. The bright sunlight reflecting through the waterfall sent a shower of rainbow colors dancing on the cave walls.

"I can't believe it," she said, turning around and drinking in the beauty. "What a marvelous place this is. I can only imagine the wonderful hours you spent here."

He watched her face and wondered if she knew how lovely she was. To look upon her made him believe in princesses, in dragons, in happy endings. "You like my secret place then, Valentina?" he asked.

"I have never seen anything like it. Does it always reflect the colors of the rainbow?"

"No, only at certain times of the day. I would be willing to bet there is not another cave to rival this one anywhere in the world."

"I wouldn't think there was, Marquis," she agreed. "What kinds of things did you dream here as a boy?"

He took her arm and seated her on a smooth rock, then sat down beside her. "I dreamed of growing up and being a great don, just as my grandfather is. At one time I wanted to travel the world, but not any longer. Everything I will ever want is right here on Paraíso del Norte."

"Did you know that your face lights up when you talk

about Paraíso del Norte, Marquis? You love this land, don't you?"

"Everything can pass away—people you love, family; generations of Vincentes have gone on before me, but the land remains. It will be here long after you and I are nothing but memories."

"How sad in a way. It makes me wish we could leave our mark in this world—that we could do something that would live after we are dust."

His eyes sparkled. "We can. Let me show you something that will make you feel very young. Turn around and look on the wall of the cave," he told her.

Valentina turned, seeing nothing for a moment; then her eyes fell on what appeared to be two handprints—one large and the other small. "Is this what you mean?" she asked, bewildered.

"Yes. At some far off time, a man and a woman found this cave. Most probably it was before any white man ever set foot on this land. They left their marks to last through all eternity. Like the pyramids in Egypt and the great Colosseum in Rome, these handprints have endured."

With a delicate finger, Valentina traced the small outline of the feminine handprint, then went on to outline the obvious male handprint. "What a pity we don't know anything about the man and woman who left the handprints. Do you think they loved each other?"

Marquis's eyes sought hers and he nodded. "There are words here, Valentina. See the strange markings. Look closely because time has faded them."

"Yes, I see them. I wonder what they mean."

"As you know, the Indians have no written words as we know it, but some tribes used symbols such as these. We had an old Indian working for us when I was a boy. I copied down the markings, just as you see them here. I showed them to Manalio and asked him if he knew what

419

they meant."

She held her breath. "Was he able to tell you what they said?"

"Yes. He told me it translated to something like, 'I pledge to you my everlasting love.'" Marquis's eyes touched Valentina's lips. "You see, they were lovers, just as you and I are."

Valentina's heart sang as his head dipped. When his lips settled on hers, her arms moved around his shoulders. She could almost feel the presence of those lovers who had once found this cave as their haven.

Marquis raised his head and chuckled. "If you do not stop tempting me, I will have you right here on the floor of the cave."

Valentina felt her face burning and turned back to the cave writings. She touched the strange markings, feeling as if she were breathing the same air that the two lovers had breathed so long ago. She was overwhelmed with the kinship she felt for the unknown man and woman. "What do you suppose happened to them?"

"Only the whispering wind and the golden California sun know, Valentina; and they are not telling."

Tenderly he gathered her into his arms while his lips brushed against her sweet-smelling hair. "Shall we leave our mark for some far distant lovers to find, Valentina?" he whispered against her ear.

"Yes, please," she breathed. "But how can we?"

"That is easy." Taking his knife out of his pocket, he picked up her hand and cut deeply around it, pressing down hard so the outline would remain in the stone wall. He then repeated the process with his hand.

Valentina marveled as she watched him. How out of character this display of sentimentality was for Marquis! she mused. He was almost loverlike today. "What words shall we write, Marquis?"

He lowered his dark eyes so they were shaded by thick,

curling lashes. "Nothing," he said almost coldly, taking note of the hurt that etched her soft lips into a frown.

Standing up slowly, sensing that his mood had changed, Valentina could feel him distancing himself from her. "I thank you for showing me your secret place, Marquis. If you don't mind, I would like to go back to the house now."

As Valentina turned away, she did not see the look of naked yearning that flamed in the dark eyes. In two quick strides he was at her side; then he took her by the shoulders and turned her to face him. Dipping his head, he lightly ran his lips over her thick, black lashes. A shudder of delight ran the length of Valentina's body as his tongue swirled around the outline of her lips.

"Are we going back to the house?" she questioned breathlessly, realizing his intention. Even though his lashes were lowered and only a sliver of brown showed, Valentina could read the raw passion that pulled her to him like a hummingbird drawn to the nectar of a rose.

"Not just yet, Valentina," came his whispered reply. "I want to make love to you here, where two other lovers once found delight in each other's arms."

Wild excitement throbbed through her body as his hands slowly moved across the contours of her face. His touch was so soft, so gentle, and the look in his eyes so disturbing, that it evoked a physical pain in her heart. She did not pull back when he began removing the pins from her hair. As the golden curtain cascaded across her shoulders and down her back, his eyes worshiped her beauty.

"You set my blood on fire and take my breath away, Valentina." He spoke against her ear. "I cannot think of anything else but you when you are near me." His hand slipped inside her gown and with a velvet-soft touch he caressed her breasts. He drew in a tight breath. "I can feel your heart beating against my hand. Admit that you want

421

me as much as I want you."

Wave after wave of delight passed through her body. Raising her head, she met his eyes. "Yes, Marquis, I admit it."

He pulled her toward him and his mouth descended to lightly brush against hers. As the fire smoldered in his blood and his passion ignited, the kiss deepened. Their breaths mingled and their heartbeats became as one.

Valentina pressed herself tightly against Marquis, craving a closeness that was denied her by their clothing. She was weak with desire when he pushed her riding habit from her shoulders. A tremor shook her as he dropped to his knees and pulled her down with him. Clasping her hands behind his back, she raised her head in ecstasy when he buried his face against her soft breasts, his breath gently teasing the rosy nipples into hard peaks.

Valentina sucked in her breath and felt her lungs fill with air. Naked to the waist, she boldly allowed her hands to wander down the front of Marquis's shirt, then pulled it free of his trousers. Pushing his snowwhite shirt aside, she moved her fingers to glide across his smooth chest.

Marquis, breathing deeply of her sweet scent, raised his head to stare at her lovely face. Taking her hands, he kissed each fingertip. "There is magic in your touch, Valentina. You have the ability to reach inside a man with the brush of your hands. Did Salamar teach you some ancient ritual on how to drive me out of my mind?"

She shook her head in confusion. "No . . . I . . . no, Salamar wouldn't do that."

"No." He smiled slightly. "You needed no one to teach you how to please a man, Valentina. Some women are born with that knowledge—you are one of them." Gently he lowered her back onto the soft sand that covered the floor of the cave. "You came into this world knowing how to flirt with a man and steal his heart."

She blinked her eyes, not understanding his teasing. "I never flirt."

His finger traced the outline of her lips. "No?" He held her gaze and she saw the fire burning in his eyes. "You are not even aware that you have me where you want me, are you, Valentina?"

"I am never sure where you want me, Marquis."

"Oh Lord, I am tempted to tell you. I wonder what you would do if you really knew how I felt about you?"

"I'm not sure I want to know."

His lips twitched in a smile, but when his eyes moved over her creamy flesh, the smile left his face. He felt his body tremble when Valentina's gaze shifted to his tight-fitting trousers and she saw evidence of his arousal and his need for her. Slowly reaching up, she laced her fingers through his dark hair, parting her lips enticingly.

"Vixen," he moaned. His lips burned into hers as his hands deftly removed her remaining clothing. Valentina was so caught up in his kiss that she was only vaguely aware that he was removing his own clothing.

A fine mist from the waterfall sprayed gently over their bodies, while bright rainbow hues reflecting from the cascading water seemed to encase them in magnificent color.

In awe and reverence, Marquis allowed his eyes to roam over her soft curves. A streak of red was slashed across her face; a kaleidoscope of colors softly touched her mist-covered body. He held his breath. "Oh God," he cried, looking deeply into her eyes, "how can anyone be so beautiful?"

He wanted to tell her how his heart sang when he made love to her. He wanted to let her know how she filled his heart. He ached to speak of the love that burned within him. Instead he said, "Since first I saw you, your beauty has touched my heart. I knew then that I wanted to possess you. Little did I know it would be you who would possess me."

Each word he spoke fired her blood; every time he touched her with his dark gaze it was like a caress on her tingling skin. She ran her fingertips over his mist-covered face, brushing a damp lock of hair from his forehead. She felt joy when he trembled at her soft touch. She was dizzy with desire when Marquis pulled her tightly to him, kissing and caressing her until she thought she would die of need.

Valentina was almost mindless when he pushed her back against the damp sand that covered the cave floor and nudged her thighs apart. She gasped when she felt the heat of his spear as he buried it deep inside her. Biting her lips, she threw her head back, allowing pleasure to wash over her like a tidal wave of desire.

Gently he nipped and teased the pink crests of her breasts, swirling his tongue around the nipples, licking the moisture from her skin, while he moved slowly within her body, carrying her away in a storm of glorious feelings. Her love for this man was boundless. He was her life—her reason for being. As he filled her emptiness, she was engulfed in a soft, unexplainable, languorous feeling.

Clasping Valentina's hips, Marquis drove deeply inside of her, caressingly arousing her with sensuous feelings. He was soothing the aching need that burned within her, making her giddy and faint with desire. He was thankful for the mist that sprinkled his face and ran down his cheeks, for it disguised the tears of love that filled his eyes. His body had never burned as it burned now. He had never felt the joy of fulfillment so strongly as he did at that moment.

With the roar of the waterfall echoing in their ears, amid the spraying mist, with the colors of the rainbow reflecting off their bodies, Marquis and Valentina reached for—and found—perfection. As they emitted soft gasps of delight and moans of pleasure, their love took on a dreamlike quality. Valentina's body found a release at the same time that Marquis's body reached a trembling climax.

Wrapped tightly in his arms, her face softened by lovemaking, Valentina wished this magical moment would never pass. She wished she could stay close to Marquis, have him hold her like this forever. Sadly she realized that even though she was wife to this hot-blooded Spaniard, their worlds could sometimes touch, but she would never be anything to him but a woman he would use when the mood struck him.

"Today I have touched the morning mist and held a rainbow in my arms," he said with feeling. Raising her face to him and giving her a smile that melted her heart, he added, "No man could say as much, except perhaps the ancient Indian warrior to his lover."

Oh yes, Valentina thought to herself. Today I, too, have held a rainbow. But like all rainbows, this one will fade into nothingness with the setting of the sun.

In that moment she could almost feel the spirits of the long dead lovers who had once occupied this cave. Looking into Marquis's eyes, she knew he felt them also.

As if a curtain had fallen across Marquis's face, he frowned and then stood up, offering Valentina his hand. "It is getting late. We should return home now," he told her. His voice sounded so dull, and the look in his eyes was so cold and distant. It was as if he had again shut her out completely.

Valentina drew on her gown and wound her hair in a tight knot, pinning it at the nape of her neck and trying all the while to hide her hurt. She had reached the heights of glory today; she was now descending into the bowels of hell. Marquis had a way of putting her in her place with a single glance. And, for the moment, she did not know where her place was.

As they rode back to the house, there was a tense silence between them. Gone was the lightheartedness they had started out with that morning. Gone was the desire and closeness they had shared in the waterfall cavern.

Chapter Twenty-Seven

After the morning Marquis had taken Valentina to the cave, he had not asked her to accompany him again. Every day he would ride out on his midnight black stallion, and she would not see him until that evening. At night Marquis would still take her in his arms and their passion would ignite into flames. She fell more in love with her husband, and he grew farther away from her.

Now that Marquis could walk, he ate most of his meals with his family, but Valentina was never invited. Although she tried not to feel hurt by the obvious insult, she was.

Valentina was sitting in the garden with her sewing in her lap when she heard the jingle of spurs. Turning around, she watched Marquis approach. He walked with only a slight limp now, and she had not ceased to be amazed at his speedy recovery once he had started walking.

"You enjoy the garden, do you not?" he asked, stopping just in front of her.

"Yes. It is my favorite spot in the house."

"How is your mother, Valentina?" he asked, sitting down on a bench, watching with interest as she made tiny stitches in her tapestry.

Marquis had not inquired about her mother until now, and his question took her by surprise. "She is growing stronger. I believe she would recover completely if we could find out about my father. She hasn't been bothered by the fever lately."

"You do not see much of my mother, do you, Valentina?"

"No," she stated flatly, not feeling inclined to criticize Marquis's mother.

"I realize you have not been treated with the respect that you should receive as my wife. My mother is set in her ways and does not adjust readily to new ideas."

"Meaning I am a new idea?"

"Yes, to her you are. I would like to tell you that, given time, she would come around, but I just do not know. I do not want you to be hurt because of her coldness toward you."

Valentina gave him a sideways glance. "I have accepted your mother's coldness, Marquis. I know I will never sit at her table or be high in her regard. It is your neglect that I find hard to live with. I am your wife, but you don't wish to treat me like it."

He reached for her hand and laced his fingers through it. "I know I have not been the ideal husband. While you have been here, you have suffered much from the Vincente family. I have found you to be steadfast and loyal, with many qualities to admire. You are a good wife, Valentina. You have not complained, though you have had much cause. I wish I could tell you that everything will be better, but I do not know if it will or not."

She felt warm inside from his generous praise. Still, she did not know why he chose today to say these things to her. "Sometimes, Marquis, I believe we should never have gotten married. We are too different, and there is too much standing in our way."

He watched as a golden curl blew across her mouth and he reached up, pushing it aside. "At night it is good with us, Valentina. It is just when the sun comes up—when we face reality—that we drift apart."

"Yes, but we cannot live in the dark for the rest of our lives, Marquis. We have to come out in the sunshine sometimes. There are some realities that we are going to have to face soon."

"Are you referring to your baby?"

"Yes, my baby. It will not be long until everyone will know that I am with child."

His face grew grim. "I do not like to think about the child."

"I have tried not to think about it myself, Marquis. But it is becoming harder and harder to ignore with each passing day."

"I do not want to talk about the baby," he said, drawing in a deep breath. "I want my baby to fill your belly, not . . ." His voice trailed off.

"You knew when you married me that I was with child, Marquis. I don't know what you want from me. I will tell you this. I was born a fighter. I will take whatever I have to, as long as I can endure it. But be warned: I can take care of myself if need be. I do not intend spending the rest of my life as just your bed partner. I am a person—my baby is a person. You cannot make us go away by ignoring us."

Valentina and Marquis were so deep in their conversation that they did not hear Tyree approach until he called out, "What would a man have to do to get himself invited to dinner around here?"

Valentina came quickly to her feet, laughing up at Tyree. "For a dear friend like yourself, I'm sure no invitation is necessary."

He held her at arm's length. "You are radiant. Is that

429

healthy glow the latest style this year?"

She hugged him and planted a kiss on his cheek. "It is for me. You see before you a contentedly married matron."

Tyree did not miss the fact that Valentina had said "contented," not "happy." His eyes clouded for the briefest moment, then he smiled at Marquis. "I don't have to ask you how you are doing. It shows on your face as well. Don Alonso tells me you are walking with only a slight limp."

Marquis was not at all pleased by the overly friendly way in which Valentina had greeted Tyree. As he came to his feet, his voice was cutting. "What brings you to Paraíso del Norte, Tyree? Did you take a wrong turn on your way to the Crystal Palace?"

Tyree caught the possessive way Marquis pulled Valentina against him. "As it happens"—he laughed— "I have a surprise for your wife that I believe will add to her happiness."

"Not a wedding present, Tyree. You didn't need to get us anything. You have given so much already," Valentina said, linking her arm with his.

"Ah, but you see, this is something I believe you will like very much. It comes to you by way of a South Sea island. If you don't want it, I'll send it away."

She looked at him, puzzled. "What can it be?"

Tyree's face beamed as he called to someone standing in the arched doorway. "Come out and see if Valentina wants to keep you or throw you back."

Valentina held her breath as a tall man stepped into the sunshine. Marquis did not take his eyes off Valentina, who seemed rooted to the spot. He saw the sob catch in her throat. The man was handsome, with golden hair and dancing blue eyes. For a moment Marquis felt bitter jealousy, wondering who this stranger could be. Was he some man from Valentina's past? Could he be the father of her baby?

"Father!" Valentina cried at last, running into the man's outstretched arms. "Father, you are alive!"

Ward Barrett clasped his daughter in his arms as tears sparkled in his eyes. She touched his face to make sure he was real and not a figment of her imagination.

"Where did you find him?" Marquis asked, wishing he had been the one to bring Valentina such joy.

"I kept checking the ships as they came into dock, until I got lucky. "He had been shanghaied all right, but not on the *Southern Cross,* as you were told, but the *Tradewind,* out of Jamaica."

"How did you secure his freedom?"

"With enough money, you can buy almost anything."

"I will pay you whatever it cost to buy his freedom, my friend. Thank you for this."

"Neither thanks nor money is necessary—this is my wedding present to your wife. My satisfaction comes from seeing this story end happily."

"You are a good friend, Tyree. I know how you feel about Valentina. I do not want it to come between the two of us." A hint of threat ran through his words and a glint of bitterness clouded his eyes.

"It won't come between us unless you let it, Marquis. I know she is your wife."

Both men fell silent as Valentina led her father over to Marquis, proudly introducing the two of them. "Marquis, this is my father. Father, my husband, Marquis Vincente."

Ward Barrett extended his hand and gripped the young Spaniard's. "I'm pleased to meet you, Marquis. Tyree filled me in on all you have done on my behalf. I have only to look at my little girl's face to see that she is happy."

431

"I am happier than you know, sir, that you are reunited with your family," Marquis declared earnestly.

Ward looked into the face of the young man who had married his daughter. He was struck by the dark, foreign looks of his new son-in-law. Marquis Vincente was the exact opposite of the husband he would have chosen for Valentina. But being a firm believer in love, Ward smiled. If his daughter was happy, what else mattered?

"Valentina," her father said, holding out his hand to her, "take me to your mother. I understand she has been ill, and I am impatient to see her."

Valentina brushed a tear from her cheek and turned to Marquis. "If you and Tyree will excuse me, I won't be long."

"Go," Marquis told her, smiling. "Be with your family. I will see you at dinner."

Valentina looked at him questioningly. "Where will we be dining tonight?"

He smiled. "When Tyree comes to visit, we always have a big family dinner." He lowered his voice. "Tyree would think it strange if you did not dine with us."

"Are we to put on a show of family tranquillity for Tyree?" Valentina asked. "I have not been invited to your mother's table before now."

Marquis frowned. "That will all change soon."

"Not on my account, Marquis. I am just as happy with the present arrangement."

"Will you come to my mother's table tonight, Valentina?"

Seeing how much it meant to him, she did not hesitate with her answer. "Yes, I will come."

He smiled. "Good. Now run along with your father while I talk to Tyree."

"Would you like to come with me and Father?" Valentina asked. "You would be most welcome."

"No. I will stay here with Tyree. Go and be with your family. You have been too long separated."

Valentina felt her father's arm go around her. Happiness danced in her eyes, and she had to touch him again and again to make sure he was really there. As they walked away, Marquis and Tyree stared after them.

"Here's a happy ending," Tyree said, leisurely stretching out his long legs.

"Yes, it would appear so," Marquis said, turning his gaze on his friend. "You seem to deal in happy endings. Have you taken to arranging everyone's happiness?"

"God forbid," Tyree retorted with a grin. "I would much rather find my own happiness."

"Do you ever think of settling down to a wife?" Marquis asked.

"Not me. What woman would want a scoundrel like me? I would rather spread myself around, so I can reach as many ladies as possible."

"Not a very long-lasting prospect. You cannot live that way forever."

Tyree folded his hands and gave his friend a disbelieving glance. "This coming from you—you, who had so many women you often got their names mixed up?"

Marquis watched Valentina disappear through the archway. "Yes, but that was before I met the one woman who could be all things to me. When I think of the others, they were as nothing."

"How fortunate for you." Tyree's eyes gave nothing away. He would hide his love for the wife of his best friend, although he knew Marquis suspected how he felt.

Marquis turned dark eyes on Tyree. "I will win her, Tyree. One day the man she loved will be only a bad memory."

Tyree stared at Marquis, astounded by his confusion.

433

Apparently, he reasoned, Valentina still had not told Marquis her secret. Why had she allowed Marquis to torment himself, thinking she had another lover? Why had she not told him that he was the lover in her past? What was going on here? Tyree knew he had to see Valentina alone. He would have to convince her to tell Marquis the truth.

Marquis's voice broke into Tyree's thoughts. "I sent word to you to find Jordanna, Tyree. Have you?"

Tyree reached past Marquis, picking up a bottle of wine that was on the table. Not looking at his friend, he poured a glass of the ruby liquid and took a sip. "I have not found her, Marquis. You aren't the only one who has been searching for Jordanna. Half the men in California would like to know her whereabouts."

"This is no joking matter, Tyree. I want you to keep looking until you find her."

Tyree raised an eyebrow. "And if I find her, what then?"

"Just let me know. I want to take care of her."

"That would be cozy—just you, Valentina, Jordanna, and—"

Marquis's eyes narrowed. "I do not care for your little jests, Tyree. Just find Jordanna for me!"

"Mother never gave up hope that you were alive, Father," Valentina told him as they climbed the stairs. "She knew you were alive, even when I doubted it."

"I understand you had several mishaps trying to find me. A carriage accident and a cave-in."

"As you see, I survived."

His eyes were laughing, and she stopped on the landing to be crushed in his arms. "Not only have you survived, but you've grown into a beautiful young lady. I always

434

knew you would be lovely, but you surpassed my expectations."

"I was but a child the last time you saw me, Father."

"Yes. How long ago that seems. I thought I would never see you or your mother again. I still can't believe I have found you both."

"Thank God, Father. Now that you are here, Mother will get well."

Valentina opened the door of her mother's bedroom to discover she was asleep. Placing her finger to her lips, Valentina opened the door wider so Salamar could see her father. Salamar's face brightened, and she came quickly to her feet. Valentina motioned for Salamar to follow her out of the room so her mother and father could be alone for their reunion.

Ward stared for a long time at the face of the woman he loved. Only the thought of seeing her again had given him the courage to survive the long sea voyage. How pale she looked—how fragile. Going down on his knees, he touched her face gently so she would not awaken too suddenly and be startled.

"Evonne, my darling, it's me—wake up."

Her eyes fluttered open. For the longest time, she just lay there, wondering if she were dreaming. Her bottom lip quivered as she reached out her hand and touched warm flesh. "Ward," she whispered. He was real! She was not dreaming. "Oh, Ward," she cried out as he gathered her in his arms.

Valentina sat across the table from Marquis at dinner. Doña Anna, who sat beside her son, was sullen and cast seething glances in Valentina's direction. Don Alonso was the perfect host, laughing and entertaining. Rosalia sat on one side of the grandee and Valentina on the other,

435

while Tyree was placed on the other side of Valentina.

Don Alonso raised his wine glass to Valentina. "We are delighted, my dear, to hear your parents have been reunited. I am sorry they couldn't join us tonight, but I certainly understand their wanting to be alone after being separated for so long." His eyes twinkled. "I am glad you came to dine with us, Valentina. You light up the room, more brightly than the candles."

She flashed him a dazzling smile. "I thank you for the pretty words, Don Alonso. My parents send their regrets. As you know, my mother's health will not permit her to stay up for very long periods at a time."

Don Alonso turned his attention to his daughter-in-law, and Tyree, taking advantage of the opportunity, leaned close to Valentina and spoke in a whisper. "I want to see you alone as soon as possible."

Valentina watched Marquis's eyes move across her face and darken with displeasure. "I cannot."

"Meet me tonight in the courtyard. I must talk to you," he urged.

". . . I'll try."

The remainder of the meal was spent with Don Alonso trying to convince Tyree, as Marquis had done, to give up his wicked ways, settle down, and take a wife. No one seemed to notice that Valentina and Doña Anna added very little to the conversation. Valentina could feel Marquis's mother's displeasure in every heated glance she cast her way. Uncomfortable and feeling out of place, she wished she had made an excuse not to join the family tonight.

After the meal, the men remained at the table with cigars and brandy, while the women went into the living room. Doña Anna picked up her sewing, moved to a corner chair, and pointedly ignored Valentina. Rosalia, trying to make up for her mother's rudeness, asked

Valentina to walk with her in the garden.

The night was ablaze with hundreds of stars. Rosalia stared up at the heavens with a wistful look on her face. Sensing she was troubled, Valentina spoke to her. "What is the matter, Rosalia?"

"No one would understand."

"Try me."

"It is just that I . . . am betrothed to Sergio Martinez, and I do not like him. I have told my mother this many times, but she will not listen. She says that it is a woman's duty to marry where her family chooses. She says love is not necessary in a marriage . . . can that be true?"

"The customs of your people are strange to me, Rosalia. I know there are a few arranged marriages in England, but to me it is an outdated custom." Seeing the stricken look on the young girl's face and fearing she had been too critical of the Spanish customs, Valentina hastened to add, "As I say, your ways are new to me."

"Valentina, would you want to spend your life with a man you . . . despised? A hateful man who made you cringe every time he came near you?"

Valentina took Rosalia's hand. Her heart ached for her gentle little sister-in-law. "No, I would not like that. Have you talked to your grandfather about your feelings?"

"I could never do that. Grandfather would be very angry if he thought I did not want to honor my betrothal. Especially after Marquis . . ." Her voice trailed off. "Grandfather can be very stern."

"There must be something you can do."

"I have thought of going into the church and taking my vows, but I do not think I would make a good nun. I love children and have always wanted many of my own."

"I do not know what I can do, Rosalia, but I will think about your problem. If there is any way, I will help you."

"Valentina, there is more I have not told you. You will think I am wicked and evil."

Valentina smiled into the angelic face. "I do not think so, Rosalia. What could you have done that would be considered evil?"

"I"—she ducked her head—"I love someone else."

Valentina raised the young girl's chin and searched her face. "Is this wise?"

"No, it is not wise, but I cannot help myself. Felipe is Sergio's younger brother. We have known each other all our lives. We did not mean to love each other. We could not help it—it just happened."

Valentina thought about her love for Marquis, and how she would have felt if she had been forced to marry someone else. "Oh, my dear little sister. My heart aches for you, but I do not know what we can do about this."

"I have no hope," Rosalia cried. "I would rather be dead than marry Sergio."

Valentina took Rosalia by the shoulders. "Do not say that. Give me time to think about your situation. In the meantime, do not see Felipe—if you are discovered it will only make matters worse for you."

Rosalia smiled through her tears. "I feel better after talking to you, Valentina. I just knew you would understand what Felipe and I are going through."

"I have to go see my mother and father now, Rosalia. I want you to know you can talk to me anytime you want to."

"I am so glad my brother married you. I did not like Isabel."

Valentina smiled. "Dry your eyes. I have to go and pay my respects to your mother. You do not want her to know you have been crying."

Rosalia caught Valentina's hand. "Did I not tell you that you would be the one who would help my brother walk. It was a miracle when you came into this family. My grandfather thinks so too."

"I'm glad. Let us go in before your mother comes looking for you."

Valentina waited until she heard Marquis's steady breathing before she slipped out of bed and quietly dressed. Silently she made her way down the balcony stairs and into the garden.

A crescent moon hung low in the sky, casting long shadows across the garden. Valentina waited half an hour, feeling perplexed that Tyree did not come. Deciding he had forgotten their meeting and gone to bed, she was startled when he stepped out of the shadows behind her.

Marquis had silently watched Valentina dress, wondering where she could be going at that time of night. Pretending to be asleep, he had heard her walk out on the balcony and descend the stairs into the courtyard. He visualized wild images of her meeting Tyree behind his back, but he pushed them aside. No, Valentina and Tyree would never betray him.

The longer he waited, the more tortured his thoughts became. He could not just lie there, not knowing what was going on. Rising out of bed, he walked out onto the balcony. He could hear voices, but he did not see who was talking. Then, through a haze of agony, he saw Valentina and Tyree standing near the bird cage. Tyree held Valentina's hand, and their voices reached Marquis on the balcony. His eyes burned and his heart ached as he witnessed what he thought was the betrayal of the woman he loved and his best friend.

"I feared you wouldn't come, Valentina," Tyree said, clasping her hand in a firm grip.

"I shouldn't have. This is wrong, Tyree. Marquis would be furious."

"I got the impression today that you haven't told Marquis about our secret. Why, Valentina?" Tyree asked.

"I can't bring myself to tell him, Tyree. He would hate us both if he knew the truth."

"I think he should know," Tyree insisted. "It's only fair."

"Don't ask it of me. Let this be our secret. The only other person who will ever know about the baby is Salamar, and she will never tell."

"I don't understand you, Valentina. Love should heal everything."

Marquis turned away, unable to listen any longer. He had been a fool. He had trusted a woman enough to lay his heart open to her, even though he had known she had loved another man. It was obvious that the man was Tyree. Making his way slowly back to bed, he collapsed in a world of swirling pain and betrayal.

Valentina and Tyree could go straight to hell for all he cared. He no longer had a friend, and he no longer wanted a wife!

In the garden below, Valentina and Tyree had no notion that Marquis had overheard their conversation. Nor did they see him slip quietly back into his room.

"Don't you think Marquis should know that it is his baby you carry, Valentina? He has had me searching for Jordanna. He is tormented."

"I have tried to tell him, but he will not listen. If only I could find the right time. I kept hoping he would grow to love me. Then he would understand why I had to deceive him."

"Grow to love you!" Tyree exclaimed. "Hell, he does love you!"

"No," Valentina said, "he doesn't."

"But—" Tyree protested.

Valentina lifted a silencing hand. "Believe me, Tyree, I know. He doesn't love Jordanna, and he doesn't love me."

Tyree thought it wasn't his place to convince Valentina of Marquis's love, so he would try another tack. "He needs to know about the baby, Valentina."

"Finding out about the baby wouldn't be the big shock for him, Tyree; the thing that would be hard for Marquis to accept would be learning that I am Jordanna. I cannot tell him just yet."

"If that's the way you see it. I think you're making a mistake though." Tyree bent and kissed her cheek. "I won't see you for a time. I'm off early in the morning."

"Why are you leaving so soon?"

"I have a church to build," he said with amused laughter.

"A what?" she asked in surprise, thinking she had heard wrong. "Did I hear you correctly? You are helping build a church?"

His laughter filled the air. "If you think you are shocked, how do you think I feel?"

"Do you want to tell me about it?"

He considered for a moment before shaking his head. "No, you wouldn't believe me if I did."

She laid her head against his shoulder and felt his arms tighten about her. "Tyree, you will always be so dear to me. You came to me at a time in my life when I needed a friend. I don't know what I would have done without you. Now you have even given my father back to me. You

441

will always have your special place in my heart."

He dropped his arms. She would never know that she occupied all his heart. With a stab at being lighthearted, he spoke past the lump in his throat. "You might like to know that the whole town of San Francisco is weeping and wailing over the disappearance of their most famous dancer."

"Let her just disappear, Tyree. She served her purpose."

"Indeed she did, Valentina. Indeed she did."

Later, when Valentina crawled back into bed, she was glad to find Marquis still sleeping. Perhaps Tyree had been right and she should tell him about the baby. It was a hard decision to make. The feelings between the two of them were still too fragile, and she was afraid of doing anything to upset the balance.

Turning toward Marquis, she watched his face. If only he knew how much she loved him. She thought of Rosalia, and how she would not be permitted to marry the man she loved. This was a strange world she had married into. Many of the customs she would never understand, but the child she carried was a Vincente and would live and grow up in this golden, sun-kissed land.

Marquis could hardly bring himself to lie beside Valentina, knowing she had betrayed him with Tyree. He felt sick inside. This was the last night she would ever share his bed. To save his pride, he could not let her know he had seen her and Tyree together.

Pain such as he had never known circled his heart. He hated the fact that loving Valentina had made him a weak, spineless fool. He had mooned after her like a lovesick animal. Tonight he had found out that she was nothing but a cheat and a fake. Valentina would never again get close enough to him to cause him pain, he vowed.

Marquis decided he would wipe Valentina out of his heart so thoroughly that not even her memory would remain.

Chapter Twenty-Eight

Valentina was awake bright and early. Marquis was still sleeping, so she quietly slipped out of the room and moved down the hallway to see her mother and father.

Marquis waited until Valentina had gone before he opened his eyes. He knew Tyree was leaving early this morning and thought bitterly that Valentina must be sneaking out to bid her lover good-bye. What did it matter? He would guard his heart against Valentina—she would not hurt him again. The one thing about this whole ordeal that made him sick and angry at the same time was the fact that Valentina's child would have the Vincente name.

Knowing her parents had always been early risers, Valentina knocked lightly on their door.

When her father's voice bid her enter, Valentina stepped into the room. To her surprise, both her father and mother were dressed. Her mother rushed to her and hugged her tightly.

"Isn't it wonderful, Valentina? We have your father back with us."

"You always knew he would come back, Mother. You

445

were the one with the faith."

Ward Barrett put his arm around his daughter and his wife. "We Barretts are unbeatable, are we not?"

Valentina laughed happily. "Indeed we are. Let the world try to separate us." She had been looking at her father as she spoke and saw the troubled glance he cast her mother. "What's wrong?" she asked, looking from one to the other. "Has something happened?"

Taking Valentina by the hands, her father led her to the bed and seated her. "Nothing is wrong, honey. It's just that your mother and I have decided to return to England."

"When . . . how . . . I don't understand."

"Immediately. We are leaving for San Francisco today."

"But Mother isn't well enough to—"

"I will take care of your mother, Valentina. We have decided we want to go home."

"But why the rush?" She looked at her mother. "Must you go so quickly?"

Ward forced Valentina to look at him. "The reason for the haste is that the *Berengalia* sails for England in three days and we want to be aboard her."

"I . . . will Salamar go with you?" Valentina asked, feeling as if she were being deserted.

"No, my love," her mother said, brushing the tears away. "Salamar already informed us she would never leave you. Of course, we wouldn't want her to. We feel a certain amount of comfort knowing she is with you."

Valentina stood up in a daze. "I have money to give you. You will need it."

Ward Barrett shook his head. "We will never want for money again. Before my partner, Sam Udell, turned on me, we'd made the big strike. Most of the gold is in a bank in San Francisco. Because of the agreement Sam and I drew up, all the money now belongs to me. Now that I know about Sam's character, I am sure he wanted the agreement so he would have been the beneficiary after he had me shipped off."

Valentina was only half listening to her father. She could not believe they were leaving today. "I hardly got to see you, Father. Must you go today? Neither you nor Mother has had the chance to get to know Marquis."

"I regret that, Valentina, but we have to leave. As a matter of fact, we must leave immediately," her father said, taking out his pocket watch and checking the time.

Valentina felt very much as she had when her parents had left her in England—abandoned. She was now old enough to realize that though they loved her, they loved each other more. They were the kinds of people who should never have had children. Not that they did not love her—they just did not need her. She vowed at that moment that she would be a better parent to her children. She was going to make sure the child she now carried would always feel wanted.

Pushing her unhappiness aside, Valentina smiled. "At least we can have breakfast together before you leave."

"This is a strange house as far as meals are concerned, Ward," Evonne said. "As you have seen, there are two separate parts to the house. This wing is independent of the other, having its own kitchen—only the kitchen in this wing is not yet set up, so the food we eat is prepared in the main kitchen."

Ward glanced at his daughter. "Can you live in this chaos?"

"It won't be so bad once I make the kitchen operational. You see, Father, in the Vincente family, the heir apparent always brings his new bride to these quarters. Don't ask me why. It is just the tradition. You will find the Vincentes are steeped in tradition. Besides, who are you to talk about living in chaos? You and Mother thrive on upheaval."

Valentina sent word by a servant that they would breakfast in the courtyard. When she went to the bedroom to see if Marquis wanted to eat with them, she found the room empty.

She learned from Carlos that Marquis had ridden away and was not expected back until after dark. She wondered why Marquis had not told her his plans. She was disappointed that he was not going to dine with her family. Of course, Marquis had not known her family would be leaving today.

Over breakfast the Barrett family laughed a lot. Ward Barrett told his family of his adventures aboard the *Tradewind*. Don Alonso later joined them and tried in vain to talk Valentina's mother and father into staying on a while longer.

By the time Valentina's mother and father were ready to leave, Valentina had resigned herself to their going. She and Salamar walked with them to the waiting carriage, waving good-bye until they drove out of sight over the hill.

"You seem in a strange mood, Valentina," Salamar observed. "I know you are grieving over your mother and father's hasty departure. They live their lives in haste. You know that."

"It's not that, Salamar. I will miss them, but I know they will be happy together. Mother seemed to have miraculously recovered, and they are off on another adventure." Valentina turned her eyes on her maid. "The only thing that would have made me grieve is if you had gone with them, Salamar."

"Only death will take me from you," Salamar said with feeling. She glanced at the hill where Valentina's mother and father had just disappeared. "I wonder how long they will be content to remain in England."

448

Valentina laughed. "Father suddenly fancied himself a country squire. I think they will soon be bored with life in Cornwall. England will be too tame for them."

Glancing toward the house where her future lay, Valentina wished her parents a happy life. They had each other, and that was all they would ever need.

"Your mother never knew of the sacrifice you made on her behalf, Valentina. She never suspected that you were forced to dance at the Crystal Palace to buy her medicine."

"Thank God she never knew where the money came from. No one but you, me, and Tyree will ever know my secret."

Marquis had ridden to the top of a hill and dismounted, and there he watched his vaqueros rounding up strays in the valley below. The day was hot, and he moved his mount beneath the shade of an oak tree. He knew he should join his men, but he needed time to think about Valentina and Tyree. His heart ached, and there was an emptiness deep inside him.

He heard a rider in the distance and glanced at the far ridge to see Isabel riding toward him. He had not seen her since that day in the barn. Now, as she drew even with him, her eyes stared boldly down at him.

"Will you not help a lady down?" she asked, holding her hands out to him.

Marquis gripped her waist and swung her to the ground. As his eyes assessed her, he found her more appealing than he had when they had been betrothed. Her red riding habit clung to her overripe curves. Her lips, the same red as her gown, were moist and inviting. The look in her eyes promised him anything he wanted.

"What are you doing here, Isabel? You are a long way from home."

"As a matter of fact, I was looking for you. I often visit your mother. She and I have become good friends." Isabel watched his face. "I am told by your mother that all is not well with you and your little wife."

Marquis turned away from her searching eyes. "Has my mother become a gossip lately? I believe it does no one good to listen to foolish tales."

Isabel moved closer to Marquis and ran her hand up his arm. "Are you saying you are happily married?"

His eyes moved to the low cut of her bodice. From his angle he could see the dusky tips of her breasts. "I do not believe my marriage should be a concern of yours or my mother's."

Her laughter was lusty, and she pressed her body close to his. "That is no answer at all." Her lashes swept her cheeks, and her tongue flicked out to moisten her lips. "Do you never wonder how it would have been between us, Marquis?"

He grabbed her by the shoulders and crushed her in his arms. His lips bruised and punished. Striking out at her in his torment, he ground his mouth brutally against hers. Isabel moaned as her hands laced through his hair. This was what she had dreamed of for so long. Her body was burning with desire and need. Her intuition told her that when Marquis made love to her, he would fill the void that no other man had been able to fill.

By midnight Marquis still had not returned to Paraíso del Norte. Valentina was beginning to be concerned. His leg was not healed well enough for him to be on it all day.

As the clock ticked off the minutes, Valentina began to pace the floor. She tried to read a book but found herself jumping up at every noise. She considered asking Don Alonso to send some men to look for Marquis, but she decided against it.

Finally, after one o'clock in the morning, Valentina fell asleep from exhaustion. She did not hear Marquis when he came in. She did not know he limped across the room to stand over her for a long time before he shook her by the shoulder to wake her.

When Valentina opened her eyes sleepily, Marquis was leaning against the bed, unbuttoning his shirt. Jumping up, Valentina tried to help him, but he shoved her away. It took her a moment to realize he had been drinking.

"I was worried about you, Marquis. You shouldn't have been on your leg all day."

He tossed his shirt aside. "Why should you care?" he asked in a harsh voice.

She reached out her hand to him. "I don't understand what you are saying. Of course I care. How could you doubt it? You know that—"

"Spare me your demonstration of wifely devotion, Valentina. I am neither impressed, nor am I interested."

Her face whitened, and she looked at him carefully. "You have been drinking, Marquis. Is that why you are—"

"Damned right I have been drinking. I had to get drunk before I could bring myself to come home and face you."

Her heart skipped a beat. "I don't know what you mean. Did you think I would be upset because you had been gone all day? I was just worried that—"

He held up his hand, silencing her. "You have not asked me where I have been." He staggered forward and fell on the bed. Valentina rushed to help him, but he shoved her away again. Pulling himself up on the pillow, he looked at her through narrowed eyelashes. "I have been with a real woman," he said, slurring his words. "Isabel knows how to make a man feel like a king. You make a man feel like a beggar."

Valentina stepped back a pace, looking as if Marquis had struck her. This was not the Marquis she knew. Surely it was the liquor talking. "Are you ill?" she asked with concern. "Does your leg hurt?"

"You are not listening to me, Valentina. I said I have been with a real woman."

"I heard you, Marquis. I just don't believe you."

He laughed sarcastically. "Do you think that you are so much woman that you can keep me tied to you? Do you know how I feel when I make love to you, knowing you are carrying another man's bastard? I feel sick inside."

Valentina gasped with disbelief. "Tyree urged me to tell you the truth, but until now I didn't think it was a wise decision. Perhaps it's time I told you everything."

The eyes that burned into her seemed to glow with hatred. "I do not want to hear anything you have to say about your baby or my friend Tyree. I just want you out of my sight, and out of my life."

"Marquis, please listen to me. I realize I have made a mistake in not telling you about the baby—I know that now. I didn't realize how you felt. You seemed—"

"I seemed like your puppet," he interrupted. "You had me in a daze, but I can see clearly now. I see you for what you are. I know all about you, Valentina."

Her hand went to her throat, thinking Marquis was implying he knew she was Jordanna. "You couldn't know unless you overheard—"

"Overheard you and Tyree in the garden," he finished for her. "You did not know I overheard your meeting with your lover, did you?"

"Marquis, Tyree isn't my lover; he never has been. If you overheard us, you know that."

"I do not want you in my life any longer, Valentina. I do not want to have to look at you while your belly swells with the child. You are welcome to stay on at Paraíso del

452

Norte, but not where I can see you. I despise the sight of you."

Valentina backed toward the door, wanting nothing more than to flee from the room. She felt like a wounded animal, needing to crawl off to lick her wounds.

"Marquis, are you saying you want our marriage to end?" she asked, holding on to the last straw blowing in the wind.

His lips curled in contempt. "Ours was a marriage built on lies. It is no marriage at all. Get out of my sight, Valentina!"

Spinning around, Valentina wrenched open the door and fled down the hall. Deep sobs were building up inside her, and she clamped her hand over her mouth so they would not spill out. Running into her room, she closed the door and threw herself on the bed. She had never thought to see such malice directed toward her. Dear God, how Marquis must hate her!

Crying into her pillow, Valentina felt her whole body tremble with emotion. Marquis had wounded her beyond reason. What had he thought he had overheard in the garden to make him turn on her this way? He had called Tyree her lover—surely he knew that was not true.

Valentina sensed Salamar standing over her. Looking up at her with tears streaming down her face, she cried out, "Marquis doesn't want me anymore. He despises the sight of me. He thinks Tyree and I were lovers."

Salamar dropped down on the bed and shook her head. "Did you tell him about the baby?"

"He wouldn't let me. He's been drinking and said he doesn't want me near him. What shall I do?"

"If he was drinking, he was not thinking clearly. I believe you should get a good night's sleep and talk to Marquis again in the morning."

Valentina rose up on her elbow with a flicker of hope shining in her eyes. "Perhaps that would be best. I could tell him everything tomorrow. Would you go with me?"

"You do not need me to help you save your marriage, Valentina."

"I . . . Marquis said he was with Isabel today."

Salamar's eyes snapped. "He what?"

"He implied he had been . . . intimate with her. If he has, I will not stay with him, Salamar. I hope it was just the liquor making him say things he didn't mean."

"Try to get some sleep now. It is not good for the baby if you get upset."

"Everything will be all right in the morning, won't it, Salamar?" Valentina asked in an almost childlike whisper.

"Let us hope so. Now let me help you into bed. You need rest for tomorrow."

Long after Valentina had fallen asleep, Salamar sat beside her, staring into the night. She was fiercely protective of Valentina. No man, not even Marquis, was going to treat Valentina badly. Growing up in a harem, Salamar had seen too many women ill used. She would never allow that to happen to Valentina. If Marquis was seeing Isabel Estrada, Valentina would not stay here and be humiliated.

Marquis was not as drunk as he had led Valentina to believe. He now took a bottle from the side table and raised it to his mouth. He wished he could get drunk enough to forget the sight of Valentina in Tyree's arms. The image of them together had haunted him all day.

He was also haunted by Jordanna. How could he be so attracted to two women? They were so different, yet both pulled the same emotions from him. God help him, he wanted them both. He also wanted the child Jordanna was carrying.

454

The need to uphold family tradition ripped into his soul, tormenting him. What about his baby? What if it turned out to be a son?

Valentina awoke to bright sunlight streaming into her room. Rushing to dress, she hurried down the corridor to Marquis's room, rapped lightly on the door, and entered on his command.

He was already dressed and had his booted feet propped on a stool so that he could buckle on his silver spurs. His eyes met hers with cold indifference. "I trust you slept well, señora?" There was no warmth in his inquiry.

Seeing he was having trouble fastening the spur because of his injury, Valentina dropped down in front of him to help. His icy glare made her pull back. "If I want your help, I will ask for it. In the future, you would do well to remember that. I told you last night to leave me alone."

She stood up slowly, knowing he was cold sober today; therefore, he meant whatever he said. "I had hoped that it had been only the liquor talking last night, Marquis." She had to know what had changed him from lover to cold stranger. "Could we talk about whatever is bothering you?" she asked nervously.

By now his spurs were in place and he stood up. "Yes, let us talk about what is bothering me. I might as well say it straight out so I will not have to repeat myself. I no longer require you to be my wife. You have been a bone of contention between me and my mother and, since your coming, have upset this house."

Valentina could not believe his cruel words. Marquis had never loved her, but he had never before been deliberately cruel. He knew that his mother had been

455

unreasonable since their marriage. It was not all Valentina's fault. "Are you asking me to leave, Marquis?"

"You know what I want, Valentina. Do not make me say it."

"I can't know unless you do say it. What have I done to turn you against me?"

He shrugged his shoulders and turned toward the window. "You and I are not suited to each other. I thought I could live with the fact that you are carrying another man's child, but I find I cannot."

"I believe it's time I told you the truth about the baby—"

He spun around and faced her, his eyes blazing like fire. "Spare me the details, Valentina. Just get out of my sight."

Valentina stared at him for a long moment. Then she raised her head, letting her pride carry her through this heartbreak. "If it is your wish, I will leave your house."

She saw his eyes widen in surprise. "I did not say you had to leave Paraíso del Norte. I have merely decided to move to the other wing, giving you free reign here."

"I see." Was her heartbreak showing? she wondered. Did she sound calmer than she felt? "What you mean is you can hide me away in a corner of your life and forget I exist."

"I doubt I will ever forget you exist, Valentina." His tone implied he was handing her no compliment.

It was too late to tell Marquis that he was her child's father. He would never believe her now—he would think she was making it up to stay in his good graces. "Do you wish to put an end to the marriage?"

He avoided her eyes. "I am a Catholic."

"I'm not."

He raised his brow. "I never knew that."

"There are a lot of things you don't know about me,

456

Marquis. You never bothered to ask."

He shrugged his shoulders. "Be that as it may, I will not be finding out now, will I?"

"Should I look forward to years of being held prisoner in this wing of the house?"

He pulled on his leather gloves and brushed past her. "You will be free to come and go as you will. Today Carlos will transfer my belongings to the other wing of the house."

Valentina could not believe it was all ending like this. What had brought it on? "Marquis, why are you doing this? I thought—"

His eyes narrowed. "You thought that I was a fool, Valentina. You thought you would use me to give your baby a name."

Her anger was stirred now. "As I recall, it was you who asked me to marry you, Marquis. I never pursued you."

"Well . . . anyone can make a mistake."

Her silver eyes were dancing with dangerous lights. "If this is your way of saying you cannot live without Isabel, why don't you just come out and say it. You said you were with her last night—if she is what you want, you are free of any obligations to me."

Marquis's voice caught in his throat as he watched her eyes come alive with fury. He wanted to rush across the room and beg her to stay with him at any price. He loved her, and he wanted her more than ever. Hating this weakness he had for her, he hardened his heart. "Let us leave Isabel out of this. When a man has had too much to drink, he often says things he does not mean."

Marquis held the door open, silently indicating that Valentina should leave. She moved across the room like one in a dream—a nightmare. There was no reality in what was happening. Marquis wanted her out of his sight and out of his life, and her pride would help her do what had to be done. She would never stay where she was not wanted.

"Good-bye, Marquis," she said, stopping in the doorway and glancing up at him.

His dark gaze moved across her face. "Not good-bye, Valentina. Even though this is a big house, we still live under the same roof. I suppose we will cross each other's path from time to time."

Without another word, she turned and walked away. She ignored the impulse to run to the safety of her room so she could cry. Proud and strong, Valentina was mentally assessing hers and Marquis's relationship. There was nothing to salvage. Her father would have told her to cut her losses and throw in her hand.

She had to think this through. It did not pay to be hasty. A marriage was supposed to be forever. Even though Marquis had struck at her pride today, she had to give him every chance.

Isabel had been in a rage since the day before. Servants tiptoed past her bedroom, and her family tried to avoid her at all cost. She had been spurned a second time by Marquis Vincente. Now her fury knew no bounds. She had thrown herself at him yesterday. After he had kissed her and made her want him all the more, he had shoved her away. How dare he say she could not fan the flame that had been lit by his wife!

Isabel's eyes were shooting sparks now as she raced down the stairs, calling for a servant to bring her horse around to the front.

Valentina moved down the stairs to the garden, searching for Rosalia. Seeing her by the bird cage, Valentina called out to her. When she neared her sister-in-law, she could see that she had been crying.

"What is wrong, Rosalia? Has something happened to make you sad?" Valentina asked.

Large brown eyes looked at her beseechingly. "Is it true that Marquis is moving out of the . . . leaving you?"

Valentina did not bother to deny the truth. "Yes, that is so."

"I do not understand. I thought the two of you were so happy."

Valentina did not know how to answer the young girl. "Sometimes things go wrong in a marriage, Rosalia. I am not without hope that your brother and I will be able to work out our differences in time."

"Why does growing up have to hurt so badly, Valentina? When I was a child, life was so simple. I thought my family was so wonderful. Now I find they have faults like everyone else."

"Yes, Rosalia. We are all human. We all have feet of clay. If you have learned this, you are halfway to being grown up."

Rosalia's eyes were troubled as she raised them to Valentina. "I have made a decision that will make me an outcast in my family, Valentina. I had to . . . I cannot marry Sergio."

"What have you decided to do?"

"Felipe and I are going to run away and be married. We cannot live without each other."

"I do not know if that is the right solution to your problem, Rosalia. Shouldn't you first try to reason with your family?"

"I talked to my mother, and she insists that I marry Sergio in three months. That is why Felipe and I have to run away."

"Oh, Rosalia, my heart is breaking for you. I wish I could tell you what to do, but I do not even have the answers for myself. Are you sure you have thought this through carefully? A great deal can happen in three months."

"Felipe and I do not care if we are disowned by both our families. We must be together."

"I will not try to stop you, but I hope you understand what you are doing. I have found that the Vincente family are not very tolerant or forgiving of others' mistakes."

Rosalia clasped Valentina's hand. "You have been hurt by us, Valentina. I wonder if my brother fully understands what a treasure he has in you. I fear it will be too late when he discovers your worth."

Valentina's eyes stung. "When would you and Felipe leave, Rosalia."

"I do not know—soon, I think. We still have plans to make."

Valentina hugged Rosalia to her, wishing her all the happiness in the world. "I give you my blessing, for what it is worth."

"My, my, here's a touching little scene," Isabel said, walking up behind them. "How fortunate someone in this family approves of you, English woman," Isabel said sarcastically, using the name by which Marquis's mother always referred to Valentina.

Rosalia turned to the visitor, trying to remember her manners. "If you have come to see my mother, she is in the living room."

"So I discovered. I have already had a nice visit with Doña Anna. I have come to talk to Marquis's wife. Do you mind?"

Valentina could hardly bear to look at the woman Marquis loved. She was beautiful and cold. Something about her made the hair on the back of Valentina's neck stand on end.

"I am sorry," Rosalia said, telling a lie for the first time in her life. "Had we known you were coming, we would not have made plans. Valentina and I are just leaving.

Please come another time."

Valentina smiled to herself, knowing that the lie had come hard to Rosalia. To help her friend, she added, "Yes, do come again. We would be happy to receive you at a later date."

Isabel's fury ignited. "I will not take up much of your time, Valentina. I just wanted to speak to you alone for a moment."

"You can talk in front of Rosalia, Isabel. We have no secrets from each other."

"Very well, but you will not like her hearing what I have to say."

"I will chance that."

In Isabel's pacing, she slowly circled Valentina and Rosalia, forcing them to turn to face her. "We all know Marquis is tired of you, English woman," Isabel said at last. "He knows it was a mistake for the two of you to marry. Doña Anna has told me that he has moved out of your bed. Surely you know when you are not wanted."

Anger threatened to choke Valentina. How dare Marquis's mother talk about intimate family problems with an outsider. "I cannot believe my husband would like it if he had overheard you just now, Isabel. What happens between me and my husband is no concern of yours."

Isabel's lip curled in a snarl. "Do you think not? Ask Marquis if the two of us did not meet yesterday. Ask him if we just sat and talked . . . or if—"

"Enough," Rosalia interrupted. "How dare you come into this house and utter such vicious lies. Go away." Rosalia did not raise her voice, but she made her point all the same.

Valentina felt hurt and confused. Surely Marquis would never betray her with this woman. He might love Isabel, but he would not . . . he could not make love to her. Dear God, no, she prayed, please let this be a

461

nightmare from which I soon wake.

Isabel saw that she had accomplished what she had intended. "By the way, I overheard your plans to run away with Felipe Martinez, Rosalia. I wonder what a word from me to your mother would do to upset that little scheme."

Rosalia's face whitened. "What are you going to do?"

Isabel's eyes moved to Valentina. "Nothing for now." She looked at Valentina. "Ask Marquis about yesterday, English woman. I happen to know he is moving away from you because he cannot bear to hold you now that he has made love to me."

Hearing Rosalia gasp, Isabel turned away in a swish of green taffeta, and moved hurriedly toward the arched doorway.

Valentina was visibly shaken. She was feeling sick inside and grabbed hold of the iron bars of the bird cage for support.

Rosalia, in spite of her horror, tried to comfort Valentina. "She was lying, Valentina. Marquis would never do what she implied."

Valentina needed to be alone. She knew if she did not run, she was going to be sick right there in the courtyard. "I must go," she said, clamping her hand over her mouth and rushing toward her quarters.

It was late afternoon when Valentina had the opportunity to face Marquis. He was in the stable rubbing down his mount when she entered. With a proud tilt of her head, she approached him.

He watched her, saying nothing. Without any pleasantries or greetings, she asked the question that had been preying on her mind all day.

"I just want to know one thing, Marquis. Did you meet Isabel yesterday?"

He swiped the brush across his horse's hindquarters without looking up. "I already told you I saw her."

"Did anything happen between the two of you?"

"Why would you want to know?"

"I am your wife."

"More went on between me and Isabel yesterday than any wife with pride and self-respect would accept. Take that for what it is worth and leave me in peace."

Without another word, Valentina turned and walked away. She had the answer she had come for. Without fanfare or advance notice, she would be leaving Paraíso del Norte.

Valentina did not know that as soon as she was out of sight, Marquis mounted his horse and rode away. He had decided to search for Jordanna himself.

When Valentina told Salamar what had happened with Isabel and how Marquis had confirmed it later, Salamar did not question her. She merely nodded her head and helped Valentina pack the trunks. Helplessly, she watched Valentina move in a dreamlike state, knowing the hurt she was feeling but unable to comfort her.

Valentina hated sneaking off like a thief in the night, but she did not want to face Marquis and his mother. She would have liked to have said good-bye to Don Alonso and Rosalia, but she dared not risk it.

Salamar had persuaded Carlos to drive her and Valentina to San Francisco. The young Spaniard had promised he would tell no one about taking them until he returned.

After leading the horses to the side of the house, a sad Carlos loaded the trunks and helped Valentina and Salamar into the buggy. Long before the sun came up, they pulled away from the house, heading for San Francisco.

No one questioned their leaving, not that Valentina expected anyone to stop them. She assumed Marquis and his mother would be glad when they learned she had disappeared from their lives. Valentina truly believed she would never see Paraíso del Norte again.

The road to San Francisco was well traveled, and Valentina and Salamar breathed more easily when they had left Vincente land behind. Where the future would lead her, Valentina did not know. She only knew that she could no longer live with Marquis, and he no longer wanted her. Valentina knew her parents would be in San Francisco and she wanted to avoid them until they sailed for England. They had their own life to lead and she had hers. She wanted them to leave Calfornia believing she was happily married.

Salamar saw Valentina's troubled expression. Smiling slightly, she patted her hand. "You will soon be returning to Paraíso del Norte, Valentina. You will only stay away until Marquis deserves you."

Chapter Twenty=Nine

Valentina rapped on the Lawtons' door and stepped back, waiting for an answer. She dreaded facing the reverend and his sister, but if the cabin was vacant, she wanted to see if she could rent it.

The door swung open and Prudence Lawton glared at Valentina over the rims of her glasses. "I'm not at home to you, miss. You are no fit person to deal with."

"I don't know what you are talking about, Miss Lawton. I came to see if your cabin is available."

"Not to you it isn't." Prudence drew her stingy little mouth up tightly. "You led my brother a merry chase and then broke his heart. He's taken to drinking and hanging out at the Crystal Palace. He's gone plumb crazy, drinking and carousing. Percival is a ruined man, and you're to blame!"

Valentina backed down one step, almost losing her footing, but managing to grab onto the porch post to break her fall. "I never led your brother on, Miss Lawton."

"Sure you did. He told me so. You had all the men chasing after you with their tongues hanging out. You was like a bitch in heat, and from the looks of you," Prudence declared, looking pointedly at Valentina's

465

rounded stomach, "I'd say you got what you deserved."

Valentina backed down the steps, shaking her head. "You are wrong about me. I am—"

"You go on and get," Prudence said, moving back into the house and slamming the door shut. Valentina was stunned. How could Mr. Lawton have turned from his faith? Why would his sister blame her? She had never encouraged Reverend Lawton in any way. She had not even liked him.

Slowly moving down the path to the street, Valentina walked toward the hotel where Salamar was waiting for her. As she passed the Crystal Palace, she pulled her blue woolen shawl across her face and quickened her steps. She did not want to come face-to-face with Tyree. Since he was Marquis's friend, it would not be fair to place him in the middle of their trouble. Besides, he would ask too many questions she was not ready to answer.

Glancing up the street, she was shocked to see Percival Lawton go reeling into the Crystal Palace. His sister had been right; he was drunk. How could a man who had considered himself so self-righteous and pious fall so far from grace? she wondered. She stepped off the boardwalk into the muddy street, for she definitely did not want Percival Lawton to see her.

Marquis dismounted, tossing the reins to Enrique, issuing him an order. "Rub her down, and do not give her water for at least an hour. I rode her hard when I got my mother's message to come home at once. Cool her down slowly."

Noticing that the mare was lathered, Enrique nodded. "*Sí, patrón*. Your mother wanted to know the minute you came home. She asked to see you at once."

Marquis had been in Santa Barbara for two weeks. He had ridden away from Paraíso del Norte right after his quarrel with Valentina. "What is wrong?" Marquis asked with dread in his heart. Removing his leather gloves, he slapped them nervously against his thigh. "Raynaldo did not know why my mother sent for me."

The vaquero looped the reins around his hands. "It is very sad, *patrón*. Your grandfather . . ."

Fear gripped Marquis's heart. He brushed Enrique aside and rushed to the house. He hardly dared breathe as he raced down the hallway and up the stairs. Stopping before his grandfather's room, he pushed the door open dreading what he would find.

Silence filled the room where only a single candle burned. Marquis stepped to the bed, his eyes glued to his grandfather's face. His heart ached at the frail, blue-veined hands that were crossed over his grandfather's chest. He looked dead.

Doña Anna rose from her kneeling position, dabbing at her eyes. "He is sinking fast, Marquis. He has been asking for you. I feared you would not get here in time. That is why I sent Raynaldo to bring you home."

Marquis touched his grandfather's talonlike hands, finding the skin cold and clammy. "What does Doctor Anza say about his condition?"

Doña Anna lowered her voice. "He says he will not last the night."

Marquis felt his eyes sting with tears. He could remember very little about his father, but his grandfather had always been there for him, teaching him, shaping him so that one day he would become head of the family. The time was near when Marquis would have to step into the grandee's place. Tonight, as his grief ripped at his insides, he doubted his ability to replace his grandfather.

"Where is Rosalia?" Marquis inquired, wondering why his sister was not present at the death vigil.

Doña Anna's eyes brimmed with tears. "Everything just fell apart after you left, Marquis. Your sister is in disgrace; she no longer belongs to this family."

"What are you saying, Mother?" Marquis was still reeling from the sad news about his grandfather. He wondered what sweet, gentle Rosalia could have done to bring down digrace upon her head.

"Your sister ran away with Felipe Martinez!" Doña Anna declared. "The shame is almost too much to endure."

Marquis's jaws clamped tightly together. "What do you mean, she ran away with Felipe? Do you not mean his brother, Sergio?"

Doña Anna pressed her handkerchief against her mouth. "No, she has gone back on her word and married Sergio Garza's younger brother, Felipe."

"Where is Valentina?" he asked, wishing he dared go to her. She always brought him comfort. She was like a cool stream running through a burning desert. He had decided in the two weeks he had been away that he could not live without her. He was prepared to go down on his knees and beg her forgiveness if need be. She would have to forgive him when he admitted that nothing had happened between him and Isabel.

Noticing that his mother had not answered him, he asked again. "Why is Valentina not here with Grandfather? He would want her to be here."

"She has gone away," Doña Anna said at last. "I do not know when." There was no satisfaction in his mother's eyes, no joy that her unwanted daughter-in-law had gone away. "We discovered she had gone just after you left."

Marquis felt the weight of the world on his shoulders. Life had dealt him one blow after another—each harder to withstand than the last. He could not deal with another crisis tonight. Dropping to his knees beside his grandfather, he bowed his head in prayer.

The beloved old grandee did not stir or wake. In the early morning hours Don Alonso's soul silently and peacefully slipped the bonds of earth.

It was a bright, sunlit day when Don Alonso was laid to rest in the shadows of the great Sierra Nevada Mountains. He had been well loved. So many people came to pay their last respects that the line stretched half a mile down the road.

Marquis, standing tall and silent, welcomed the guests as the new head of the family. If people wondered why his new wife and younger sister were not in attendance, they were much too wise to ask.

Many friends thought the brooding look in Marquis's eyes was because of the death of his grandfather. Doña Anna knew it was more than that. He was also grieving over his sister's disgrace, and he was haunted by Valentina's disappearance.

Doña Anna knew that after the last guest left, Marquis would leave to search for his sister. For the honor of the Vincente family, he would have to deal with Felipe Martinez. She did not know what her son would do about his missing wife. She was beginning to see that Marquis loved the English woman. Rosalia had told her what terrible things Isabel had said to Valentina. For the first time since her son's marriage, Doña Anna was ashamed of the part she had played in chasing Marquis's wife away.

She now saw things more clearly. Marquis might never have walked if Valentina had not made him. The English woman had believed Marquis would walk even when Doctor Anza had given up hope.

In the following days, Doña Anna watched Marquis ride out each morning to search for his sister. She knew he was torn between having to find Rosalia, and needing to search for Valentina. Doña Anna prayed each day that

Marquis would not find his sister until his temper cooled, and that Valentina would come home to stand beside her husband in his time of need.

As Doña Anna stood by the window gazing down at her son in the garden, she could almost feel his hurt. He was living in torment. Tomorrow she would urge him to give up searching for his sister and concentrate on finding his wife.

Spurs jingled and leather creaked as Marquis dismounted in front of the Crystal Palace. His eyes burned with anger as he shoved the swinging doors aside and walked to the bar. "It's nice to see you, señor Vincente," Ted Hutcheson, the bartender, greeted him in a friendly manner.

"Where is your boss?" Marquis asked, reaching for a bottle of whiskey and pouring a liberal amount into a glass. Downing it in one swallow, he waited for an answer.

"Tyree's in his office, I reckon. Leastwise I ain't seen him go out this morning."

Marquis tossed a silver coin on the bar. "You might want to tell Tyree that his whiskey does not go down smoothly. He might want to consider a better quality."

Ted whistled through his teeth. Something had Marquis Vincente all heated up, he mused, figuring Tyree and his friend were in for a tiff.

Marquis shoved open the office door and moved across the room to stand before the desk where Tyree was pouring over a ledger.

Tyree looked up, his brows coming together. "Marquis, I'm glad you are here. I heard about your grandfather, but it was too late to pay my last respects. You know how I felt about the old grandee. We will all miss him."

Marquis slapped his leather gloves against the palm of his hand. "You might be interested to know that when his will was read, my grandfather left you five thousand dollars, and two hundred acres of river bottomland."

Tyree shook his head. "I'll not take it, Marquis. I can't accept such a generous gift."

Marquis leaned closer and flicked a stack of papers. "It was his to give. If I were you, I would accept it."

Tyree was becoming aware that something was bothering Marquis. There was something in his cool manner that he could not define. Was it anger? "Where is that lovely wife of yours? Did you bring her to town with you?"

Marquis's eyes narrowed to dark slits. "Do you take me for a fool?"

Tyree puffed on his cigar. "I have taken you for a fool on occasion—especially lately."

"I do not find you as amusing as I once did, Tyree. You were like a brother to me. Now, I would hesitate to turn my back on you."

Tyree came to his feet. "I think you had better explain what you mean. I still consider you my friend, however much you abuse the privilege." Picking up a bottle from the side table, Tyree poured Marquis a drink and extended it to him.

"Where is she, Tyree?" Marquis pushed his hand away. "I did not come here today to drink your cheap whiskey or play games."

Tyree lifted the glass to his lips and took a sip. "This happens to be very good whiskey . . . and I leave the playing of games to you."

"You haven't answered my question."

"What was the question, Marquis?"

"Where is Valentina?"

Tyree set the glass on his desk, looking puzzled. No, he thought, this was not a game. "If you have misplaced

471

your wife, why would you expect me to know where she is?"

"In the name of past friendship, give me the courtesy of telling me the truth."

"I don't consider our friendship in the past, Marquis, but I get the feeling you do. When last we met, I thought our friendship was still intact. What happened to change your mind?"

"Do not make me say it, Tyree. At this moment it takes all my willpower to keep from slamming you against the wall. I know Valentina and you were lovers. It is only natural that she would come to you."

Tyree gritted his teeth. "You bastard, Marquis," he said, moving around the desk within reach of Marquis. "If you don't think highly of me, the least you could do is have more faith in Valentina. I am not now, nor have I ever been, her lover. I have not seen her since the night I spent at Paraíso del Norte."

"I know about your little meeting with my wife that night in the garden, when you both thought I was asleep," Marquis bit out.

"Did Valentina tell you?"

"No, I saw you with my own eyes."

"Then you must have heard what we were discussing. I'm sure Valentina is glad it's out in the open. You are a fool if you drove her away, Marquis."

"I somehow get the feeling you and I are not having the same conversation, Tyree. You are saying one thing and I am hearing another. If Valentina did not come to you, then where is she?"

"As God is my witness, Marquis, I have not seen Valentina in three months. If she has disappeared, I believe you should be concerned, because, to my knowledge, she didn't come to San Francisco."

"Are you telling the truth?"

"I swear it. If you like, I'll help you search for her. I'm as worried as you are about her. Why didn't you come to mc sooner?"

Marquis sank down in a chair. "So much has happened, Tyree. If I am wrong about you and Valentina, then what were the two of you talking about that night in the garden?"

Tyree stubbed out his cigar. "How much did you overhear?"

"Enough to believe the two of you were discussing something Valentina did not want me to overhear. I thought at the time you were the father of her child."

"Not likely!" Tyree exclaimed with a hard set to his jaw. "If I were, you wouldn't be married to her now—I would."

"Yes, that's the part that had me puzzled."

"You and I both know, without saying, how I feel about Valentina. If she were having my baby, I damned sure wouldn't have let her marry you."

"But you know who the father is, Tyree?" There was a clipped tone to Marquis's question.

Tyree met his friend's eyes. "Yes, I know who the father is. Don't ask me though. I can't tell you."

Marquis stood up and moved toward the door. "Keep your damned secrets, Tyree. Just do not get in the way of my finding my wife. If you do, you will get trampled underfoot."

"It's always nice to see you, Marquis," Tyree stated ironically. "Drop by anytime, so we can pass pleasantries."

Marquis paused at the door. "I will tear this town apart searching for Valentina. If you see her, tell her . . . tell her—"

"Yes?"

Marquis walked out the door, closing it behind him.

"I'll be damned," Tyree exclaimed to himself. "Where in the hell could she be?"

* * *

Five months had passed since Valentina had disappeared. In that time, between Marquis and Tyree, San Francisco had been searched from the docks to every road leading out of town. They inquired at hotels, asked questions of shopkeepers along the boardwalk and at the fish markets. Even strangers were stopped on the street and asked if they had seen a woman of Valentina's description. Both men gave up each sundown, only to renew their search the next day.

Two miles out of San Francisco, down a sandy beach, Reverend Percival Lawton was having better fortune than Marquis and Tyree. In the early morning he had awakened by the docks, having no recollection of how he had gotten there. The last thing he remembered was going into the Crystal Palace.

His mouth felt dry; he needed a drink badly. He had moved out of the house because he could not face his sister's preaching at him. Prudence had become stingy, withholding his money. He now slept anywhere his mood took him.

Squinting his eyes against the early morning glare, he watched the woman passing by him, thinking she looked vaguely familiar. Dropping back behind a packing crate, he watched her buy fresh fish from a small boat. It was Salamar, Valentina Barrett's maid!

Slinking into shadows, flattening himself against walls, he followed her. She moved quickly for a woman her age and Percival had trouble keeping up with her. After an hour of steady walking, he spotted a whitewashed cabin just off the beach. Dropping back into a cove that jutted out to the ocean, he watched Salamar climb the steps to the cabin.

Blinking his eyes, he saw a second woman come out on the porch. It was Valentina Barrett! Percival's watery eyes fastened hungrily on the lovely face. When his eyes moved lower, he noticed with a sinking heart that she was

474

heavy with child. He slammed his fist against a rock over and over, yet he felt no pain. When blood dropped from his fingers and soaked into the thirsty sand, he still did not notice. The angel he had adored and worshiped was having some other man's baby.

Staggering back down the beach, he made his way to town. He knew where Prudence kept her marketing money, and he sorely needed a drink. He could sneak into the house and be gone before his sister discovered him.

Misery weighed him down. Valentina had turned out to be just another slut, and it broke his heart.

Every day after that, Percival walked to the cabin, hoping for the chance to see Valentina. Some days his vigil was rewarded, while other days she did not come out of the house at all. He would often catch a glimpse of her moving along the beach, playfully darting in and out of the waves. Even as she grew heavier with child, she was still the most beautiful, the most desirable, woman he had ever seen.

Valentina walked down the beach soaking up the bright sunshine. The cool ocean breeze kissed her rosy cheeks, and her bare feet sank into the warm sand. It was tranquil here by the blue Pacific. She could open her mind and commune with the beauty of nature, forgetting about her own troubles for a time. She could walk for hours, watching the sea gulls in their continuous flights. Sometimes a playful sea otter would bounce along the beach until its mother scoldingly called it back to sea.

"Valentina-a-a," Salamar called, waving a wide-brimmed straw hat in the air. "You are going to get as dark as I am if you do not stop going out without your hat."

Walking toward Salamar, Valentina obediently took the hat and clapped it on her head, tying the silk ribbon beneath her chin. "Wouldn't it be wonderful if we could stay here forever, not worrying about freckles and dark skin, not caring what gown is in style in which season?" Valentina asked laughingly.

"No, I cannot say I would like it. One can only stand so much solitude. I thought you had your fill of solitude in Cornwall. You are going to have to face reality before long."

Valentina picked up a handful of sand, allowing it to sift through her fingers. "There will be time enough for reality when the baby comes."

"Captain Williams, who allowed us to rent this cabin, will want it back by the end of summer."

"We are fortunate to have had the cabin this long. If you hadn't always insisted on shopping for fresh fish at the docks, you never would have met Captain Williams, and we never would have known about this wonderful place."

Salamar nodded in the direction of the house. "I have prepared cool melons and hot tea. I do not want you eating heavily today."

"Why?"

Salamar gazed out to sea. "You will go into labor in the early morning hours."

Valentina felt a weight settle on her shoulders. The thought of the baby brought reality rushing back. It had been five lonely, aching months since she had seen Marquis. She remembered the short happiness they had shared—at least she had been happy when he hadn't been ignoring her. With a heavy sigh, she linked her arm through Salamar's and moved toward the house.

"If I am soon going to be a mother, we had better make preparations."

"Everything is in readiness," Salamar said. "We have but to wait."

"I will be glad when it is over. I feel fat and ugly. It will be nice to be able to see my waistline again."

"Your husband should be with you tonight, Valentina. You have been very clever in hiding from him. It is said in town that he and Tyree both search diligently for you."

"I don't want to talk about Marquis, Salamar. As soon as this baby is born, we are going home to England."

"You are making a mistake," Salamar warned.

"It won't be the first and, if I live long enough, it won't be my last."

Salamar took Valentina's arm and helped her up the steps. "If we all had our mistakes stacked end to end, they would probably reach to the moon," Salamar observed.

Valentina walked into the house and stood at the window. Soon she would become a mother, and Marquis would never know he was a father.

Percival Lawton bellied up to the bar, licking his lips, staring at the bottle of rum that had been left there. He could almost taste the soothing liquid sliding down his throat. He needed a drink to help him get through the night.

Tyree Garth was walking past, greeting customers and passing a few comments with friends. When he saw Percival Lawton, he stopped short. Tyree had kept a watchful eye on the man for the last few months. Percival was steadily losing his grip on reality. Tyree did not like the man, but he thought someone should give him a helping hand. The pathetic creature never drew a sober breath. He hung around the Crystal Palace, begging for handouts.

"Why don't you go on home now, Mr. Lawton?" Tyree said, glancing into the red, watery eyes, then at the rumpled and dirty clothing. "You need to pull yourself together, Reverend. Get back to the fire and brimstone you used to preach."

"I'm lost," Percival muttered, laying his head on the bar. "I need a drink and I don't have the money."

No one in San Francisco liked the dull-witted little preacher. Many joked about him getting his just desserts, but Tyree was not among those. He had seen enough men lose their grips on sanity to know that Percival was in a bad way and needed help.

Tyree gathered him up by the shirtfront and pulled him off the bar. "Come on, Reverend, I'm going to take you home. Chances are that your sister can deal with you."

"Can't go home," Percival moaned. "I need a drink. If you will give me a bottle, I'll tell you something you want to know."

"All I need is for you to stay out of my place," Tyree said, hoisting the man upon his shoulder. "You don't belong here."

"You want to know about Valentina and I know where she is," Percival murmured, slurring his words. "I see her every day."

Tyree plopped the reverend into a chair and snapped his fingers, motioning for Ted to bring a bottle of whiskey. Percival's beady little eyes lit up. "I got your attention now, didn't I?"

"That you did, Mr. Lawton." Tyree poured the liquor into a glass and held it out to him. "Tell me where Valentina is and the bottle is yours."

"She's a soiled angel," was his sniveling reply. "I see her every day walking along the beach, her stomach swollen, hiding from the world in her shame."

"Where did you see her?" Tyree held the glass within Percival's reach. "Tell me where to find her."

"The drink?" he reminded Tyree, licking his lips thirstily.

"After you tell me where I can find Valentina."

Percival greedily watched the amber liquor as Tyree set down the glass. He could almost feel it burning a trail of forgetfulness down his throat. He had sunk so low that he was no longer particular what he drank—he would do anything to reach that state of oblivion. "Valentina lives in a cabin down the southern beach, just out of San Francisco."

"I know the place," Tyree said thoughtfully. He was impatient to be off. He had to know Valentina was all right.

"I worshipped Valentina Barrett, thinking she was good and pure." A loud cry of frustration escaped Percival's lips. "I turned my back on God when she left. I fell from grace when I saw her tumble off her pedestal."

"Shut up!" Tyree snapped, realizing others were listening to his drunken rambling. He waited until Percival had gulped down the whiskey before he gathered him up, motioning for Ted. When the bartender appeared, Tyree spoke in a low voice. "Take him to his sister."

"But, Boss, he don't live with his sister anymore. He tells me every day how she would hound him to give up drinking. He thinks if she was to get her hooks into him, she'd watch him like a hawk."

"It's time someone watched him and got him back on the right road. I will leave his redemption to Providence —and his very able sister. I doubt we will see much of him around the Crystal Palace after today."

Valentina slipped in and out of awareness. When the pains came, her stomach would contract, and she would grip Salamar's hand tightly. Bathed in perspiration, she moaned, rolling her head from side to side. Licking her cracked, dry lips, she murmured in a painful voice, "I did not know bringing a child into the world could be so—"

479

At that moment another pain struck, ripping through her body. She arched her back, gasping for breath, her mind a swirling tide of pain.

Salamar lifted Valentina's head, pouring some evil-tasting liquid down her throat. "This will help dull the pain. Try to rest between pains. Doctor Cline should be here soon."

Valentina ran her tongue along her lips, feeling the pain subsiding. "What time is it?"

"Just after five."

"In the morning?"

"No, afternoon."

Valentina closed her eyes. She had been in labor for over sixteen hours. Would this baby never come? She could hear a sea gull crying just outside and wished she could walk along the beach, free of pain, feeling the cool water washing over her like a cleansing tide.

With a worried frown, Salamar watched Valentina drift in and out of sleep. There was something wrong. The pains were coming too often, lasting too long. She walked to the window where a cool ocean breeze touched her face. She felt drained, and aching, as if she herself were having the pain. In desperation, her eyes searched the beach for some sign of Doctor Cline. Why had he not come yet?

Hearing the neighing of a horse, Salamar rushed out the door expecting to see Doctor Cline. Stopping short, she watched Tyree Garth dismount. Frantically she reached out to him. "Go for the doctor quickly! Valentina is having the baby and all is not well!"

Without stopping to consider, Tyree bounded onto his mount and kicked it into action. As he raced full speed along the beach, his horse's hooves sprayed granules of sand high into the air.

*　　　*　　　*

Valentina felt as if she were floating on dark wings of pain. She could hear voices around her, but she could not fully comprehend the meaning of the words they spoke.

"The baby is breech," Doctor Cline's voice floated to her.

"Then turn it!" Salamar demanded. "Either you do it, or I will."

The voices meandered amid searing pain that seemed to rip her stomach apart. Unaware that she was screaming, Valentina at last found herself drifting into a peaceful world where pain could not enter, a tranquil world where cooling waves of water bathed her fevered body.

Tyree stood on the beach, tossing seashells into the foamy ocean. His eyes went often to the cabin, and he feared the worst. Just at sundown, when the tide splashed heavily against the sandy shores, Tyree heard the cry of an infant.

"My God!" he breathed with relief. "A new Vincente has been born into the world. Marquis is a father and doesn't even know it."

Valentina opened her eyes as Salamar laid a tiny bundle in her arms. "Your daughter, Valentina," she said softly, pushing a damp curl off Valentina's forehead.

"It's all over?" Valentina questioned, hoping she would not have to endure more pain.

"It is over," Salamar assured her.

Glancing down at the baby, Valentina felt her heart open to a flood of feelings. Her helpless little daughter was thrusting her fists into the air, already searching for something to eat. Soft, downy black hair covered the perfectly shaped little head. Valentina kissed the child as motherly love flowed through her body. It was difficult to tell what color eyes the child had, but her skin was dark and she had the look of a Vincente.

"She is wonderful," Valentina said, lightly touching

481

the soft, bow-shaped lips. "Oh, Salamar, she is so dear."

A heavy mist rolled off the Pacific Ocean, blocking out most of the sunlight. Valentina and Tyree walked along the beach, just out of reach of the plundering waves.

Tyree glanced up at Valentina, noting the smile that curved her lips. He knew she was thinking about her daughter. The child had brought a new maturity to Valentina. She was more sure of herself, more determined about her future.

"I'm surprised you named your daughter Jordanna. Weren't you afraid some people in San Francisco might connect her name with the dancer?"

"No, I'm not worried, because I will not be staying in San Francisco."

Tyree felt his heart constrict. "I had feared you were thinking in that direction. Have you decided to return to England?"

"Yes. That's what I wanted to talk to you about. I would like to dance one more time at the Crystal Palace. I need the money to buy passage to England."

He took her hand. "You don't have to dance if you don't want to. I would gladly give you whatever money you needed."

She smiled, lacing her fingers through his. "I knew you would say that, but no. I want to earn the money myself."

"I don't suppose you would reconsider telling Marquis about the baby?" he asked for at least the twentieth time. "A man needs to know when he becomes a father."

"No, Tyree. I do not want Marquis to know about Jordanna. As far as I am concerned, I will never see Marquis again. That part of my life is over."

Tyree saw the pain in her silver-blue eyes and knew she still loved Marquis. She had not yet succeeded in forgetting him. "I wish you would at least talk to Marquis. He has searched for you diligently. He is a desperate man, Valentina. He loves you. Give him a chance to tell you how he feels. I told you about his grandfather's death and Rosalia's running off with Felipe Martinez. Marquis has been through hell."

"I am sorry about Don Alonso, and I grieve for him. He was an exceptional man. The world will never know his like again. He is a dying breed." Valentina's eyes narrowed through the mist. "However, I am not sorry about Rosalia. She is married to the man she loves, and I wish her every happiness."

"You don't understand the Vincentes' kind of honor. As far as they are concerned, Rosalia broke her word; she is dead to them. Rosalia can never find true happiness unless her mother and brother forgive her and take her back."

"Oh, how well I understand the Vincentes' misplaced honor and their stubborn pride. I am still reeling from the effects of it," Valentina admitted.

"Marquis is hurting, Valentina. Will you be able to turn your back on him? Can you just block him out of your mind?"

Not a day had gone by during which thoughts of Marquis had not dominated Valentina's thinking. Nor a night during which she had not ached for his touch. She had to get away from California so she could start putting her life back together. She had to think of her daughter. "I don't want to talk about Marquis anymore, Tyree; my mind is made up. I am going back to England."

Tyree knew by the toss of Valentina's golden head and the tightening of her jaw that her decision was final. "Very well. Let me know when you are ready to dance, and I will arrange everything."

Valentina placed her hand on his cheek. "I wonder if you know how special you are to me? No one has ever had a better friend."

"Always the friend," he said, smiling, certain that was all he would ever be to her.

Valentina would miss this wonderful man who had appointed himself her protector and had never deviated from that path. Tears moistened her eyes, and she knew she would have to change the subject or risk bursting into tears. "I should be ready to dance in another month. By that time my daughter will be three months old and ready to make the long sea voyage to England."

"San Francisco will welcome back their Jordanna with raving enthusiasm. You can't know how you have been missed. I expect your last performance will be the biggest event to hit this town since the discovery of gold."

Chapter Thirty

San Francisco . . . 1851

The Crystal Palace was crowded to overflowing. Men were standing in the street, trying to push their way inside. The word was out that their Jordanna had returned and would be performing tonight. From hundreds of miles away, men came to worship their beautiful dancer.

In the dressing room backstage, Valentina held her breath while Salamar tightly laced her corset. "Your waist will never be as small as it once was, Valentina. You owe this to the birth of your child."

Valentina looked lovingly at the bed where her daughter gurgled and cooed. "I owe many things to my daughter. Most of all, I owe her for helping save my sanity. I don't know how I would have made it through these last months if it hadn't been for Jordanna."

Salamar slipped the frothy white costume over Valentina's head and fastened it up the back. "Are you sure you feel up to dancing tonight?" she inquired with concern. "After all, the baby is only three months old."

"I feel wonderful, but a little nervous. I just hope I don't miss a step. It has been a long time since I danced before an audience."

"From what I can hear, your audience is giving you a rousing welcome back."

Valentina could hear the loud voices that drifted backstage. She slipped into her satin toe shoes and looked at herself in the full-length mirror. Reaching for the white sequined veil, she fastened it across the bottom of her face. A frosty white net covered her golden hair, making her disguise complete.

The music started, and a hush fell over the crowd. They waited with bated breath for their star to appear. When Valentina walked out the door and approached the stage, she could feel the emotional intensity.

The music rose in volume, and she leapt across the stage and landed with a graceful bow. The audience was in a frenzy. Jumping to their feet in a standing ovation, they applauded and yelled their joy that Jordanna had returned to them.

It took a full five minutes for the crowd to finally quiet so Valentina could perform her dance. She was touched by this love that the Californians sent her way. She would dance her best for them tonight. This would be her final and, hopefully, her best performance. After tonight, she would hang up her dancing shoes forever.

Her gestures were poetic and beguiling. The audience was bewitched, completely under her spell, as she whirled and turned, defying gravity.

Valentina displayed a piercing beauty from the tips of her elegant feet to the top of her delicately poised head. She used every part of her body to communicate with the audience. She dazzled them with daring turns, captivated them with graceful pirouettes. Leaping through the air, she seemed weightless, graceful, magnificent. Without any visible effort, Valentina gave a high leap and appeared to float to the stage.

On one of her turns, she saw dark eyes watching her

with notable intensity. She felt her heart skip a beat and almost missed a step. Marquis was in the audience! Dear God, she cried inwardly, not having anticipated that she would ever have to face him again. She should have known that she was risking discovery when she had asked to dance for Tyree this one last time.

Turning in a breathtaking pirouette, she went spinning across the stage while the music slowed. A drumroll filled the room and men held their collective breath in anticipation. Valentina seemed to fly across the stage as a floor-to-ceiling flag of California was unfurled.

Tyree felt his heart melt as he watched Valentina. He knew she had never danced better. Before, she had been beauty in motion; now she brought something deeper to her dance—a sensitivity that touched men's hearts, reaching clear to their souls. He knew anyone watching Valentina dance tonight would never forget her performance.

Up on her toes, extending her leg, Valentina spun around and around while the audience gasped in awe and reverence. Her arms were graceful as she crossed them over her breasts and then lifted them over her head. She was dancing for Marquis. It was her way of telling him good-bye.

Leaping higher than she had ever leapt before, she split her legs wide while still in the air. Silence followed as the lights dimmed and she walked to the end of the stage. Her audience was reaching out to her with love.

The usual tribute of gold dust and flowers fell at her feet. She picked up one white rose, knowing it was from Marquis, and curtsied. Unlike the first time he had thrown her a rose, she did not kiss it. Her eyes rested, for a brief moment, on Marquis. His face was impassive and she could not tell what he was thinking. Throwing the audience a kiss, she waved her hand and hurried off the stage.

For a long moment the audience was stunned, for they sensed they would never again see the lovely, mysterious Jordanna. Strangely the audience remained silent. The feeling in the Crystal Palace was heavy. This time there was not the usual cry for Jordanna to continue—each man knew in his heart that she would never return. Most of the men filed quietly out to the street, still gripped by the beauty of what they had just witnessed.

Valentina ran into her dressing room and shut the door. Salamar laid the baby down and stared at Valentina's stricken face. "It is no great tragedy if you missed a step, Valentina. No one but you would have known."

"He's here, Salamar. I saw him."

"Marquis?"

"Yes. I will not see him alone, Salamar. I have nothing to say to him."

"Just stay calm. If you do not want to see him, then you will ask Tyree to keep him away."

Valentina placed her hands over her face. "I thought if I ever saw him again I would be able to ignore him. I didn't know I would feel so devastated."

"Perhaps you should see him, Valentina. Remember, he thinks of you as Jordanna. He will not know you are his missing wife."

Watching Valentina exit the stage, Marquis stood up. His eyes were expressionless as he pushed several men out of his path, making his way to Tyree's office. Without knocking, he entered the familiar room to find Tyree sitting at his desk.

Tyree looked up from his ledger and tossed down his pen. "I did not know you had returned to San Francisco, Marquis. I would have thought you would be sticking close to Paraíso del Norte with your duties as grandee."

Marquis propped a booted foot on the rung of a chair. "You should have known I would be back," he stated flatly. "Did you think I would give up searching for Valentina?"

Tyree looked at him through a haze of cigar smoke. "How do you judge my dancer? She is better than ever, don't you think?"

"You know damned well she's good, Tyree—she is the best. I want to talk about Valentina. Do not lie to me, Tyree. I know she came to see you."

"Don't push it, Marquis. I believe you and I have said all there is to say on this subject. I wouldn't tell you where Valentina was, even if I knew."

"You know," Marquis stated. His eyes were dark and brooding. Many things had become clear to him tonight. He did not know how much he could trust Tyree. Most probably Tyree would protect Valentina at all cost.

Tyree stood, moving to the window. "I am surprised that you are not interested in Jordanna, even though she had your baby."

All the life seemed to drain out of Marquis. "Have you seen the child?"

"Of course. Jordanna is always proud to show off her daughter."

"You said daughter?"

"Yes, you have a daughter."

Marquis slumped down in a chair and stared at Tyree. "I have begun to believe that the Vincente line will die out with me. Rosalia has run off and married Felipe Martinez. Valentina has vanished. I have been thinking a lot of the child I fathered by Jordanna." Marquis was watching Tyree's face carefully.

"What do you mean by that statement?"

"I would like to see the child. I have been wondering if Jordanna would let me take the child to Paraíso del Norte."

"You bastard," Tyree ground out. "You didn't once think of Jordanna while she had your baby alone. You never considered Valentina's feelings when you drove her away. Why should anyone show any consideration for you?"

Tyree expected Marquis's angry retaliations; he did not expect him to admit total defeat. "You are right, Tyree. Nothing you can say will be as bad as what I have already said to myself. I love Valentina. Life has been meaningless without her. I have searched everywhere but cannot find any trace of her. I have decided she must have returned to England. I had even considered going to England to search for her. If I have to, I will sail to hell and back to find her."

Tyree was in no mood to forgive Marquis. "You made some very unflattering statements concerning myself and Valentina. I don't know if she will ever forgive you, and I don't know if I want to either."

"I know this is no excuse, Tyree, but I was crazy with jealousy. I know now that you would never have betrayed me. I just was not thinking clearly. I hope the time will come when you will forgive and forget."

"I may forget, but I doubt if Valentina ever will. If you were to find her in England, what makes you think she would return to California with you? She knew only unhappiness with you. You bullied her into marrying you, then insulted and ignored her. Your mother was unkind to her, and you treated her like she had the plague."

"I know. No hell is as dark as the one I have dug for myself. I would do anything to get Valentina back— *anything*."

"And her child?"

"I will take the child."

After studying Marquis's face for a time, Tyree walked toward the door. "You wait here. I don't know if I can find Valentina for you, but it just may be that I can talk Jordanna into allowing you to see your daughter."

Valentina had just removed her veil when the knock came on her door. Moving behind the dressing screen, she could not keep her heart from beating frantically as she waited for Salamar to see who it was. When she heard Tyree's voice, she was overcome with relief.

"You did the Crystal Palace proud tonight, Jordanna," he said, smiling brightly.

"I missed a step," she said dully.

"No one would have noticed," Tyree said, taking her hand and raising it to his lips. "They loved you tonight."

"That is what I told her," Salamar interjected.

Valentina searched Tyree's face. "I saw Marquis in the audience."

"Yes, he is in my office. He has asked to see you."

"I don't want to see him," she said forcefully. "Marquis and I have nothing to say to each other."

"That may very well be, but he wants to see the child. Can you deny him that?"

"He has no right, Tyree. How can you ask me to see him?"

"To be fair, Valentina, Marquis acted no different from any man who loved a woman and believed she was having another man's child."

Valentina caught her breath. "Marquis does not love me. He never did. He loves Isabel."

"No, he does not now, nor did he at any time, love Isabel. He has loved you almost from the first time he saw you. I don't know why he never told you, but he told me many times."

He saw hope fan to life in Valentina's eyes. "If Marquis loved me, how could he have been so cruel?"

"He was striking out at you—trying to hurt you like he

491

was hurt. I can tell you one thing—he never expected you to leave him. You heard how diligently he has searched for you all these months. What you may not know is how doggedly he has searched for Jordanna. He is a proud man, but a loving one. He loves you, but also wanted to make things right for Jordanna and his baby."

Salamar's eyes met Tyree's and she nodded before she spoke. "Valentina, perhaps it is time that you see Marquis. See him as Jordanna, and then you can judge for yourself if you want to see him as Valentina. The two of you have a daughter to consider. Put your personal feelings aside for a moment."

"How can I? I'm frightened of seeing Marquis again. I have just pulled my life back together; he could destroy me again."

"I am going to slip out the back way," Salamar said, blowing out all the candles but one. She then handed Valentina her veil. "Put this on. It is time to face the past. You cannot have a future until you put old hurts to rest."

"Salamar is right," Tyree agreed. "Get ready and I will send Marquis to you."

Before Valentina could object, Salamar disappeared out the back door, while Tyree left through the front. Valentina panicked, wanting to leave herself. How could she face Marquis after all that had passed between them?

Rushing across the room, she scooped up the baby. Undecided, she stood there for a moment, calling herself a coward. Bravely, she tried to face her fears. Perhaps Salamar and Tyree were right—it was time to close the door on that chapter of her life.

Laying down her infant daughter on the bed, she pulled her veil in place. Her stomach felt like thousands of tiny butterflies were beating their wings inside it. Several times she considered picking up Jordanna and fleeing into the night, but she did not.

When the knock came on the door, Valentina almost jumped out of her skin. Her muffled "come in" barely reached Marquis's ears. Calling on all the courage she possessed, Valentina waited for the door to open.

Marquis was bigger than life as he stood in the doorway, smiling at her. Her heart caught in her throat, and she could not breathe. She had never stopped loving him for one minute. His pull on her was as strong as it had always been. Unable to speak, she stepped aside and allowed him entrance.

"I thought your performance was the best ever, Jordanna. If it is possible to improve on perfection, you have done so."

"Thank you," she said, remembering to use her French accent.

Marquis's eyes were drawn to the baby who lay on the bed. His heart was drumming in his throat as he walked slowly forward. It was dark in the room, and he knelt down to get a better look at the child. Soft, fatherly feelings enveloped him. Carefully he picked up a tiny hand and watched it curl around his finger. Rosebud lips gurgled and cooed. Curly black hair covered the tiny head, and he thought her the most beautiful baby he had ever seen.

"What is her name?" he asked, glancing up at Jordanna.

"I have named her Jordanna."

His eyes moved over the child's face. "I am glad. I always thought your name unusually beautiful."

Valentina said nothing. For the longest time he stared at her. Finally, breaking the silence, he spoke. "I wonder if you would mind if I held her?" he asked softly.

"You may hold her if you like," Valentina said, watching him carefully. Was he playing some kind of trick on her? Was he pretending an interest in the baby?

Marquis lifted the child, finding she weighed hardly

493

anything. How little and helpless she was. She smiled at him and his heart melted. "Is she a good baby?" he wanted to know.

"Yes. She hardly ever cries."

Marquis turned his attention to Valentina. "I wonder if you would consider allowing me to take the baby home with me."

With fear in her eyes, Valentina took a hesitant step forward, wanting to take the child from him. "No, you cannot have my baby! You have no right to her!"

"I meant to include you in my invitation also, Jordanna. You have my word that if you will both come home with me I will take care of you. I will endeavor to be the kind of father my daughter deserves. I have so much to make up to you both. I have been a blind fool and am asking you to forgive me if you can."

Valentina saw tears in Marquis's eyes and shook her head skeptically. How could this be? Was it possible that Marquis was feeling regret for his past actions? She had always thought him to be so strong and decisive, but at the moment he was humble and repentant.

"I cannot go home with you, Marquis. You have a wife. What role would I play—that of your mistress?"

He placed the baby on the bed and turned to her. "I know I once asked you to be my mistress, but I was a fool then."

"What role then, Marquis?"

"I love you," he whispered. "I would like you to be my wife." His eyes were shining as he captured her hand.

Her heart was racing madly. "As I just said, you have a wife."

"Let me tell you a few truths about myself, Jordanna. You are right about my having a wife. Valentina was everything a man could want in a wife, but I was too blind to see it. I would fly into jealous rages for no reason.

494

While I worshiped her beauty, I was envious of every look she gave to others. I was unworthy of her."

His voice caught in his throat and he had to wait a moment before he could continue. "You see . . . I love Valentina. She is the only woman I have ever loved. I realize she may never love me, but if she would come back, I would do anything to make amends. I have lived through hell, searching for her."

Valentina jerked her hand free and wiped the tears from her eyes. Turning her back, she whispered, "If you love your wife, how can you also claim to love me? Why would you want me and my baby?"

He clasped her shoulders and turned her to face him. "I have searched for both you and Valentina with no success. No one would tell me where either of you had disappeared to. I had heard that the famous Jordanna was giving her farewell performance at the Crystal Palace. I had to see you dance one last time. As I watched you tonight, I realized what a blind fool I had been. I must have been out of my mind not to have seen the obvious. There could never be two women like you . . . Valentina!"

Reaching up, he unhooked her veil and stared at the face that had haunted him for so long. "It is hard to fool a husband when it comes to his wife's body, Valentina. I knew your body so well that the moment you stepped onto stage tonight I realized you and Jordanna were one and the same. No one could be as beautiful and as graceful as you."

"I—"

He placed his hand on her lips. "Shh, let me finish. When the truth hit me, I began to tie all the loose ends together, Valentina. Can you imagine how I felt as I watched you dance tonight, knowing the truth at last? I was remembering that Jordanna had given birth to my baby, therefore making the baby Valentina was carrying mine!" He passed his hand over his face. "God, what a tangle! I recalled the envy I had felt for the man who had fathered my wife's baby—all along I was my own rival."

"I know I should have told you the truth, Marquis. I tried to when we were trapped in the mine, but you chose to misunderstand me."

"Did you?"

"Yes."

He looked puzzled for a moment. "That time is so vague in my memory . . . I do not recall much that happened. Why did you not tell me later?"

"I couldn't."

He sighed. "Why should you have told me? I had done nothing to win your trust."

He reached out to her with a trembling hand. Valentina saw the haggard look on his face and wanted to soothe him. "Oh God, Valentina, come home with me," he pleaded. "I love you."

Her sobs were smothered against his shoulder, and his hands were comforting as they ran up and down her back in a caressing motion. She was almost afraid to believe he loved her. How did she know he would not hurt her again?

Raising her head, she looked into soft brown eyes. "What about Isabel?"

He smiled. "I am told she was sent back to Spain, but I do not know for sure. Isabel never meant anything to me. It pains me to confess that I used her to hurt you, but it was only because I thought you loved Tyree."

"You implied that . . . Isabel said . . ."

"I know what Isabel said. My mother told me. I admit I kissed her that day, but it was done in an attempt to drive my demons away. You have my word I did no more than kiss her. My heart was too full of love for you—there is no room for anyone else in my bed or in my heart."

Valentina was still afraid to trust him. "You are not mad because I tricked you?"

"I wish I had inspired your trust from the beginning so you would not have felt the need to keep secrets from me. I will strive to win your trust and your love in the future." He touched her face so softly, and his eyes looked deeply into hers. "Give me another chance, Valentina. I promise you will not regret it." His eyes moved across her face lovingly. "I seem to remember one thing that gives me reason to hope."

"What is that?" she asked shyly.

"I recall your telling me that you loved the father of your child. Is that true, Valentina? Did you love me?"

She looked into his dark eyes, knowing that the time for lies had passed. "Yes, Marquis. I've always loved you."

His hand trembled as it brushed her cheek, then moved to softly touch her lips. "My own little Silver Eyes," he whispered. "I have been to hell and back searching for you. Tonight I will be in paradise. I've discovered I had your love all along but was too blind to see it."

"Oh, Marquis, if only there were hope for us. We have hurt each other so deeply. I don't know if we will ever trust each other."

"I would trust you with my life, Valentina. You admitted that you loved me in the past. Do you still have feelings for me?"

Tears ran unchecked down her face. "It was always you, Marquis. Why else do you think I would have married you? I was afraid that you would find out that I was Jordanna and despise me."

Tenderly he brushed her tears away with his fingertips. "My dearest love, we have wasted so much time. Could we start all over again? Will you give me a chance to make everything up to you?"

"If you are sure you want me."

He picked her up in his arms and swung her around the room, his face bright with happiness. "*If* I want you? God knows I want you, Valentina. Why do you not know? I cannot wait to take you home. I want the world to know that we have a daughter. I want the world to know that I am loved by Valentina Barrett Vincente."

Suddenly his face became serious and he dipped his head to taste the lips that had given him so much pleasure in the past. He now knew why he had felt so alive with the dancer, Jordanna. His body had known that she was his love, even if his head had not.

"Will you come home with me, Valentina?"

"Yes, my love—oh yes!"

"I will not expect you to forgive me right away, Valentina. I know I will have to win your trust."

She was crying and could do no more than nod her head. When she could speak, her voice was a soft whisper. "We both have much to think about, Marquis."

"I would like to start for Paraíso del Norte tomorrow. Will you be ready by then?"

"Yes. I will have to tell Tyree."

Marquis held Valentina tightly for a moment before releasing her. "I do not want to let you out of my sight. Even now I half fear you will vanish again."

She smiled. "I ran away from you before, my Spaniard, but be warned; you will not get rid of me so easily the next time."

His laughter was deep, and his eyes kept darting to the baby who was gurgling happily. "I am happy, Valentina. I feel like I own the world."

Suddenly Valentina felt shy before this darkly handsome man who was her husband and the father of her daughter. "I should take the baby to the hotel now,

Marquis. She needs to be in her bed."

He stood looking down at her tensely, as if he were waiting for an invitation to go with her. Valentina could read the question in his eyes. "I can't rush this, Marquis. Will you be willing to give me time?"

He nodded. "How much time would you need, Valentina?"

A mischievous light danced in her eyes. "I will need the time it will take me to change out of my costume. Is that too long?"

He grabbed her, pulling her into his arms. "So you think to torture me, Valentina. You know I have ached for you for months. I do not know if I can wait another night."

Tyree heard the laughter coming from Valentina's dressing room and realized he had lost his dancer again. Smiling sadly, he walked away, wishing his two friends the best of everything.

Clapping his hat on his head, he walked out into the street. San Francisco was growing. She was no longer the sleepy little town that the Spaniards had first established. Nor was she just another bustling gold-rush town. She was becoming respectable. Husbands were bringing their wives and children to California. Schools were being built. This was a city of the future, a place to raise a family.

Tyree's eyes moved up the hill and focused on the site of the church he had had built. He thought of the new pastor's lovely blue-eyed daughter, Molly. Perhaps it was time he sold the Crystal Palace and settled into an acceptable job as a storekeeper, or perhaps a rancher. Then again, he mused, he had always wanted to be in the banking business.

His footsteps quickened and he found himself anxious to see Molly. He could tell she liked him. She was just a little frightened of him because of his reputation, but he would court her in the proper manner and she would soon get over her fear.

"Yep," he said under his breath, "it's time to settle down."

Chapter Thirty-One

It was a strange procession that moved toward Paraíso del Norte. Salamar sat in the buggy with Jordanna, while Marquis and Valentina rode horseback.

There was little chance to talk, but Valentina could feel Marquis watching her. The previous night she had been disappointed when Marquis had stayed in a hotel room down the hall from hers. She had wanted him to stay with her, but she had been too shy to ask.

As the sun rose high, her heart soared with it. She was on her way home to Paraíso del Norte, the only real home she had ever known. There had been bitterness and mistrust between her and Marquis, but that was behind them now.

Late in the morning, they stopped so Valentina could feed her daughter, and Marquis rode away to give her privacy. He seemed distant, as though something was bothering him.

It was almost sundown and dark clouds were gathering in the west when they reached Paraíso del Norte. Marquis helped Valentina dismount, then turned to Salamar, taking the baby from her.

Valentina's heart filled with dread when she saw Doña Anna coming slowly down the stairs toward them. As she drew near, Valentina saw before her a changed Doña Anna. Her dark eyes were dull and lifeless. There was no sign of her usual airiness.

Marquis's mother met Valentina's eyes. "I hope you will believe me when I say I am glad my son has found you."

Valentina was tempted to say that, based on past experiences, she doubted the truthfulness of her statement, but she held her tongue. She saw sincerity and a certain humbleness in Doña Anna. "I am glad to be home," Valentina replied instead. "Thank you for making me feel welcome."

Doña Anna glanced at her son, and her mouth gaped open in surprise. "What is this? Whose is this baby?"

Marquis proudly held out the child to his mother. "This is a new generation of Vincentes, Mother. Welcome your new granddaughter, Jordanna Vincente."

The old woman's eyes filled with tears as she pulled aside the blanket and stared at the child. There was disbelief and shame in her eyes as she looked at Valentina. "I am so sorry. I did not know you were with child. Can you forgive me?"

"There is nothing to forgive," Valentina answered, glad the battle between her and Doña Anna was over.

"May I hold her?" she asked hopefully, glancing at Valentina for permission. Being a grandmother was a new experience for Doña Anna. She could hardly wait to get her hands on the child.

"Of course. She is your grandchild," Valentina told her.

Doña Anna carefully lifted the child from Marquis's arms and held her as if she were the most precious jewel. "Let us get her out of this night air. It is not good for a baby's lungs."

Valentina and Marquis smiled at each other as his mother took charge of the child. Salamar was directing

502

the unloading of the trunks, and Marquis led Valentina up the steps.

"I dreamed of your return," he whispered near her ear. "I cannot believe you are really here with me."

Her eyes moved across his dark face and she felt her heart melt with love. "This is where I will always want to be, Marquis."

Valentina was surprised when she was led up the main stairway. "I am head of the family now," Marquis explained sadly. "These are the quarters always occupied by the grandee."

Valentina and Marquis were right behind Doña Anna as she entered the bedroom. Even with the darkness of the coming storm, it seemed a bright, cheerful room where yellows and cream colors blended together. The room was twice the size of the bedroom Marquis had occupied in the other wing.

"After grandfather died, I had this part of the house redecorated in colors I thought you would like, Valentina," Marquis said, pulling her into his arms. "I always hoped I would find you and bring you home."

Doña Anna was happily changing her new granddaughter. She was giggling and smiling at the child, her eyes dancing with joy. "It is so good to have a child in this house again, Valentina. You and this baby will chase the gloom away that has been hanging over our heads lately," Doña Anna declared. "I cannot wait to tell Doña Carmela Lopez about my granddaughter. Her two daughters and one son have been married far longer than you and have yet to produce a grandchild."

Suddenly Doña Anna fell silent. She stared at the child and fresh tears filled her eyes. "Look, Marquis, the child has the Vincente mark. She is blessed as you are!"

Marquis looked at the child and there, on her upper leg, he saw the red heart-shaped birthmark. His eyes caught and held Valentina's. Doña Anna smiled, knowing

503

there would never be a question in anyone's mind as to whether or not Jordanna was Marquis's daughter.

Doña Anna wrapped the child in a blanket and picked her up. "Do you mind if I take Jordanna with me?" she asked hesitantly, as if fearing Valentina would refuse her request. "I would like to show her to everyone."

Valentina nodded. "You can keep her until she needs to be fed; then bring her to me."

Marquis's mother hurried across the room with her precious bundle clasped to her breast. Her spirits were lighter than they had been in months. There had been so much grief hanging over this house with don Alonso's death and Rosalia's running away and disgracing the family. Now happiness, in the shape of a precious granddaughter, had come to chase away all the gloom.

A bolt of lightning flashed across the sky, illuminating the room. Marquis walked to the door, then looked back at Valentina. "I need to see about something. If you are hungry, ring for a maid."

"Shouldn't I wait for you?" Valentina asked, feeling out of place in the huge bedroom and wondering why Marquis was acting so distant.

"No, do not wait for me. I have many things to do and may be late."

Valentina watched him leave, hoping he had not withdrawn from her again. Salamar was directing the men with Valentina's trunks. When they were placed to her satisfaction, she left. Valentina stood in the middle of the empty room feeling abandoned.

The rain pattering against the window did nothing to soothe Valentina's frayed nerves. Marquis had been gone for over an hour. His mother had already brought Jordanna back and the child was now asleep at the foot of the bed in a cradle that had been in the Vincente family for generations.

Valentina removed her riding habit, slipped on a pale

pink nightgown, and pulled on her robe. The rain had stopped moments ago, and now Valentina thought she heard the sound of soft Spanish music below in the garden. It was too late at night for a party, she thought. Her footsteps were cushioned by the thick yellow rug as she moved to the balcony and glanced down.

She drew in her breath as she saw several troubadours strumming guitars. When they saw Valentina, they broke into a beautiful old Spanish ballad.

The night air had been washed clean by the rain, and a wonderful, drugging aroma came from the garden, filling Valentina's senses. Leaning forward, she listened to the music. She had the feeling that many Vincente brides before her had stood in this very spot being serenaded by the soft music of Spanish guitars.

Marquis stepped out of the shadows and stared up at her with adoration in his dark eyes. "I come as a beggar, señora, hoping you will accept this small tribute of my love." He tossed her a white rose. She caught it and placed it behind her ear. Joy danced in her eyes, for she now knew why Marquis had acted so distant earlier. He was courting her in the Spanish tradition!

Slowly he climbed the steps toward her. The guitarists dropped back into the shadows, but their music still filled the garden. Marquis's eyes were hypnotizing as he came nearer. She could tell by his expression that this was no game he was playing. When he took the last step that brought him even with Valentina, he bowed gallantly. "My lady wife, I come to you as I should have the first night I took you as my bride. I give you my heart and pledge eternal love. Will you accept this from me?"

"You couldn't," she reminded him. "You couldn't walk at that time."

He smiled. "I should have crawled to you." Suddenly he wasn't smiling. Holding out his hand, he asked, "Will you accept me, Valentina?"

Her hand trembled as she offered it to him. "I accept with all my heart. I love you, Marquis." Her voice broke. "I always have."

His eyes flamed as his hand tightened on hers. Without a word, he led her inside. Holding her at arm's length, he hungrily ran his eyes over her soft curves. "Who will come to my bed tonight—the dancer, Jordanna . . . or Valentina?"

"They are both me, Marquis—they are both married to you."

He lifted her in his arms and placed her on the bed. Her heart was thudding so hard in her chest that she could hardly breathe when he started slowly to remove his clothing, piece by piece. When he stood before her in all his magnificence, she held her hand out to him.

Dropping on the bed beside her, he slowly removed the pins that secured her hair and a curtain of gold tumbled across her shoulders. He then ran his hands through the tresses caressingly, as if it were the most delicate and priceless spun gold.

His eyes flickered as he took the white rose from behind her ear. When he moved the soft, fragrant petals across Valentina's lips, her senses were filled with its sweet aroma.

Marquis's dark eyes stared into Valentina's, thrilling her to her toes. He saw no resistance in her silver-blue eyes when he slipped her nightgown up her legs and over her head.

Valentina's body readily responded to his feathery touch. Her head was whirling when he touched her mouth lightly with his. He was treating her like a piece of fine porcelain, fearing she might break. Slowly he was stirring the fires of passion within her. Gently moving down her arm, across her breasts, he followed her velvet curves with his eyes. His fingertips circled her breasts, inviting the gathering tide of passion that surged inside her body.

"I am happy," he breathed hotly against her mouth. "That which I treasure most in life has been returned to me. I will never let a day go by that I will not remind you that you are my greatest treasure."

Valentina felt her heart swell with so much love that she thought it would burst. As his wonderful hands worked magic on her satiny skin, he filled the emptiness of her body with his pulsating shaft.

Marquis took her body leisurely to paradise, knowing they had the rest of their lives to love each other.

Valentina closed her eyes as waves of ecstasy passed through her. She knew that after tonight she would never again be intimidated by Marquis's domineering personality, for she had found the softer side of his nature. She would never again doubt that he loved her.

After the storm of passion had passed, leaving Marquis and Valentina breathless, his dark eyes swept her face as tender feelings melted his heart. "The first time I saw you, Valentina, I knew I was to love you. I would never have found happiness had you not loved me."

"I loved you as Valentina, but I could only show that love through Jordanna, the dancer," she admitted.

His smile was heartwarming. "Sometimes, when we are alone, perhaps you will dance for me. I will never allow you to dance for anyone else."

"Are you not ashamed of me because I danced for money?"

"No, not now. I would like it if the whole of California could know that the beautiful dancer who won every man's heart belongs to Marquis Vincente alone."

She laughed and cuddled up in his arms. "We will have to keep this our secret. Jordanna will never dance for anyone but her husband. She has retired from the stage—permanently."

Marquis heard the baby awaken and he moved off the

bed to pick her up. As he placed her beside Valentina, his eyes misted with happiness. He watched, fascinated, as the hungry rosebud mouth nursed at Valentina's breast. His arms went out to bring them both within the circle of his love. He was captivated as he saw his tiny daughter drift off to sleep. With the tip of his finger, Marquis traced the heart on his daughter's upper leg. She was so beautiful, so important to him already.

Marquis shivered when he thought how different his life would have been if he had married Isabel Estrada. He knew he would thank God every day of his life for his beautiful, silver-eyed wife. As his eyes locked with Valentina's, he saw she was troubled.

"Are you happy?" he whispered.

"I would be completely happy but for one thing, Marquis," Valentina admitted.

"You have but to tell me what would make you happy and I will give it to you," he said, kissing the tip of her pert little nose. "Ask anything of me that you will."

"I want Rosalia to come home. Please send for her, Marquis. If you have forgiven me for deceiving you, then forgive your sister for marrying the man she loves."

She could see the conflict in his dark eyes. It was not easy for him to forsake the ways of his ancestors. Finally he smiled and nodded. "I will send for Rosalia and Felipe tomorrow."

Valentina basked in Marquis's tenderness and love. Now he was allowing all his defenses to fall away, one by one, leaving himself open and vulnerable. He was an honorable and loving man, yet it was these two admirable qualities that had caused such opposing emotions to war within him. He had tried to uphold his family's traditions, while wanting to follow his heart.

This golden land of California had taken Valentina to its bosom; she had borne a child of this land—a daughter—whom Salamar had predicted would one day return to England to fulfill her destiny.

Sighing contentedly, Valentina felt Marquis's lips settle on hers. Laughing delightedly, with happiness overflowing her heart, she watched him lift their sleeping daughter and place her back in the cradle.

Returning to Valentina, Marquis enfolded her in his warm embrace and once more stirred her passion to life. She felt Marquis's lips move across her breasts, sending delightful tremors through her body.

"You are mine, Silver Eyes," he murmured. "I will never let you go again."

Oh, yes, she thought joyfully, she was Marquis's by conquest—by way of possession! She remembered a time when that thought had frightened her . . . but not any longer.

SWEET MEDICINE'S PROPHECY
by Karen A. Bale

MORE SIZZLING ROMANCES
by Carol Finch

CAPTIVE BRIDE   (1984, $3.95)
Feisty Rozalyn DuBois had to pretend affection for roguish
Dominic Baudelair; her only wish was to trick him into
falling in love and then drop him cold. But Dominic had
his own plans: To become the richest trapper in the terri-
tory by making Rozalyn his *Captive Bride*.

WILDFIRE   (1737, $3.95)
If it meant following him all the way across the wilderness,
Alexa had to satisfy the sensual agony Keane ignited in her
soul. He was a devilish rogue who brought her to *Wildfire*.

DAWN'S DESIRE   (1340, $3.50)
Kathryn became a road bandit to pay the taxes on her once
magnificent plantation. But she never dreamed her victim
would steal her heart and her innocence before he let her
go.

ENDLESS PASSION   (1155, $3.50)
Surrounded by boring suitors, Brianne Talbert finally
found love in the lusty gaze of Seth Donovan. Only this
innocent beauty could warm his cold heart, make him forget the wounds of his past, and bring him to the peaks of
rapture's pleasure.

SATIN SURRENDER   (1861, $3.95)
Dante Fowler found innocent Erica Bennett in his bed in
the most fashionable whorehouse in New Orleans. Expecting a woman of experience, Dante instead stole the innocence of the most magnificent creature he'd ever seen. He
would forever make her succumb to . . . *Satin Surrender*.

*Available wherever paperbacks are sold, or order direct from the
Publisher. Send cover price plus 50¢ per copy for mailing and
handling to Zebra Books, Dept. 2007, 475 Park Avenue South,
New York, N.Y. 10016. Residents of New York, New Jersey and
Pennsylvania must include sales tax. DO NOT SEND CASH.*